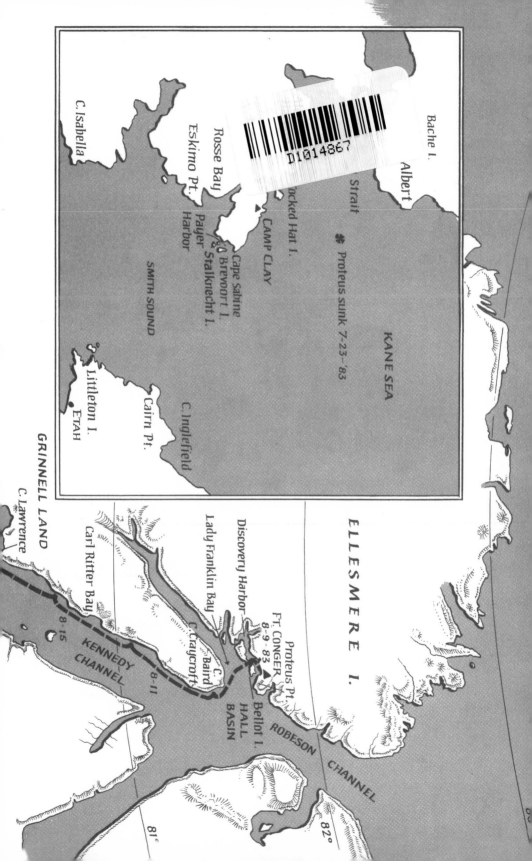

More praise for *Starvation Shore*

"Laura Waterman's story of a forgotten Arctic expedition is gripping, scholarly, textured, and gives penetrating insight into the bravery, cowardice, and terrible hunger that characterized this all-but-forgotten nineteenth-century disaster. *Starvation Shore* is destined to become a compelling classic of the Far North."

Jon Waterman, author of *Arctic Crossing and Running Dry*

"A novel with the accuracy of a history, a history with the psychological depth of a novel. . . . This book is thrilling, terrifying, and unforgettable."

Jonathan Strong, author of *The Judge's House*

"A compelling and engaging dramatization of what is arguably the most tragic and least known episode in the annals of Arctic exploration."

Geoffrey E. Clark, producer of *Abandoned in the Arctic: The True Story of the Greely Expedition*

"I loved the book and found it an engrossing, heartfelt, and compelling story. Laura Waterman should be congratulated for embarking on such a monumental task as relaying such an intricate history, and for doing it justice."

Andrew Evans, author of *The Black Penguin*

"Like the best historical novelists, Waterman is in love with her story and her characters, even (sometimes especially) when those characters behave badly. She understands how the wild can seep into our lives: changing us, destroying us, saving us."   Clint Willis, editor of *Ice: Stories of Survival from Polar Exploration*

"Through Waterman's unflinching eye and evocative prose, we can see, feel, and understand what could well have occurred in so remote a time and place, at the extreme of human experience."

Charles W. Johnson, author of *Ice Ship: The Epic Voyages of the Polar Adventurer* Fram

"A finely textured account of the expedition that often goes missing from the history books. Here the men of Cape Sabine are brought to life."
Michael Robinson, author of *The Coldest Crucible: Arctic Exploration and American Culture*

"Laura Waterman unfolds a tragic tale of nineteenth-century polar exploration, immersing us in the richness of human frailties—and supreme heroism—that was the U.S. Army's Lady Franklin Bay Expedition."
Glenn M. Stein, author of *Discovering the North-West Passage: The Four-Year Arctic Odyssey of H.M.S.* Investigator *and the McClure Expedition*

STARVATION
SHORE

Laura Waterman

THE UNIVERSITY OF WISCONSIN PRESS

Publication of this book has been made possible, in part,
through support from the Brittingham Trust.

The University of Wisconsin Press
1930 Monroe Street, 3rd Floor
Madison, Wisconsin 53711-2059
uwpress.wisc.edu

Gray's Inn House, 127 Clerkenwell Road
London EC1R 5DB, United Kingdom
eurospanbookstore.com

Printed in the United States of America

This book may be available in a digital edition.

Library of Congress Cataloging-in-Publication Data

Names: Waterman, Laura, author.
Title: Starvation shore / Laura Waterman.
Description: Madison, Wisconsin: The University of Wisconsin Press, [2019]
Identifiers: LCCN 2018045753 | ISBN 9780299323400 (cloth: alk. paper)
Subjects: LCSH: Lady Franklin Bay Expedition (1881-1884)—Fiction.
| Arctic regions—Discovery and exploration—American—Fiction.
| Brainard, David L. (David Legge), 1856-1946—Fiction.
| Greely, A. W. (Adolphus Washington), 1844-1935—Fiction.
| LCGFT: Nonfiction novels.
Classification: LCC PS3573.A8145 S73 2019 | DDC 813/.54—dc23
LC record available at https://lccn.loc.gov/2018045753

Lines from "After great pain, a formal feeling comes" by Emily Dickinson are reprinted by
permission from *The Poems of Emily Dickinson*, edited by Thomas H. Johnson, Cambridge, Mass.:
The Belknap Press of Harvard University Press, Copyright © 1951, 1955 by the President and
Fellows of Harvard College. Copyright © renewed 1979, 1983 by the President and Fellows of
Harvard College. Copyright © 1914, 1918, 1919, 1924, 1929, 1930, 1932, 1935, 1937, 1942, by Martha
Dickinson Bianchi. Copyright © 1952, 1957, 1958, 1963, 1965, by Mary L. Hampson.

Endsheets: Map of the Arctic showing the Ellesmere Island coastline and Lieutenant Greely's
retreat from Fort Conger to Cape Sabine. Reproduced by permission from Theodore Powell, *The
Long Rescue* (Garden City, NY: Doubleday, 1960). Courtesy of Gregory C. Powell.

RON WYDEN
SENATOR FOR OREGON

LIBRARY OF CONGRESS

"I cannot live without books."
-Thomas Jefferson

for

Tommy

beloved brother

There is a something—I know not what to call it—in those frozen spaces, that brings a man face to face with himself and his companions; if he is a man, the man comes out; and, if he is a cur, the cur shows as quickly.

Admiral Robert Peary, *The North Pole*, 1910

Contents

Part One: Fort Conger

Illustrations

Acknowledgments

I owe Clint Willis a debt of gratitude. It was in his *Ice: Stories of Survival from Polar Exploration* that I first read Sergeant Brainard's diary entries, which ignited this project. I offer thanks to Arctic expert Glenn M. Stein, FRGS, FRCGS, my guide from the beginning through this ice-clogged wreckage of Arctic history. In particular, I thank him for his generosity in sharing with me before publication his "An Arctic Execution: Private Charles B. Henry of the United States Lady Franklin Bay Expedition 1881–1884," *Arctic* (December 2011), as well as his expert assistance with the images for this book. My thanks to Greely enthusiast Dr. Geoffrey Clark. His book *Abandoned in the Arctic: Adolphus W. Greely and the Lady Franklin Bay Expedition, 1881–1884* and documentary on Greely's expedition was very helpful. I particularly thank him for sharing with me material from Private Henry's diary, as well as for the image used here. I acknowledge the late Jim Lotz, an Arctic explorer scientist whose book *The Best Journey in the World: Adventures in Canada's High Arctic*, as well as our correspondence, gave me insight into the physical and psychological reserves necessary for survival above the 80th parallel. My thanks to Michael Robinson for his correspondence with me, so full of encouragement and support. I extend grateful thanks to Gregory C. Powell for granting permission to use the endsheet maps from his father's book, *The Long Rescue* by Theodore Powell, as endsheets here.

I thank Jay Satterfield and his ever-responsive staff at the Rauner Special Collections Library at Dartmouth College for the use of Sergeant Brainard's original Camp Clay diary and the resource material bearing on the Greely Expedition in the Stefansson Collection. I thank the Scott Polar Research Institute, University of Cambridge, for material by Raymond Priestley that made vivid the terrors of going hungry over a long period in a frigid climate. I extend my grateful thanks for their help in the beginning of this project to Brainard family members Ellen Brainard and Marshall David Brainard.

I thank Ken Linge, former librarian of the Blake Memorial Library, East Corinth, Vermont, and his successor, Emily Heidenreich, both of whom never failed to turn up everything—in print or digital—I asked for, a valued service for a writer who lives in a rural setting. Eleanor Kohlsaat pointed me toward *The Biology of Human Starvation* by Ancel Keys. Annie Bellerose put Clint Willis's *Ice: Stories of Survival from Polar Exploration* in my hands. My wonderful readers offered encouragement and invaluable critical comment: Annie Bellerose, John M. Daniel, Alvin Handelman, Mary Hays, Eleanor Kohlsaat, Martin Magoun, Jonathan Strong, and Sally Tomlinson. My thanks to all, and to Jeremy Hawkins, who after I was well along on this project gave me an absolutely first-rate critique that pushed the manuscript over some final hurdles. My grateful thanks to my friend Dr. John Dunn, who guided my understanding of Dr. Pavy's use of ergot and other medical practices of the late nineteenth century. I thank Jon Marken for his digital assistance with the illustrations and maps. Jacob Maki supplied invaluable digital assistance with the manuscript.

I thank my amanuensis, Sue Foster, whose work for me is beyond telling.

The steadfast enthusiasm, discerning guidance, and just plain patience through the long haul of my agent, Craig Kayser, has been, for this writer, a lucky, happy journey. It's a giant-sized pleasure to extend to him my thanks.

I thank my editor Raphael Kadushin at the University of Wisconsin Press for taking a chance on this true-life Arctic story. Grateful thanks as well to the competent and creative staff at the UW Press—Amber Rose, Adam Mehring, Michelle Wing, Kaitlin Svabek, Jennifer Conn, and my vigilant, sharp-eyed editor Sheila McMahon.

Author's Note

What went on at Camp Clay as winter turned to spring can never be entirely known. That cannibalism took place is undisputed, but when it started and how it was carried out is probably unknowable. The men did not record it, not Lieutenant Greely, not Private Henry, not Sergeant Brainard, who kept up his diary entries daily to just hours before their rescue. In an attempt to understand how the men of Camp Clay reached this point, I turned inward to an imagining based on fact. I wanted to break through to an essence of our natures that could emerge only under the extremity of physical and mental distress. Who took responsibility for executing Private Henry remains unanswered, as does the debated question of whether Sergeant Brainard knew of Private Henry's criminal past, but a kind of truth can be reached indeed by telling the story of these twenty-five men through the novel form.

In part, I have used the medium of letters (Lieutenant Greely and Dr. Pavy) and journal entries (Sergeant Brainard and Private Henry) to give expression to individual points of view. Both Brainard and Henry kept journals and Greely wrote letters to his wife. Dr. Pavy's letters are entirely fiction, but his character and how he was perceived by the men come from the writings of Greely, Brainard, and the few others whose diary entries we have. The letters and diary entries I created mix fiction with fact, since I have retained certain original phrases where they served the narrative. Especially useful to me was hearing each man's individual voice as it came through in his writing. Private Henry made few diary entries—or few have come down to us—but his distinctive voice conveys character and personality of the type I've given him here. Sergeant Brainard used his diary entries to report weather and to comment on daily life. His reporting is factual but he could be frank about the men, his commanding officer, and his own feelings. Lieutenant Greely used his letters to Henrietta to express his frustrations, to review his thinking, and to justify his actions. Lieutenant Lockwood's obsession with food at Camp Clay comes from his diary entries.

I have kept very close to the facts with the Greely Expedition. However, when I read Lieutenant Lockwood's diary entries, I came away with the impression that he had, in nineteenth-century terms, a "close attachment" to Mary Murray. I learned later that Mary Murray was his sister, but since it fit my purposes for Lieutenant Lockwood to have a sweetheart, I let it stand.

Greely's *Three Years of Arctic Service* was useful here, as was his *Report of the Proceedings of the United States Expedition to Lady Franklin Bay, Grinnell Land*. Lockwood's diary and Brainard's are found in Greely's *Report of the Proceedings*. Henry's diaries are located in the U.S. National Archives, and Brainard's diaries were published in *Outpost of the Lost* and *Six Came Back*, both edited by Bessie Rowland James. I can only admire the force of mind it took for these men to keep up their diaries, in particular David Brainard, who at Camp Clay made entries daily despite freezing fingers and the uncertain shadowy light of the blubber lamp. In the early stages of working on this book, I started off my day by reading one or two entries of Brainard's diary and making a transcription of it. This is now available at the website of the Dartmouth College Library.

Alden Todd's *Abandoned: The Story of the Greely Arctic Expedition: 1881–1884*, Leonard Guttridge's *The Ghosts of Cape Sabine: The Harrowing True Story of the Greely Expedition*, and Theodore Powell's *The Long Rescue* were essential tools, as was Jim Lotz's *Canada's Forgotten Arctic Hero: George Rice*. Michael Robinson's *The Coldest Crucible: Arctic Exploration and American Culture* clarified for me America's role in nineteenth-century Arctic exploration. I relied on Winfield S. Schley's *Report of Winfield S. Schley, Commanding Greely Relief Expedition of 1884* and his *Rescue of Greely* for a firsthand account of Greely's rescue. These were chief among the numerous books and articles I happily read for this project, though since the age of twelve, when I read Maurice Herzog's

Annapurna: The First Conquest of an 8000-Metre Peak, I've been an avid reader of expedition books and stories of travel, adventure, and hardship anywhere. This project allowed me to indulge this desultory habit.

My own experience with cold is as a winter climber in the White Mountains of New Hampshire, where on frigid days above treeline, when the wind blows hard enough to knock you down, you can feel, despite the layers of fleece and wind gear, that you have nothing on at all, and even a short stop for water and a quick snack numbs your fingers in seconds. I drew on all my knowledge of cold, of wind-driven ice and snow, of the breathtaking, often frightening beauty to be found there to make the experience of these twenty-five men become real for me. Though, in truth, their story is impossible to duplicate.

The Roster of the Lady Franklin Bay Expedition

First Lieutenant Adolphus W. Greely, aged 37*, in over his head
Second Lieutenant Frederick F. Kislingbury, aged 33, should not have signed on
Second Lieutenant James B. Lockwood, aged 28, looking for adventure
Octave Pavy, physician and naturalist, aged 37, came for the North Pole
Sergeant George W. Rice, photographer, aged 26, impossible to dislike
Sergeant David L. Brainard, aged 24, most trusted
Sergeant Edward Israel, astronomer, aged 21, youngest and most innocent
Sergeant Winfield S. Jewell, meteorologist, aged 30, Mt. Washington winter veteran
Sergeant David C. Ralston, meteorologist, aged 32, went through his wife's money
Sergeant Hampden S. Gardiner, meteorologist, aged 24, most religious
Sergeant William H. Cross, engineer, aged 37, an alcoholic who missed his wife
Sergeant David Linn, probably not yet 30, a strong man who caved in
Corporal Nicholas Salor, aged 30, least distinctive
Corporal Joseph Elison, aged 31, most uncomplaining
Private Roderick R. Schneider, probably not yet 30, their dog man
Private Charles B. Henry (true name: Charles Henry Buck), aged 25, their biggest, strongest, and hungriest

*Ages given when the expedition left St. John's, Newfoundland, July 7, 1881.

Private Maurice Connell, aged 29, a fault-finding bully
Private Jacob Bender, aged 29, Henry's picked-on buddy
Private Francis Long, aged 28, popular cook and hunter
Private William Whisler, aged 24, stood up to the doctor
Private Henry Biederbick, hospital steward, aged 22, their most
    empathetic
Private Julius Frederick (known as "Shorty"), aged 28, most dependable
Private William A. Ellis, aged 40, oldest man
Jens Edward, hunter and dog sledge driver, aged 37, native of Greenland
Frederik Thorlip Christiansen, hunter and dog sledge driver, aged 34,
    native of Greenland

Starvation Shore

The Lady Franklin Bay Expedition team in the Washington studio of Moses P. Rice, brother of expedition member George Rice, June 1881. *Seated, left to right*: Maurice Connell, David L. Brainard, Frederick F. Kislingbury, Adolphus Washington Greely, James B. Lockwood, Edward Israel, Winfield S. Jewell, George W. Rice. *Standing, left to right*: William Whisler, William A. Ellis, Jacob Bender, William H. Cross, Julius Frederick, David Linn, Henry Biederbick, Charles B. Henry, Francis Long, David C. Ralston, Nicholas Salor, Dr. Octave Pavy (*pasted in*), Hampden S. Gardiner, Joseph Elison. Roderick Schneider is missing, as are the Greenlanders, Jens Edward and Frederik Christiansen. Courtesy of the National Archives and Records Administration.

Prologue

Mount Hope Cemetery, Rochester, New York, and the Greely Home on Prospect Street, Newburyport, Massachusetts

14 August 1884

The men arrived by carriage. The horses, following with the coffin in the wagon, had worked themselves into a lather on the hill, rutted and muddy from recent downpours. The driver pulled up before the chapel door, his horses' flanks steaming, damp harness leather filling the air with a tangy smell.

The two brothers of the deceased, the two who lived in Rochester, mounted the granite steps to throw open the chapel's double doors. The undertaker jumped down from the wagon to direct the off-loading of the iron coffin, his assistants grunting, their footsteps loud on the slate floor as they stumbled to maneuver the dead weight down the aisle and up onto an oak table positioned below the altar.

The editor of the *Rochester Post-Express* stood off to the side, already at work with his pad and pencil. The two medical examiners turned up the gas lamps and the stained glass flared, revealing the royal blue in the Virgin's robe, the blood red of a Wise Man's cloak. But these costly windows admitted little light, and it was cold. The moisture-saturated air beaded the men's beards and left a slick sheen on their black cloth suits and tall stovepipe hats.

The undertaker and his helpers set to work unscrewing the iron bolts that held the lid clamped in place. The coffin was made of iron. On one end was the deceased's name etched on a brass plaque: Frederick F. Kislingbury. He had been dead eleven weeks. These bolts, fifty-two in total, were not meant to be removed. The brothers knew this. They had been so instructed by the United States government.

The man from the *Post-Express* was very aware that all the caskets that had been shipped back from the Arctic were hermetically sealed, but since his newspaper was paying for the exhumation in exchange for the story—the arrangement worked out by the brothers—he pushed in to gain a clear line of sight. "Stand back, man," the elder of the two Kislingbury brothers said. "Be respectful of the dead." The newspaper man racked his fingers through his mustache, a droopy walrus in need of a trim.

A bolt clattered to the slate and one of the undertaker's assistants raised his hand, knuckles bloody. "Watch yourself," he said to the other men at work on the bolts, "they bite."

One of the doctors handed him a handkerchief. "It's all I've got. Didn't think I'd need my full complement of medical supplies today," he said, risking a smile.

"He never should have left," the second brother said. He was tall and sandy-haired with a strong jaw. It was said of the four Kislingbury brothers, he most resembled the one in the coffin.

"Young Harry should be here," said the elder.

"You would put Frederick's son through this?"

"He's the eldest. It would have been his right."

Another clank on the slate and a bolt rolled under the brothers' feet. "How many have you got off?" the younger asked.

"About half," said the undertaker.

"He told us he intended to return to them a new man," the younger went on. "Lieutenant Greely wanted him, hell, he invited him. They'd strung the telegraph lines together across the Western Plains."

"That's no preparation for an Arctic expedition," one of the assistants, his wrench around a bolt, offered.

"My brother, Frederick Kislingbury," the elder said, "had a great familiarity with ice and snow from his tour of duty at Fort Custer."

One of the medical examiners said, "That was a tragic story."

The brothers nodded. The doctor meant the sad misfortune of Frederick losing his second wife at Fort Custer. Their brother had brought the four boys out there in May 1879, along with Jessie, the sister of his first wife, whom he had married only a few months after the first wife's death. Frederick was on a scouting mission in the late fall when word was got to him that Jessie was dying. The snow was deep and the cold intense and he didn't make it back to the fort in time to say good-bye.

"He should have stayed to be a father to his sons," the elder brother said.

"How many bolts left, undertaker?" one of the medical examiners broke in.

Every bolt that was unscrewed the undertaker took and placed against the chapel wall. He ordered them in lines of ten, so as to more easily keep count. "Only five left now," he said.

"He was burning to join that expedition, you know that," the younger sandy-haired brother said. "But my wife and I didn't have the means to take care of his boys. And neither did you," he said to the elder.

The elder sighed and brushed a hand down the front of his coat, scattering tear-like drops of moisture. "I'll regret what happened for the rest of my life. But at least Fred left thinking we could."

"What happened?" the undertaker asked.

"They got split up, separated among relatives from Detroit to Ontario."

"That's awful," one of the undertaker's assistants said.

The brothers exchanged glances. "Well, at least we're here today to set our minds at rest. To find out just how true those rumors we've been hearing are," said the elder.

The newspaper man said, "What are the boys' names? The boys of the deceased, I'm talking about."

"Well, Harry. He's the eldest. You heard that."

"How old?" the editor had his pencil aimed at his pad.

"I don't know. How old is Harry?" the younger brother asked.

"Well, let's see," the elder went on. "Wheeler's the youngest. Then Douglas, and then Walter, going in reverse order. Dammit all, what do you want to know how old they are for?"

"We've got it," the undertaker announced. He strode over to the wall with the last bolt and set it in the line below the stained glass panel of the Virgin cradling the baby Jesus.

The reporter from the *Rochester Post-Express* sprang forward.

"Back, man," the elder Kislingbury shouted. "You'll get your story." He motioned to the medical examiners to step up as the assistants began to manhandle the lid.

"Watch it," the undertaker said. "It's as heavy as a caboose."

The brothers and the doctors moved in to help. "Don't crowd," ordered the undertaker and swung up his arm. "Give my men room. One false move could take your leg off." The lid was making a grating sound, like a rasp drawn against a knife blade.

The brothers and the doctors could not restrain themselves from pushing forward again as the lid slid back. Already the coffin had opened enough to give them a glimpse of what was inside.

✱

The doctors had pronounced him well enough to travel from the Portsmouth Navy Yard to his mother's home in Newburyport, and Lieutenant Adolphus W. Greely had left at dawn to make the short journey with Henrietta and their two young daughters by the navy's launch. As they steamed down the New Hampshire coast, the mists thinned to reveal Rye Beach and Hampton against a shoreline of tall, dark pines and the lighter greens of maples and oaks. A small fleet of fishing boats passed them as they turned up the inlet to his boyhood hometown, a familiar scene, though he had spent little time here since he had left to join the fighting in 1864, underage at seventeen.

His mother was waiting for him on the pier, along with his brother, John, with the wagon. Both had been at the festivities in Portsmouth on the weekend of August 2 and 3, just ten days earlier, but now he was being welcomed home, truly home, with a celebration his hometown promised would outdo the city of Portsmouth's.

Lieutenant Greely had with him the other survivors, five of the men he had gone to the Arctic with in 1881. They stood stiffly in their dark suits on the cobblestones, heavy carts rumbling past, still not at ease in the bustle. But when John began stowing their baggage in the wagon, Sergeant Brainard and Private Frederick sprang to assist. Greely watched his mother smile at that. Her hair had gone white while he was away, but she was as sharp as he remembered, and as neat in her dark-blue calico with the cameo at her throat she only donned for holidays. Henrietta had told him of their correspondence, that they had become good friends when he was in the Arctic.

"That's enough load for the horse," Mother Greely said. "We'll walk," and giving a hand to each of her granddaughters, she led off, taking a side path between the wooden buildings of the shipyard. Her son, his arm linked in his wife's, followed with his men, soon reaching the house on Prospect Street. It was not changed, he saw with relief, except on this day the white, two-story clapboard was swathed in red, white, and blue bunting. John was already hitching the horse to the wooden post.

"Why," Sergeant Brainard said, his hand on the picket fence that separated the house from the dirt street, "it didn't take us any longer to walk up to your front door, Mrs. Greely, than it did for us to walk from the ice foot up to our fort at Lady Franklin Bay."

"What's an ice foot?" Antoinette asked, looking up at the tall sergeant with the kind face. She was the eldest at five and full of questions. Henrietta had taken both daughters to live with their grandfather in San Diego, when her husband had gone north. The baby, Adola, named after her father, Adolphus, had been only a few months old when they made the long rail trip from Washington across the country.

Sergeant Brainard dropped down on one knee to explain an ice foot to Antoinette. "That's where the shore ice reaches out into the ocean, just like a large foot," he said.

"Can you walk on it?" she asked.

"Oh, yes, a very long way sometimes. When the *Proteus* landed us at Lady Franklin Bay, we unloaded all our stores into small boats and rowed to the ice foot, and from there we carried everything to dry land."

"That sounds laborious," Mother Greely offered. She understood hard work. After her husband sickened, she had turned to factory work to support her family. This man, Sergeant Brainard, she liked. She knew him to have been her son's true friend when they were undergoing such a hard time. "From what my son told me, you were about as far north as it was possible to be and remain on dry land," she said, as the one called Private Biederbick stepped forward to help John unload the wagon, along with Private Long, who had been their hunter, Dolph had told her. She had mastered these men's names. She thought this important. They were the only ones left.

"Sergeant Brainard," Private Frederick said, "was with Lieutenant Lockwood when they reached the Farthest North and beat the British record. What I mean to say, ma'am, is that the land extended farther up from where we were, even." He frowned. What he said had come out awkward. She liked him, too. This short man his messmates called Shorty. He had an earnest, serious face that gave one confidence.

"Lockwood. Lieutenant Lockwood," said the fifth man lounging against the picket fence. "There was no man who could talk better about food. He knew more goddamn restaurants, begging your pardon, ma'am." His Irish accent gave him away. This was Private Connell. But Lockwood—Mother Greely recalled how Henrietta had written her from California that Lieutenant Lockwood's father, the general, had been most helpful in spurring the government to bring her son back home. She studied Connell. He was big-boned with a shock of thick, black hair. His mustache was well trimmed, but he looked a ruffian all the same.

Henrietta had her eye on Connell, too. He was the one who had accepted a reduction from sergeant to private, so eager was he to join her Dolph's expedition. But this Irishman had not lived up to the high recommendation given by his previous company commander. At their starvation camp, Connell had saved his energy by doing little work.

"John will take you men around to the inn," Mother Greely said, "so you can rest up before the parade." She worried about these survivors. She was sure they tired much too easily, even that broad-shouldered man, Connell. Dolph was still wearing his fur vest under his summer linen suit. They were all so thin, their hands boney. Dolph's hands, long and slim-fingered, looked more—she hated to think this—like the talons of a bird of prey.

✳

The day had come off well. Greely and his five men sat in the lead carriage, the horses raising dust off the dirt lanes, then clattering on the cobblestones as the parade marched from the waterfront to the town hall. The band stirred patriotic hearts with the song written by Francis Scott Key as he had watched "bombs bursting in air" over Fort McHenry. Only town officials presided, unlike the celebration in Portsmouth, where there were speeches by Navy Secretary Chandler; the Governor of New Hampshire; Senator Hale and Representative Randall, who had shepherded the Greely relief bill through Congress; and General Hazen, Greely's boss in the Army Signal Corps, who had worked so hard to bring him home.

The day had ended with fireworks filling the darkening sky and now it was over. Greely's men had returned to the inn and their leader had sought out the swinging seat on the back porch of his mother's home. It was fully dark. The air remained mild, but filled with an enervating moisture that concentrated the scents coming from his mother's roses. There was no moon and the wisteria shading the porch blocked out any stars that might have been visible. He felt safe here, but the swing was making a terrible creaking noise. He couldn't seem to stop it.

Greely heard her step coming down the stairs. The screen door opened and Henrietta came out in a shaft of light from the gas lamp in the kitchen. She sat on the wooden seat beside him and the back and forth slowed and settled. "Your mother is so good with them," she said. "She read an Uncle Remus story. Such a battered book. It must have been yours. Adola fell asleep but Antoinette would have kept her at it till morning." She took his hand in hers. "You are so preoccupied, Dolph." She turned toward him, but it was too dark to see his face. "The news today was only on your homecoming."

"Those were the local papers," he said, the swinging seat beginning to groan.

She understood what he meant. She had seen the *New York Times* headlines of two days ago: HORRORS OF CAPE SABINE.

"I'm concerned about General Hazen," he said. "The *Times* has blamed him for the hard time we had."

She was aware of this, but this wasn't the thing that made him start when she brought him the morning papers, like a small wild creature, sensing danger, uncertain where to dart.

The crickets whirred and churred. The air grew closer and a distinct smell of tobacco announced a visitor. Sergeant Brainard ducked under the wisteria and was beside them on the porch.

"Sergeant! You were one of the nonsmokers at Fort Conger," Greely said in surprise.

Brainard's smile made a flash of white as he settled himself on the porch railing facing them. "It's the real thing, not the thrice-steeped tea leaves those desperate men rolled at Camp Clay." He noticed Mrs. Greely had not let go her husband's hand. The white of his shirt cuff and her blouse told him that. "Perhaps," he said to her, "Lieutenant Greely mentioned how hard-pressed our smokers were after the tobacco gave out." And to his commanding officer he said, "You don't smoke, but I've brought you a cigar." He passed the Havana and struck a match, a flare in the darkness that lit up both their faces, glinting off his commanding officer's steel-rimmed spectacles, and filling the air with the smell of sulfur. "I leave tomorrow on the early morning train for Albany," Brainard said, flicking out the match.

"Dolph told me you grew up on a dairy farm, Sergeant Brainard," Henrietta said. "Your family will be glad to have you back."

"There were always cows to milk." The cigar end glowed. "My father and I built a sidehill barn. I need to walk under its beams again."

"I told you, dear," Greely said to his wife, "how Sergeant Brainard fished for us when few others would stir themselves to carry water."

Brainard's smile flashed out. "The men needed to eat, just as the cows needed to be milked."

The smell of roses blended with cigar smoke and their talk of the recent past. Brainard saw that Mrs. Greely now held her husband's hand in both of hers.

"Your farm," Henrietta said. "You must have thought about it often."

"Oh, I did. I saw how it sat on the land. I'd go over each of our cows in my mind when I was down at the ocean's edge with my burlap net. It kept me going." He shivered. He didn't want to think about that miserable cold. Leaning toward the Greelys from the porch railing, he said, "Wasn't that a grand feast tonight? Biederbick said it rivaled his best meals at the Vienna Café in Brooklyn."

The menu before each place in that gaslit room had the survivors of the Lady Franklin Bay Expedition laughing. It had been drawn up in the spirit of the menu Private Henry had created for their first Christmas in 1881. Roast Beef à la Lieutenant Greely, Musk Ox Roast à la Frederick, Arctic Salmon. "Your plum puddings, Mrs. Greely," Brainard went on, "we had them for every holiday and blessed you for them." His cigar end glowed.

"Making them gave me a chance to be a small part of your life there," she said.

"I remember," Greely said, "George Rice saying he had helped his family pick apples in their orchard on the day he left."

They were silent and comfortable together. They felt protected from the world beyond by the darkness.

Brainard spoke suddenly as the crickets' whir intensified. "He also said that to pick the wrong man when there's a lengthy voyage ahead is inviting disaster."

"Rice saw too deeply. He thought too much," Greely muttered.

"I must talk to you," Brainard said. He slapped his fist in his palm.

Henrietta stood up, the swing creaking. "And I must check on the children," she said, extending her hand to Sergeant Brainard. "I'll see you in Washington. I know you'll be working with my husband there, sorting out the records you've brought back. He has a book to write. You must come and have a meal with us."

He jumped off the railing and took her hand. "Thank you, I'd enjoy that." He wanted to say more but she had moved into the gaslight that turned her silk skirt to the color of plums as it swept the floor. He leaned back against the railing. "I wanted to tell her I know about what she did to bring about our rescue. I wanted to thank her."

"She's remarkable, isn't she?" Greely said, and stubbed out his cigar. The darkness around him grew as deep as a well, his full black beard, his black hair, the blackness of his suit making him nearly invisible. Brainard managed to locate his cuffs, a rim of white, and spoke the words he had come to say.

"We should say nothing, don't you agree, Lieutenant Greely?"

The other was silent, a silence that stretched out until Brainard wondered if his commanding officer had fallen into a doze. At Camp Clay, Lieutenant Greely could sink away like this. But Brainard had learned that their commander knew very well what was going on around him. He waited. The crickets kept up their pulsating song. The wisteria rustled in the light breeze.

Lieutenant Greely finally spoke. "The news has spread like a virus. If we try to explain ourselves, we are dead men." Brainard heard the old authority. "When I get to Washington," Greely went on, "I will make sure you get your commission. I promised you that at Fort Conger, after your victory of the Farthest North."

"Not just mine. Lockwood's . . ."

"I am aware of that."

"But you agree? We will say nothing?" Brainard pressed. Out of the darkness, he sensed Lieutenant Greely had reached out, the swing creaking and the white cuff flaring toward him. Brainard leaned to bridge the gap, meeting his commanding officer's hand with his own.

Part One

Fort Conger

1

A Question of Luck

Fort Conger, Lady Franklin Bay

26 August 1881

> I feel that perhaps we should never be so happy if you gave up
> the opportunity for you would always think of what you had
> missed.
>
> Henrietta Greely **in a letter to her husband before the expedition**

The spot they had reached, Lady Franklin Bay, a long and narrow penetration in the Ellesmere Land coast, was eleven hundred miles north of the Arctic Circle, and only one hundred miles short of the top of the North American continent. Captain Pike had butted and wedged the *Proteus* through rotten ice up to ten feet thick into the indentation of Discovery Harbor, rimmed by cliffs shooting well over a thousand feet. Cascades of water thundered down the solid rock, splitting into smaller streams before plunging into the sea. In the harbor's center sat a rugged island named Bellot by the British, its summit snow-crested in mid-August. The ship, looking for a landing spot, turned to place this island on its starboard side while keeping Cairn Hill, on the mainland, to port. High on the hill's steep slopes musk oxen grazed, while lower down at a brook-fed open pool a large flock of eider ducks splashed and flapped. The expansive shoreline was studded with rocks, the largest rivaling in size the motor launch Lieutenant Adolphus W. Greely had brought up in the *Proteus* for coastline exploring. These boulders, fallen from the cliffs since the commencement of time, presented a formidable obstacle to moving about this raw and unknown land. Back beyond, over the cliffs, the terrain steepened to mountains, revealing glaciated slopes. Where the ship dropped anchor below Proteus Point, midsummer greenery flourished: sedges and grasses, clusters of purple flowering saxifrage, and patches of yellow Arctic poppies. But no trees; none at all.

The light was constant, only dimming around midnight. In those first few days after landing the men worked sixteen hours of the twenty-four, unloading the ship and beginning construction on their house. An army barracks was already framed, sitting solid on a stretch of level land, its gable ends riding north and south, its long bank of windows facing east toward the sunrise and the sea. The *Proteus* had made several attempts to leave the harbor, but a storm from the east had driven in ice from Lady Franklin Bay, and though the ship had battled her way to Dutch Island, two miles from Proteus Point, she was forced back. She lay now nearly within hailing distance from the huddle of tents, giving the men a last opportunity to pen notes to be carried back home.

They had arrived easily enough through seas that could wreck ships: the crosscurrents of Smith Sound, the turbulent Kane Basin, finally the long, narrow ice-choked Kennedy Channel. These twenty-five men comprised only the fourth expedition to make it through the treacherous pack ice this far north. They were well prepared: precut lumber, glass windows, two heating stoves, a cooking range, a boiler, and a bathtub. Lieutenant Greely was concerned about diet and hygiene. He wanted his men to be healthy and comfortable.

Dr. Octave Pavy, who had spent the winter living in Greenland with the natives, learning their ways and their language, had already fought with Henry Clay. Clay, the grandson of the great orator, had also spent the winter there, contracting sled dogs for Greely. Both men had been picked up by the *Proteus*. Greely wanted Clay to remain, but Clay said, "I can't get along with the man. You'll need him. He's a decent physician. I'll return with the ship." Greely knew he had lost a good man.

Lieutenant Frederick Kislingbury had become a source of concern, too. He had been with Greely when they laid the military telegraph line across the Dakota and Montana Territories. Kislingbury had done excellent work, and they had discovered a mutual interest in the Arctic when their small party had nearly frozen in a late-fall snowstorm. Kislingbury, born in England, knew all about the Franklin tragedy, and was on Lady Franklin's side over the rumored cannibalism. "Englishmen don't eat Englishmen," he had assured Greely. "It was the Eskimos, no question." In his response to his commander's invitation to join the expedition he had written frankly of the recent loss of his second wife. She was at Fort Custer with him and had died of typhoid when he was away on an Indian raid. For this very reason, Kislingbury wrote, he looked upon Lieutenant Greely's invitation as "a godsend, giving me a wonderful chance to wear out my second terrible sorrow." He also wrote he was eager for the "overland trips through snow and ice. I'm with you heart and soul." His handwriting—festooned with flourishes reflective of his emotive nature—had not put Greely off, though perhaps it should have. Kislingbury could be impulsive, boyishly so, a trait that a thirty-three-year-old father of four sons should have outgrown.

Take the incident of the polar bear on the voyage up. Lieutenant Kislingbury had spotted the great beast resting on an ice floe. Here was formidable game seen by few except in books. Kislingbury ordered the men to lower a boat and grabbed his shiny new Remington rifle. His shot brought the bear down, and back on the *Proteus*, in front of everyone, he announced that the pelt was his trophy, to bring back for his boys, who would be so proud of him.

"You cannot claim this bear as your personal property, Lieutenant Kislingbury," Greely made clear. "It's an expedition capture and therefore belongs to the expedition." His second officer had gone white to the hairline and given him a piercing stare that would have felled a lesser man. This man's defiance was not indicative of the kind of soldierly conduct Greely demanded of his officers.

Lieutenant Kislingbury and Lieutenant James Lockwood—who had grown up at the naval academy in Annapolis, where his father was an instructor—had exhibited further shortcomings when Greely asked them to negotiate their transport in St. John's, Newfoundland. While both were trained to execute a superior's orders and to handle men, neither possessed the management skills needed for securing their ship, the steam sealer *Proteus*. He had to take over, and at the absolute worst moment with Henrietta coming to term with her second pregnancy.

Despite these initial setbacks, the men of the Lady Franklin Bay Expedition were working well together. Their barracks was a sixty-by-seventeen-foot building, a living arrangement these men, mostly Indian fighters off the Plains, were used to. They had kept at the backbreaking task of unloading the lumber, the wooden boxes and barrels of canned and dry food, and all their scientific equipment with jokes, laughter, and a healthy dash of swagger in the shakedown of who could hoist the heaviest load. Greely dispatched hunting teams for the musk oxen. But these enormous shaggy beasts ignorant of men just stood and faced the gun barrel, no sport at all. They hung the meat on tripods of poles brought on the ship to this treeless land, well out of reach of the jumping dogs they had picked up in Greenland.

Within a week of their arrival they had moved into the fort, named Fort Conger to honor the senator from Michigan who had sponsored the bill that had pushed a reluctant government to fund the Lady Franklin Bay Expedition. The privates already were at the job they had been brought here for, taking observations—temperatures, wind directions, currents, tides, clouds, movement of the ice—some five hundred a day in support of the three meteorologists, plus an astronomer and a photographer. The photographer was Sergeant George Rice, and the whole expedition, gathered in Washington, had sat to be photographed at Rice's brother's studio.

Every man was well aware their expedition was one of a dozen stations, composed of teams from Germany, Austria, Norway, and Russia, that were all part of an enterprise called the International Polar Year. Greely's men, near the top of Ellesmere Land, were the farthest north, the coldest, the most isolated, the hardest to reach, and the loneliest. Greely had told his men that they were a part of the most important effort of scientific discovery and exploration since Lewis and Clark had opened up vast new territories for the United States under the Jefferson administration. That was seventy years ago. The data they would bring back to Washington would be pondered, analyzed, and stored for years to come.

They were here to collect rocks, plants, birds, animals, and insects. They were here to record celestial occurrences like auroras and parhelions. They were here to discover new lands, study glaciers, to find out if Greenland extended clear over the pole. They were not here to reach the pole. But they were here to set a new Farthest North record and best the British. In sum, they were here to learn all they could about the Arctic, this adversary that for the last three centuries had sunk ships and killed men who searched for a feasible trading route through the great North American archipelago—a Northwest Passage.

The Civil War had changed the country, exhausted it. Their older brothers and fathers had fought in it. Lieutenant Greely had himself, and had the battle wounds to prove it. The bankers had taken over. The railroads had split the land up and opened the West where a man could make his fortune in mining, or on the great river systems, or in the forests of tall, straight trees. The nation had rushed into a period of immense wealth, its politics prey to scandals, corruption, and greed. The agrarian way of life was fading into the past. Those who had grown up on the farms felt uprooted, adrift in a world they did not understand. Volunteering for this Arctic assignment was going to give them *their* chance.

✳

In the last few days they had already done something that had never been done in the Arctic: begun construction on a sturdy building that could house twenty-five men safely and with enough comfort to see them through a winter on land. When men overwintered previously, they had lived on their ships. Every man at Conger knew, if he came back, he would be famous, or at least he would be assured of a rise in rank and pay. None of them were ordered to be here. But each thought it worth the risk. Each man knew how tough he was. They had survived fifty below zero in the Plains forts. Like the men who had panned for gold in '49, these men had come to make a stake.

Sergeant David Brainard stood on the top of Cairn Hill, the thousand-foot rise behind their fort. He had come up to gaze down. He

David L. Brainard, Company L, Second Cavalry, Montana Territory, 1879. Courtesy of Glenn M. Stein, Fellow of the Royal Geographical Society and the Royal Canadian Geographical Society.

wanted this bird's-eye view of where they were and what their new home looked like from above. He gave the men a task, nailing up the precut siding, and told them he would be gone an hour. He put Private Julius Frederick in charge. He knew he could trust Shorty—as they affectionately called him—with his life as he had done in the Plains Wars.

He was puffing by the time he clambered over the rocks, and wished he had given himself another half hour. But that was all right, the exercise was good for him after the two months spent on the *Proteus*. He needed to make this a habit. If he was going to keep a clear head and be true to his responsibilities, he needed to get off by himself now and then. It was his way of gaining perspective on situations, and right now, at the top of Cairn Hill, he could gain a very clear perspective in the literal sense, for there was their fort taking shape below.

He crouched down, his hand on the stony top, and relished the view. The fresh breeze was drying out his shirt and he passed a hand across his forehead to help the wind dry his sweat. The men looked like ants down there, each one of them at some task or other. He could hear the hammer blows, and smiled to himself. He was glad that Shorty Frederick was with him, and Francis Long, too. They had all been privates together at Fort Ellis, fighting the Sioux and the Nez Perce.

He stood up and looked around at the great country they had come to, turning his gaze inland, toward Grinnell Land, a great sweep of the Arctic that carried through to the Western Ocean. He smiled again. He couldn't see thousands of miles. *But, damn, it feels as if I could. The air is so clear. I feel so good. I'm so happy to be here.* He raised his arms in the joy of it and tried to absorb the sight of these mountains—they must be three thousand feet high, a great barrier of glaciated peaks on the horizon. Lieutenant Greely was going to send exploring parties into them!

The breeze picked up and he shivered. He had run up without his jacket and now that his sweat had dried he felt a chill that caught his breath. *It's so huge, this land. So vast.* He searched his mind for the words that could possibly describe the scene of cliffs that rose out of an ice-choked sea, of peaks that in all his experience in the West could not approach this grandeur. *It's too immense to grasp. It's so empty.* And then he corrected himself. This land was anything but empty! There was an overpowering fullness to it. He felt nearly drowned by the wildness. *But no people*, he said aloud. *Nature herself reigns here. No humans other than ourselves.* The thought sobered him: the immensity of this Arctic land, the distance they had come from home.

A rush of shadow flashing over made him look up to see a broad pair of black wings. A raven. A single bird. *Oh my God, it's so beautiful.* The bird circled back over him, much lower this time, and Brainard's eyes connected with the black pinprick of the raven's eyes. *How thankful I am to be here.* He spoke the words aloud, like a prayer.

Discovery Harbor, beneath his feet, gleamed in the sun. The ship that had brought them up, the *Proteus*, was still there, held fast by ice. Brainard was both glad for this sight that connected them, still, to home—the ship would carry back their mail—but wishing for the day that Captain Pike would break free and leave them, truly, on their own. *Then we'll find out what we are made of,* his thoughts ran. *This is the beginning of something new. We will make history here. We are expected to accomplish meaningful work, work that will expand human knowledge.* He looked down at his boots, embarrassed at his own great ponderings, and the opening lines of *David Copperfield* flooded his mind: Will I, he wondered, be the hero of my own life? That was the question Copperfield had asked himself, and David Brainard, another David, posed the same. *Just keep your head straight and feet on the ground,* he lectured. *You're here to perform a duty, to carry out orders, and give your strength and loyalty to Lieutenant Greely, and now you must descend the mountain and get to work.*

He let his eyes follow out to the far, far horizon. The raven was there, high up, a black dot, headed somewhere on business of its own. He waved to the great bird; he could not help himself. He had experienced such a surge of joy to be in this land with a bird like that. *I'm in this raven's home. I'm just a visitor, yet I want to learn how to become comfortable here.* He searched for the black dot again, but the raven had vanished, absorbed into the wildness of the landscape. David Brainard set a fast pace down Cairn Hill.

⚹

"You are late, Lieutenant," Greely snapped, leaning over his pocket watch positioned before him on the breakfast table, "by twenty minutes."

Lieutenant Kislingbury had overslept on the boat coming up and continued to oversleep most mornings since. Greely had sent a man to wake him. Today he would put an end to this officer's insubordination.

"I would prefer to stay in bed and do without breakfast, sir," articulated the lieutenant.

The man's crisp accent grated on Lieutenant Greely's ear. He sprang up, jostling the table. "Lieutenant Kislingbury," he pronounced in a voice he knew how to make carry. "I would willingly lose every officer and do my work with enlisted men alone rather than have men disposed to question my orders." He swept up his watch and dropped it in his pocket. "Are you willing to continue on this basis?"

While his superior was speaking Kislingbury had sat down on the bench—Private William Whisler moving over to make room—and helped himself to oatmeal, now congealed, from the bowl on the table. "I am not." His words emerged, separate and distinct. He was a good-looking, sandy-haired man with a trimmed mustache. "Matters have gone too far." He stayed seated while he said this. Lieutenant Kislingbury had the advantage with his accent; Lieutenant Greely, topping out at six feet, the advantage in height, so the Englishman remained seated.

"Then I relieve you, Lieutenant, of your position on this expedition." Kislingbury rocked back on the bench as though struck, but continued to masticate his cold oatmeal. "You are excused, men," Greely addressed the table, aware that every eye was trained on him. "There are the meteorological readings to take on the hour, and you are late." He ran a hand down his bushy black beard in a smoothing action. "It is past eight o'clock. The beds must be aired as today is Tuesday; dishes cleared, washed, and put away, the floor swept and the coal boxes filled." He had taken off his spectacles to run his eyes down the table, black eyes, soft, lustrous, and full of highlights. They were his best feature. He swerved on his left heel and strode in a military manner out of the common room, every eye fixed upon his arrow-straight back.

They had been here just seventeen days.

David Brainard rubbed a hand across his freshly shaved chin. He had seen this coming. Their commanding officer had to nip insubordination if he were to hold his men. But Brainard had his doubts about how Lieutenant Greely had handled this. Colonel Doane would never have let the situation escalate in a way that put his whole expedition at risk. Colonel G. C. Doane had led men like these around the breakfast tables—Indian fighters. He had served under Doane during the Nez Perce War. Doane had the kind of confidence that made men want to follow him anywhere. He had set himself apart from an ordinary army commander when he confirmed the great geysers and boiling springs of the Yellowstone. Colonel Doane had the temperament of the true explorer. Greely's experience in leading men was directing the logistics of placing the telegraph line for the Army Signal Corps. The stringent discipline he had just exhibited toward Lieutenant Kislingbury was as though Fort Conger were under imminent Indian attack. These men were just starting to work together. Just getting to know each other. Brainard hoped his commander, when he cooled down, might see a way to defuse this situation with Lieutenant Kislingbury. Colonel Doane had been approached to lead the Lady Franklin Bay Expedition. He had turned it down. Lieutenant Greely was the second choice.

Sergeant Brainard stood up. He had his commissary to look after. His tins of food were still in their packing crates. They needed to be in order on their shelves.

Lieutenant Kislingbury, who had just been stripped and so had no official duties, shoved aside his half-consumed oatmeal and pulled a small book out of his breast pocket. Private Charles Henry, sweeping the floor, saw this and came over, Private Jacob Bender at his heels. "What book is that?" Private Henry asked, leaning over the lieutenant's shoulder. He liked to read, and write as well. He told everyone he was writing up their expedition for the *Chicago Times*. Most of them didn't believe him, but when Charlie Henry swung through the Windy City on his way east to join the expedition in Washington, he arranged with the editor to be that paper's special correspondent. He invested in pens, paper, and an ink pot. He went to the trouble of having cards printed up bearing his new title: Special Correspondent to the *Chicago Times*. He mailed one to his old commander Captain Price. He wouldn't have minded visiting Mina, his married sister who lived in Chicago, but her husband asked entirely too many questions. It was pretty important, right when he was on the verge of leaving the country, that the less anyone knew of his plans and whereabouts the better.

"Here, I want to show you men something," the fallen lieutenant said, and turned his book toward the two privates. "See? See what my Harry wrote on the flyleaf?"

Bender nudged Charlie. "Read it out loud, would you?"

Private Charlie Henry stared at him. "Can't you read?"

"Please, just read it," Bender said in his squeaky voice.

Bender sounded so like his sister Mina, Charlie was ready to comply when Lieutenant Kislingbury said, "*I'll* read it." He held the book so the men could see. "'To My Dear Father.'" His precise pronunciation re-flected the well-formed letters written in the schoolboy's penmanship. "'May God be with you and return you safely to me. Your affectionate son, Harry Kislingbury.'"

Poor illiterate Bender let out something that sounded like a sob. Kislingbury moaned, "Oh, how I miss them all," and pocketed his son's gift. "On the ship I wrote my boys that Papa has but one thing he dreads. The long night. One hundred and thirty days of darkness. My God!" Lieutenant Kislingbury buried his face in his hands. "I cannot die now. I *must* get back for my little men." A few of the other privates, Maurice Connell, William Whisler, and Roderick Schneider—who was in charge of the dogs—drifted over.

"Dr. Pavy should be in charge," Kislingbury said. He pounded his fist on the table.

Connell laughed a disrespectful laugh, baring his teeth under his bushy black mustache, indicating he was in agreement with the demoted lieutenant. The others stayed silent. This sounded too dangerously mutinous.

"The doctor lived in the Arctic," Kislingbury went on. "He came up with the Howgate Expedition in the *Gulnare* last year. Colonel Doane was to lead. You've heard all that. He brought eleven men east with him from Fort Ellis, including Sergeant Brainard; you ask him if he wasn't with Doane. But when the naval officers examined the vessel they pro-nounced it unseaworthy. Captain Howgate, though, he sent the *Gulnare* up anyway, to drop off stores for next year."

"The doctor's told us about his winter with the Eskimos," Private Bender said. He was short, slight, and baby-faced, and needed to be in the middle of things.

"Bet they lent him their wives." Connell, their lone Irishman among these German privates, leered. "Eskimos can be awfully generous that way." He got an appreciative laugh. They had given up women to come here. Or said they had. It's doubtful, if they were not married like Lieutenant Greely or the doctor or the meteorologist Hampden Gardiner, who had married his sweetheart just two months before he left, that their relations with women had been little other than with the "ladies of the night" in Deadwood or such lawless towns accessible from the army forts on the Plains.

"What did you do with your four motherless boys?" Schneider asked.

"I left them in the care of my brothers, as I've told you. My three brothers will look after my poor boys." He glared at the privates gathered around. "I'm not going to serve under a man who tells me to my face that subordination is the most important qualification for Arctic service. I'm not like Lieutenant Lockwood."

"Yeah, but Lieutenant Lockwood apologizes for being late," Whisler said. He had a way of standing, an erect carriage that gave his words authority.

"He's an insomniac," Charlie Henry explained.

"What's an insom . . ." Bender stumbled over this new word.

"Means he can't sleep, you dumbkoff," said Charlie.

"Lieutenant Greely will promote him now," Connell said. "He'll take over as the C.O.'s second officer."

"That's right," said Schneider, smirking. "In a position to command."

Kislingbury rose abruptly. He wanted to strike the man but settled for overturning the bench and stalked out.

He was fired up to leave. He couldn't wait to see his boys again. It was a miracle that the *Proteus* was still in the harbor. Captain Pike had tried daily to extricate his ship. It was nearly September and he and all his crew were still above the 82nd parallel. Kislingbury waited outside Greely's quarters. He stared at his boots, scuffed and unpolished. Lieutenant Greely's boots reflected light like a mirror. The Englishman rocked back and forth on his unshined footware. They had enjoyed each other's company during the telegraph assignment. Greely had changed. Lieutenant Kislingbury could hear the C.O. scratching away with his pen on the order relieving him from the expedition. The C.O. was a methodical man and Kislingbury damned him for taking his measured time with the I-am-sir-your-most-obedient-servant, etcetera, as was required in the official forms. He began to sweat.

Meanwhile, Captain Pike on the *Proteus* seized his chance. A lead had opened between the floes and he had his men firing up the boiler, spreading the sails, and hauling up the anchor. Pike had no notion of Lieutenant Kislingbury's predicament; all he was concerned about was taking advantage of this lead and gaining the open water.

✗

Top Sergeant David Brainard had the men on the roof, hammering down tarpaper. It was a good day for finishing this job, not too windy, and they had discovered that Lady Franklin Bay was a windy spot. This country was a lot more rugged than the Plains or even the Rocky Mountain ranges. One swell or uplift looked like another. It was hard to establish landmarks in a landscape composed of rocks and snow and ice and no trees. It was often foggy, shutting off visibility. A man could die pretty quick if he got caught out with no place to hide.

When Brainard had commented on the sameness of the terrain to George Rice, their photographer, Rice had said, "It's the light. It's always changing." They were standing on the ice foot that stretched from the shore at the high-tide line and looking out toward a pair of icebergs the size of upended boxcars. "Lewis and Clark had an artist along," Rice went on. "But I'm working in this new artistic medium with glass plates." And Brainard caught the photographer's excitement, the challenge of capturing the beauty of this monochromatic land.

The men finishing up the roof were working well together. Brainard was glad to see that. Their chatter was of exploring trips they would be going on and whether the thermometer would hit colder than the fifty below zero they had experienced on the Plains. Brainard sensed concern about the twenty weeks of darkness. But they had kerosene for their lamps and Lieutenant Greely had brought along a library. He was eager to read Elisha Kent Kane's *Arctic Explorations* and Charles Francis Hall's narrative as well. Both men had searched for Franklin and their books had made them famous.

Suddenly Private Bender shouted, "Look! It's Lieutenant Kisling-bury! He's got his duffle." Brainard looked up. So, Lieutenant Greely had followed through, and the lieutenant was too bound up in his pride to apologize. Two wrongs don't make a right, that's what he had learned at home on the farm and in school, too. They all watched the lieutenant running at breakneck speed, blasting through snowdrifts, falling over himself, his canvas gear bag catching on the rocks, waving his free hand.

"By God, he's trying to flag down the *Proteus*," Private Henry shouted. And they all started talking at once.

"He told the C.O. he was going to keep that polar bear's pelt."

"Shot it with that Remington *given* him by the firm. Told us that fifty times."

"He just wants to get back to his boys."

"He never should have left them," Private Frederick said. He was their shortest man with a quiet voice that always got their attention.

"You're right, Shorty," Whisler said. "Goddamnit. He never should have come up here."

All work on the roof stopped as they watched Lieutenant Kisling-bury drop his heavy load and hurl himself forward. They lost him in a dip, but he appeared again, growing smaller until he reached Dutch Island, a rocky dot a full two miles away. But the *Proteus* was beyond Lieutenant Kislingbury's reach, and the men on the roof went back to work. Now and then they glanced up to spot the lieutenant as he limped slowly back. He flung around to see what the ship was doing, but she only showed him her backside. When he reached his kit bag he hoisted it and staggered. It seemed to Brainard that poor Lieutenant Kisling-bury had taken up a weight too great to bear.

"I'd say our Englishman is stuck and stuck good," Private Connell said in a tone that betrayed his amusement at the lieutenant's misfortune.

"Brought it on himself." Private Henry chuckled. "His timing's about as disastrous as General Custer's, leading his Seventh Cavalry into the Indian trap at Little Big Horn."

Bender joined in the laugh and got a frown from Brainard. The ser-geant was well aware that this private was impressed by these two men. The Irishman, Connell, had a blasphemous mouth that was not going down well with the C.O. Charlie Henry was built like a prizefighter. He cultivated a droopy mustache and spooned down food like a starving

Charles Henry Buck, alias Charles B. Henry, Cheyenne, Wyoming, ca. 1879–80. Courtesy of Dr. Geoffrey E. Clark.

man. Their conversation brought out the worst in Private Bender, who attempted to make up for his height deficit by puffing out his skinny chest.

✶

Brainard found out that Private Charles B. Henry had gotten off on a poor footing with his commanding officer. He was in his commissary unpacking the crates of canned food meant to keep them well fed and healthy. He enjoyed this task of making an alphabetical arrangement of his cans, starting with anchovies and ending with zucchinis. Lieutenant Greely had come in to talk with him about hanging the musk oxen meat to keep it out of reach of jumping, hungry dogs. He was about to leave, when he turned to his sergeant. "You should know Private Henry came to me on the trip up to say he wanted your position."

"You mean he wanted to be placed in charge of all of this?" David Brainard waved his hand over a compressed acre of cans and jars, the burlap sacks of tobacco, extra clothing, sledge harnesses for men and dogs, snowshoes, axes, extra thermometers, and countless other items.

The C.O. laughed at the incredulous expression on his top sergeant's face. "The private said he'd been the chief clerk under Captain Price at Fort Sidney. George Price is a fine man and a splendid officer. It was on the strength of his recommendation that I took Private Henry."

Brainard nodded at this and returned to his cans.

"Private Henry told me I was making a mistake by not giving him the position. The way he looked at me—the man is large, he can appear quite threatening—when I told him he was the last to sign on and lucky to be here at all, I really think he expected me to make the change." Lieutenant Greely drew a hand down his black beard. "He thinks highly of Price, and Price tried to discourage him from coming to the Arctic. According to Henry, Price said, 'If I had a yellow cat and was mad with her, I wouldn't send her out to the Arctic seas.' The private thought this was very funny. Then he said, 'So, I'm just here to fill out the roster.' I didn't like the look he gave me then either."

Brainard had stopped sorting cans. "I'll keep an eye on him," he said. He recalled how this private had made an imposing presence in the back row of the photograph taken in George Rice's brother's studio. Private Henry was one of the Germans. There was no trace of an accent, but Brainard had picked up in the privates' conversations that Henry had immigrated with his family. Others here came from immigrant backgrounds. Army life suited men who had experienced little stability, had in their early days in America gone hungry. Such men knew that a certain amount of pillage was tolerated on army posts. Private Henry made a lot of noise about how much he loved the musk oxen roasts, proclaiming the musk oxen was nearly as tasty as his favorite dish, hamburg beefsteak. He stowed away three times as much as his friend Bender. Yes, Sergeant David Brainard promised himself he would keep a close eye on Private Charles Henry.

It was clear to all from his talk, however, that Charlie Henry was proud to be a part of this expedition. Weren't they based a mere five hundred miles from the North Pole? Didn't they all know about the Englishman Sir John Franklin? Why, whole nations had been looking for him for the past thirty-five years, way before they were born. Lady Franklin Bay was named for his widow. Sir John had sacrificed his life, his ships, and all his crew in his great search for the Northwest Passage. This Englishman was a hero with a tomb in Westminster Abbey and an epitaph composed by the poet Tennyson, which Henry recited, one hand thrust between the buttons on his uniform coat:

> Not here! The white North has thy bones; and thou heroic sailor-soul
> art passing on thine happier voyage now toward no earthly pole.

But he, Charlie, didn't intend to die up here. He planned to return to his army mates famous.

✶

As he watched Kislingbury struggle back, Sergeant David Brainard was concerned that his commander's disciplinary action did not fit their situation. The word martinet had crossed his mind as a description for Greely's leadership. If that was what they were up against, a man's stripes were worthless, as the Englishman's case had proved. They were in an isolated world that was becoming colder and darker by the day. It seemed to Brainard this called for an easing of strict adherence to army regulations, not the harshest punishment for a minor infraction. His commanding officer could not permit oversleeping. He just wished that Kislingbury had taken the hint from Lieutenant Lockwood, who admitted his fault and expressed a willingness to correct himself. Then Lieutenant Greely could restore him to duty.

His C.O. was known for handling men with fairness and prudence when he was pushing through the telegraph lines for the Army Signal Corps. Yet this quality was called into question the very week they arrived, when Greely announced that the men were expected to wash the officers' clothing. "I ask for volunteers," he said. No one stepped forward, and Brainard watched as Greely massaged his chin through the black beard that covered the lower half of his face, where the bullet had passed through his jaw at Antietam. He had observed this gesture his superior officer resorted to when confronted with a situation that veered unpleasant. Greely turned to Sergeant Brainard. "I order you, Sergeant, to detail men to this duty." Then he faced the men standing around the breakfast fire, awaiting their work assignments. "I am not a man to be trifled with," Greely said, "and in the case of mutiny I would not stop at the loss of human lives to restore order."

Tension clogged the air, every eye on Greely. Brainard heard the ice floes in the bay thrashing and growling and punching each other about. He held off detailing a washing crew and Greely said nothing more to him about it. They were preoccupied with settling in. Taking the meteorological readings, some five hundred in a twenty-four hour period. Transporting coal from the seam Captain Nares of the British Royal Navy had discovered at Watercourse Bay that made living here possible. Schneider was already working with the dogs. They would be pulling sledges for the exploring trips. And so the incident passed. Brainard hoped his commanding officer would see his error and ameliorate his actions to those appropriate to their situation. These men were trained fighters, while Greely's previous military experience had been the logistical laying out of telegraph lines. The situation at Fort Conger might call for a similar kind of leadership, but the men themselves had come from recent combat on the Plains. Brainard desperately hoped his C.O. could find his way with these men.

✴

Fort Conger

15 September 1881

My Dear Wife,

I will write you my present thoughts though you will not read them until the relief picks up our mail in a year from now. But keeping this running journal gives me the double comfort of a means to relieve my mind as I keep you close to me.

I have instituted a Psalm reading at ten o'clock on Sunday mornings. I will as well, on Sundays, cut down the men's duty to what is only strictly necessary. I will, however, permit no games, in particular no card playing. As you know, I abhor betting, and have restricted the men, if they must bet, to their tobacco. Do you think me overly strict? The Sabbath should be observed with reverence, but I will excuse those with scruples of conscience. Edward Israel, our youngest at twenty-one, and a Jew, attends our services, but I want him to know he is not compelled to do so. You remember how pleased I was to welcome this young graduate from the University of Michigan as our astronomer, and how difficult for his parents, aware of the hazards of our expedition, to entrust him to my care. He possesses a lively intelligence, and I predict I shall enjoy his company. Though I'm not sure how he will enjoy ours. These army men—I'm speaking of the privates— are a species he has never encountered. But Ned Israel possesses a gentle nature that will, I'm sure, tame these rough beasts.

I cannot say the same of Lieutenant Kislingbury. He is intelligent enough but has disgraced himself over a minor matter. I had to break the man. It appears he is not cut out for the disciplined teamwork I require and that is needed in our harsh Arctic situation. I blame myself for this miscalculation. I judged the man to be industrious, competent, and worthy of trust. I singled him out for special commendation for the excellent job he did for me leading the men stringing telegraph poles through the remote Western Territories. But it seems that fifteen years of military training have not taught Lieutenant Kislingbury to execute his superior's orders with absolute and unhesitating obedience, no matter what that order might be. I want a willing compliance. I require it. I can only conclude that the recent loss of his second wife has unbalanced his mind, the more so as he calls *my* demands unreasonable. Perhaps Lieutenant Kislingbury finds our Arctic life too rough and was looking for a way out. Already when the men discuss the coming darkness, I hear the dread in their voices. Lieutenant Kislingbury left four young sons. He cannot stop talking about them. The men at first heard him out with sympathy, but his harping on the sad tale now only annoys them. It pains me to reveal to you the cause of his offence—a trivial matter of refusing to arise at seven and take breakfast at the same hour as the men. As I require this of myself, I do not hesitate to require this of my officers. But Lieutenant Kislingbury surprised me by saying that he would remain in bed and do without his breakfast. I said that he would get up whether he chose to eat or not. It was a regulation of the expedition and must be complied with. He said that he would do so only if it was insisted upon. I said to him that this was no place for an officer to say that he would obey an order only if it was *insisted on*, that cheerful compliance was expected, and when an officer could not yield it, his usefulness as a member of the expedition was destroyed. He commenced discussing the question, and I was twice compelled to say that I would listen to no arguments. The situation is awkward, but I have resolved that the discomfort will be Lieutenant Kislingbury's, not mine. It distresses me, as you can imagine. We have hardly begun our work here and my second officer has become useless to the expedition. I am quite sure he despises me. I will close now, as I fear I have overburdened you with this matter of Lieutenant Kislingbury.

How I miss you, my dear wife. My body aches for you. I did not know I could miss you this much, and so I kiss you. And I ask you to kiss our sweet babes. I wonder if little Antoinette has already forgotten me.

Your own,
Dolph

I add this postscript a few days later. The situation of Lieutenant Kislingbury has been much on my mind. I have encouraged him to engage in unofficial activities, such as hunting. The Englishman, true to his race, is a born sportsman. His rifle, given him by the Remington firm, is his proudest possession, I would judge, as he displayed it on the voyage up, telling everyone of the gift. I am sure he wants to be a part of all we will accomplish here, and so I hope my leniency will show him I am willing to listen to an apology. If such is forthcoming, I would restore him to his rank. But he must bend. I fully expect it. Lieutenant Kislingbury's attitude is a setback to the expedition, but it cannot last. Ah! So much is a question of luck in this world. But if I had not thought that I was lucky I should never have come up here.

2

Benches without Backs
Fort Conger, Lady Franklin Bay

Early Winter 1881

Human beings are not ideally designed for getting on with each other—especially in close quarters.

Sir Ranulph Fiennes, *Mind over Matter: The Epic Crossing of the Antarctic Continent* (1993)

Sergeant David Brainard—Sergeant Davy, as the men were already calling him—strode toward Dutch Island. It made a good destination, a four-mile round trip, a labyrinthine course the men had worked out, threading the boulders and chunks of shore ice—a horizontal talus slope. They had been here over a month, and, now, deep into September, the sun was only slightly elevated at midday, then sinking to a profound twilight and darkness. The dark was putting them on edge and snappish. Except for George Rice. Their photographer from Cape Breton, their Canadian, remained cheery, exhibiting the sweetest temperament of anyone Brainard had ever met, and he recognized the value of this where they were now. The men were already joking about how accident prone he seemed. Cutting himself when he sharpened his pencils with his penknife, falling out of his top bunk, landing face first on the floor. But Brainard saw how Rice used his role as photographer to go off by himself. He envied Rice this. He wasn't the loner Rice seemed to be, but he chaffed under the close regulations of army life.

The C.O. was more of a stickler for army regulations since the Kislingbury episode. Every man at Conger was alert to the black notebook he carried in his right breast pocket, in which he recorded who, and for how long, had held up, for instance, the sledging parties hauling coal back from Watercourse Bay. The C.O. muttered, "4:08 p.m. Connell's knee gives out," as he carefully extracted his spectacles from the same breast pocket, fitted the wire rims around his ears, and made a notation. Everyone was aware of Private Connell's convenient bum knee, yet Connell had taken a drop in rank to volunteer for this expedition. He was strong and could work hard if he wanted, but the C.O.'s little black notebook came out often when Connell was involved in a detail. Lieutenant Greely made a note of who was late for meals or Sunday service. To manage an Arctic expedition as if it were a body of troops before the enemy seemed absurd, Brainard thought.

His route to Dutch Island took him close under the cliffs. The wind, swirling in crazy gusts, pushed him against a boulder covered with hoarfrost on the windward side. He brushed off the white flakes and pulled up his jacket hood, cinching it closed with the toggles, awkward with mittened hands. He was dressed in wool long johns top and bottom, wool pants, wool shirt, and a thick, blue wool sweater that his mother had knitted for him. Everything else: three pairs of socks, mukluk boots, his windsuit of close-weave cotton, was army issue. He butted into the wind. Sergeant Winfield Jewell, one of the meteorologists, who came from his Signal Corps posting on the summit of Mt. Washington in the White Mountains of New Hampshire, said that summit was pretty damn windy. Brainard had a party outside in the wind at the time, building up the snow-block wall around the fort. "How windy?" Connell had asked, sticking out his neck, hands on hips—one of the Irishman's favorite poses—as a gust slammed into them, lifting the shovel Connell had dropped off the ground and ramming it against the building.

"Windier than here." Jewell laughed. "You have to crawl. You put out your arm and the wind holds it horizontal. You have to face away from that kind of wind to breathe." Jewell paused as if catching his breath in the wind he had just described. Then he added, "Anything else you want to know about the winds on Mt. Washington, Private Connell?"

Connell straightened. He was tall to start with, but stretching himself out he barely came to eye level with Sergeant Jewell. "I don't believe you," he snapped.

Brainard thought about this conversation as he walked toward Dutch Island. He had hit the outgoing tide and could skip across the seawater rushing between the gravel. They had seen no slabs of rock, the earth's surface here seemed to be composed of gravel and very little top soil. Yet the yellow Arctic poppies were blooming when they arrived, and there was the shrubby silver-leaved willow the musk oxen ate and a plant that Rice called wild rhubarb that grew in dense clumps around the base of rocks. The land wasn't entirely barren. But to Davy Brainard, who had grown up in dairy farm country of New York State—richly green, redolent of newly mown hay—this terrain took getting used to. His western postings on the Plains or the forested mountains of Montana Territory, despite its ruggedness, had not prepared him for this absence of growing life.

Dutch Island was only thirty yards across, a bald head of shale bare of vegetation. His thoughts went back to Jewell. He liked Jewell, a quiet man and a steady worker born in the hills of New Hampshire, a farm boy like himself. Brainard had picked up unsavory talk about Sergeant David Ralston, another of the meteorologists. He had married a widow, emptied her savings, and the family was after him. Brainard wondered how many of the others were running away from something. He wondered why he himself had come. He had fulfilled his contract to the army, he had meant to rejoin civilian life, but an Arctic expedition! He had read too many Horatio Alger stories to pass it up. These meteorologists were in their element up here, excited to be contributing to science and obsessed with collecting data and recording it in ink on the specially printed forms. Their third meteorologist, Sergeant Hampden Gardiner, who had married just before he left, couldn't stop talking about the pendulum they had brought up to measure the earth's gravitational pull. It weighed one hundred pounds and was housed in a wooden case.

On Dutch Island, Brainard crouched down to give a lower profile to the battering wind and stared out across the Hall Basin toward Greenland. Charles Francis Hall lay buried over there, poisoned by his doctor, a German named Bessels. Dr. Pavy knew Bessels. No one could prove the murder, or those who could weren't talking. Dr. Pavy said Bessels had been given a laboratory on the top floor of the Smithsonian in Washington, where he continued his scientific work.

If, Brainard told himself, he had learned one thing in these few short weeks, it was that living in this inhospitable place where no humans had ever lived, or not for long, would either bring out the worst or the best. Rice, for instance, was good to start with. He could count on Rice to stay good.

A strong blast nearly flattened him. He waited for the wind to let up and then stood. He had stayed out too long. The purple twilight was deepening into darkness and the air was full of noise as the wind beat the waves into a chaos of ice chunks. He looked toward the zenith, hoping for unclouded light to guide him home, and Emerson's words from "Nature" that he had learned in the Cortland Normal School flooded his mind: "If a man would be alone, let him look at the stars." He said these words out loud, filled with a sudden joy. Cold, too. He was cold standing in the wind, and he would be facing into that wind now. Time to head back. But he had thought it out. His job here was to keep his eye on the worst.

✳

They had seen the sun for the last time. When they went out they cracked their shins on sharp-edged ice cakes pushed up on the beach. Monstrous black rocks littered the shore. They stumbled against them. They cursed them. But they talked excitedly about being the first to walk among them. The shadows confused them. They stepped in holes and fell. This northern land was empty. They saw only themselves. They were alone in a great void. Their ties to home were broken, vanished with the last puff of black smoke when the ship dropped beyond their view.

✳

Fort Conger

15 October 1881

My Dearest Lilla Mae,

I dislike Lieutenant Greely. I should be the leader of this expedition. He is the son of a shoemaker. I will not take orders from a man whose father was a shoemaker! I am here as a civilian specialist under contract at $100 a month to serve as doctor to these men. The lieutenant knows he has no power over me. He assumes because I am French and studied medicine in Paris that I am intimate with the bohemian life. True enough! I flaunt it because he disapproves. He is a New England puritan and exudes a moral superiority. For that I hold him in contempt. I am the best-educated man here but have found a suitable companion in George Rice, whom I know from our time in Greenland. He has an inquiring mind, though shares not my lust for the pole. I have the best grasp of Arctic lore, better than Greely's, though he acknowledges the importance of Dr. Elisha Kent Kane's Arctic work. You know how I admire poor Kane, dead, from tuberculosis, two years after his return. He was awarded a hero's welcome, though he did not find Franklin, nor reach the pole—his great dream. He was criticized, yes! His equipment was miserable, inadequate. Most of his dogs died of bad food, men had scurvy from the same bad food, and frostbite, snow blindness. Terrible sufferings! "An Arctic night can age a man more rapidly and harshly than a year anywhere else in this weary world." I quote Kane from memory. But he was the first to pass through Smith Sound and into the enormous basin—one hundred miles wide—now named for him. We passed through it on our way up, a sea of swirling currents, of churning, towering ship-crushing ice. A dangerous place, my dear wife, I assure you.

I envy Kane that hero's welcome. But I, too, have survived an Arctic winter. They rely on me to speak with our two Eskimos who know no English. I am the Arctic expert here. I have rid myself of Henry Clay. "Greely," I said, "I give you this ultimatum. You must choose between Clay and me." "You must," he informed me, "present what you have to say as a 'complaint' not as an 'ultimatum.' You might be here as a civilian specialist,

Doctor, but I remind you that you are serving an army expedition and I expect you to show respect for military command." Ha! Ha! I laugh in his face. But Henry Clay said, "Having a doctor is most important. I have no particular skills you need." I was sorry I did not like Henry Clay. He was well connected. He was a gentleman, like me.

I, too, dream Kane's dream. I was on my way to the pole with the great explorer Lambert, when we were both called to serve in the Franco-Prussian War. Poor Lambert was killed. I found another expedition. The leader agreed to test my theory. Kane's theory of the Open Polar Sea. A warm current that sweeps northward from the tropics would carry us to the pole. But we lost our financial backing when our patron was murdered by his valet. That's what some said. I do not know, but my dream was shattered. I lost my direction. A black time. I try to forget. Perhaps I went a little mad. I kept myself alive by fishing on the banks of your great Mississippi River, near St. Louis. How can this be? I asked myself. I am cleverer than other men. I am Octave Pavy, born in New Orleans, son of a Frenchman, a wealthy plantation owner. Your father found me. A minister and a kind man. Wealthy, too, and generous. He took me into his home. He paid for my medical studies. You were there, an educated beautiful woman of good family. You are my ideal in a wife. And I have left you for so long! But the pole! We are only five hundred miles away. I can smell it. I can nearly touch it. By God, I will touch it! I will not let the U.S. government stand in my way. When I return to your arms, I will be a famous man!

In my letters to you, my precious Lilla Mae, I will tell you everything.

> I caress you, I kiss you.
> Octave

✶

Before winter closed in, Greely sent out parties to establish depots for spring exploring. Brainard, along with Privates Connell and Bender, were with Lieutenant Greely, carrying forty-pound packs up a cold valley, when Greely fell, his knee smashing on a rock. They helped him up, but when he put weight on his leg he nearly passed out. They eased him to a snowy hummock, and Brainard knelt down, carefully working his hands around the knee.

"You've not cracked the kneecap, sir. Just a bad knock."

"I hope you are right, but it's clear to me we must abandon this effort," Greely said. His body sagged. "Sergeant Brainard, I command you to take over the leadership."

His C.O.'s face was ashen, and it ran through Brainard's head that Greely rarely joined the men for walks to Dutch Island. He didn't think their commander enjoyed physical exercise. Well, *he* didn't welcome this leadership position. It was not his wish to be in charge.

"I'd be much obliged," Greely said in a strained voice, "if the three of you would be willing to share a bag." He was nursing his knee that was rapidly swelling.

"Of course, sir," Brainard said. "It will give you a little more room if you have a bag to yourself." The other two said nothing, though Connell let out a snort. This forced the three of them into a two-man bag.

Brainard located the pemmican, attacking it with his knife, slicing off the frozen hunks and passing them around. "Private Connell, please get out the spirit lamp and melt some ice for water. Find the tea leaves and make us a cup each." They had not stopped to carry out this process, so had drunk nothing all day. He wanted to get them in the sleeping bags. No one should stand around with the temperature dropping. Lieutenant Greely especially must be cared for. He addressed Bender, who was sitting on his pack staring into a white void. "Private Bender, make yourself useful and lay out the bags." Most of their sleeping bags were made of buffalo hide, heavy and stiff in the cold. They swallowed their tepid tea, made Lieutenant Greely as comfortable as they could, and crawled in themselves. They were cramped, and after a period of thrashing, Bender suggested, "Let's slit open the bottom and I'll sleep with my head out that end."

"That means your stinking feet will be in my face," Connell was quick to point out.

On the slow march back to the fort the next morning, Brainard pondered what he should have done to make the night less of a fighting match with Bender's feet. But he could only conclude that he was never going to repeat that experiment.

✶

They were becoming accustomed to their routines, even the once-a-week washes in the bathtub Greely had brought up. Large, white, and heavy, sitting on porcelain feet, it had been wedged by the men into the washroom, comfortably located against the double chimney near the center of the building. They had nearly completed the six-foot snow-block wall, one-foot thick around their living quarters, and had filled the space between the blocks and the tar-papered wood with light snow for insulation. They were working in twilight in the early November dark, with the temperature mostly below zero. But the C.O. wanted Lieutenant Lockwood to lead one more trip. They were all standing outside the fort in the frigid air, Lieutenant Greely shaking Lockwood's hand, the sledges lined up, the dogs, and men, too, harnessed, and ready to start dragging. Schneider was running around breaking up dog fights that filled the air with barking.

Sergeant Brainard was looking forward to this trip with Lockwood. The lieutenant was twenty-eight, four years his senior, but he did not feel the age difference. Lockwood was so approachable. They were to haul the whaleboat on a sledge and then row over to Thank God Harbor on the Greenland side and check the condition of old caches laid down by Nares and Hall, in preparation for the spring trip to determine if Greenland was an island or a landmass that might expand to the North Pole. "I'm immensely keen to set a new Farthest North record, Brainard," Lockwood said. His eyes took on a faraway look. "I do this for the expedition and for my family, too. They will be so proud of me."

It was impossible not to like Lockwood, he was so open and forthright. He said things like "I want to trod where no man has ever trod before." Brainard doubted the lieutenant had the drive or the ability to oversee and carry out a large endeavor the way Greely did. Their C.O. was a master of detail, an essential skill in keeping the men healthy and the expedition focused on its goal. Lockwood's flair was for leading in the van, on the trail of adventure with the men behind him. At Conger, Brainard watched Lockwood shine the buttons on his uniform. He put energy into polishing his boots. He kept his mustache waxed to a fine point.

Lockwood's party of nearly a dozen men, four sledges, and the dogs took nearly a week to reach Cape Beechy, their ferrying point to Greenland. He was standing with Lockwood at the shoreline, trying to penetrate the gloom. The sky above appeared purple in the semidarkness of midday.

"No exploring party has ever tried to cross the Robeson Channel so early in the winter," Lockwood said. He had assumed a heroic pose, hand on hip, the other hand shading eyes. "But I am confident." His handsome face broke into a radiant smile, and Brainard found himself envying his friend's seemingly boundless confidence. "I never complain of hardship, Brainard. The sweetest victory can only be bought with difficulty and effort. The danger lies in the unfrozen mid-channel, but I'm sure the whaleboat will carry us through that mass of drifting ice. You know about Charles Francis Hall, don't you, David?" Lockwood went on in a confidential tone, as though they were in the lieutenant's home, before the fire, drinking brandy. "He was a small-time printer from Cleveland. He knew nothing about the Arctic, but he became obsessed with finding Sir John Franklin. No luck there, but he lived with Eskimos and adopted their ways, and there was nothing for it but he must reach the North Pole." His lively face dissolved into a look of frustration. "But *we're* not to try for the pole, you know that, Brainard." And Brainard saw his friend was nearly crushed to miss such a prized adventure. "Well," he went on in a resigned tone, "it's all because of Lieutenant Commander De Long. My father told me before I left that all of Washington is concerned that this navy man is lost. That's why Lieutenant Greely was told to keep away from the pole. Wouldn't do for us to lose men on a polar push and have the navy laugh at *us*."

They all knew the story of the *Jeannette*, De Long's ship that had left from San Francisco two years ago and had not been heard from since. Lieutenant Greely had asked them to keep a sharp eye out for signs of De Long. He showed them the letter Mrs. De Long had given him to deliver to her husband. It was startling to see Mrs. De Long's handwriting, as if they might run into her husband in this vast, shapeless land over the next snowy hillock.

Lockwood swerved on his heel and raised his right arm. "Let's try it, men!" he shouted to the others. It was amazing, Brainard thought, how hard these men worked for Lieutenant Lockwood, straining to launch the whaleboat, calling out to watch for ice chunks, hoots of laughter as they crashed through an icy barrier. In mid-channel they became hopelessly entangled in a quantity of sludgy ice slamming into the boat's sides. Lieutenant Lockwood was compelled to call off the attempt. The next morning he was eager to try again and asked Brainard to walk down with him to look at the crossing. He stared at the ice that appeared the same as yesterday, and disappointment flooded his handsome face. "I so much wanted to report our success to Lieutenant Greely."

"Lockwood," Brainard said, in an effort to cheer him, "we've been camped out for a week at 25 degrees below zero. The men have done well."

"Oh yes," he said "we're all hardening up." He was pleased, Brainard could see that, but it wasn't the victory he wanted.

✷

"Why are we condemned to sit on benches?" Connell grumbled. "I need something with a back." They had lost the light now. Those big-paned windows that spanned the east side of Fort Conger only reflected back their own faces. Their coal stove kept them warm enough but the intensity of the frigid air as it emanated through the hard glassy surface made them more in need of their inside comforts.

Connell was sitting at the table where they had just had dinner, a hearty meal cooked by their excellent red-haired chef Private Francis Long: roast beef, mashed potatoes, green beans, and pickled onions, with a tasty brown gravy slathered over it all. Long was a wizard as a baker, too. Fresh bread, fruit pies, and Parker House rolls that Lieutenant Greely pronounced nearly as good as his wife Henrietta's, who made the best Parker House rolls east of Chicago's Parker House. Their food came in tins, dried or pickled. Greely had seen to the antiscorbutics meant to prevent scurvy, and to fresh meat as well: musk oxen and more than one hundred eider ducks they had shot in Greenland. Their two Eskimos, Greenland natives Jens Edwards and Frederik Christiansen, here to drive the dogs and hunt for them, had caught seals. But the seals had gone south now.

Lieutenant Greely's diet gave each man five thousand calories daily, the amount calculated to sustain health and energy at these subzero temperatures. Even Dr. Pavy could say nothing against it, though he made up for this agreeableness by describing scurvy in graphic terms. "Your teeth will loosen," the Frenchman said, waving his arms and spreading his fingers in a way that evoked his foreign authority. "Your gums will soften and turn black. You will fall into a gloom, you will irritate each other. Sudden movements will make you dizzy. You can't plan, you can't *do* anything." His arms spun and his fingers widened, mesmerizing the men around the table. "In the last stages," the doctor continued, his voice elevated and nasal, "your *blood* will seep through your pores. Old *wounds* will open." Several of the men probed their old injuries. Lieutenant Greely's hand flew to his jaw. "Hah!" the doctor crowed. "Perhaps I will see this phenomenon." He lowered his voice to a bare, hissy whisper. "Then, you will go mad and die."

"I've got it. I've got scurvy," Bender shrieked. "Look!" He swung, mouth open, toward his buddy Charlie Henry, who placed his hand on Bender's forehead, tilting back his head, and peered in, probing with a finger. "God, you stink," Charlie said. He extracted a raisin, embedded near the gum line, waving it around for public view. That broke the tension in a swell of relieved laughter. But Sergeant Brainard sat with his arms folded across his chest. He really did not like how the doctor could stir up the men.

✷

Dinner over and the table cleared, some of these well-fed men were writing in their diaries, compliments of the army. They had been told the army wanted their firsthand impressions of life in this intensely cold, isolated, white-and-gray place. Some of them took to this journal writing, but Connell didn't, though tonight he said, "I'll write about having no chairs. I want those generals to know how uncomfortable I am."

"The C.O. has a rocking chair," Bender pointed out. He was pleased to have made them all laugh and relieved to know he didn't have scurvy.

"See? It's not fair!" Connell banged his fist on the table.

"Well, you don't have to look at it," Charlie Henry remarked. "It's in the officers' room. What do you bet Lieutenant Kislingbury sits in it when the C.O.'s not around."

"So would the doctor." Schneider, their dog man, hooted.

"But not Lieutenant Lockwood!" Charlie's voice boomed, and the rest snickered.

Their three officers and the doctor shared a fifteen-by-seventeen-foot space—about the size of a garden shed—that must feel pretty tight these days with Lieutenant Kislingbury disgraced. He and the doctor had taken to spending time together, making the two-mile trudge to Dutch Island, talking in low voices in ill-lit corners away from the rest of them.

"Bender," Connell prodded, "what do you write about?" His teeth flashed white from under his black mustache.

Bender stared at Connell's teeth, his hands clamped between his knees. "I can read and write," he said. "Just not in English."

"Then write in German, you dolt," the Irishman said.

Sergeant Brainard looked up from where he was writing, slightly apart from the privates. He had a girl at home, or hoped he still did. Her family lived on the nearby farm and she had been a classmate of one of his sisters. Lena was her name. They had made no commitment to each other. He couldn't have asked her to wait for him, besides he wasn't ready to settle down like that yet. Still, he liked writing to her.

"Lay off him," Charlie rasped out. "He fixes our lamps when you break them." Private Charlie Henry was not in the habit of sticking up for anyone, but a buddy could come in handy and Bender had attached himself to him.

"He's taking up space," Connell whined. "Anyone who can't write shouldn't be sitting here. There's not enough room. You have to get right under the damn lamps to see." Connell leaned toward Bender, breathing in his face. "So, if you could make our lamps brighter, that would be one useful thing an illiterate like you could do for this great expedition."

Charlie sprang to his feet, shouting. "You son-of-a-bitch! Leave him—" George Rice strolled in. "Hey fellows, what's the row?" He was carrying his case and smiling, but not the kind that encouraged Connell to go on abusing poor Bender. Rice's smile let these privates know he expected better from them. Charlie sat down. Connell made room for Rice on the bench. "Thank you," Rice said, opening his case. They all knew what this leather case contained. Rice had a voluminous correspondence with members of the fair sex.

George Rice intrigued them. He learned photography in the West Indies. He went to Greenland as photographer on the *Gulnare* expedition just last year, where he met the doctor and Henry Clay. When Lieutenant Greely heard about this photographer with Arctic experience he had invited Rice to come along. "I was happy the way things turned out," Rice told them. "I've never found that routine work suited me." What about those fat law books you've lugged along, they asked him. "Oh, I was enrolled in law school, Columbia University in New York City." Yes, he had gotten along with Dr. Pavy. It was too bad about Henry Clay, though. And, yes, like the doctor, he was under contract to the army, not enlisted. The men knew this meant that neither Rice nor Pavy were subject to the kind of strict discipline they were. Lieutenant Greely couldn't break those two as he broke Lieutenant Kislingbury. It was an important point. Basically, the C.O. had no control over Rice or the doctor.

"Writing your mother?" Whisler quipped. They had recently celebrated Whisler's twenty-fifth birthday, and that had everyone excited about birthdays. Lieutenant Greely's idea to vary the winter tedium was working. The birthday boy was relieved of all duties, allowed to choose his birthday meal from among their delicacies, and the C.O. himself presented him with a quart of rum. Whisler took a swig and passed the bottle. He got it back empty. But as he had suddenly acquired a reputation as a jolly good fellow, his sacrifice had paid off. He had heard himself referred to as the runt of the expedition. He didn't like this, but he was, weighing in at 156 pounds.

"This letter, Private Whisler, is for my dear friend Maud," Rice answered, nodding toward Whisler. "She and I grew up together on Cape Breton."

"How will Florence and Alice feel about your writing Maud?" Charlie asked, elbowing Whisler aside with his 203 pounds. They were all big men here, especially the Germans. The C.O. told them their average weight was one hundred and seventy-six pounds. "How about Florence and Alice," Charlie insisted, though what they all wanted to know was how Miss Helen Bishop would feel about Rice writing these other ladies. Word got around that George Rice had formed an attachment with this lady before they left Washington.

"They will get their letters, don't you worry about that, Private Henry."

The *New York Herald* had hired Rice to write dispatches about their adventures at Lady Franklin Bay. When Charlie found this out he wasted no time telling Rice he was writing for the *Chicago Times*. Rice, to Charlie's delight, took this seriously and had even consulted him on one of his dispatches. Being treated as a fellow journalist by Rice made Charlie very happy and gave him a leg up on the others.

They all knew that their letters wouldn't get mailed until the relief came next August. But that didn't stop them from writing. Most of the men had some family member who would prize a letter written from practically the North Pole. Charlie Henry had three sisters. He had a brother, Wilhelm, or William, since the family was American now. But he was not going to write any of them. Writing in this diary the army had so thoughtfully provided was more his style. He meant to tell the true story. He didn't care if generals read it. He was going to write about *what really happened on this expedition*. He was calling it "The True and Accurate Account of the Lady Franklin Bay Expedition According to Private Charles B. Henry."

Sergeant William Cross, their engineer, wrote to his wife. He was a morose man who hid behind a hedge of black beard. He had a thick stack of letters ready to send to his wife. He talked about her too. The men were as sick of hearing about his wife's Welsh rarebit as they were hearing how much Lieutenant Kislingbury missed his four poor motherless boys. Cross got as little sympathy as Kislingbury because the engineer lived up to his name: he was always cross. By nature a surly man, he was brought along for one reason only: to keep the motor launch, *The Lady Greely*—the C.O. had named it after his wife—in tiptop working order. But Sergeant Brainard had apprehended the man drinking the launch's fuel. Good God! *Now* they find out that Cross was a damn drunk. It was a good thing they had Sergeant Davy. Their stores sergeant was on the job. Their observer Ralston had caught Cross drinking the alcoholic fluid the meteorologists used to preserve their specimens, the lichens and mosses, even some caterpillars and a few flies. They needed *all* fuel. No resupply up here. Any man who stole expedition supplies put everyone in jeopardy.

Lieutenant Lockwood's favorite topic was his family. He wrote to all of them, his father the general, his mother, who was the best cook in Maryland, his brother, his married sisters and the unmarried ones and his sweetheart, Mary Murray. Everyone knew *her name.* "Here in the Arctic I can make myself worthy of Mary Murray's love, whose virtues I have extolled to all of you." He told them this in his soft southern tones. He didn't often join them in the common room, preferring to write his letters in his own bunk space, but when he did they felt the honor. Lieutenant Lockwood lent his patrician class to the whole expedition.

"Hey!" Private Henry shouted out to everyone. "Listen to this. I've just written up the story for the *Chicago Times* of how our own Lieutenant Kislingbury—ex-lieutenant, I should say—shot the polar bear. I'm calling it 'The Officer and the Big Game.'" He drew himself up and fixed his audience with a burning eye. "You want to listen to this story?" he asked. And immediately pens were put aside and talk ceased.

"You never know," Charlie began, "what might be waiting for you in the frigid Arctic wastes. This unforgiving land can prove the worth of a man, or as easily bring him down. I offer a tale about a man and a beast, and you, my readers, can plumb the moral as you see fit." He paused to create dramatic effect. "Our big-game hunter spotted the great white bear stretched at his ease on an ice floe. Large he was, as large as a buffalo and an elephant combined, and Lieutenant Kislingbury seized his Remington. He commanded four men to lower the boat and was over the side of his ship in a leap and a flash. I was an eyewitness to this event and have never seen a man move faster. As swift as a gazelle, was Lieutenant Kislingbury."

Bender interrupted. "Gazelles are usually prey."

"Well then, like a hyena," Charlie countered.

By this time Kislingbury himself had emerged from the officer's bunkroom. Schneider moved over, making room, and Private Henry waved an arm and said, "Our star attraction has arrived. You're going to be in the *Chicago Times*." The lieutenant shrugged and sat.

Charlie picked up his tale. "Lieutenant Kislingbury had his men row right up to that floe. Cool as an icicle he raised his rifle. The bear rose to his full height, blocking out the sun. The men at the oars grew faint, but Lieutenant Kislingbury held his ground. The polar bear let out a deafening roar and moved in a lunging pace toward the lieutenant. 'My God,' our hero muttered, 'this beast is a worthy prize. He will make a rug for my boys.' The men in the boat crawled under the thwarts, but our David stood firm against Goliath. One crack from the Remington and the bear pitched into the sea in a great gush of blood and gore. The men towed the beast to the ship, where eager hands hauled the monster aboard. And our hero stood, modest yet proud, to receive their praises."

Private Henry stopped reading and looked out on his audience. There was complete silence, their faces eager with attention. Lieutenant Kislingbury was smiling a pleased smile. Charlie went on in his story-telling voice. "Like any good tale, this story has a moral. As the Fates would have it, Lieutenant Kislingbury was not destined to"—there was a movement near the officer's room that made him quickly squeeze in the words before he broke off—"take home the bear's pelt to his sons . . ."

"Go on, Private," Lieutenant Greely said. He was leaning against the bunkroom door, arms folded across his chest. He had on his night-shirt, visible below his uniform jacket. It was red, as was his nightcap. "A moral, you say? I've always enjoyed stories with a moral. Please go on." He did not smile.

Private Henry picked up his papers. He scratched his head with his pen, fumbled with a button on his jacket that had come undone. The room was very still.

"Bender!" Connell shouted and rapped the table, making everyone's ink pots jump. "How about it if I write Bronco Moll for you." He reached across Bender to grab Charlie's pen out of his hand. "You dictate." This got the expected laugh. "Bronco Moll," Connell went on, teeth flashing, "Bender's favorite lady in Deadwood. Does she give you a good ride, Bender?" He waved the pen, splattering ink on Bender.

This made sufficient disturbance so that when Charlie cast a glance toward the officer's bunkroom door, Lieutenant Greely was gone, apparently back inside. The private gave Connell a grateful look. But Bender just sat with his head bent, hands between his knees, next to Charlie.

"Bronco Moll doesn't know German," he muttered. Sergeant Brainard watched as Private Charles Henry kept balling and unballing his fists. He and Connell had become a tight duo. He felt they shared a general contempt for human nature. He had seen them exchange dissatisfied looks under Lieutenant Greely's too-firm hand. The meteorologists had told him that both these men were adept at collecting the daily reading. Private Henry especially, Gardiner had said, exhibited a real interest in the science. Brainard nodded. He had not forgotten coming across Private Henry on one of his walks. The private was standing stock still, twenty paces back from the black cliffs, staring up at their frozen, frosted verticality, his arms stretched above his head. His figure was so massive, Brainard at first mistook him for a polar bear until Brainard caught the words this figure was shouting into the wind:

> And there they lay till all their bones were bleached,
> And lichened into colour with the crags . . .

Brainard ran up, clapping Private Henry on the shoulder, saying, "You're quoting Tennyson!"

The private spun away. "Are you going to report me for that?"

"Why, I was delighted to hear those lines. How well they fit into our situation."

"I hope they won't."

"I share your feeling," Sergeant Brainard replied. The private had omitted the customary "sir" and Brainard saw in the closed, stern face of Private Henry a strong dislike. They had separated, each going his own way. *I believe he hates me,* Brainard thought. *But there is a poetical streak in this man's nature and it would behoove me to turn it to the good of our party.*

Rice hadn't missed any of this interchange among these privates, and he smiled his cheery smile. But his eyes weren't smiling, and Connell lowered the pen, pulled out his army issue handkerchief, and put some effort into blotting up the splatters on Bender's shirt. Ah, yes, Bronco Moll. The joke had passed into crudeness, not so bad in itself—Brainard was no prude—but crudeness at Bender's expense. Bender was, after all, one of the Germans. And Connell was not.

Brainard decided he had heard enough of these privates' talk for one evening and stood up.

"Sergeant Brainard," Schneider said, "there is a story going around about how you happened to join the army. That you'd run out of money. You were in Philadelphia and couldn't get home."

Brainard sat down again. He might as well just tell the whole silly thing straight out. "That's right, Private Schneider," he said. Schneider was a good man and very good with the dogs. He was turning out some well-trained teams that would be useful to them when the time came for spring sledging. "I'd traveled there for the Centennial Exhibition in '76. They had some fine displays on agriculture and especially industry, showing our country's ingenuity since the Civil War. They say we're in the machine age now. But to my surprise I found myself standing in front of the U.S. Naval Observatory's exhibit, reading about the Franklin tragedy. I was actually looking at the relics Charles Francis Hall had brought back!"

"Like what?" probed Connell. "Any bones?"

"Copper cooking pots, Private, and some of the silver plate. Those poor men must have hauled heavy sledges. I'm sure those weights con-tributed to the disaster."

"Go on, Sergeant Brainard," Schneider said. "I want to hear how you joined up."

"I was heading home by train, Private Schneider, but when I got to New York, where I had to change, and went to pay, I found nothing but an empty pocket. I stepped out of line. Embarrassed, I can tell you, and I couldn't figure out what had happened to my money. I could write my parents for funds, but that didn't seem right. I shouldn't make them pay for my stupidity. Even at nineteen I knew that much. Then I remember that when my older brother Henry joined the army during the Civil War, he was younger than I was. So I took the free ferry out to Governor's Island. But here's the really silly part. While changing into my new uni-form I located my lost money. Right in my civilian shirt pocket! I stared at that ten-dollar bill thinking, Now what have you gone and done? But I wasn't going to back out. I had just become Private David Brainard."

"Well," said Private Henry, "you knew where your next meal was coming from. Damn it all, that's why I joined!"

"You can always get lucky breaks and advance," Whisler said.

"I did. I was sent out to Fort Ellis, Montana Territory, to fight the Sioux."

"Cleaning up after that bastard Custer," Connell sneered.

"The fiasco at Little Big Horn was pretty hot news," Whisler said.

"I was a keen enough soldier at the time. Glad to see the West and what opportunities awaited a young man from the East out there. I served under some good men, too. Colonel Miles, I learned how to be a good soldier under Colonel Miles. He was a brave and decisive fighter. He taught me that orders concisely given should be obeyed. When Colonel Miles discovered Lame Deer's village near the mouth of Muddy Creek, he ordered us to attack at dawn. We stampeded their pony herd, so most of the Sioux managed to escape our fire by disappearing into the hills. Colonel Miles wanted to communicate with Lame Deer and stopped the shooting. But something broke up their parley and the shooting started. Lame Deer took a shot at Colonel Miles, but the bullet went wide by a few inches and killed his orderly. I witnessed that and witnessed as well Lame Deer's flight up a rocky hillside—his head-dress made him a visible target—and he was brought down. My Second Cavalry suffered four casualties and nine wounded, one of them me." Brainard stopped speaking, partly to catch his breath. He surprised himself with how caught up he had become in these memories, only three years ago, but so much had happened in the last few months that his Indian fighting days felt very far away.

"What happened to you?" Schneider asked.

"My right hand was hit and I received a gunshot wound to my right cheek, Private Schneider."

"How about your eye," Whisler asked.

"I didn't lose my sight. So I was a lucky man." He smiled at these men. "I'm sure you've all got war stories, and I hope you'll spin me a tale or two." He stood up then, and left them.

✴

He had finished reading *Arctic Explorations*. The C.O. had told him the book sold sixty-five thousand copies the year it was published. Kane lost his ship, most of his scientific collections, and three of his men died. *I'd say Kane's expedition was a colossal failure,* Brainard said to himself, and when he put Kane's book back on the library shelf, he found next to it another book about Kane's last expedition by William Godfrey, one of the crew on the *Advance.* He had read that and knew he wanted to talk with Lieutenant Greely about Elisha Kent Kane. Brainard was aware his commander's position kept him cut off from easygoing conversations. His only interactions, as far as Brainard could see, were to give orders that kept the fort running like a well-oiled clock.

Brainard knocked at the officers' bunkroom door. "Come in," came the muffled response. Brainard entered and looked around. It was cold in the bunkroom, and damp in a way that made the cold more penetrating. Brainard had never been in the officers' quarters. Lieutenant Greely had hung thick curtains as partitions between the living spaces of Lieutenant Lockwood, Kislingbury, and the doctor. Still, it must get awkward with the four of them in here. Lieutenant Greely sat in his rocking chair, the afghan his wife had made for him over his knees. The shelves over the bed were lined with books and papers were stored neatly in cubbyholes. Brainard admired the arrangement. An American flag hung on the wall over the desk. From the letter paper Brainard was sure Lieutenant Greely must be writing to his wife. He must miss her terribly, he thought, and was glad he had broken down the barrier between officers and enlisted men to come talk to Lieutenant Greely about Elisha Kent Kane.

"No, I have not read this book," Greely said when his sergeant showed him Godfrey's account. "But I wouldn't put much stock in it. The man was a common sailor. Kane's book was so extremely popular. No one paid much attention to what this man had to say."

"I get the idea from Godfrey that Kane was an unpopular commander."

"Well, Godfrey was one of the deserters," the C.O. said, leaning back in the rocking chair that made a domestic creak.

"Kane lost a good portion of his crew, but he nearly leaves this out of his book," Brainard continued. "He calls the men who left a 'withdrawing' party. It sounded like a mutiny to me."

"Elisha Kent Kane was one of the most celebrated men in America when he died," the C.O. pronounced, looking up at the stars and stripes above his desk.

"After his ship became trapped in the ice," Brainard said, "it was the Eskimos at the settlement of Etah on the Greenland side that saw them through the winter. Kane didn't give them much credit for that."

"We passed Etah on the way up," the C.O. said. He picked up his pen. "Littleton Island is just off Etah, on the Greenland side. It's only around thirty miles across Smith Sound to Cape Sabine. We could see the cape on the Ellesmere coast." He smoothed down his black beard.

"I felt Kane wasn't very fair to people who had saved his men's lives. He treated those Eskimos like children in his book."

His C.O. made a move toward his inkwell. "I can tell you, news editors profited from Kane's return. When he came sailing out of the Arctic in those small whaleboats he was hailed a hero."

"I guess I just don't see him that way," Brainard said. "We have our two Eskimos, Jens and Fred. It must be hard for them, not knowing English." He felt he was dangerously close to an argument with his commanding officer. "Thank you for recommending that I read Kane." He thumbed through Godfrey's book. "It was this other fellow's that set me to thinking." Brainard started toward the door, then turned and smiled at Lieutenant Greely. "You have everything so neatly arranged here, so homelike, even. I envy you." Lieutenant Greely gave him an acknowledging nod. "I've been lucky with the men who have had command over me," Brainard continued. "I've learned from them how important to the well-being of the men is the experience a leader brings with him."

Lieutenant Greely made no reply. He had already dipped his pen and resumed his letter before Sergeant David Brainard was out the door.

✳

Fort Conger
Expedition Journal of David Brainard

15 November 1881

Weather mild -6 degrees. A wolf seen within a hundred yards of the station was shot by Lieutenant Kislingbury.

We recently celebrated Sergeant Jewell's birthday. Jewell has more experience with cold and wind than anyone here, including the doctor, though Pavy would never admit this. We celebrated Mrs. Greely's birthday on October 7. She had sent along wine for this occasion and we drank to her health.

The excessive use of profanity is becoming ridiculous. The oaths of Privates Henry and Connell show considerable imagination. Private Bender tries to keep up with them, but he is not a born blasphemer. To rein them in and because I know how blaspheming disturbs Lieutenant Greely, I've started an anti-swearing society. We have, at present, eleven members. The offender pays a fine of five cents for each oath and a committee will agree on a suitable use for the proceeds when we return to the U.S. Already there is enough to finance a dinner in a fine restaurant.

Many are depressed. It's the effect of the increasing darkness. They growl for no reason. The commanding officer is trying to counter sour moods by directing each man have at least one hour's exercise daily. By this he means more than the routine walking we get with our regular weather observations. Lieutenant Greely's intent is to drag out the indolent who devote their time to sleeping, eating—and grumbling. I doubt he will be successful with the more obstinate cases. I am thinking of Privates Henry and Connell, but could include Private Bender, who is under their influence. I, too, find it hard to keep up my spirits. But to this end, Lieutenant Greely has organized a school. This will be very useful for poor Private Bender, who has pulled down contempt for his inability to read and write in English. This is unkind, but I am learning by the day that when we are under stress the worst in our natures comes out.

I must express my foremost concern. I know more about Private Henry than I would like to know. I will disclose here what I do know and why I have acted as I have in case something happens to me. The man who calls himself Private Henry is not as he presents himself. While in the Seventh Cavalry at Fort Buford in the Montana Territory, Private Henry forged his commander's signature on commissary orders to facilitate his own preying upon supplies. He was caught and sentenced to two years at hard labor, but escaped and showed up in Deadwood, Dakota Territory, where he killed a Chinaman over a gambling debt. He evaded the law, changed his name, and reenlisted in the Fifth Cavalry. Charles Henry Buck became Charles

Buck Henry. Such a small change! How he managed to get by Captain Price, who recommended him for this expedition, I can't fathom, except the man is big and strong; he's a crack shot and quick to carry out orders. He knows how to defer to rank, and so would give the appearance of splendid soldier material to an officer. So we have a man here under an alias, who is a forger, a thief, and a murderer!

How do I know? Henry was recognized from our group photograph that was published in *Harper's Weekly*. A cavalry officer, a friend of mine, wrote me. His letter arrived the day we sailed and as we were all preoccupied with departure I put it aside. I confess I forgot about it. Then upon landing we were driving ourselves to build our fort and settle in, so it was another few weeks before I again put my hand on the letter from my officer friend. It is most unfortunate that I did not turn it up before the *Proteus* steamed back to St. John's since I would have informed Lieutenant Greely, and Private Henry could have returned to the U.S. Now, if I disclose Henry's past, it would appear that I was calling into question Lieutenant Greely's decision to take him. I understand now why he was so covetous of the chief clerk position. I believe he dislikes me just because I hold it. This man is driven by his stomach. Here at Fort Conger our food is finite. We are not like the Plains forts, receiving regular visits from the post traders. It is my responsibility to my commanding officer and to the men to make sure our food lasts until the resupply comes next summer. It is my obligation to keep a close eye on Private Henry. I would not hesitate to punish him if he resumes his thieving ways.

✳

When the sun dropped below the horizon on October 16, the men at Conger entered the four-month period explorers called "the white darkness." A symptom of the darkness and their indoor confinement was to crave sleep, and to counter the resulting boredom their commander kept them at the outside work well into the deepening twilight. Not so bad in itself, Brainard realized. They would gain confidence with the cold and with the landscape. A familiarity with the landmarks would pay off when the wind blew up the snow or the fog settled, blotting out visibility. The C.O. ordered the observers to position their instruments far from the fort, necessitating a walk that got them into the air after the outdoor work shut down. The men were still hacking the bituminous coal from the outcrop at Watercourse Bay, a five-mile trudge east along the coast over the rubble ice and between the headlands. Already several tons of coal were piled within the walls of Conger, and a daily task was to shovel coal in the stove and clear out the ashes. But coal mining was filthy, exhausting work. If there was a moon—Miss Luna, the men called her—it went well enough as they could walk without falling over the upheaved surface. But the work itself had their arms dropping off from swinging the picks and mattocks. At first the C.O. had permitted daytime napping when they crawled back, dragging the heavy sledges. But as the fury of winter set in—all storms and darkness—Greely cut off this comfort. The men felt themselves pinched in the vise of a netherworld where the cold shut down the mind. Brainard saw this, and he heard the mutterings: "Damn the C.O., he's too hard on us. Lets us nap, then stops us."

"All I think about is my bunk," said Corporal Joe Elison, one of their most uncomplaining men. "I want to crawl into it like a little hibernating animal."

"Me, too," echoed the other corporal, Nicholas Salor, whom Brainard knew to be a silent man, though a steady worker, and faithful about writing his father, who lived in Europe somewhere, not Germany.

When Dr. Pavy, hearing this talk, stepped into their midst, Brainard heard the doctor say, "He makes up the rules. He don't know what he does."

And Kislingbury took up the theme. "Our doctor's right, men. Greely's enforcing discipline to gratify his own personal vanity." And spacing out his words in his clipped English accent, he added, "And I should know."

That brought out an expected bark of laughter from the two corporals that caused Brainard to grit his teeth. Yet, Elison and Salor were decent men. He was sure of that. He knew he could do nothing. Nothing *now*, except keep alert as they entered the white darkness.

3

"Our Great and Marvelous Adventure"

Fort Conger, Lady Franklin Bay

Winter 1881–30 August 1882

By Thanksgiving the darkness was complete, or nearly so. If it was clear, but it was rarely clear, a rosy glow could be caught at the horizon. Or a greenish light that was eerie and strange. The man who saw this felt both lucky and haunted and told everyone what this green light looked like until he was told to shut up. But a horizon glow relieved the darkness. When there was fog, the darkness turned solid. Thick and sludgy. The meteorologists, the observers as they were generally called, told them the fog was caused by the warm air rising from the open ocean — the spaces between the bergs and heaps of ice. But the fog unnerved the men. It crept along with whoever ventured out to take these myriad of daily readings. Surrounded by its cold, clammy breath, they could see nothing at all. No one objected when the C.O. insisted they go out in pairs when it was foggy.

The C.O., in his wisdom, declared Thanksgiving a day of rest and relaxation. The men need perform only the most basic duties. A wise move, Sergeant Brainard thought. Everyone would welcome a day of relaxation. The disciplinary problem of Lieutenant Kislingbury, not unexpected in army posts, was especially troublesome here in their isolation. Normally Lieutenant Greely could have sent the man to a nearby fort. But Kislingbury, with no function, no role to play with the expedition, spent much of his time playing cards with the enlisted men.

Demeaning himself as Brainard saw it. Now and then the sergeant caught bits of their conversation. "He's waiting for me to apologize," Kislingbury said, laying down the jack of spades.

"Well," said Connell, "why don't you?" He sat at an angle that gave him access to Bender's cards.

"Dolph should apologize to me!" Kislingbury snapped, his clipped English voice rising, and scooped up the pile.

It was not the first time Brainard had picked up that the men called their C.O. "Dolph." This showed a lack of respect. Since the C.O. had stripped his second officer, the men obeyed orders out of fear rather than a willing spirit. Brainard had debated pointing out to Kislingbury that if he apologized, it would benefit the expedition. But he might cause more harm by interfering. If they could just get through the winter, the fallen lieutenant could board the ship that was sure to bring them supplies and fresh men in the summer. Lieutenant Greely could not apologize. A commander couldn't lower himself like that. He would lose the men's respect.

The other problem was the doctor. The men were aware the C.O. and Dr. Pavy affected each other like oil and water, and that Lieutenant Greely had, ultimately, no control over their doctor. If he laid down the law, Pavy could refuse to treat them. The doctor held the trump card. A very bad situation. But it had made sense to pick up Pavy in Greenland, as Greely had been directed by General Hazen, his boss in the Army Signal Corps. By now, though, Greely must be wishing he had taken an army physician, subject to his command. The result was that Dr. Pavy and ex-Lieutenant Kislingbury had been thrown together in common cause against a leader they held in contempt. Brainard forced himself to wrench his mind out of this line of thinking. It only wore him down. They had been here only a little over three months. They were still in the shakedown phase.

This holiday was exactly what the men needed, and most of the men were as excited as pups to be here. Lieutenant Greely had them out after breakfast setting up lanterns in the sharp starlight for the day's events. The complete absence of humidity accentuated the brilliance of the stars displayed in the Arctic sky domed above them. Even the Indian fighters had never experienced such a display—the heavens ablaze, with pricks and stabs of light beyond the counting. Their young astronomer Ned Israel was jumping and pointing upward, shouting, "There's Ursa Major and Minor, too, and look, we can see Cassiopeia in her chair and, oh my! That great sweeping curve of stars is Draco's long tail!"

At -33 degrees, men and officers were hopping around in an effort to keep warm despite their standard issue expedition outfit: a double suit of underclothing, thick wool pants and jackets with attached hoods, three pairs of socks—but still the cold was too much for their canvas or leather boots. Lieutenant Greely got their blood stirring with a race, some on foot, some on snowshoes, their breath filling the air in front of their faces, freezing on beards and eyebrows, and coat collars. When Jens and Eskimo Fred began circling the fort in a dog sled race, the air became denser still from the dogs' frosty breath, and their sharp yips seemed to be coming out of a fog. With the dogs in a frenzy of running, the betting started up. Only tobacco, on which the C.O. turned a blind eye, but Brainard chuckled to himself since tobacco was more precious than gold at Fort Conger.

Private Charlie Henry won the marksmanship contest, a regulation paper target pinned inside a box with a candle burning directly in front of the bull's-eye. He racked up fifteen out of fifteen, a perfect score causing Sergeant Brainard to ponder why this soldier, perhaps their strongest man and a good worker when he put his mind to it, had the soul of a sneaking thief. Already he had noticed the occasional missing can of sardines or beef stew. He couldn't be sure it was Private Henry, but by God, he was keeping his eye on him. One evening he had been sitting working on his lists of supplies when Connell and Charlie walked in, Charlie saying he aimed to put on twenty-five pounds. "Look," he explained, "the Eskimos said this was a 'good ice year.' Well, as I see it, that sets us up for a bad ice year next year when the relief is to show up. *I'm* not taking any chances of going on half rations."

"Sergeant Brainard, he's got his eye on you." Connell snickered.

Charlie snorted. "He'll have to have lynx eyes to catch me."

Connell laughed. "I'll bet the sergeant can see in complete darkness."

This made Sergeant Brainard laugh too, nearly giving himself away in his dark corner. He watched as Connell leaned toward Charlie. "I was known to lift a can at my old postings," he said.

Their red-haired cook came up for high praise when Thanksgiving dinner was served with a bill of fare worthy of the Parker House. That's what the C.O. said, and Lieutenant Lockwood agreed. Oyster soup, salmon, eider duck, boiled ham, asparagus, deviled crab, lobster salad, peach and blueberry pie, raisin and jelly cake, vanilla ice cream, dates, Brazil nuts, figs, and coffee. With the coffee, Long set before his C.O. Mrs. Greely's plum pudding. She had sent along several of these delicacies, made by her own hand. When Lieutenant Lockwood dug into it, he declared Mrs. Greely's plum pudding to be equal, or nearly, to his mother's. "Next year or the year after when I'm home again," he said in his soft southern drawl, "I'll tell my family how excellent your wife's plum pudding is, Lieutenant Greely. It was most kind and thoughtful of her." He paused with his fork in the air. It was clear he had more to say, and they were silent, because what Lieutenant Lockwood said often reflected what was in their own minds. "I am thinking of my family today," Lockwood began. "There are two turkeys, or a roast and a turkey. My dear father is carving at one end of the table and my oldest brother at the other. My sweetheart, Mary Murray, is sitting between my sisters, and . . ." Lieutenant Lockwood broke off. He dropped his knife and fork—standard issue army silverware—and brought his hands to his face, overwhelmed by this home scene. Ned Israel began to sniff and the meteorological observer Gardiner moaned, "I'm not home to celebrate my first Thanksgiving with my wife."

"What a bunch of babies," Private Henry blurted out, and he began to laugh. But for once no one laughed with him.

Sergeant Brainard was stunned at how quickly this private could blight the cheer of this day of giving thanks.

"Well, well." The C.O. stepped in. "We are all thinking of our families." He rose to get their attention. "I propose we conclude our festivities with twice the usual order of our Sunday rum." This was well received, but what brought back the cheer was George Rice, master of ceremonies, who hopped around the tables in a tattered swallow-tailed coat distributing prizes for the day's events: cans of preserved peaches, rum, tobacco, extra towels, and fancy bath soap. Most seized on the rum and tobacco, those being the items that kept life at Fort Conger tolerable.

✳

The very next day Dr. Pavy was back to his old tricks of baiting Lieutenant Greely. The C.O. expected a yes, sir or no, sir answer. His military training wouldn't stand for evasion. The doctor liked to give his unsolicited opinion, and Brainard had never known Lieutenant Greely to ask his officers for their opinions. General Custer was like that. Never consulted with his officers and they hated him.

They were having their midday meal when Lieutenant Greely said, "I want your opinion of this sauerkraut, Doctor. Most of the men haven't touched it. If it is not good, I want you to tell me."

"It is old," Pavy said, not looking up from his heaping plate of food.

"That goes without saying, Doctor. But is it harmful? I want your medical opinion here."

"Freezing might have injured it." He muttered through a mouthful.

This conversation had the men's attention. Their C.O. was trying to engage, and Dr. Pavy wasn't cooperating. As they watched, the C.O. rose up and strode to the doctor's end of the table. He leaned over him, all six feet. "Is this sauerkraut, Doctor, improper food? Answer me: yes or no."

Pavy looked the C.O. right in the eye and said, "You are the son of a shoemaker. I do not have to say if it is proper or improper." His black eyebrows shot upward as did his shoulders in a Gallic manner that caused a suppressed snicker from Private Henry. "It is food." The doctor wiped his mouth with his cloth napkin and continued. "I have, myself, never liked sauerkraut, not because of its taste but because it is a *German* food. I do not like Germans. I have shot Germans in the Franco-Prussian War. Perhaps you forget?" He looked around the table.

The son of a shoemaker. All eyes jumped to their commander. Pavy had insulted Lieutenant Greely's father! Pavy had killed Germans! There were bursts of nervous laughter among the Germans. The C.O. straightened himself and his black beard bristled. "I expect an apology, Doctor Pavy." His black, luminous eyes widened and grew blacker. Pavy ran a hand across his broad forehead from which the hair had receded, pulled the hand down his face and through the beard he kept cut to a sharp point. Why, Sergeant Brainard thought, what a ferret's face our doctor has. Pavy let his hand wave in the air, a motion apparently meant to dismiss his remark, and Connell muttered to his buddy Charlie, "Oooh. That was good entertainment." To which the private responded, to Brainard's surprise, "But it's not *good*." Turning to Pavy, Charlie said, "Does that mean we German boys are at war with you, Doctor?" Pavy spread his fingers in what might be taken for a conciliatory gesture. "I am finished with all that," he said.

✳

Private Henry's True & Accurate Account of the LFB Expedition

7 January 1882

Pretty boring around here. Nothing going on but the mindless weather readings. Take this morning. I was freezing my fingers writing down Jewell's measurements when the meteorologist said, "Damn, the mercury's frozen at -38 degrees Fahrenheit." We had another type of thermometer that could record lower and he sent me back for it. That's when I got my bright idea to test the freezing point of other substances. I corralled Schneider because his little dog Gypsy—we all love Gypsy, she's so bright and cute—had lost her last pup when another mother killed it. Schneider was most broken up on Gypsy's account, so to cheer him up I had him help me test the coal oil, which became the consistency of syrup at -25 degrees F. We swiped the oil of peppermint from the doctor's medical supplies and it froze solid at -30 degrees. But our discovery that could change the world— I'm not kidding—was that the New England rum, ninety proof it was too, at -41.7 degrees F showed a thin coating of slush, at -47.4 degrees F left a syrupy substance in the bottom of the vial, but at -49.7 degrees F, I could upend the container without a drop spilling out. Schneider was most admiring and went off to tell Biederbick, who came and told me he had found one or two of the brandy bottles, part of the hospital stores, frozen solid and the bottles cracked. "I tasted some of the frozen spirits, Charlie," he reported. "Then you'd better watch out the C.O. doesn't accuse you of being a hard drinker like Cross." Ha! Ha! I'm just doing my best to lighten things up around here.

Christmas is behind us and the New Year too. I'm glad. I was getting sick of hearing so many of them going on about missing their homes.

I've started a newspaper. I'm calling it the *Arctic Moon*. George Rice is a contributor and Lieutenant Lockwood drew a pen-and-ink sketch for our masthead. These two men are a cut above anyone else here and I am doing myself a good turn by associating with them. In fact, Lieutenant Lockwood has taken me into his confidence. When we were sitting together at the table penning our stories, me thinking how impressed the *Chicago Times* editor will be when I show him my grand little newspaper, he said in his southern tones that draw wild beasts like me to him, "Charlie, I will confide that my spirit longs for adventure. My family expects great things of me." He has this high style of address that I would mock in anyone else. He waxes his mustache, indicative of vanity. Well, perhaps Lieutenant Lockwood is vain, but he is kind to me. So, what is my reaction? I, Charlie Henry, who cares nothing for noble striving? Whose main concern is filling his own stomach? When Lieutenant Lockwood drew me toward him with personal talk, I felt myself no better than some low scavenging animal—a weasel—who preys upon small and defenseless creatures. With the *Arctic Moon* I've constructed a trap. I've caught Lieutenant Lockwood. And George Rice as well. Rice praised me—"very clever, Charlie," he said—for an advertisement that Connell, Whisler—all my friends, including poor Bender—had told me to my face was in poor taste. I copy it out here for the world to judge:

> Information wanted of the Greely Arctic Expedition. It strayed away from home last July and was last heard from at Upernavik, Greenland.
>
> Address:
>
> Bereaved Parents.

✳

By now the men at Fort Conger were in the cold crucible of winter, deep and dark. When the sky was clear and the moon bright, they could take the *Arctic Moon* outside and read it. But most of them saw no point in going out unless they had to. It was unpleasant enough in their bunkrooms, despite the second stove at that end of the common room, despite their work to insulate the walls the frost wormed its way in, like white puss. Masses of it seeping through the wood like a damned infection. Impossible not to roll up against at night in your narrow bunk. The top bunks were the warmest, so they changed around. The C.O. had located the station only one hundred yards from the water's edge. This forced the light sleepers—Sergeant Brainard fell into this category, as did Lieutenant Lockwood—to listen to the pack ice grind and growl and smash itself to bits.

As the weather grew meaner the conversations around the tables did too, and Sergeant Brainard had ceased to be surprised by any sort of unpleasant talk. He had taken to sitting out of their lamplight, working on his supply records. He was very orderly about it. He found it satisfying to note what they had consumed and what was left on the shelves to be consumed, the kind of work that let him tune in and out of the men's conversations. This evening Connell and Charlie were working over poor Whisler. Any man generous enough to pass around his birthday rum was bound to be made sport of by those two. Not Private Biederbick, a decent chap, who made the fourth man in their bunkroom and was sitting next to Whisler at the table.

"You know what happened to Sir John Franklin, don't you, Whisler?" Connell started off. Whisler remained silent. "Driven to the last resource." Connell let out a grim chuckle.

"No need to go into it," Biederbick said.

"You know what that means, don't you, Whisler?" Charlie pressed on, ignoring Biederbick.

"Huh?" Whisler said.

The Irishman waved his arms in Whisler's face. "Ha! Ha! He has no idea what we're talking about," Connell chortled. "Their camp. Strewn with corpses. Mutilated. Human flesh and bones in the cook pot."

Whisler started to get up, but Connell grabbed his arm and pulled him down. "Only thirty-five years ago, Whisler. You weren't born. But the C.O. was. So was the doctor. One hundred and twenty-nine Englishmen. Vanished."

"Give it up, boys." Biederbick tried again to get them to stop.

"Staaaarrrrved." Charlie drew out the word, leaning into Whisler's face. "A Hudson Bay Company man brought to light what happened. Acquired relics from the Eskimos. It was the silver plate stamped with Franklin's crest that proved it."

"Lady Franklin," Connell said, "refused to believe the Hudson Bay man. *She* blamed the eating on the Eskimos."

"Civilized folk don't eat civilized folk. Not with crested spoons." Charlie guffawed, pounding the table.

"If they were man-hauling they should have ditched the silverware," Whisler said.

"Smart boy, Whisler." Charlie whacked him on the back. "The success of any sledging party depends on its ability to reduce the constant weights. The C.O.'s very big on that, you heard him."

"Why," put in Connell, flashing his teeth, "Franklin's men would have improved their chances if they'd dumped their pocket watches."

Whisler sat there, picking at the coal dust under his fingernails. "Doesn't it scare you, Whisler?" Charlie said.

"It's just nasty. You fellows are nasty," Whisler said. He rose again and stood.

Charlie tried to keep the game going. "We're just telling you these Arctic wastes have the power to deliver a good story. All the better if you don't come back."

"Sir John Franklin is a hero today. You want to be a hero, don't you, Whisler?" Connell was forcing it now.

"I just want to get home," Whisler said. That stopped it. Probably they agreed with him, Brainard thought.

✳

By March the light became stronger daily in a way that seemed to soften the landscape around the fort. This increasing light that had some warmth pulled the men out of the building. The cold was still keen and the wind brisk but because of the light they were inclined to stay out after taking the hourly readings of temperature and barometer, wind and tide. The sky shone with a brightness that compelled them to look up and then quickly down as the sun, from its position on the horizon, hit them at eye level. Sergeant Brainard, on such a foray, found musk oxen scat and clumps of the great beasts' hair on the shrubby willow they fed on. He wondered if this meant that the musk oxen didn't migrate south as was thought, but holed up in some well-sheltered valley during the long dark. A cloud covered the sun, and the air suddenly thickened with snow. The temperature plunged and Sergeant Brainard found himself turning for home. *I am not like the musk oxen*, he thought, and he smiled to himself for his human weakness. When he pulled the door open he was greeted by the familiar sour smell of men who have been living in close quarters far too long.

But spring *had* come and Dr. Octave Pavy's chance for the pole arrived. The sledging season slotted itself between the return of continuous daylight and before the sun could turn the winter ice to slush. Temperatures still sank into the negative 40s, yet the sun was strong enough to burn exposed flesh and melt the surface to standing pools of water. The C.O. planned to equip two parties and both knew they were expected to surpass the Farthest North record set by Commander Markham of the British Royal Navy six years ago.

Greely turned the leadership of the sledging trips over to Dr. Pavy and Lieutenant Lockwood. Brainard imagined that Lieutenant Greely would not mind the doctor's absence. He was delighted that Lockwood had requested him second-in-command. Eskimo Fred would drive a dog team. They would have man-hauling parties as well. Lockwood's orders were to retrace their route of last fall, sledge across the Robeson Channel to Greenland, and continue north until they had surpassed the British. They would be out for two months, mapping and exploring. "Finally," Lieutenant Lockwood said to his friend Brainard, "we're getting down to the real work of this expedition."

✗

Fort Conger

15 March 1882

Dear Lilla Mae,

My chance for the pole has come. It will be difficult. Harder than anything your Octave has ever done. Already I am at a disadvantage. I will tell you.

I have my own fine team of dogs I brought from Greenland. But for the pole I need more. Dogs can wear out and die on the trail. Already we have lost half of our dogs from disease. But, as I was leaving before Lockwood, I could outfit myself from Lockwood's team. A brilliant plan! Lockwood had no dogs to spare, but this was to my advantage because by shorting him I prevented him from making a polar dash, if he had such a thing in mind. I did not know. But I am always a careful man, you know that, Lilla Mae. I started to congratulate myself—but, ah, too soon.

I will tell you more. I saw two privates making life miserable for this other private, Whisler. Whisler was going with Lockwood! I would make this weak man get Lockwood's dogs for me. This would be easy, I told myself.

You can imagine my amazement when I laid out my plan and this spineless private said, "Steal, you mean, Doctor Pavy. I will not do it."

I cursed myself. I tried harder. I said, "You impute to me a motive far from my mind. I have my own dogs, and Lieutenant Greely has lent me his team, but I need Lockwood's dogs as well."

"Ask him yourself. You won't get me to do it." He started to walk away.

"Wait!" I shouted. "You may accompany me to the pole, Private Whisler," I said. "I can make you famous."

"Lieutenant Greely said to stay away from the pole, Dr. Pavy." He stared at me. I told myself, "Damn! This man has principles." But every man has a price. I said, "Fame will make you rich, Private Whisler." I gave him my most meaningful smile to make sure he understood. He said nothing, compelling me to say, "Private Whisler. Think again. Bear in mind that I am your physician."

"You mean you would refuse to treat me if I got sick?"

"Certainly." And I added, "I could make it even worse if you told Lieutenant Greely of our conversation."

"How so?" His face was stony, rigid. I damned him in my soul.

"My medicines are powerful." I made my face stony, too. "I might have difficulty in estimating an accurate dosage in your case, Private Whisler."

"You threaten my life?"

"If you get me Lockwood's dogs, you won't be troubled by this concern." But this stubborn man would not bend. Lilla Mae, your Octave was defeated by this lowly, stupid private. I am on my way to the North

Pole, nonetheless. It is too far, too cold, too hard. It is impossible, but I know that I will do it.

Your loving husband,
Octave

✳

For the past month everyone at Conger had been working to get the spring trips—the Farthest North trips—launched. Lieutenant Greely, at his desk, drew up lists of supplies. Lockwood studied the maps and writings of Markham and Beaumont of the British Royal Navy, who had set the past records. Bender, their tinsmith, repaired lamps, stoves, and copper cooking pots, counting out plates, cups, and eating utensils. The common room tables were turned into a factory for the stitching of tents and harnesses for dogs and men. Shorty Frederick was in charge of leather repairs: knife scabbards, buffalo-hide sleeping bags, gloves and mittens, moccasins and boots. Cross reinforced the Hudson Bay sledges with a stronger design he had worked out with Lockwood. They would be hauling tentpoles, snow knives, axes. And rations for two months. Brainard had been grinding up beans for flour for days. They would be eating stews of ground meat and hard bread, heating with cooking alcohol whatever came out of the cans. He had picked up grumbling about the man-hauling. They had dogs; the dogs should be doing this work. It was true they had dogs, but not enough dogs. Schneider had been working with the puppy teams, dogs born at Conger in November. Everyone loved the puppies and Schneider was proud of the teams shaping up under his direction, but these were not mature, trail-hardened dogs.

Dr. Pavy and Rice's party left on March 19. On April 3, Lockwood's men lined up with their loaded sledges in front of the fort. Lieutenant Greely made a speech—he had a talent for making an occasion of something, Brainard noted. "The boat *Valorous* is beached on Dutch Island," he said. "We did this to set us, at Fort Conger, ready to come to your rescue if the ice breaks up while you are still on the Greenland side. We have done this to give you peace of mind." There was some cheering, and the C.O. walked around with Lockwood, making final checks on sledges and men. They stopped, and the C.O. shook his lieutenant's hand. "I charge you," he intoned, "with full control of the most important sledging and geographical work of the expedition." He raised his arm in a gesture that seemed to sweep up to the North Pole. "I know you will extend our knowledge regarding lands beyond the Arctic Circle."

"But, Lieutenant Greely," Private Henry barked, "we're eleven hundred miles above the Arctic Circle already!"

Brainard, anxious to blot out this private's rudeness, let out a rollicking cheer. This was picked up by everyone.

Lieutenant Greely gave the order, and as ten men harnessed to four sledges struggled against the inertia of their loads, they began moving, slowly gaining momentum as they traversed the uneven surface of broken ice, hummocked snow, and gravel.

Brainard, in his harness, turned to look back to catch a last glimpse of Lockwood, who was not to leave until the 5th, two days later. He was to drive the dog sledge with Eskimo Fred, the sledge Greely had named *Antoinette*, after his firstborn. To Lockwood was entrusted the flag made by Mrs. Greely that they would plant at their Farthest North. Even though Brainard could not see Lockwood, he knew his friend was smiling and would be waving, along with the men left at the fort, until he had lost sight of the sledges, grown too small to see.

✶

Lockwood was prompt and Brainard breathed a sigh of relief about that. They left the next morning, Lockwood's dog team hauling eight hundred pounds, each man dragging about 116 pounds. In spite of the weight and the driving wind, they reached Cape Beechey on April 6; Whisler, complaining of illness, showed his spirit by keeping at the drag ropes. The temperature was -49. The corned meat at dinner barely thawed, and Brainard remarked to Lockwood, as he scrapped his tin plate, the ice crystals forming, "Chilled sledgers want hot food—a lot of it!"

During the marches, their sleeping bags froze iron hard from their moist body heat given off at night. They were moving in the nighttime hours, according to the clock, and sleeping during the day when the sun was most intense, but they still spoke in terms of night and day. Frozen bags meant the dreaded task of thawing their way back into them. They were doubled up, some tripled, in the bags, but nonetheless, Connell had frozen one of his toes in the sleeping bag. He kept limping along in his traces with surprising good spirits. "I think you actually enjoy hauling, Private Connell," Brainard said. "I do. I'm like the dogs," the Irishman explained. Brainard wasn't sure what Connell meant by that, but as the private was so often full of complaints, this was a welcomed change. They had been out a week and were on the Greenland side.

Cooking, if it could be called that, was the worst detail. That evening when Brainard was setting up the stove, Ritenbenk, the king dog, and Gypsy, the queen, stole their ration of meat. As no allowance could be made for thievish dogs, they went without meat, and Brainard received glares that matched the strong wind searing his fingers as he ladled out their slim portions.

After bolting his dinner, Private Henry insisted that he be allowed to return to the fort. He was doubled up with rheumatism and they would be hauling him if they didn't, so they let him go. Then Connell, who had been bravely struggling with his frosted toe, asked if he, too, could return to the fort. Lockwood sought out Brainard. "I really don't think he's faking it," he said. "He was nearly in tears. I'll take him on the dog sled, catch up with Henry, and the two can walk back together." When Lockwood returned, he reported that they had not overtaken the private. "I didn't even see him in the distance," Lockwood said. "Remarkably speedy for a man afflicted with rheumatism."

"I've got my eye on him," Brainard assured his friend.

They were sitting side by side in the buffalo bag, pushing their feet through the frozen hide by centimeters, losing feeling in their toes, when Lockwood said, "My father told me that you were with General Sherman on his western trip in '77. I wish you'd tell me about that."

"Generous of you to ask," Brainard replied. "General Sherman is no friend of southerners. Your father fought against him."

"Oh, I know!" Lockwood said. "But you saw a different side of the general. That's what I want to hear about. Besides, telling stories is a good way to forget how damn uncomfortable we are."

The wind hammered the thin tent canvas as Brainard began. "Yellowstone had just been declared our first national park. Colonel Doane's doing, you know. He had brought back word of those geysers, great fountains of steam shooting upward for hundreds of feet into the air. I saw them myself. You'd have been burned to death if you'd fallen into one of those boiling potholes."

"What about General Sherman? What he was like. My father told me that unlike Custer, he was popular with his men."

"I'll start at the beginning and spin out this tale. We have a long way to travel before we reach the foot of this sleeping bag." Brainard smiled at Lockwood. The lieutenant was in his element on this mission. His beard was growing out, tangling with his mustache, now untrimmed and unwaxed. Lockwood loved driving the dog sledge. He cut a dashing figure, too, a figure of romance.

"The general wished to go into the park in the most democratic way possible," Brainard continued. "He asked for five men, a corporal and four privates from my Second Cavalry troop at Fort Ellis. I felt very fortunate to have been chosen as one of the privates. He had his own men as well, Colonels Poe and Bacon, and his son Tom. I liked Tom. He was not a fighter like his father. He was studying to become a priest. He loved to fish and we kept our camp supplied with first-class trout dinners. Colonel Norris, who was the superintendent of the park, tipped us off as to the best spots. We used grasshoppers for baits and were pulling out two-and-a-half-pound trout. Can you believe it? Colonel Bacon said he'd never seen such sport; he said he doubted it could be excelled upon earth."

Lockwood laughed. "My father met Colonel Bacon. He must have been a good fellow to have along."

"They were all good fellows," Brainard said. "We were to be out eighteen days but the general wanted to keep our camp equipage simple. We had our own saddle horses and five pack mules. We carried no tents. The general slept under a tent fly; the rest of us slept in the open with a good supply of bedding and our overcoats we could spread over us on the frosty nights."

"Ah!" Lockwood laughed. "I wouldn't mind a merely frosty night. That sounds like heaven."

"What was most thrilling for me was to listen to the general as we sat around the campfire at night. He'd made sure the liquor ration was adequate, though I never saw him abuse it. He was an old man by then—or seemed old to me—with a wrinkled face from his outdoor life. I wouldn't mind looking as he looked when I grow old." Brainard stopped, aware of the tent being rocked back and forth in the wind. They had banked the sides with snow, now blown off, and the gusts blasting under the rubber ground cloth ballooned out the sides and chilled them.

"Please go on," Lockwood urged.

"The general loved the camping, the 'roving about,' he called it. It had a charm for him he couldn't describe. I knew what he meant, I felt that way too. It was wonderful how he could launch into historical accounts. Napoleon he admired greatly, and our own General George Washington. Even at the time I remember thinking what a lucky dog I was, and how I should take in everything since it wasn't going to happen again."

"I envy you the experience," Lockwood said. "Did you see much game? I hear there are antelopes."

"Surprisingly little. We were all amazed and disappointed because the grazing appeared to be of the very best."

"How about the Indians. Any encounters with them?"

"Our party did not, but we met a party of tourists our first day in the park, under the direction of a guide. We found out after we returned to Fort Ellis that they had been attacked by the Nez Perce and two killed, one being their guide."

"How unfortunate," Lockwood exclaimed.

"When General Sherman heard this he said, 'The only good Indian is a dead Indian.'" Brainard turned to his friend for his reaction.

"Do you agree?" Lockwood asked. "I know you fought in the Nez Perce wars."

"My older brother Henry fought against your father in the Civil War," Brainard said. "Yet you and I are friends."

"That's because we know each other, and like what we know."

"I can say the same about the Indians I've gotten to know," Brainard said.

"I'm glad we have our Greenland natives," Lockwood said. "They work hard and I sense they want the best for us. It's a great pleasure for me to be on a sledge with them. I'm learning how to drive the dogs."

"We'll never be as good as they are at it."

"Oh, I know," Lockwood said. I wish they could speak English." Brainard watched his friend frown, perhaps over the obstinacy of Jens and Eskimo Fred being so slow at learning English words. I'll have them teach me their language, Brainard thought, and that would help them learn English, too, I bet.

"I think my feet have reached down to the bottom of this bag," the lieutenant said. He yawned and then shivered. "I hope I can sleep. They feel like icicles."

"I'm just going to slip out and see how the others are doing," Brainard said.

✳

On April 8, they were doing some mapping along the coastline when a storm, coming up from the southwest, hit them at alarming speed. The men were knocked down by the force of the wind, and Lockwood had them make camp early on the lee side of a huge floeberg. The temperature was -16. When Privates Salor and Biederbick did not appear—they had passed through some narrow passages of pack ice and no one remembered seeing those two after that—Lockwood asked Brainard to go and look for them. "We'll have the tents up and the stove going by the time you return," he said.

Brainard stumbled along hardly able to keep to his feet, shaping his course by compass, until he came upon their tracks and began sorting out how they had become confused in the intricacies of the pack. This threw his thoughts to Colonel Doane and how the colonel talked to the men he trained to be Indian fighters. Brainard could see his tall figure, his square-jawed handsome face, his eyes piercing into your very soul, his mustache waxed into points three inches long, standing outside Fort Ellis, addressing the new recruits. Telling them in his deep rumbling baritone what he expected of them: "I will turn you into men of versatility and toughness. You will make your own clothes, drive teams, pack and travel on foot or horseback, by sledges or on snowshoes, you will never get lost or bewildered; you will regard as a laughingstock the severities of winter on the Plains, where the thermometer goes down to fifty degrees below zero." This was followed by a fit of nervous laughter. Brainard remembered that feeling of being scared, yet tremendously excited when he first heard Doane's words. "I will mold you into the bone and sinew of the Plains," Doane promised those who served under him, and Brainard was quite aware Colonel Doane had done this for him. He knew as well that Long and Shorty Frederick, who had also been trained by Doane, could be doing what he was doing, following these wind-blown tracks that ended in a snowbank where Salor and Biederbick had burrowed in with only a rubber blanket to fend off the wind and the cold. They had done the smart thing, Brainard assured them, stopping before they became hopelessly lost and waiting for rescue. These two were able enough, especially Biederbick who put extra effort into his work assignments, but Brainard was aware that men who had come through the crucible of Doane's training brought an uncommon degree, not just of toughness, but of spirit that would be there for them, and for their comrades, in the pinch.

By the time they reached their camp, the storm was a raging gale, the tents weighted down with snow, narrowing the living space, crowding the inhabitants. The temperature, risen to ten degrees above zero, had thawed out the sleeping bags, turning them soggy. Held down by the wind, they spent forty-five hours in cramped misery, their one attempt to cook ending in an upset fuel can.

Despite these setbacks, they made progress, following the British route up the Greenland coast. Reaching Stanton Gorge on April 26, they found forty rations, a can of rum, and the note Lieutenant Beaumont left in the cache he built in the spring of '76. Lockwood unscrewed the brass canister that contained Lieutenant Beaumont's message. "Let us see what this Britisher has to say," the lieutenant said. "Those men were riddled with scurvy by this time." Linn and Eskimo Fred, intent on breaking into the rum, stopped to gather around Lockwood. "'All have done their best.'" The lieutenant's soft, cultivated Southern tones were at odds in this Arctic wasteland. "'We will go on as far as we can and live as long as we can. God help us.'"

"Sounds pretty grim," Sergeant Linn said. "Some of them died, didn't they, Lieutenant Lockwood?" The lieutenant was silently staring at the message he held in his ungloved hand. Why doesn't he say something, Brainard thought. The men's faces had gone blank, taken over by their own exhaustion in this lonely, forbidding place. Lockwood shook himself. "Get that rum open, boys, we'll celebrate reaching this spot, and I'll write our own message to leave in the cairn."

✳

The daylight was continuous, no relief from the sun's direct rays, even at midnight. It was strange to watch the sun dip to the crest of the northern hills, rest there briefly, then curve slowly upward to resume its course. All the while they paced off the miles northward, moving on the frozen coastline from headland to headland, mapping when they could.

On April 29, Lockwood turned back his support team with orders to await his return, while he continued with the single dog sled, Eskimo Fred Christiansen, Sergeant Brainard, and rations for eighteen days. They traveled along the ice foot, winding among the hummocks and crossing tidal cracks, always hounded by the wind. They named the capes they passed: Distant Cape, Dome Cape, and Surprise Cape.

By the middle of May, they had exceeded Beaumont's record by a hundred miles and were eating down their rations. Brainard and Eskimo Fred caught a hare, providing a fine stew, saving half of the hare for their next meal. A mistake, as the lead dog Ritenbenk consumed the morsel "deliberately as an epicure," Lockwood put it, while men and dogs looked on from a respectful distance. The men themselves were eating only every sixteen hours, their rations and fuel almost used up. That night Ritenbenk burrowed under their tent and made off with one of the remaining bags of pemmican. By that time they were sure they had bested Captain Markham's Farthest North, and celebrated that event—it was Sunday, May 14—with cold chocolate and frosted musk ox stew. The next day Lockwood and Brainard climbed to the summit of the cape, nearly three thousand feet above the sea. In a raw wind, they erected as big a cairn as they could construct around their flagpole. Brainard stretched out upon the snow with the sextant, pencil, and notepaper, looking up at Lieutenant Lockwood, who was deep in the calculations that would give them their latitude. The wind tugged at Brainard's paper. In the distance a confused mass of snowy peaks lifted above the fog. "We've exceeded Captain Markham by four miles," Lockwood said. "I estimate we're at latitude 83 degrees 24 minutes North." He looked north then, and Brainard, lying on his stomach, followed his leader's hungry gaze to the next headland. "It's probably only eight miles away," the lieutenant said.

Brainard laughed. "You have never been satisfied by just glimpsing at what lies ahead."

Lockwood smiled down at his friend. "This time I will have to be. But, oh!" he exclaimed, his eyes alight with joy. "My father will be so proud of me!"

They descended then, back down into the fog, though the sun's reflection could be seen on the summits of far-off mountains. "We broke it," Lieutenant Lockwood shouted, running up to Eskimo Fred, who was hitching up the dogs. "We broke the record the British held for three centuries!" Fred gave his broadest grin, though Brainard knew he could not understand the words. But words mattered not. Fred understood, as he demonstrated by jumping into his position behind the dogs, his whip raised. The other two took their places and braced themselves as Fred cracked his whip. The dogs took off like lightning, pointed south and heading home.

✳

Fort Conger

5 May 1882

My Dearest Henrietta,

I have returned from a successful trip into Grinnell Land, where I had the honor of naming several geographical features after those who were paramount in launching the Lady Franklin Bay Expedition. In particular, I was pleased to give General Hazen's name to a lovely 500-square-mile frozen lake. I wish you could have stood next to me on the shoreline, my love, and watched the lake's snowy surface shimmer like diamond dust in the midnight sun. I named a fjord for my friend William Chandler, secretary of the navy, but will name nothing for the secretary of war, Robert Lincoln, who, as you know, did nothing but show a distinct lack of interest in all Arctic endeavors. He would have killed our expedition if he could have. I am saving the best news for last. From the Garfield Mountains—I do hope our president recovered from the attempt on his life—descends a spectacular river of ice that I deemed worth of carrying your name on the maps: Henrietta Nesmith Glacier!

I arrived to find Dr. Pavy back. He failed in his attempt. He got no farther than Cape Joseph Henry on the frozen Lincoln Sea, far short of Markham's record. He is a tricky, double-faced man, idle, unfit for any Arctic work except doctoring and sledge travel and not first class in the latter. I will admit, he is an excellent doctor. You may rest assured on that score. I will go further and say he and Lieutenant Kislingbury consort together. I know they are united by the common wish to break down my command. I will leave my remarks at that, except to add you must have no fears for my safety.

This comes with all my love to you and the children,
Adolphus

✳

Fort Conger

5 May 1882

Darling Lilla Mae,

I will tell you, my dear wife, if we had not run into open water I would have broken the British record. We were back at Fort Conger one month before we were expected. Greely welcomed me by saying, "I gave you my dog team, Doctor, to ensure your success. You erred in your choice of departure point for crossing the ice. You should have pushed to the northernmost land, Doctor. Then your party would have avoided the polar drift."

He scolded me like a schoolboy in front of everyone! But I have ways to get at him. How much I enjoy to turn in my medical reports, due monthly, late. He terms this tardiness insubordination. He detests insubordination, and so, you may be sure, the lateness of my reports has him pulling out the hairs of his black beard.

But, Lilla Mae, you must understand: it was not my poor judgment. We were unlucky. When we left the land and got on the ice, the floes began to separate. We were surrounded by water. We were forced to abandon our tent and most of our scientific instruments. That annoyed him, too, the loss of equipment. "Listen, Greely," I told him, "you should be grateful I brought back your dogs."

I embrace you with hugs and kisses,
Octave

✶

Private Henry's True & Accurate Account of the LFB Expedition
5 June 1882

Lockwood was back on June 1, but it's strange. Lieutenant Lockwood, the hero of our expedition, has flattened out. He's best leading the action; he thrives on derring-do: the glorious charge. "Our great and marvelous adventure," Lieutenant Lockwood called our expedition, and now that we've achieved our big goal of beating the British, the heart has gone out of the adventure for Lieutenant Lockwood. He's sunk back to being very late for breakfast.

The main topic of conversation here is Lockwood's victory yet the doctor and Kislingbury haven't even shaken his hand. I know why. The doctor is eaten up with jealousy. His trip came to naught and he's not likely to get another opportunity for the pole. By now we know the doctor came on this expedition for the pole. Whisler let it out when he told us the doctor wanted him to steal Lieutenant Lockwood's dogs. I'll reveal what else I know about our good doctor. He has a little daughter in France whom he hasn't seen since she was three. This comes by way of Whisler, too. "Pavy's a bigamist then," I said. "If he married the woman. And if he didn't, that's worse." "The doctor told me he was superior to other men," said Whisler. "That's why I should steal Lockwood's dogs." "He's as bad as Ralston," I told him. "What a bunch of deadbeats we have on this expedition. Not you, Whisler." I was thinking of myself. But none of them are going to dig out my inglorious past.

I shiver as I write this, but I know nothing colder than crawling out of a bag after a poor night's sleep to stand in line at 40 degrees below zero waiting for the cook to dish oatmeal onto my tin plate. Our food was never more than barely warm. I had to bolt it before it froze. We sweated from the man-hauling, and when we stopped, our shirts froze to our backs. We slogged through meltwater soaking our footgear. I changed to dry socks until I ran out of socks. Our bags froze stiff as iron during the day from the moisture our bodies gave off at night. So at the end of a day's hauling, when we were ready to drop, what we had to look forward to was the dreaded business of thawing our way into our bags. Connell and I were sharing a bag to combine body heat, yet Connell frostbit his great toe in the bag. What was worse, the hair on the bag's inside, whether buffalo, deer, or dog, became slimy from moisture and sloughed off in clumps. Connell and I lay like cordwood shivering through the night. I never knew if I slept. I suppose I must have. Whenever Connell rolled over he started up cold drafts that woke me. He said I did the same. "You kept me awake all night," I told him. "Just trying to find a comfortable position, Charlie," he said. "It wasn't so much that," I said. "It was the beating of your heart." "Impossible," he said. "It did," I said. "The beating of your heart kept me awake."

I lost weight. We all did. The brutal hauling made us hungry as wolves. But my lost weight made me ask Lieutenant Lockwood to send me back before my time. My rheumatism, I explained; they'd have to haul me on a sledge. The lieutenant marched off to consult with Sergeant Brainard and I heard the sergeant say, "So much for large men for Arctic service, eh, Lockwood?" I didn't like them taking me for a coward, but even worse was what Captain Price would think.

But I could not help myself, and with Brainard out among the ice hummocks, I'd have no trouble, back at Conger, replenishing my weight, and my peace of mind.

Connell was sent back too, because of his frozen toe. "I tried to catch up with you, Charlie, but you must have run like a sledge dog," he said. "I bet you frosted it on purpose," I told him, but he assured me he hadn't. He said it killed him to be sent back. "I thought I was going to shed tears in front of the lieutenant," was what he said. The sledging was the only thing he liked about being here. I told him I didn't believe him. "You bastard, you froze it on purpose," I said.

Soon as I got back, I padded into Sergeant Davy Brainard's storehouse nightly after the fattest meat I could sink my jaws into. My aim was to stuff myself until my skin had a silky sheen and was as smooth as a prize hog. But he's back on duty now, so I'd better be attentive.

✻

Midsummer now and it was never dark. There was no respite from the daylight. At first the men welcomed the novelty of eternal light. It was strange not to see the stars. But this light had no softness. It was all glare. Even on cloudy days, they were surrounded by the glare reflected from the snow remaining in the hollows. Glare rose from the roiling sea. Glare came at them off the bank of windows of their own fort. Because of the glare, the sky had no color at all, no softening blue. The wide expanse of sky above Fort Conger radiated a burning platinum, a steely harsh brightness that oppressed them as much as the darkness ever had. They could not retreat from this searching light. The men's internal clocks rebelled at being ordered to their bunks in the fullness of this light. The densest fog could not restrain it. The Eskimos could have been out hunting for seals during any hour of the twenty-four, if the C.O. had not been so rigid about sending everyone to bed. Their C.O., they grumbled, could not restrain this light but discipline must be maintained!

Overriding all was the hope of the relief. Each man wanted to be the first to spot the ship. All eyes were on the sea, where the light played its most fiendish tricks. The ship was there, and then it wasn't. When a man awoke at night to relieve himself, he would spot the ship in a flash of wave and wake his bunkmates. Each morning they expected to see their savior ship sitting in the harbor, sunlight benignly flashing off its flags. This expectation gave them the vigilance of an Eskimo over a seal hole.

Every man at Conger was on edge. All they thought about was the ship, coming soon, carrying news, fresh men, food, and letters from home. *Letters from home.* But the channel remained choked with pack ice. The wind blew it clear, raising hopes, but it never stayed open long.

Lieutenant Greely asked his top sergeant to call the men together. This was after dinner and most of them were at the tables, seated on the benches. Dr. Pavy and Kislingbury were in their usual corner, using the wall as a backrest. Brainard hoped, for the disgraced lieutenant's sake, the ship would show soon. When Greely was out exploring, he had left the fort in Sergeant Ned Israel's charge. This could only have humiliated Kislingbury more, and it had not helped that Lieutenant Greely made a point of coming up to camp at Watercourse Bay to await Lockwood's arrival. A generous gesture, but it only served to drive the wedge in deeper between the C.O. and his former second officer. At Watercourse Bay they had all heard the C.O. say to Lockwood, "Three lives paid for the English discoveries. You have beaten them and lost none." Brainard, despite being completely fagged and frustrated by a sledge lashing he was at that moment trying to repair, had been struck by Greely's remark. Not so much the words, but the tone. It said to Brainard that Greely had picked the right man, and that this man's achievement cast a glory on its leader that would carry him into what he coveted most: respect in Washington and a brilliant career.

When Lieutenant Greely made his entrance into the common room, he chose not to sit but stood before them, his fingertips balanced on the table. "I have gotten our records in order," he said in a ringing voice. "You men have accumulated a storehouse of data in meteorology, astronomy"—he gave a nod to Ned Israel—"physics, oceanography, biology, anthropology, and more; sometimes with surprising results." He raised his eyebrows in an attempt at jocularity. "The overall snow-fall, for instance, was scant. Living in the Arctic, in terms of precipitation, is equivalent to living in a desert. February showed a mean temperature of 40.1 degrees below zero. I have worked out a tidal schedule, which, when combined with data from the other International Polar Year stations, will enable scientists to set tidal patterns in all Arctic waters. Lockwood's tidal measurements taken on the Farthest North will, I'm sure, prove that Greenland is an island. You remember this was in dispute when the expedition set out. I will say again how delighted I am with Lieutenant Lockwood's achievement."

At these words Lockwood straightened himself. He had shaved off his beard and trimmed his mustache, which was carefully waxed again. "Lockwood, your party," Greely went on, "was absent from Conger for sixty days. You traveled almost one thousand miles, mostly in temperatures far below zero. You have returned in perfect health." The C.O. made the Farthest North heroics sound as if they had been the sole feat of the lieutenant himself. Brainard looked to see how Pavy and Kislingbury were taking this. Both were staring at their boots, sitting with their legs crossed at the ankles, backs to the wall.

"But our real achievement"—the C.O. actually clapped his hands together—"the one that will mean the most to future exploring parties, is that this party has just come through a year of Arctic living in safety, comfort, and in excellent health. The great Arctic killer, scurvy, that ravaged the Nares expedition only five years before, we held off with our diet of fresh meat and the pemmican treated with lime juice." Greely gestured toward Dr. Pavy. "The doctor can take much credit for this triumph." Pavy, at hearing his name, looked up. But his stony expression did not change. The expression on Kislingbury's face that he turned toward his card-playing friends seemed to say: What a fool our C.O. is.

But Greely, Brainard was quite sure, took in none of this.

He was standing before his men looking happier than he had looked since the expedition began.

"It sure would be nice to see some mugs other than our own," Private Bender squeaked.

"The Eskimos said we'd arrived in a 'good ice year,'" Private Henry shouted.

"So that sets us up for a poor one now!" Connell drove his friend's point home.

Practical Whisler spoke up. "But Lieutenant Greely said we had food for three years."

"He'll cut our rations, I bet," growled Henry.

"Can't we survive *without* cutting our rations?" Bender's squeak was close to panic.

"Men, men." The C.O.'s stentorian tones sliced through and Brainard was relieved to hear that their leader could bring the room to silence. "Let me address your concerns. Not only do we have food for three years, but we can stock up on fresh musk oxen meat. I'm sure Lieutenant Kislingbury would be glad to put his Remington to our good use." Greely smiled at the fallen lieutenant, who kept his eyes on his scuffed boots. "No one will go hungry." He gave a little laugh to show how ridiculous they were to even think of it.

"Lieutenant Greely," Brainard said, "would you remind us all of your plans laid down in Washington if the relief fails?"

"I was coming to that," Greely said with a startled look. But it was clear to Brainard that his C.O. had not been coming to that at all.

"If the relief ship cannot get through this summer, or even next, I have set it up in Washington that stores will be left for us at Cape Sabine. You saw this elbow of land on the way up, two hundred and fifty miles south of us now."

"Greenland is only thirty miles from that point," Lieutenant Lockwood said, "across Smith Sound. I believe you directed the relief to leave rations at Littleton Island, too, Lieutenant Greely, right off the Greenland coast."

"That's correct, Lieutenant." The C.O. nodded at his second officer.

"But how will we get there? We can't swim," Bender's high-pitched voice cut through, making the men laugh.

Greely smiled at Bender. The kind of smile, Brainard thought, a slightly annoyed father would lavish on a son who was not that smart and had to be looked after. "Private Bender," Lieutenant Greely said, drawing his hand down the length of his black beard, a gesture Brainard knew revealed his agitation. "Sergeant Cross has kept our motor launch in excellent shape. The *Lady Greely* will come to our aid." Cross's eyes registered something impossible to read behind that bushy black beard.

Schneider spoke up. "But, sir, the *Lady Greely* weighs nearly ten tons. We can't possibly sledge her if we are blocked by pack ice."

"I have accounted for that contingency." Greely hurriedly addressed this difficulty. "We have the *Narwhal*, the whaleboat, built to my orders in New Bedford. We have the English jolly-boat *Valorous* we took on board near Cape Hawks when we came up. We have the small Whitehall boat that can carry supplies and needs only one or two men to man it. But"—their C.O. paused—"abandoning Fort Conger is very unlikely." His fingertips, which had returned to the table, beat a tattoo in the silent room. Brainard knew, and was sure the others understood as well, that what those generals drew up in Washington could be ground to splinters here. He had learned, on the Plains, how to be flexible and alert. Now he would be more so.

Doctor Pavy was on his feet, stretching out his arms, spreading apart his fingers, the gesture he made in extreme agitation. "Men, listen to *me*, I am your doctor who is telling you. The ship, it was never sent!"

Lieutenant Greely took a step back, as if pushed by the doctor's words. "Please, Pavy," he said. "You know nothing. You are only upsetting these men." His hands found his beard. "Of course the ship was sent," he said, and began the stroking motion. "I made sure of that. *The ship was sent.*" But these last words were drowned by a babble of talk as to whether the ship had been sent or not sent, who was right, who was wrong, the doctor or their C.O., with Bender's ear-splitting squeal overriding all: "Listen to Dr. Pavy! He's our doctor!"

They are all terrified, Brainard thought. *And if Lieutenant Greely doesn't gain control soon, I will, though I will get reprimanded for it.* Dr. Pavy sat down, and as the energy began to drain out of this fruitless discussion, Lieutenant Greely put up his hand, and, to Brainard's relief, the room silenced. "If it is needful," Lieutenant Greely said in his fatherly voice, "for us to spend another winter here, we will do so. But I assure you, our government will not abandon us." He abruptly turned and strode toward his bunkroom, shoulders squared, heels loud on the wooden floor. The doctor turned toward Kislingbury, and, making no effort to keep his voice down, said, "As a Frenchman I put no trust in your men in Washington."

✳

On July 21, Shorty Frederick, loved by all because he volunteered for any duty, turned thirty. But more momentous, Sergeant Brainard caught Private Henry. Brainard wanted like anything to catch the pilferer (or pilferers) before the ship arrived so the rascal could be sent back. If it were Private Henry, as Brainard strongly suspected, he would breathe a sigh of relief to be rid of him. The sergeant found it difficult carrying the weight of Henry's past crimes on his conscience. If half rations were called for, Sergeant Brainard knew he could not forgive himself if they ran into real trouble, especially as he had chosen to withhold this information from his C.O. He must catch the thief *in the act* and had been shorting himself of sleep, going to bed at the proper hour, then getting up, creeping into the storeroom and kitchen area in his socks. That the sun never slept made his job harder.

On the night of July 21, he stood motionless in the shadowy entrance, listening to the sound of jaws grinding on bone. He quietly moved forward. Private Henry was sitting on a stool, masticating the remains of the musk oxen roast served at Shorty's birthday dinner. The private gnawed attentively, engrossed to the point of stupefaction over the joint. "You have put on weight, Private," Sergeant Brainard said. "Now I see why." Charlie looked up, juice running down his chin. His eyes took in the pistol strapped to his sergeant's belt, making him gnaw faster, until suddenly he dropped the bone and, wiping his greasy hands on his shirt, stood up. His mouth tilted crazily and he shrugged, a Pavy-like shrug of shoulders and hands that said without words: *You catch me red-handed.* "Come with me," Sergeant Brainard said, and marched the private off to Lieutenant Greely.

"You admit freely of your visits to the stores, Private Henry?" Greely asked. Charlie said he did. "You show no repentance for your crime?" No, the private did not. "I will say then," Lieutenant Greely continued, "that you are worse than a pilferer. You have the soul of a thief. Here, where we cannot easily replace our food supplies. I cannot tolerate a thief. You will return on the ship." Brainard saw the same crazy smile cross the private's face, and he realized that this man had had enough of what Lieutenant Lockwood called their great and marvelous adventure. Sergeant Davy Brainard went back to bed in the broad daylight and slept the soundest sleep since arriving at Lady Franklin Bay.

On August 7, the C.O. had Sergeant Cross ignite the motor of the coal-burning *Lady Greely*. He took Lieutenant Lockwood with him a short way down the coast where they could obtain a good view to the south. They returned to report they saw no ice, and no ship either. Sunshine and calm continued into the next week. The men climbed Cairn Hill behind the fort daily and ran down to say they had sighted a vessel, they had heard a steam whistle. But it all came to naught. These flights of fancy had them all stretched to the breaking point. On August 30, Lieutenant Greely issued the order to prepare the station for winter.

Interlude

William Beebe Does His Best
St. John's, Newfoundland

Summer 1882

Tiny details imperceptible to us decide everything.
W. G. Sebald, *Vertigo* (1990)

Private William Beebe was seasick. He felt himself the most miserable wretch alive. He began thinking that long before July 8, 1882, when he boarded the *Neptune* and sailed out of St. John's. In Washington the chief signal officer, Beebe's boss, General Hazen, told him the ship must sail by July 1. Every day the vessel was delayed added to the pressure Beebe already felt: that the lives of the men at Lady Franklin Bay rested upon his ability.

Now, in St. John's, William Beebe realized that his low rank was not adequate to his assignment. The general had assured him that this re-supply for the Greely Expedition was a routine operation; he was merely in charge of securing the ship. He needed go no farther than Disko in Baffin Bay on the Greenland coast, where he would take on additional stores—the sealskin pants that could only be procured there. But when General Hazen cabled him to take the ship up into the Kane Basin, William Beebe knew that as a private, he was not in a position to give orders to the army sergeant in charge of the men who were to relieve

Greely. He cabled Hazen back. "It will be embarrassing. I should be made a sergeant, or better still, a lieutenant." But the promotion never came.

Another troubling matter: he had been sent to St. John's before the appropriations bill to cover the expense of buying the ship had passed in Congress. Secretary of War Robert Todd Lincoln saw Arctic exploration as a drain on his main concern: wrapping up the Indian Wars. Exploration was a waste of money, men's lives, and no useful scientific work emerged from it. The war secretary claimed he was aware of "no understanding" about annual relief visits to Fort Conger.

Beebe went ahead and chose the *Neptune* at six thousand dollars a month. The ship's captain was a man named Sopp. James Norman was chief mate, an advantage; Norman had been ice pilot on the *Proteus* that dropped the men at Lady Franklin Bay last year. Nonetheless, Beebe cabled General Hazen: "This mission is so entirely different from any former experience, I would give five years of my life if I could back out." He added, "I would like to purchase pigs, cows, and sheep to take up to Fort Conger so that Lieutenant Greely's men might have fresh meat." He called Norman into his cabin to request he set up the decks to receive this livestock.

"Are you daft, man?" Norman boomed. Beebe found the ice pilot overpowering. The man was so full of the sea—this northern ice-infested sea so entirely foreign to Beebe's experience. "The dogs, Private Beebe, you forget the dogs have the run of the deck," Norman bellowed. "Those dogs will pull down the sheep and the cows, too, before we're out of the harbor. You can pen the pigs. You can keep them in the hold, but I'd stake a year's pay they'll all be dead before we reach Lady Franklin Bay."

Private Beebe cabled Hazen to cancel the livestock.

✱

When General Hazen wired that the appropriations bill had passed, Captain Sopp got the *Neptune* under way in a blinding rain. Beebe became seasick before they lost sight of the St. John's lighthouse. He had gotten off a week late, not his fault; he felt his entire trip in jeopardy. He took to his bunk. What the cook brought him came right back up.

He was too embarrassed to appear on deck. Every time he tried to stand, he was forced to his knees with the dry heaves. When Norman stuck his head in his cabin to inquire, he could not stop himself from saying, "I don't care whether we float or sink."

"You'll gain your sea legs in a day or two," Norman assured him. "The *Neptune* is faster under steam than the *Proteus*. Her boiler is new and she is a more powerful iceboat."

But Beebe was not cheered by Norman's words. He felt the ambiguity of his position with every churn of the heaving ship. He did not gain his sea legs; the possibility of it appeared as unattainable as possessing the rank he needed to be in command. Yet, if he was not in command, who was? Captain Sopp commanded the ship and his sailors, but who was responsible for the overall command? General Hazen had thrust upon him the duty to reach Lieutenant Greely's men. He would do his best. After all, Hazen had seen to his reinstatement when he was accused of abusing alcohol and forced to leave the army. But Hazen had owed him a favor. Beebe had sprung to his general's defense when Hazen was accused of cowardice under enemy fire at Shiloh during the Civil War. As he lay on his bunk unable to control the tumult in his gut, Beebe wished to God he had never spoken up for General Hazen.

Before they reached Disko on the Greeland coast, the *Neptune* hit the first ice fields. Beebe watched as the ship sliced her way through, like a plow through a farmer's field was how his landlubber eyes saw it. He took hope from this but lost it when the inspector in Disko, who oversaw the loading of the sealskin pants and the dogs, said, "You're aware, sir, last winter was unusually severe."

"What are our chances of reaching Lady Franklin Bay?" Beebe asked.

"Not much hope of that," the inspector said. "The ice is so thick the sealers have been unable to penetrate to their accustomed sealing grounds."

He sought out Norman. The ice pilot spread his hands, displaying calloused palms rough as barnacles on a ship's bottom. "The ice will move soon enough before the northerly wind, Private. Then you'll see how the *Neptune* can push through the ice-pans." Beebe had never seen pan ice, and would not show his ignorance by asking. He presumed it to be ice piled like pancakes on a plate.

When the *Neptune* pulled out of Disko's harbor on July 20, Beebe retired to his cabin to reread his orders. If a ship could not reach Lady Franklin Bay in the summer of 1882, Lieutenant Greely had designated points where supplies could be dropped. These were at Cape Hawks on the Ellesmere side and Littleton Island off Greenland's coast. But, he read, if the *Neptune* failed to reach Greely, he was to bring all food and equipment back to St. John's. Rather stinting on the army's part. If those men were to travel by boat down the coast, their lives might depend on these food drops. He was determined to leave caches at the points Lieutenant Greely had designated, but those apparent contradictory orders only increased the desperate pressure Beebe felt. Somehow he must reach those men at Lady Franklin Bay.

When Littleton Island emerged from the mists on July 29, Captain Sopp came to Beebe's cabin to find him stretched upon his cot. He was vomiting as soon as they left Disko. "We can go no further, sir," said Sopp. "If you come on deck I can show you why."

Beebe struggled into his outer clothing. From the deck he saw an unbroken barrier of ice. "This ice," the captain explained, "is twelve- to twenty-feet thick. It extends across the head of Smith Sound. I can anchor the ship and we can wait until the ice decides to move. Right now the southwesterly gales are against us."

At the end of the week the ice had not budged and Captain Sopp pronounced the ice impassable. The *Neptune* was blocked twelve miles short of Cape Hawks, where Beebe had hoped to leave a depot for Greely.

But at midnight on August 12, as Beebe stood at the *Neptune*'s rail with Norman, the pilot, picking up the bell-like cracking of the young ice near the ship, shouted, "By God, look! Water! The water's trickling through," and he ran off to stir Captain Sopp to start the engines and force open the lead. Beebe remained standing in the weak warmth of midnight twilight, staring into the black, glary depths. He felt the ship strain and gather speed as she forced her way between the imprisoning floes. Here was hope! But the forward movement ceased and Norman returned. "We've sprung a leak in the boiler. She's overstrained. So much for the new boiler, eh?" And Norman laughed.

"I cannot find what you report funny, Mister Norman," Beebe said. "It only adds to my anxiety." He stalked off to find the captain. If Beebe could not reach Cape Hawks, he would have Sopp retreat south to Cape Sabine where he would leave a message for Greely explaining why he had not placed stores here. "I am determined," he penned, "to turn all my efforts to land supplies and whaleboat as far north as possible."

They reached the end of August. The short summer shut down. New ice formed every night and held fast during the day. The heavy floes crashed together with each change in wind and tide, making a chaos that even this rough seal-hunting crew swore would crush the ship. Beebe found it terrifying. The noise, the unpredictability of the colliding ice swept him back into the heavy combat of Shiloh. It seemed to William Beebe he had always been on the losing side of things.

His great fear now was that Littleton Island would be ice blocked, so he changed his mind and left two hundred and fifty rations at Cape Sabine, aware this would feed Greely's party of twenty-five men for only ten days. But his hands were tied. He dared not leave more.

When Sopp crossed back to Littleton Island, Beebe left the same amount there. The ship was starting to leak, but Beebe prevailed upon the captain to cover the thirty miles across Smith Sound to the Ellesmere coast one last time. He had the men unload the whaleboat at Cape Isabella, thirty miles south of Sabine. He wrote Greely a final note. "I leave the whaleboat here as a last resort, in hopes you will be able to reach this point and use it for crossing to Littleton Island."

By September 5, the *Neptune* had thrashed back and forth through the ice-infested waters of Smith Sound for forty days. Beebe had left all he dared, a total of five hundred rations for Lieutenant Greely that might never be found. He was steaming home with at least two thousand rations in the hold, food that could have fed Greely and his men for three months. Even if he had been made lieutenant, Beebe doubted he had the courage to disobey these orders. Everyone in Washington had assured him Greely had adequate supplies at Conger to see him through another winter. He wished for the thousandth time that he had never been sent. He hated the Arctic. He dreaded facing General Hazen, and, God knows, he was at an utter loss how to explain his failure to Mrs. Greely.

4

"Our Inglorious Second Winter"

Fort Conger, Lady Franklin Bay

Winter 1882–9 August 1883

They were living in the kind of darkness found at the bottom of wells, the underground darkness of caves deep in the earth. If it was clear, the stars in the desert-dry Arctic air pulsated with the hard brilliance of diamonds, that rare and precious mineral consisting of nearly pure carbon in crystalline form, usually colorless. But color lived in this darkness. Streaks, streamers, bands of electrical discharges that throbbed in the ionized air could produce fountains of eye-shattering color, flower beds of rose and greens, yellows and blues. One afternoon, or it could have been at night—there was no distinction—their astronomer Ned Israel burst in shouting, "Come out! You must come out!" The men, slouched around the table on the backless benches, barely glanced up. This was their second winter, by now they had seen it all. Whatever the sky had to offer, they just weren't interested. "Please!" Ned persisted, his face flushed from the cold. "Now! Before it's gone. My heavens, men, this aurora nearly struck me in the face!" To humor this likable young man they shuffled to their feet and followed him out of the building to find themselves under a blinding, throbbing, dancing, vibrating sky awash in a raging artist's palette of colors. They began jumping and leaping about, hooting like boys released from school, arms raised to touch the colored streamers, Ned shouting, "Isn't it glorious? It's why we're here!"

But the colors faded and the jumping stopped, and the men filed back into the fort, back to living in their white-and-gray world where nothing changed. Back to arguing over senseless things, barking and growling at each other like dogs. Sergeant Brainard knew this wasn't good, but he told himself this was their second winter. No expedition had ever spent two consecutive winters in a building of their own making, at a latitude where the sun was absent for so long.

The observers made note of a meteor that fell from the northern sky, leaving behind a blue trail. Shorty Frederick reported frost had collected at the head of his bunk, causing his bunkmates to remark that they wished nature would freeze Shorty's snores. The coal oil, which they had dug from the bituminous shale at Watercourse Bay and used for their lamps, congealed and needed to be thawed. Sergeant Brainard noted that during the previous month alone they had consumed 14,159 pounds of coal.

The darkness was intense. It was hard to describe. They noticed just how dark the darkness was when they were given the relief of a thin new moon. This particular new moon appeared on the shortest day of the year, a sliver of light that made it a fraction less dark. From this day forward, they consoled themselves, the sun drew closer.

This day of hope marked Sergeant Brainard's twenty-sixth birthday. He celebrated by spending it in his storeroom, where he spent most days, arranging and counting cans. It separated him from the arguments and provided a certain solace to the tedium of life in the prison of an Arctic winter. He had discovered Richard Henry Dana's *Two Years before the Mast* in the library. Dana wasn't even twenty when he signed up as a common sailor aboard the brig *Pilgrim*, and up in the crow's nest he read Washington Irving's *Tales of the Alhambra*. Brainard would read that next.

He wished he could talk to Dana because his voyage around Cape Horn to California was so like theirs here: the confined living, the same unvarying faces, a male world, yet a manly one too, as he had discovered on the Farthest North with Lockwood. Dana had witnessed men flogged for no reason other than the captain's whim. At Lady Franklin Bay they were not under the sway of a bad man—Greely was no sadist—but as a rigid rule follower in a place that called for imaginative bending of the regulations, the outcome could be as destructive. Brainard could not help his thoughts turning to Colonel Doane. He was convinced they could have thrived here with Doane. The colonel would not have let plans laid down in the war offices in Washington affect his decisions when the circumstances had changed. Brainard was learning from Dana how the sea takes and gives a man's measure; he was here to learn how the Arctic does the same.

Corporal Salor celebrated his thirty-second birthday on the 24th.

And then: Christmas day. It was a failure. The thoughtfulness of Mrs. Greely's gift of English plum pudding had Lieutenant Lockwood wiping his eyes, his heart overfilled with images of home. The men plowed through Private Long's excellent feast as if it were their last meal. Any attempt to raise a song fell flat. Forced cheer seemed to mock the day itself.

✷

On the evening of January 27, dinner was punctuated by grumbles, eyes shifting to their C.O. and back to their plates heaped with canned ham, baked beans, potatoes, gravy, all of them forking in the food as if this were a race to the finish. After dessert (canned peaches), Greely removed himself to his own quarters.

"You can all blame me." This was Linn, who back in October managed to get himself reduced from sergeant to private through an act of insubordination, the offence, along with blasphemy, that brought out the worst in the C.O.

Brainard spoke up. "We can blame it on the bear." If there was any humor in that long-ago incident, he was determined to bring it out.

"It's really my fault," said Shorty Frederick.

"I never blamed you, Shorty," Linn said. "If that bear hadn't been so close to the fort, I never would have seen him in the twilight. I had the hunting rifle, then you're at my elbow telling me the C.O. had ordered you to take my weapon. Goddamn!" Linn's solid palm slapped the table. "It still makes my blood boil. He gave no reason for it."

"I was standing right next to him," Shorty tried to explain. "I wish I hadn't been."

"Well, I should have swallowed my pride. It was really my fault he cut off our walks to Dutch Island."

Schneider said, "When you walked up to the C.O., Linn, and said, 'Lieutenant, did you order that I should give up my gun?' and he said,

'Yes,' and you said, 'Well, I don't think much of it.' And he said, 'Sergeant Linn, do you realize what you are saying?' And you said—gosh, I couldn't believe it—you said, 'Yes! And I still don't think much of it.'" Schneider started to laugh.

Suddenly they were all laughing, and Brainard, though it was not noticeable, laughed the hardest because if you can laugh at something bad, it helps to get over it.

"He said . . . he said . . ." Schneider could hardly get the words out for laughing.

"I know what he said. He was saying it to *me*." Linn hooted. "He said, 'I shall reduce you to private.' He said, 'I'll have you court-martialed on our return, if you don't come around.'"

"The damned thing was," Connell said, "when he read your reduction order out at dinner that night and announced that I'd been raised to sergeant . . . me!" He jabbed a dirty finger at his chest. "Oh, God! I wish me old mum in County Kerry could've heard that!" This had everyone howling, Connell wiping his eyes. "I think old Dolph felt sorry for me," the Irishman managed to bark out, "because my frozen toe had sent me back to the fort. He told me then I was an excellent sledgeman. He said I was 'one of our best men.'"

"Well, bad things came of it," Rice said, and Rice never said much, so when he did he was listened to. The bad things were that no enlisted man could pass more than five hundred yards beyond the station without asking Lieutenant Greely's permission. He had given no explanation, and Brainard knew that was what annoyed them the most. True, that polar bear was hanging around and it was dark and cold. If there was a safety issue, there was also a health consideration. The men valued their walks to Dutch Island. While the C.O. had not cut these off, asking for permission for something they had never needed to ask permission for before was demeaning. He was treating them like schoolboys and life at Conger had come to feel even more like a prison camp.

The notice on the bulletin board on January 27, three months after the initial incident, Brainard thought absurd. Extending their walks to three-quarters of a mile did nothing. Dutch Island was outside that radius. They were still confined to the same unvarying round, a square footage of ice and snow that was numbingly familiar. That was the trouble with the army. One must adhere to commands, whether the reason is stated or not, sanctioning a means of disciplining men that shut down the pathways to loyalty, a willingness to perform one's duty, even camaraderie. Why couldn't Greely see that by this meaningless extension of their walks, he only rubbed in the salt? Worse, he let the disciplining of one man—a man with a spotless record—serve to punish all of them.

✷

On February 1, the mean temperature registered negative 44 degrees. Discovery Harbor was seen as sufficiently frozen for a small team to measure the depth of the ice. They returned to report a thickness of fifty-two and a half inches. It was a day of light, too. A day of such clarity and brightness that when Sergeant Brainard walked out with Lieutenant Lockwood before lunch, only two stars of the first magnitude, Capella and Vega, and the planet Jupiter were visible. There was no sign of light on the horizon, but the extreme darkness was beginning to recede, prompting Lieutenant Lockwood to confide in his friend Brainard how much he was looking forward to going northward again in April and how he hoped Brainard would accompany him, along with Eskimo Fred, same as last year. "I expect to achieve great things," he said.

But if the darkness had appeared to weaken, the cold had strengthened, with daytime readings reaching the fifty below mark. Those Indian fighters knew what fifty below in a stiff breeze felt like. They knew how hard it was to keep toes, fingers, and faces from frostbite. But *this* fifty below felt intent on killing you. It was the darkness; Brainard was convinced of that. This deep cold that came at you out of this bottomless dark felt endless. Every time he woke up and the fort's windows only reflected back his own thin face, it hit him once again that it might be day, but it wasn't going to get light. He should be used to it. They had been living in it long enough. His thoughts took him back to his bedroom on the farm, shared with two of his brothers. In the dead of winter it was dark when their mother woke them, but he knew it would be light by the time they finished the milking and came in for breakfast.

✷

They were, as usual, sitting on the benches around the common room tables. Dinner was over, dishes washed up and stacked away. This evening at Fort Conger was a repeat of the evening before and of the ones to come. The aroma of the men's tobacco—cigarettes and pipes—hung in the air. "Our inglorious second winter," as Lieutenant Lockwood called it, had not seen a change in Dr. Pavy, who continued to provoke Lieutenant Greely. The doctor's preferred venue for these baiting conversations was the common room, where everyone could listen in.

"Doctor Pavy," Greely said, "you are behindhand with your monthly medical report." He was sitting at his usual spot at the head of the table.

"I don't believe so." The doctor, who had just walked in, feigned a look of surprise, eyebrows raised as high up as they could go.

"Yes, Doctor, it was due yesterday." Greely's fingers drummed on the table.

"Oh? Yesterday? Tomorrow? Time means so little here." The doctor spread his hands to indicate how meaningless was the passage of time.

"I spoke to you about this last month, Doctor," Greely said, his fingers finding his black beard.

"What difference? The men are healthy. Anyone with half an eyeball can see." Dr. Pavy began to move toward Kislingbury, sitting on their bench.

"Doctor, we are a military command here. I think you forget this." He stood up.

"Ah!" The doctor gave an exaggerated sigh. "I wish I could forget."

Brainard, sitting with Rice, both of them occupied with the lists of rations, watched his commander's hand move up to his chin, massaging his black beard where the musket ball had cut a swath through his jaw. The men at the tables exchanged glances, most barely able to contain their laughter, as the C.O. headed into the officer's quarters.

"You men want to hear the story of Sir John Franklin?" Private Henry said.

"Sir John Franklin," said Gardiner. He had just walked in from taking the evening temperatures. "Wasn't he the man who ate his boots?"

"The very one," Charlie said. "On his first expedition. His book's in our library. Some of you fellows might like it. They just missed starving to death. That's why Sir John ate his boots. But I'm going to tell you about his second expedition. He was still hell-bent to discover the Northwest Passage and get himself a statue in Trafalgar Square."

"You already told us what happened to him," Whisler cut in.

"Yeah, Charlie," Connell prompted. "Tell us some good cannibal stories."

"Well, Sir John was a portly man," Charlie said, his eyes flashing over his audience. "The fat ones get picked off first."

"Did they shoot him?" Schneider was leaning forward, elbows on knees.

"If they were starving, I bet he wasn't fat anymore," Bender said.

"Their ships had got frozen in, see. They couldn't move a goddamn inch. They couldn't get out of the Arctic and Sir John had 128 men to feed.

"Well, Lieutenant Greely has only us," Bender said. "Sir John shouldn't have taken so many men."

"They should have taken more food," Whisler pointed out.

Salor, who said very little, spoke up. "They should have blasted their way out of that ice."

Private Henry put up his hands. "Hold on, fellows, I'm telling this story."

"Tell us what happened then," Whisler urged.

"You know what happened, Whisler," Henry went on. "When those men tried to walk out—I'm talking about a couple of hundred miles hauling sledges across the Arctic wastes, half-starved—they dropped in their tracks. The Eskimos found their bones in the cook pots."

"Listen here," Bender squeaked. "Somebody'd better come up for us." He began to sniffle.

"Take it easy, Bender," Charlie said. He reached across the table and patted his friend's arm. "We're not going to starve. At least I'm not."

"Who wants to eat a crybaby," Connell sneered. "But, Charlie, you're a husky fellow. I might start with you!"

Brainard put down his pen. He didn't like where this conversation was going, and nodded to Rice.

"Now the C.O.," Charlie said, ignoring Connell, "he'd be one tough morsel."

"All gristle," Connell picked up. "I'd start with the young ones. Like Ned." Connell made a show of smacking his lips as Ned Israel walked in, his outer gear frosted from making celestial observations. Everyone stared at Ned.

"What's going on?" he asked with a smile. He had a pleasant voice. He was different from them, having studied astronomy at college, but he got on with everyone.

That defuses this conversation, Brainard thought.

"I'm telling them about the Franklin expedition," Charlie explained. Some of the men had gone back to writing their letters or in their diaries. Bender lit the cigarette Connell had given him. He began to cough. Connell rolled his own and used a strong mix.

"Was that the one where the man ate his boots?" Ned asked.

"That's the one," Charlie responded. He sent a lopsided grin in Connell's direction. But Connell just frowned and began playing with the candle wax that pooled on the table.

Brainard leaned toward Rice. "They're nervous the ship's not going to show up."

"They're right about Lieutenant Greely," Rice said. "He would yield a pretty unsatisfying first course." And the two men grinned at each other.

✻

Fort Conger

15 February 1883

My Dearest Henrietta,

You had written, when I was wooing you, "I would rather be your wife as you are, than your widow as the most revered man you could become. I am *not* a Lady Franklin. You will be terribly disappointed in me, dear, but remember that I do not even *suggest* that you stay. I feel we should never be so happy if you gave up the opportunity. You would always think of what you had missed. I love you too well to mar your life."

I keep your letters close to me, my dear wife.

Remember, I had assured you, should any such trial come to you as came into Lady Franklin's life, I would never leave. I still believe this, even though the promised relief has not come. The doctor has been telling the men he thinks the ship was never sent. This alarms them, but they know that I worked out a scheme for an independent retreat before I left Washington. On our voyage up, we deposited caches containing rations along the Ellesmere coast and on the Greenland side at Littleton Island. Littleton is 250 miles from Fort Conger, a taxing journey for the open whale boats and the launch named for you, my love. But I doubt we will have to travel so far. We are likely to encounter the ship as we come down the Ellesmere coast. If not, and we make it to Cape Sabine, we could stop there. I will find stores waiting for us, left by the relief, if the ship could not get through to Conger. Or, we will cross to Littleton, a straight thirty-mile shot across Smith Sound from Sabine. Eskimos winter there and the island is visited in summer by the whalers.

I will stop here, for now, and send my love,
Your Dolph

Private Henry's True & Accurate Account of the LFB Expedition

3 March 1883

Ha! Ha! The C.O. was in the observers' room making an entry when I stalked in. "You're noting the mock moon, sir? I saw it myself."

He stared at me. "It was an aurora," he pronounced.

His tone set me off. "It was a parhelion, Lieutenant. That's what the observers call a mock moon." I had overstepped myself. But I really didn't care.

"You contradict me? Go out and look again, Private."

I obliged him by going out. "It's a parhelion, sir," I said on return.

"Your sight is poor, Private," he barked. "I have studied astronomy. I know what I saw."

I stood there and watched as he completed the entry in ink in the observers' book.

The next day Ralston grabbed me. "I know what happened. I saw you in there with the C.O. He messed up our record book by recording something that never existed."

"Are you going to tell him that?" I asked.

"Not me." Ralston snickered. "I don't want him to break me as he broke Kislingbury."

Ha! Ha! This is rich! I will send this little tale to the Chicago paper!

✴

By the end of March, the observers could read the instruments in the meteorological shelter by natural light at midnight. The air had softened. The wind seemed, if not less, at least less punishing. The men were pulled out of the fort by the imperative of an Arctic spring. Everyone was excited because the C.O. had said there was time before the expected relief to go exploring again. Lockwood's energy returned. But Dr. Pavy, who had argued for a retreat since last October, stepped up his attack, insisting on laying more caches down the Ellesmere coast. "Your government will never send a ship for you," the doctor snapped. This brought Kislingbury into action, his King's English slicing the air of the common room. Greely must send a sledge party down to Littleton Island. He, Kislingbury, would command. He would wait for the relief and lead it back up to Fort Conger.

The doctor's polar dreams were dead, and his suggestion, Brainard was sure, was motivated by his jealousy of Lieutenant Lockwood. Kislingbury's proposal meant dividing the party, which the C.O. would never agree to, and stank of mutiny. Behind their plans was a desperate attempt to get out of the Arctic.

✴

Lieutenant Lockwood was in his element. The depressed man of winter had blossomed with the spring and on March 27, a day of clouds and warm temperatures, they departed Fort Conger. Their two Green-landers, Fred and Jens, drove the sledges, and Private Ellis was in charge of the small support party that included Sergeant Jewell and Shorty Frederick. Brainard was glad the C.O. had so favored Ellis. As their oldest man, past forty, he was left out of the general socializing among the privates, ten or fifteen years his junior. Lieutenant Greely accompanied them to Watercourse Bay, and with a ceremony of handshakes, they took off at a fast pace. They made Cape Beechey, their crossing point to Greenland, in record time, their outer garments covered with frost from their own sweat, which promptly froze.

They moved up the Greenland coast at the same punishing pace, and four days later, a clear morning with a temperature of -30 degrees, they spotted dark but strangely luminous clouds to the north and east. "Oh," Lockwood groaned. "I so hope those water clouds come from the tidal overflow of the ice foot." He and Brainard went to see what the Eskimos might have to say, where they were hitching the dogs. Fred and Jens looked grim, and with gestures and broken English conveyed that from the condition of the ice the whole polar pack must have been in motion all winter. When they reached camp, Brainard climbed the headland, reaching the cliff top that dropped 1,300 feet into the sea. As he stood on the brink and looked out on the polar pack, he saw lanes of open water extending along the coast northward until they were lost in the haze. If the pack was broken up, they could not travel on the ice foot, and without boats they could not get around the cliffs.

He returned to camp expecting to find a discouraged Lockwood. Not at all! "I want you to have all in readiness for tomorrow. My plan is to bypass the cliff. We'll proceed up the glacier and move inland. We'll carry our load, piece by piece." Brainard said nothing; his eyes were fixed on the broken river of ice where the glacier ran into the ocean. Lockwood slowly pulled from his pocket his instructions. "I want you to read this and give me your opinion." Brainard silently read Lieutenant Greely's orders that instructed Lockwood to "turn back immediately if any disintegration of the polar pack was detected." He handed the paper back to Lockwood.

"My friend," Brainard said. "I want to reach the 84th parallel, too. It's the goal of this journey. But think of your men. Think of the dangers."

Lockwood sighed. He crumpled the instructions he held in his un-gloved hand. "You are right, David. I cannot expose my men." They stood facing each other. Brainard saw that Lieutenant Lockwood's jaw was set, his eyes clear and calm. What a noble look, Brainard thought. But it's costing him. He really doesn't want to give up his goal. The wind hissed, and snow swirled around their feet. Shorty Frederick was thawing their dinner while the others set up the tents.

Brainard's gaze went to the glacier's snout, a jumble of ice blocks churned at the pace of centuries by the sea. He could hear the grinding, and he shivered at the rawness of it. *I and the others here are farther north than anyone on earth.* The thought overwhelmed him. All his experience with the great open spaces of the Plains had not prepared him for this. The vastness, the untamed wildness was beyond his comprehension. The sea was never still, the ice in plates, all upheaved and toppling from the constant pressuring motion gave no sense of calm. Nowhere were there open grassy meadows. Nowhere a glade of sheltering trees. Nowhere comfort in human terms. Here the wind rarely calmed to just a breeze. Rather a powerful wind waged war with the pack. The wind was in league with the currents to keep the sea in eternal conflict with the ice. Here was danger. Here each puny human triumph was wrung out at the fearful cost of exertion and hardship. Yet there was beauty, and David Brainard promised himself never to lose sight of this fragile wild beauty. *Had I known how hard it would be would I have come?* The answer, still, was yes.

Lockwood had broken away and asked Sergeant Jewell to make the tidal observations. The temperature stood at -31. Jewell, down near the shoreline, suddenly swung his arm into the air, an action that had them looking up. A snowy owl was flying up the coast from the south. The great bird rounded their cape and disappeared from sight. This was the first bird sighting of the spring. "That snowy owl," Lockwood said, turning to his friend Davy Brainard, "is heading north but we will not."

The next day the small party was on the track, back toward Conger. When they stopped to camp at the end of the march, Lockwood took Brainard aside. "Listen," he said. His face was radiant. "I have another plan I will take up with our commander when we return. I want you, Brainard, to accompany me."

"You always have my willing support." Brainard smiled. Lockwood's enthusiasm was hard to resist.

"We will take the two sledges, ten dogs, both Eskimos to drive, and food for fifty days. We can sacrifice one of the dog teams to feed the other team at our northern high point, the 84th parallel. I am determined!" He smacked his right gloved fist into his left. It made a satisfying smack. "A do-or-die attempt, my friend." He drew off his glove and raked his fingers through his mustache, grown out and filled with frost. "I must persuade the C.O."

Brainard had his doubts, but he was quite sure a voicing of them would not discourage Lockwood. He had stumbled across a book in their library titled *Journey to the Ends of the Earth* by a compatriot of Dr. Pavy's. Lockwood would have managed beautifully on such a venture; why, Lieutenant Lockwood should be put in charge of a journey to the moon!

They were back in Conger on April 12, having not been away two weeks. Greely was surprised, unpleasantly so, and their welcome was not warm. "He treats me as if I had *failed*," Lockwood said to Brainard. "Well, I *did*, and I can tell you it leaves a bitter taste."

Nonetheless Lockwood persuaded the C.O. to let him expand the knowledge of interior Grinnell Land. They might reach the Western Ocean. This would be the last exploring trip of the season.

They returned to the fort on May 26. The skuas were back and the saxifrage had purple blossoms. Brainard, unpacking from their trip, sorting out and repairing the dogs' harnesses, was aware of a contentment he had not known since arriving, nearly two years ago. He understood the origins: Lieutenant Lockwood's success. Lockwood had redeemed himself not just in Lieutenant Greely's eyes but in his own. They did not reach the Western Ocean, but they had set a Farthest West record in the process of charting large areas of Grinnell Land. They named a fjord after Lieutenant Greely, and two headlands they named Cape Lockwood and Cape Brainard. An immense ice cap they named for Agassiz, the much-admired Swiss American naturalist. Most astonishing, they had traveled by sledge one-eighth of the distance around the world above the 80th parallel. On the way back, encountering deep snow, they nearly ran out of food. They were hungry, and the dogs howled from hunger. When their best dog, Disko King, weakened, Lockwood made the agonizing decision to shoot one dog to feed the others. He shot it himself, as he said to Brainard, "I cannot turn over this responsibility. I must take it on myself." This mission of exploration had made an impressive show for the whole expedition, throwing great credit on Lockwood. Brainard hoped it would sustain him in their uncertain future.

The melting snow trickled down the hillsides. The mild air drew the men outside. But despite these hopeful signs, Fort Conger was not a happy place. The men were sick of living in a landscape that never changed. Sick of the black rocks, sick of the round-the-clock daylight, sick of the unending bleakness, sick of the loneliness, sick of each other, sick of themselves. Sergeant Brainard noted in his journal on July 4: *Independence Day once more! We no longer have the imagination necessary to provide entertainment for these holiday occasions. Our lone ceremony was the unfurling of the flag.*

The men could not keep themselves from looking twenty times a day toward the channel, but the ice held as firm as prison gates. The C.O. had them pack up the scientific records, the stuffed birds, the animal skins, the pressed flowers, all in readiness for when the ship arrived. If the ship failed them, the records, the fruit of their two years of hard labor, would go with them in the open boats. Sergeant Brainard recorded on July 20: *The pack is too solid even now for a relief boat to push through.*

Also on this date, Dr. Pavy's contract expired. He informed the men at breakfast, making it known that because he was such a good fellow he would continue to act as their physician whether the ship arrived or not.

"But Doctor," the C.O. said from his position at the head of the table, "if you are to perform your duties, you must renew your contract."

"I can administer without a contract."

"If you have no formal agreement, how can I be sure of you?"

"You cannot." The doctor displayed his teeth.

"Doctor." Lieutenant Greely's fingers flew to his jaw. "If you refuse to sign a contract, you have, in effect, resigned. In that case, you must release the expedition's medical stores *and your diary* to Lieutenant Lockwood, as my second in command."

"*Not* my diary!" Dr. Pavy stood up, his black eyes sharp in his ferret's face.

"Dr. Pavy." Lieutenant Greely forced himself to detach his fingers. He tucked them into his armpits. "You were aware of the army's request. All diaries will be turned in at the end of the expedition. I repeat myself: If you refuse to sign a contract for another year, you have resigned and must turn in your diary."

"I will not!"

"I am disappointed in you, Doctor." Lieutenant Greely shoved back his bench and stood. He leaned with his palms on the table and stared down at Pavy at the other end. "I charge you with disobeying orders."

The doctor's eyebrows shot up. He made a huffing sound through his nose that showed his contempt.

Everyone had stopped eating. Brainard looked around at the men sitting on the benches at the tables. Some could hardly keep down their mirth, while others were plainly horrified. Private Bender had his hands over his ears. He was sitting next to Private Henry, who reached up and pulled at Bender's hands. There was a small struggle, which Bender lost. The private resumed his customary slump, his hands between his knees. "Men." Lieutenant Greely's voice rocketed around the room. "You have finished your breakfast. You will get about the duties of the day."

✗

Private Henry's True & Accurate Account of the LFB Expedition

20 July 1883

Ha! Ha! What a joke! I will capture the scene for the *Chicago Times*.

The C.O. had our very own bunkmate, hospital steward Biederbick, deliver the formal message and who else but our worthy Sergeant Brainard make the arrest.

How did Pavy take it? Connell and I asked Biederbick when he returned.

"You know the doctor," said Biederbick, and he shrugged, all elbows and shoulders, in an imitation of Dr. Pavy. "Oh. I want to zay zat physeecally I may accept arrest, yeess, but morally, I do not accept."

Ha! Ha! Ha! Ha! Connell's beefy hand, landing on his thigh, sounded like rifle fire.

"I weell, of course," Biederbick went on, "obey all rules and regulations, but eef some accident happens I weell not be responsible for eet."

"So if we get sick it's not his fault if we die?" Connell bellowed. "My mum in County Kerry won't like that."

"Nothing to worry about," I chimed in. "He's just playing with old Dolph, who's *the son of a shoemaker.*"

"Lieutenant Kislingbury said," Biederbick continued, "he was sure Dolph would see Pavy faces court-martial when we get back."

✳

Brainard picked up the men's concerns whenever he walked through the common room.

"I've never been in a small boat in my life," Bender said. "I'm an *army* man."

"Can you swim, Bender?" Private Charlie Henry asked.

Bender answered this by staring at the floor.

"No better than you can read, I see. How about you, Schneider?" Charlie probed. "Can you dog paddle?" Schneider shook his head.

"Well, I can't either," Charlie confessed. "And I'll be damned if I'll embark on an open boat voyage with old Dolph."

"George Rice," Connell offered. "He's a sailor. He must be. He's from Cape Breton."

"But even Rice doesn't know how to manage an overloaded boat through pack ice," Charlie said.

"But where are we going?" Schneider asked. "The C.O. hasn't told us."

"He's got no bloody idea, I bet," Charlie insisted. "He doesn't know what the hell he's doing."

"I'd have never volunteered for this stinking expedition if I'd known we'd end up in this mess," Bender moaned.

"If the ship shows up tomorrow, that will change everything," said Shorty Frederick.

"You can find something good to say about the worst situations, Shorty," Connell said.

"But no ship's going to show," Charlie growled. "The doctor keeps telling us."

✶

The C.O. had assigned Sergeant Cross, as engineer, and Sergeant Linn — to make sure Cross didn't get drunk on the fuel — to sleep on the *Lady Greely*, now ready for departure, to protect her from the heavy ice. All their records of the last two years were up to date and packed for the arriving vessel, or the boat trip. The men ran up Cairn Hill several times a day to scout the horizon. The days crawled by and no one knew what the C.O. had in mind. Brainard found this very hard to take. Not knowing Lieutenant Greely's plans weakened the men's confidence in their leader.

On August 4, Lieutenant Kislingbury shot a small seal that Eskimo Jens secured with his kayak, giving the men the first fresh meat in some time. On the fifth, Lieutenant Greely, returning from Cairn Hill, reported the Kennedy Channel choked with ice, no open water in sight. "The ice," he explained in a heavy voice, "is evidently moving north with the tide."

"Well, goddamn," sputtered Private Henry. "We're icebound." By now it had crashed down on everyone that the summer of 1881, when the *Proteus* had so easily steamed up the Kennedy Channel, had been exceptional. The channel's normal aspect was to be choked with ice.

On August 9, an hour after breakfast, the men found a notice tacked on the bulletin board. Sergeant Brainard was standing by to answer questions.

"Read it to me, Charlie," Bender said.

"I thought Dolph had taught you to read."

Bender stared at his feet. "Don't be hard on me," he mumbled.

"Okay, listen up." Charlie whacked him on the back. "'In case of the non-arrival of a vessel by August ninth,' that's today, Bender, 'this station will be abandoned and a retreat southwest by boats to Littleton Island will be attempted. Sixteen pounds of personal baggage will be allowed each officer and eight pounds to each man.' You got that, Bender? I'll read it again, if you didn't. The C.O. has beautiful penmanship, don't you agree?"

"We're leaving today? For Littleton?" Bender's voice shook. "He's not giving us much time to pack and finish closing down the fort, is he, Charlie?" Poor Bender gazed up into his friend's face. "I'm scared."

"I'll help you pack, Bender," Charlie offered. "Won't take but a minute to stow eight pounds."

"Bring your duffle out here," Sergeant Brainard said. "You can sort it on the tables. I can help out, if you want."

"I'll see what Biederbick and Whisler are up to, Sergeant," Private Henry said. "Looks like the C.O.'s in a tearing hurry to take us on a boat excursion down Smith Sound." He gave Sergeant Brainard a toothy grin. Brainard felt this comment did not need a reply. He held his post as Private Henry escorted Bender into their bunkroom and he heard the private say, "I'm helping Bender pack. What are you fellows taking?"

"I'm wearing most of it," Biederbick said. "I've got on three flannel shirts, my leather vest with my blanket vest over it, and two pairs of trousers."

"And your long johns," Whisler added. I have on two pair. Gardiner's taking his Bible. It must weigh three pounds."

"Sergeant Gardiner's a very religious man. He's an observer and can take the officers' weight," Charlie pointed out. "You two look as puffed as pigeons baked in a pie. Did you catch all that, Bender? Here." He threw his friend a pair of long johns he picked up off the floor. "Start with this."

"I don't have a blanket vest," Bender said.

"Take this one."

Brainard heard shoving and pushing, a fair amount of cursing, thumping and snickers, too, as all three privates worked on outfitting Bender. "This vest is too small," Bender squeaked.

"Here, pull the sides together, Biederbick," Private Henry directed, "as I attack the buttons. Hold still, Bender. Stop squirming."

"I can't hardly breathe," Bender wheezed.

"There!" Whisler said. "You look grand!"

"You're the fattest pigeon," Charlie hooted. "Now let's get out of here."

"But I want to straighten my bunk," Bender insisted. "We're leaving this place in a god-awful mess."

"No time, no time," Charlie ordered. "Say good-bye to your happy home." He pushed Bender across the threshold. The private tripped. Sergeant Brainard caught his arm to steady him, and watched the quartet troop past the tables. Dirty dishes from their breakfast lay in disorder with the silverware, amid open tins of coffee, tea, sugar, strawberry jam, and a scattering of crumbs. "My Captain Price," Charlie said to Bender, "would have us leave this place looking spotless." They turned into the kitchen, where Private Long stood at the stove, spooning stew into a kettle to carry down to the boats.

"We might be coming back if the ice closes in," Long said to the privates. "I'm not taking all of this." He set the huge black pot back on the stove and methodically shut down the dampers.

"Say good-bye to our kitchen," Charlie said to Bender, and Brainard watched Private Henry—one hand on Bender's arm—guide his friend through a chaos of boxes, half-empty or half-packed, depending on point of view. As Charlie slid Bender around a wooden box of scientific instruments, Brainard detected a silvery flash as the private's palm closed around a small object. Private Brainard was about to pounce when Ned Israel, working on the final astronomical observations, as fresh-faced as the day they had arrived, caught Brainard's eye and shouted, "We landed here on August 9, 1881, *two years ago to this very day!*" The privates were out the door; he would have Private Henry turn out his pockets later. Right now he must attempt to make order out of these boxes. He looked around to see if Lieutenant Greely had heard what Ned had said. The lieutenant was standing just outside the open door, his tall, stiff figure set against the background of Conger's rocks and rubble.

"On the double, you privates," Lieutenant Greely bellowed as Private Henry, still grasping Bender's arm, slunk by, carrying their eight pounds. "Lieutenant Lockwood will tell you which boat you're in when you get to the harbor." Lieutenant Greely was in full-dress uniform, down to the shoulder knots and helmet cord, his saber strapped on and revolver at his hip. My heavens, Private Brainard said to himself, I guess we're in a state of crisis. It was well known that in times of crisis, officers, in compliance with war department regulations, were required to appear in full-dress uniform.

The C.O. had appointed him the last man out, with the responsibility of nailing shut the door. He gave himself a few minutes to take in this final scene. There was Schneider, surrounded by leaping and barking dogs. "They know something's afoot," Schneider shouted to the sergeant. "I've tried to explain . . ." He broke off and went down on one knee, burying his hand in the ruff of the nearest. "You can't come on the boats. Go back home now. You'll find food. See?" He pointed to where Long had overturned the barrels. "Seal blubber and pork and hard bread. You love that. My best advice is, after you've run through it, follow your own wild natures and catch your own dinners." Schneider rested his head on the head of one of the dogs. He stood up then, and Brainard watched him stride off, passing Charlie and Bender, careful not to look back.

Interlude

The Misfortune of Lieutenant Garlington
Cape Sabine

Summer 1883

The history of navigation in those waters is little more than a chapter of accidents.

Commander W. S. Schley, *The Rescue of Greely* (1885)

General Hazen was satisfied with the choice of Lieutenant Garlington. He had shown a rare ability for command in one just turned thirty. As an army officer, of course, he had never been to sea, nor had he set foot in the Arctic, but General Hazen did not hold this a drawback. Success depended on ability to command. The setting was unimportant. It mattered little that only four expeditions, counting Greely's, had passed through the Kane Sea and crossed the 80th parallel into the Kennedy Channel and on up to the Hall Basin.

General Hazen failed to quash the stories that went around after Private Beebe's return that he, Hazen, had appointed a man known to be a "habitual drunkard." In his opinion, William Beebe was no more a drunkard than he himself was a coward. He had considered giving Beebe a role to play on this second attempt to reach Lieutenant Greely, but decided against it. Then, on August 6—Garlington was by this time five weeks at sea—Beebe was found dead in his home. He had killed himself with laudanum. General Hazen was aware Beebe had been brought down by his inability to reach the men at Lady Franklin Bay; he was taken aback by Beebe's sordid end, but what could he have done to prevent it? He was not pleased with how the relief turned out. There was no reason why the *Neptune* should have run into difficulties. Beebe was just not that competent.

The general had written Henrietta Greely in San Diego, assuring her Lieutenant Greely was in no danger. Henrietta had taken the news like a sensible woman. Greely had done well for himself. Mrs. Lockwood, however, was inconsolable upon learning that her son James would not be coming back on the *Neptune*. James Lockwood was thought very capable, and Hazen was aware that Mrs. Greely, together with General and Mrs. Lockwood, had lobbied hard for a more carefully planned relief in '83.

General Hazen had found just the man! When Lieutenant Ernest L. Garlington strode into his office on G Street at the end of January, Hazen's spirits lifted. He noted the correct military bearing—that polish of the West Point trained—and was assured that unlike the unfortunate Beebe, command came as naturally as breathing to this handsome young officer. Command, Hazen reminded himself, could not be taught. The techniques certainly, one could memorize a set of rules, but one either had the innate ability or one did not. Hazen was casting his bets that Lieutenant Garlington did. The general took in that this young lieutenant's blond hair was trimmed with a precision that reflected his overall orderly appearance. He was pleased to see how Garlington looked him in the eye with a steady blue-eyed gaze.

The general had heard the story of Garlington's luck. How when he was taking his graduation furlough at his parent's home in Georgia, and the news of Custer's defeat had broken across the nation, he cut short his furlough to join his regiment, the Seventh Cavalry, Custer's cavalry, and was quickly promoted to first lieutenant since so many officers had died at Little Big Horn. There was irony in the young man's rise, but this had not prevented General Hazen from writing Mrs. Greely that he had found the "man above all others in the army I would submit myself to command the relief in 1883. Sober, persistent, and able."

In the privacy of his office, Hazen let Garlington know that speed was of the essence. "Absolutely, sir. Lieutenant Greely instructed that the relief reach him as quickly as possible." He sat with his hands spread upon his knees, his spine curved out from the chair, a racehorse at the starting gate. The contrast to poor Beebe made Hazen smile. This was the young man's chance to advance himself. He admired this eagerness for new assignments in the young and ambitious.

"If you are stopped by pack ice," said the general, "go ashore at Littleton Island. Establish a depot there. Build shelters and await my friend Greely's arrival."

"If I cannot reach him with the ship," said Garlington, leaning forward, "I will take the sledges and the dogs up to meet him."

Hazen's smile broadened as he handed Garlington his orders. Orders drawn up by Lieutenant Greely before his departure in 1881. He took the packet to his desk and read he was to make straight for Lady Franklin Bay with adequate provisions for forty persons for fifteen months, meaning he had provisions for Greely's men, as well as rations adequate for his own crew to overwinter if they were frozen in. If they were blocked by ice, he was to leave caches along the Ellesmere coast to aid Greely in his retreat. More than that, if he could not reach Lady Franklin Bay, he was to set up a winter station at Littleton Island with telescopes focused across Smith Sound on Cape Sabine, and after the sound froze over, sledge to the cape, where Greely and his men would be expecting them.

As Garlington returned his instructions to the packet, a small piece of paper floated to the floor. He leaned down and picked it up. It was unsigned but requested that he stop at Littleton Island and leave stores. Stop at Littleton Island? *He had been expressly ordered not to stop.* Garlington sprang up and strode into General Hazen's office.

"What is this?" the general asked, taking the paper. "I have not seen this memorandum. Perhaps it is not a bad idea to stop at Littleton," the general went on, his gaze focused on a pigeon squatting on the window ledge outside the building.

"I understood, sir," the young lieutenant said, "that Lieutenant Greely's instructions demanded inflexible compliance."

"I want you," Hazen went on, "to be governed by your own judgment."

"Do I understand you want me to exercise my own discretion?"

"Yes, while at the same time carrying out Lieutenant Greely's demands."

"I can imagine situations in which those might become incompatible, sir, with what *I* might choose to do," Garlington said.

"I will add nothing more," said the general.

"I will succeed, General, you may be sure of that," he said, and wheeled out of Hazen's office. He was to take charge as he saw fit! Garlington ran his fingers through his blond hair, then smoothed it down with his palm. If General Hazen had not seen the unsigned memorandum, how had it found its way into his instructions? It contradicted Greely's orders that the relief proceed with haste. No matter. He had Hazen's trust. He had always known what to do when he was on the ground. Garlington slapped his right fist into his left hand. His spirits were high. He was looking forward to his first Arctic adventure. He was just born lucky.

✳

In St. John's, Lieutenant Garlington acquired a companion, a Newfoundland dog. He named the great beast Rover, and the dog attached himself to his new master as a barnacle to the bottom of a ship. The two made an eye-catching pair as they paced the streets of the port town on the business of preparing the *Proteus* for departure, the very ship captained by the very man who had taken Greely up in 1881. It was evident the conflicting memorandum had faded from Garlington's mind when he told his new friend, John Colwell, the navy lieutenant aboard, to lend his naval expertise. "My duty is to push as fast as I can to Lady Franklin Bay."

"Will you keep close to the *Yantic*?" Colwell asked.

"Not at all. I've discussed this with Commander Wildes. The *Yantic* isn't part of our expedition. I expect General Hazen was compelled to take her to make this voyage appear safer to the general public. After Private Beebe's disaster, you know." He shrugged. "The *Yantic* might be our tender, but she is not to interfere with my progress north."

"I would think we'd want the *Yantic* nearby in case we run into trouble," Colwell said.

"We won't run into trouble. But *should* the *Proteus* be lost I will push a boat and party south to the *Yantic*. Commander Wildes and I agreed on that."

"But Wildes has his orders not to remain longer than August tweny-fifth."

Garlington glared at this new friend. "I cannot compromise my movements. But, I'll tell you this." Garlington leaned forward, his blond hair gleaming in the sun. "This isn't a relief expedition. I've been entrusted with bringing Lieutenant Greely home."

"What do you mean?"

"General Hazen gave me a letter for Greely stating the government is discontinuing the work at Lady Franklin Bay."

"I bet it's because of what happened to De Long," Colwell said. By now the news of the commodore's death had been confirmed, the expedition deemed a failure and worse: a fiasco for the navy.

"That's what I think, too," said Garlington. "Wouldn't do to have the *army* lose men in the Arctic, would it?" He sent a sidelong glance to his navy friend. "Besides, General Hazen told me that Lieutenant Greely's stores would take him only to this August. So, I'm not stopping at Littleton."

"I understood they had provisions for three years," Colwell said.

"I had thought so myself," Garlington agreed.

Before he left St. John's, Garlington wrote General Hazen, "I will not allow myself to be retarded on my way north. All that can be done will be done to get the ship to Fort Conger." He wrote Mrs. Greely, "I will make every effort within my power to bring your husband out this season. If the *Proteus* cannot get through to Lady Franklin Bay, I most assuredly will by means of sledges. I am quite sanguine of success."

✶

The *Proteus*, trailed by her tender, the *Yantic*, departed St. John's on June 29. The weather was perfect with an offshore breeze and blue skies overhead. At seven thirty in the evening, Lieutenant Colwell came up on deck. He scanned the horizon; already their small escort was nowhere in sight.

As Colwell stood under the lifeboats mounted on their frames—the ones they would be forced into if the *Proteus* ran into trouble—he could see daylight through the seams of two of them. The ship's rigging was old, as were her compasses. The first mate, Captain Pike's son, was only twenty-one and this was his first voyage into Arctic waters. Colwell was concerned about the *Yantic*. Their tender could not keep up, nor was she constructed to enter pack ice, and her men, fresh from the Caribbean, weren't equipped for frigid weather.

On July 22, the *Proteus* passed Littleton Island. Garlington did not stop. Greely wasn't there. The coal pile Beebe had left was undisturbed. Two hours later the ship came dead up against a barrier of ice Captain Pike said was too massive to smash apart. In response, Garlington ordered a course west across Smith Sound, toward Cape Sabine, less than thirty miles distant.

As Pike dropped anchor, Garlington sprang ashore to examine the cache Beebe had left there, and supervised packing one for Greely with five hundred rations: hard bread, bacon, tea, various canned goods, tobacco, lemons to fight scurvy wrapped in newspaper, and a couple of sleeping bags. As James Norman tossed a tent fly over it, the ice pilot scoffed, "That will only last those twenty-five men for twenty days."

"It was a waste of my time to construct it in the first place," Garlington snapped. "I will reach them before Lieutenant Greely even thinks of heading south. Hand me that spyglass, would you? Just as I thought." He slapped the glass across his left palm. "The leads north look favorable."

Back on the *Proteus*, he dashed to Pike's cabin. The captain was asleep. "The lanes are open to the north, Captain. Roust yourself and get the ship underway."

Pike's feet thumped to the floor. "I am not ready to leave, Lieutenant. I need fresh water. I need to fill my coal bunkers from the ship's extra coal cargo." He rubbed his eyes, staring at this young army lieutenant who had broken his rest. "I will remain here until the ice has passed out of Smith Sound. That open water you saw is caused by the tide shifting the floating ice. It will not last." He lay back on his bunk, hands clasped behind his head. "A week's delay, Lieutenant, will not upset your relief expedition," he said to the ceiling. "There is too much ice and it is too early." His feet hit the floor again. He was too exasperated to sleep. He stood, about to push past Garlington, when two of the lieutenant's men came in to report that the sound appeared completely blocked.

"I cannot believe it," Garlington snapped. "Captain, my men will assist in filling your coal bunkers and your water casks. I order you to get this ship underway immediately."

Captain Pike was stymied. He was forced to follow this brash West Pointer's orders unless he, a master mariner licensed by the Newfoundland Board of Trade, wished to be accused of mutiny. Pike eyed his opponent. "You cause me to go against my better judgment. Yet"—he shrugged—"as I do not want to be blamed for lingering here if your expedition fails, I submit."

The *Proteus* tore northward to find herself caught in the frothing churning pack. Garlington sent Colwell up to the crow's nest to oversee the first mate, Pike's neophyte son. At midnight, with the sun on the horizon, Colwell could see how right Captain Pike was. "Lieutenant Garlington," he said to the captain's son, "would have been well advised to wait a week at Cape Sabine."

The two aloft watched as the frigid night air hardened the loose pack, and when the captain toed his iron-sheathed bow against a crack and revved his engines to ramming speed, a tremor shook the ship. Water rushed in as the crack split apart. Looking north, Colwell saw only ice, floes as tall as barns racing down Smith Sound on the shifting tide headed for collision with the rigid shelf of shore ice. They were trapped, the ship set to become jammed. Solid cakes of blue ice ten feet thick tumbled and thumped about the hull, squeezing the ship in a nutcracker vice. The nip, as sailors called it. Odysseus, caught between the closing jaws of Scylla and Charybdis, could not have felt more desperate.

The ship was splitting apart, Colwell realized, with no more effort than he would give to splitting kindling for his mother and the morning fire at home. The *Proteus*, built in Scotland in 1874, with a life expectancy in the sealing trade of fifty years, Garlington had just commuted to a death sentence at one-fifth her lifetime. The young navy lieutenant dreaded to think what might be his army friend's fate when he—*if* he—made his sorry way back to Washington.

A movement made him look down. "Father will not let the ship sink," Pike's son said. His face looked so fresh in the early light, much younger than his twenty-one years. Another bone-shattering crack and Colwell saw panic streak the young man's eyes. The dogs, all twenty-two, let loose a yelping cry driven by pure fright.

"Follow me," Colwell shouted and slid down to the deck, a turmoil of heaved-up planks, splintered seams, stumbling men, voices shrill with the edge of panic.

"Lieutenant Colwell, get the boats clear," Garlington ordered as he emerged from the hatchway, his handsome features streaked with coal dust and sweat. "Ice has crashed through into the starboard coal bunker." He waved a directing hand toward Pike's seamen. "You men throw everything overboard." Garlington could shout himself purple for all they cared. A shipwreck discharges all hands. Already their pay had ceased.

"Drop that, James Norman," Garlington intervened as the ice pilot grabbed a buffalo coat from the stores piled for Greely on the deck.

Norman went right on stuffing the coat into his duffle. "It will go to the bottom if I don't take it," he scoffed. "The ship's doomed." Garlington looked around. These Newfoundland sailors had armed themselves. He counted five shotguns and six rifles. Pike had no authority over his men now.

But Garlington had control over his and had them throwing overboard blankets, clothing, the tinned food. Even the dogs, who scrambled onto the flatter floes. Rover kept close to Garlington's heels. He put a hand on his dog's broad head in an attempt to drive Pike's men out of his mind and ordered two of his own men down on the ice to organize supplies on a firm floe. A good third of what had been flung over the side had already sunk to the bottom.

Colwell had the boats down from the davits and in the water. Captain Pike gave the order to abandon ship; his men took one side, while Garlington's took the other. Like the *Proteus*, her men had splintered in two. The boats moved out, both sides working to put distance between themselves and the suction of the sinking ship. The water bobbed with clothing, crates, and dogs, soon pushed under by the debris from the dismembered ship. Colwell, hunched over his oars, watched the ship grow lower in the water in response to the turning tide loosening the pressure of the ice. Already most of the supplies meant for Greely had sunk to the bottom—canned goods, clothing, and those precious letters from home. The men in his boat had gone quiet. They stared transfixed as the *Proteus*, maintaining her upright stance, her yards like outstretched wings supporting her on the ice floes, splintered and the great ship vanished in a final hissing cloud of steam. Colwell checked his pocket watch. The entire process, from when the pressure was first brought to bear, had taken just five hours.

✸

"Captain Pike," Garlington was forced to yell, "can you shift us a few of your oarsmen?" The lieutenant's boats were close to swamping as his men jostled each other with the heavy oars, their hands going numb in the freezing spray.

"Landlubbers. Stinking *army*," Pike's men shouted, though a few submitted to the request, and before long all thirty-seven castaways had reached the rocks of Cape Sabine, not far from the cache Garlington had erected thirty hours before. They spent the night in a stiffened state, chilled further by a cold rain. The men watched as the floe where they had left the last loads broke up, and the crates—much of it food—joined their ship at the bottom of Smith Sound.

Garlington settled himself among the rocks with his back against Rover. His dog had taken up more than his share of room in the boat, but now, on shore, was generous about imparting his warmth to anyone— army or seaman—who crawled up against his shaggy damp coat. "I suppose you've been asking yourself," Colwell said to his friend, "why you willingly exchanged your comfortable cavalry posting for this sea duty?"

"Hell, no fun fighting Indians with Custer out of the game. I don't know. Thought I'd freshen up my life with an Arctic adventure."

Colwell chuckled. "Think you'll wait here for Lieutenant Greely?"

Garlington shook his head.

"Think you'll wait on the Greenland side?" Colwell probed.

"I can't wait at all. We haven't the stores for it. Wouldn't do to eat up everything we've left for Lieutenant Greely. The men are already grumbling about how much Rover eats." He sat up straighter. "This dog smells like wet dog." He ran his hand along his Newfoundland's sodden flank. "Lieutenant Greely's orders were to leave Lady Franklin Bay no later than September first," Garlington went on. "He might have left earlier. He might not have left at all. Lieutenant Greely's an army man. He might conclude not to risk his men's lives with a boat trip."

"He'd go against orders in that case," Colwell pointed out.

"It would be worse to winter somewhere on the Ellesmere coast," Garlington countered. "He might decide to wait for spring. That's what I'd do. But it makes no difference to me what *he* plans. I plan to sledge up to him. I promised Mrs. Greely that."

Colwell gave him an appraising look. Despite Garlington's salt-stained and soggy appearance, the lieutenant continued to hold himself erect and aloof: a man capable of the kind of brash boldness it would take to sledge up to Greely. Yet the sledges had sunk and the dogs had scattered or gone to the bottom. All but Rover. The two men sat in silence while Colwell pondered whether the Arctic's lessons had penetrated Garlington's consciousness, or whether he still saw himself immune by right of his West Point education and his superior will.

Norman strolled over and crouched down beside Rover's colossal foreleg. Garlington remained silent, staring out toward the floes that continued to smash against each other, pulverizing themselves. "I'm guessing you've got forty days' worth of grub," Norman said, "and you'll need every bit of it. If you'll take my advice you'll get your men over to the other side. Be ready to greet the *Yantic*." The ice pilot waved a calloused hand toward Greenland.

"And you?" Garlington asked. "You have more men than I to feed."

"And we're not sharing any of it," Norman assured this army lieutenant. "Pike can't make us. That's why I'm telling you to stow your forty rations and run for it. Better to be safe than hungry in the Arctic. Any cabin boy can tell you that."

"My orders are to reach Lieutenant Greely," Garlington pronounced.

"All bets go by the boards when your ship goes down, West Pointer," Norman sneered.

"The lieutenant's orders," Colwell cut in, "are to winter on the Greenland coast, with the Eskimos there, if he can't get up to Lady Franklin Bay." This man Norman annoyed him. "Then no matter which side of Smith Sound Lieutenant Greely comes down, we'll be able to help him."

"You'll get nowhere ordering us!" Norman's great voice boomed into the void, "Why, you might as well tell us to stay sober on shore leave." The ice pilot laughed at his own joke, pushed up, and stalked off.

Colwell expected Garlington to cross back and wait. The *Yantic* could take back Pike's men and some of Garlington's. The rest would settle on Littleton Island or at the Eskimo village on the mainland. That would be an adventure. Colwell felt his spirits lift with the thought of it. They couldn't reach Greely now, despite Garlington's bravado.

✳

They crossed back to the Greenland side against a sleety rain that pitted their faces. Once again the two men had their backs against Garlington's great dog. Now it was a matter of waiting for the *Yantic*. But Garlington wasn't about to wait. "Wildes won't bring the *Yantic* this far north," he said to Colwell.

"What do you mean, he won't?" Colwell asked.

"I must go to him," Garlington went on. "I cannot sit here at Littleton. The season will close and Wildes's men are in cotton shirts and trousers."

"But Wildes has time to make it here. His orders are not to stay later than August twenty-fifth. That's a month from today," Colwell pointed out.

"All the more reason to reach him," Garlington illogically insisted.

"But you and the captain agreed . . ."

"No, no! Those men are in tropic-weight clothing. I must go to them," Garlington interrupted.

"You won't be here if Lieutenant Greely shows up!"

Garlington made a futile attempt to untangle his hair stuck together with salt spray. "We see this situation differently. But I am right." He got to his feet and marched off.

But his dog remained. The Newfoundland's great breaths came steady and calm as Colwell leaned against the dog's broad flank. If he were in charge, he would remain at Littleton, ready to do what he could for Greely. Relieving Lieutenant Greely, for Garlington, had sunk to second place, upended by his drive to regain St. John's. It was strange what could happen to a man when the adventure demanded more from him than he anticipated. But it was General Hazen and the others in Washington who had appointed an army man when an experienced naval officer was needed. And Colwell knew that Ernest Garlington had volunteered for this mission.

✶

Garlington persuaded Pike to give him two men, one for each of his boats, to help with the rowing. They inched their way down the Greenland coast, Garlington stopping at every headland to build a cairn and leave a message for the *Yantic*, and for Greely, a tattered effort to patch up his miscarried relief.

By mid-August, new ice was forming every night, and there was no sign of the *Yantic*.

"She's left for St. John's," Norman grumbled.

Garlington silently feared as much. His men were exhausted, their hands bloodied and blistered from urging heavy oars through choppy ice-filled waters, their backs sore, clothing soaked, sleep-deprived, and seasick. They ate half-cooked rations, then heaved it up in the nauseating swells.

"Let me make a sprint for Upernavik," Colwell offered. "We might just catch the *Yantic* there."

"Take Norman," Garlington said. "Pick your crew from Pike's men."

"We'll move fast." Colwell clapped his friend on the shoulder. "We can eat and sleep and row like hell in turns."

They covered the 500 miles down the Greenland coast to Upernavik in seven days to discover the *Yantic* had come and gone. Colwell had the men back in the boat and rowing like the damned for Godhavn, another 275 miles farther south. There, having navigated the iciest, foggiest, least-known seas in open boats, they caught up with Wildes. The captain took them on board and steamed back to Upernavik in a day and a half. Garlington was there, along with Pike and the *Proteus* sailors.

No one could have known that Lieutenant Greely was only 100 miles north, floundering in the Upper Kane Basin. But Garlington had to know what was in store for him when he reached St. John's. First: send a telegram to the war department in Washington owning he had sunk the *Proteus*. Second, let Mrs. Greely know he had failed to save her husband.

5

"Our Scenic Boat Trip into Smith Sound"

Between Discovery Harbor and Cape Sabine

9 August 1883–15 October 1883

Sergeant Brainard, entrusted with nailing shut the door to Fort Conger, was the last to leave. As he ran toward the shore, he felt an object hitting his thigh. Inserting his hand in his pocket, his fingers closed around *Two Years before the Mast*. "Ah! Dana! I'm so glad you're with me," he said aloud.

When he reached the shoreline, he found Lieutenant Greely bellowing orders, the men stumbling over each other in their hurried effort to load the four separate boats. A biting wind had lashed up a squally snowstorm, and as the last man boarded they careened into Discovery Harbor.

Out in the open water, Connell shouted, "Look!" pointing back toward the shore. The dogs sat lined up across the rise in front of the fort, watching in silence as the men in the boats grew smaller. Suddenly one broke away, skittered across the ice, leapt into the water, and started swimming toward them. "It's Flipper," Schneider said. He had raised Flipper, born last season, and trained him to haul the sledge. The C.O. didn't notice Flipper. He was in the bow with Sergeant Cross at the helm, struggling to navigate the launch through the chunky ice. The C.O.'s gold braid flashed and his saber banged against the side of the boat. The others couldn't take their eyes off Flipper. Schneider sat statue-still watching the dog struggle to keep his head above the chop. The gulf widened between dog and boat. The wind, driving ice chunks in a blistering froth, made it impossible to see when the small head vanished. "He's gone," Whisler breathed. No one could look at Schneider, who remained at rigid attention, as if for taps. And the cold and blinding darkness shifted across the face of the deep.

The snow blotted out the shoreline. Masses of ice beat against the boats, threatened to crush them. The men, seizing the oars, shoved at the treacherous blocks borne down on the tide as they emerged from Lady Franklin Bay and into the Hall Basin. They were crowded, cramped for leg room, any movement risked swamping. Soaked from the spray, jackets and trousers gone rigid as armor, they rowed with wet gloves and freezing fingers. Nothing they experienced in their army postings on the Plains prepared them for this sea voyage.

Lieutenant Greely commanded the *Lady Greely* and had with him Lieutenant Lockwood, Kislingbury, and Dr. Pavy. Sergeant Brainard was in command of the large English jolly boat *Valorous*, and Rice was in charge of the whaleboat *Narwhal*. The small Whitehall boat, crammed with supplies, brought up the rear, all towed in a string by the steam launch. The officers were armed. Lockwood carried his large army revolver, Greely had his saber, as well as his revolver on his belt. Kislingbury's Remington was never far from his hand. The steam launch had a deck with stowage space below. Already the freshwater in their keg had frozen, a mere three feet from the *Lady Greely*'s boiler. They carried rations for forty days with the plan to pick up caches down the coast, some left by the Nares Expedition in 1875, and some they had placed on the voyage up.

Already the C.O. had removed Cross and placed Rice at the tiller. While Rice showed a talent for spying out the leads, he was not an ice pilot. The men watched as their commander strained forward in the bow, trying to see through spectacles that kept icing up. He scrubbed the lenses with his damp handkerchief and fit the wire rims back around his ears. He kept repeating this action.

At Cape Baird, to the southeast of Lady Franklin Bay, they picked up the English ice boat *Beaumont* that Greely had cached there weeks ago. He put Connell in command of this sixteen-footer with runners to drag it over the sea ice.

That first night they slept in damp bags on a stony beach. They had brought no tents. In the morning Brainard was struggling with his men to launch the *Valorous*, aware of Lieutenant Greely's haste to leave, when, "Damn you, Sergeant Brainard, get your goddamn men moving," came at him like a rifle shot. Every man within hearing distance stared at their commander. Sergeant Brainard shook his head as if to clear it. In their two years at Conger, Lieutenant Greely had never lost his temper. Their C.O. abhorred profanity. Sergeant Brainard knew his conduct did not deserve this reprimand. He did not expect Lieutenant Greely to apologize. It was up to him to get on with the job and forget about this injustice. All of them were sore and stiff from a bad night. They had not had their breakfast. They were as snappish as underfed huskies. Well, Brainard thought, he has on his mind his decision to take to the boats.

Lieutenant Lockwood, who had thrown off hardship on the Farthest trips, could not stop saying how "very disagreeable" their life had turned. Brainard doubted the men would have boarded the boats if they had known they would be so cold and wet, so beset by danger. If he had apprehended this back at Conger, he might have spoken to Lieutenant Greely about spending the winter there. The doctor was right; they had the food for it. Dogs, too, to make a sledge journey down the coast in the spring. The sergeant wrenched his mind away from this unprofitable line of thought. Later that day, Lieutenant Kislingbury killed a young seal, and with full stomachs their mood improved. "I can't recall eating a more delicious dinner," Brainard said, and Kislingbury looked pleased. After all, during the last two years the poor man had had little opportunity to contribute.

From Cape Cracroft, three days after leaving Lady Franklin Bay, they took the corned beef from the cache there and continued toward Carl Ritter Bay, passing many icebergs, their upper surfaces acres in extent. "I think this is something unusual for the Kennedy Channel," Brainard said to Rice. "Bergs this big aren't generally found north of Cape Lawrence."

"The ice is packed so closely, and with the tide shoving it back and forth," said Rice, "I fear for us." Brainard gave the photographer a startled look. Rice was more inclined to laugh off the dangers.

Despite fog, flying snow, and a fierce wind that had them chilled to the bone, they had worked their way south of the 81st parallel. Here they were stopped, the pack too thick to fight and spent the night under the overhanging edges of rocks, wet and miserable. The next day the cakes of ice that had piled along the beach held them fast. Brainard spoke to Lieutenant Greely. "Let me walk down the coast. I might spot a vessel coming up to us." He knew their chances of spotting anything in this foul weather were negligible, but he needed to get off by himself. Dana had the crow's nest; Brainard had no space for solitude. "I do not consider it advisable to separate the party," Lieutenant Greely answered, shutting down his sergeant's request.

When Whisler informed everyone that Cross was drunk again on the fuel alcohol in the *Lady Greely*, Brainard pulled the engineer out of the launch and marched him to the C.O., who informed Cross he was relieved from his duties and put Shorty Frederick in charge, not to anyone's advantage since Cross was the only man there who understood engines.

The next morning as the men bolted down their oatmeal before it froze to the sides of their tins, Lieutenant Greely asked for silence, not that anyone was talking. They were gathered around a small fire made from breaking up the Whitehall boat, too full of leaks to be seaworthy. They had been out a week, their beards had grown out, their faces lined and hardened. They stood huddled, shoulders and elbows touching, in an unconscious effort to keep their body heat. Good God, Brainard thought, we look like a herd of musk oxen. This struck him as funny—those beasts were so large and hairy—and he was about to share this joke with the men when Lieutenant Greely announced, "I mean to abandon the launch. We will transfer the smaller boats and our supplies to the drifting ice and float southward." He stopped abruptly and glared at the men as if defying them to oppose him. *This is folly*, went through Brainard's mind. "We would be south of Cape Lawrence if I had done this when we were first frozen in." Everyone stared at their C.O. with slack jaws.

Bender's squeaky voice sounded from deep in the pack of bodies. "He'll hate to abandon the *Lady Greely*. Wouldn't he hate to abandon the *Lady Greely*, Charlie? He named it for his wife." Private Charlie Henry emitted a growl.

The doctor laughed in an unpleasant sneering way and the circle broke up. Dr. Pavy seized Kislingbury by the elbow and the two walked off. The men had broken up into little groups, keeping their voices down, casting glances in the C.O.'s direction. Greely himself seemed oblivious to how his directive had been received.

"It's suicide," Private Henry said to Bender, as if to address his friend's question.

"He's a lunatic," Elison said to Schneider. "Getting us into one scrape after another."

"He's a miserable fool," Schneider barked.

Connell joined their discussion. "He's jesting, right?"

"Are you kidding?" Elison said. "Have you ever heard Dolph jest?"

Brainard looked around for Rice but didn't see him. Lockwood was helping Private Long pack away the cooking gear. How we chafe under his leadership, Brainard thought. He must be aware of this. He issued no orders, thank God for that. We must forestall this crazy plan. It's still possible to turn back. He's working from his original orders he laid down himself in Washington. *Damn! I'm making excuses for Lieutenant Greely.* But if Colonel Doane had been in charge, Brainard knew they would be at Conger, stocking up on musk oxen.

Doane had been asked but he turned down the opportunity to lead the expedition. Brainard knew, if he had been in Doane's position, he would have done the same. Colonel Doane had divorced his first wife, Amelia, or she had divorced him. He was young when they married, and when the Indian Wars demanded so much of him he had no time for married life. Married officers during the Indian Wars were lucky if they saw their wives a week during the entire year. Who could blame the wives for leaving husbands who let their careers dominate their lives? Custer's debacle at Little Big Horn had provoked a change. The older officers had seen enough bloodshed, and most of the Indians had been pushed onto the reservations anyway. Doane, who had been on the front for twenty years, met, or met again, Mary Lee Hunter. She was the daughter of the physician at Fort Ellis; he had known her as a child. Now she was nineteen and Colonel Doane fell in love. He had before him the prospect of a settled life.

When Brainard had seen the new Mrs. Doane, he could see why. Mary Lee Hunter made the perfect pairing for her husband; it mattered not that she was half his age. She understood the military life; she carried herself like a general. She was tall and strong in a womanly way, shoulders broad enough to bear a load, a fine head with a heap of auburn hair, eyes as piercing as her husband's. The way she had placed her hand lightly on his shoulder, standing on the porch at Fort Ellis when Colonel Doane introduced her to his officers and men, in her touch it was clear to Brainard that she loved him. He felt he would be damned lucky to find a wife like Mrs. Doane. There was Lena he was writing to, back home. He would wait and see. He didn't want to marry the wrong woman.

Lieutenant Greely was shouting orders that broke Brainard away from his thoughts. Greely was their leader, and Brainard knew that it was his responsibility to support the expedition's leader; on the other hand, he would do whatever it took to see them through. Taking to the floes, where they would have even less control of their fate then in the boats, was an ill-advised plan, driven by Lieutenant Greely's own desperation. *If I am asked, I will tell him what I think. I know he has respect for me.* But why, he asked himself, will the United States government persist in sending fools in command of an Arctic expedition?

No more was said about making camp on ice floes. The ice had opened up again, and the C.O. had them back in the boats. Brainard was right behind the *Lady Greely* in their small procession, giving him a good view of their commander, at his station in the bow. As he watched, their leader leaned so far forward in an effort to peer out the leads, he feared the C.O. would topple overboard. Private Bender's squeak reached him on the wind: "Look at him. You need sharp eyes for this work."

"Follow the open water close to shore, Sergeant Rice," Greely ordered.

"Commander, there's open water farther out," Sergeant Ellis shouted. "We're headed for it. Don't you see it?" Ellis is a competent man, Brainard thought. He would not have spoken up if he were uncertain. Rice looked first at Ellis, then to Greely.

"Follow the lead close to the shore, Sergeant Rice," Greely bellowed.

Rice turned the launch and the ice roared as the current brought the floes crashing together in a soaking spray, snapping at their oars, at risk of swamping, and Brainard caught Private Henry's deep base rising in panic. "Christ! He bloody can't see." Rice was washed overboard. Hands grabbed to haul him out, helped him undress, and draped his wet clothing over the boiler.

"Take my extra long johns, George," Kislingbury offered. "You're the most indispensable man we have."

"He's our waterfowl," Shorty Frederick crowed. But Brainard was concerned that while Rice might be their bravest and their pluckiest, he also took the most chances.

✳

Mid-August. Some days they could barely move for the squalls, each man hunkered down in his own private misery. The spray kept them damp, condemned to dry out their clothing with their own body heat. The ice rushed by at a breakneck pace, kicking up a swirl of ice cakes that collided at every tide change. The boom and crash never ceased. Their hands were never dry. At least their commander made sure the rum got portioned out once a day. Mostly they slept on the stony beach, a chance to stretch their legs, and better than the boats, with their bottoms ridged and sloped. The relief ship should show up. It had to be on its way south by September 15 to avoid entrapment in the ice. But how could it find them in the immensity of the swells?

The sky was the same dull gray as the sea.

They had come through the Kennedy Channel, escaping a buffeting directionless wind, to emerge into a wide sea, the Kane Basin, a violent froth of crosscurrents heaving their tiny boats. They lost sight of land. They had no idea where they were. Lieutenant Greely seemed uncertain, unsure. He could not stop wiping his spectacles.

At Cape Collinson, in the rain, Sergeant Brainard took a crew to examine the English cache. Polar bears had pulled apart the stones, punctured the cans. They grabbed what they could of the bread, green with mold. Rice climbed a headland: ice closely packed, he reported, no open water in sight. All night the sleety mix fell, and Brainard, unable to sleep in his saturated buffalo-hide bag, let his mind drift.

He was with Shorty. They had become separated from their scouting party, with a full-blown blizzard sprung loose, the cold so numbing it stopped his breath. His horse shied; he was nearly pitched headforemost into a rock outcrop. Shorty, reining hard, signaled to dismount, screaming above the wind, there was no point killing themselves. They crawled to the lee side, wedged behind boulders, persuaded the horses to lie in front: windbreak and heat source. Shorty dug into his saddlebag and passed out the beef jerky. They chewed on that. No water. No choice but to put up with the salt. Eating snow would freeze their guts. The snow drove down, like sitting under a waterfall, piling up on the horses and on them. They kept pushing it off or they would be buried alive. During that long night—if they dozed off they would never wake up in this world—they told stories, shouting in the other's ear to be heard. The one that Brainard remembered was Shorty's tale of a man caught out, just like this. "He was on the point of freezing to death," Shorty related. "He hated to do it but he killed his horse, skinned it, and bedded down in the carcass, wrapped up in the hide."

Remembering this night that Shorty and he had taken in stride, a part of Plains life during the Indian Wars, just a matter of doing the right things to get through, gave him hope. Long was on that scouting party, too. None of them had made it back to Fort Ellis that night. He thanked his stars to have Long and Shorty along with him now. With men like that, Greely's party had a chance against this stacked deck.

By morning the storm had moved out, and as the clouds thinned the constant light continued to brighten until the sun was fully out. This sunlight bounced off the water, filling the surface with a glassy brilliance. It glanced off the rocks and caught every drop of moisture in the air. This strong sunlight translated the bergs into crystal palaces. A light breeze kept the cloud shadows dancing. This brightness was nearly unbearable, but the sun imparted warmth, and these storm-tossed men stripped to their long johns and spread out their wet clothes and sleeping bags in homage to this sun that would soak up the moisture. When the cooks called breakfast, they grabbed their tins, received their portion, and sat on the rocks, stretching out their legs, squinting in the bright light, chattering among themselves like so many happy sparrows after a wild night.

Brainard had not seen spirits this high in weeks. He was enjoying this scene, putting off rounding up his crew and readying for departure, when Doctor Pavy walked up and took him by the arm. He desired a private conversation, he said, and led Brainard off behind a boulder where Lieutenant Kislingbury and George Rice were waiting.

"Sergeant," the doctor started off, "I get to point." He paused, spread open his fingers, displaying his palms, an indication of his agitation, as was his disjointed English. "Us three"—he pointed to Kislingbury, Rice, and himself—"we say Lieutenant Greely is unfit for command. Crazy idea to drift. He will kill us. As medical officer I say: Lieutenant Kislingbury will take over leadership." The doctor pointed at Kislingbury, who straightened himself in an attempt to look the part. "We want your support, Sergeant," Pavy said. "You talk to men."

Sergeant Brainard's mind was made up before his support was asked. Kislingbury had no legal right to the leadership. He had no moral right, either. If Lieutenant Greely were to cede command, that role would fall to Lieutenant Lockwood.

Sergeant Brainard leaned his back against the rock. As top sergeant, these schemers needed him if they were to gain ascendency over the enlisted men. He remained silent, arms folded across his chest.

Doctor Pavy was forced to go on, his fingers flexing wildly. "I will tell Greely I must examine him. I tell him: place boats and men on floe and ride with current is irrational. *Irrational I tell you!*" The doctor's voice rose to a shriek.

"Quiet, man!" Kislingbury bit out.

Rice backed away. Brainard thought he might keep going. But Rice stopped.

Dr. Pavy, suddenly aware of his fingers opening and closing, balled his hands into fists. In a low hiss, he said, "I am the doctor telling you: Lieutenant Greely is insane."

Sergeant Brainard did not change his position. Pavy smiled a false smile. "I see you thinking over whether to join. Easy decision. With Greely out of way, we"—he pointed again to Kislingbury and Rice— "lead party back to Fort Conger."

"Lieutenant Lockwood?" asked Brainard. "What is your plan for him?"

"Arrest the damn fool," Kislingbury snapped.

Rice said nothing. He was focused on the far horizon where the pack ice was indistinguishable from the colorless sky. Sergeant Brainard wondered how committed he was to this mutiny. For mutiny it was. He, David Brainard, was not going to buy into it. If he felt it had a chance of working, *if* there was a good chance of getting the men safely back to Conger . . . but no. The time for a safe retreat had passed. The worst thing for these men would be to end up under Dr. Pavy, who cared little if they lived or died. Lieutenant Greely could hold them together. He had made some poor decisions, but he understood command. His mind flashed back to his trip to the top of Cairn Hill, when he had left Private Shorty Frederick in charge of the privates pounding nails into the siding of their fort. In the short time he had on that summit, he attempted to place himself in the context of this expedition. He felt keenly his responsibility as top sergeant to these men, and as keenly, he was aware that Lieutenant Greely, as their leader, deserved his loyalty. Loyalty was what he could offer to Greely now.

George Rice pulled his gaze away from the horizon and began to talk. "Doctor Pavy's idea is to walk along the ice foot, David. That was how we traveled when we made the trip north in the summer of '82. It was dangerous. You could find yourself adrift on ice not connected to the shore. That happened to me. It was a close shave." He threw back his head, his eyes glittering, and Brainard saw that a part of George Rice relished close shaves. "But we were a small troop," he went on, "carrying light loads." The doctor turned his cold-eyed glare on Rice.

"And now, George," Brainard picked up, "we're a large troop with heavy loads."

Rice shrugged. "Doctor Pavy didn't think we should have left Conger in the first place."

"George," Brainard went on, "Lieutenant Greely has his orders and we're best off with him. The men like you, but you are not a leader of army men." He turned to include the other two. "Your plan will not work, gentlemen. The men will not submit to your command. You cannot hold them. They will splinter into diverse groups. We'd end up killing each other." He slashed his arm through the air and wheeled out of their circle. He stumbled back toward their camp. Now he was late getting the boats launched, and if the C.O. swore at him, the reprimand would be deserved. But good god! Mutineers could be shot. Executions, at this point, could have them all shedding each other's blood. Greely must not know about this. But he felt the burden of keeping silent, a double burden, since he maintained silence about Private Henry's sneak-thief murderous past.

✼

By the fourth week of August, they were halfway down the Kane Basin, off Cape Hawks. Here they dismantled a stone cache left by the English, and filled their boats with dried potatoes, more rum, and one keg of pickled onions. But when they pried open the bread casks, they were knocked back by the hideous smell coming from a mass of green slime. They knew when they opened casks contained in cairns for several years they could not be confident that the food was edible. Lieutenant Greely, in an attempt to raise spirits, assured them they would land in two days. Cape Sabine was only fifty miles to the south.

Five hours out from Cape Hawks, they were stopped by the pack, and by morning what they feared for so long had happened. Pack ice completely enclosed the boats. Boats and men had become mere stationary specks in a frozen seascape. This pack was in constant motion, driven by winds, currents, tides, and temperatures. Brainard could feel the water moving underneath them. He searched the faces of the men. How conscious were they of the danger they were in? Pack ice was completely unpredictable. It could give a mighty heave and toss the entire party into the sea. It might break into small cakes, sending them off in different directions. Temperatures were in the teens. Twenty inches of snow covered their floe. They were cold and wet and miserable. The time dragged.

They were trapped on this floe, as far as Brainard could see, until it chose to break up. Lieutenant Greely had them chop the smaller boats free and drag them up on the floe. They couldn't budge the *Lady Greely*, so had secured her to a section of the ice that appeared stable. They could abandon the launch and try to reach water. But that meant dragging the sledges loaded with the smaller boats. Brainard didn't think Lieutenant Greely was ready to take that step. These men could be pushed and had been pushed, but it was a good leader who could judge just how much to push his men. Sergeant Brainard, because he was driven to take some useful action, collected a detail to rig a tripod. Together they raised a flag in the forlorn hope of hailing the relief. No vessel could have spotted them otherwise on the flat surface of the floe.

Rice and the Eskimos put the men to work building a house out of snow blocks. They found they were the warmest and driest. The men sleeping in the boats might have a wooden floor, but it was ridged, and the tarpaulin covering made it stuffy and cramped. The men who had made a tent out of sails and moved in with the cookstove put up with an icy floor that melted from the heat and kept their bags thoroughly soaked.

They had located a small pool of freshwater on an old floe—the meteorologists called it a paleocrystic floe—good fortune that saved them fuel. Jens and Eskimo Fred killed a seal and urged the men to drink the warm blood. Ned Israel's calculations revealed they were drifting northward with the pack and the men's talk turned nervous.

They were leaning against the barrels and crates set up to provide a windbreak, listening to Private Charlie Henry. "Goddamnit, if we're swept back up into the Kane Basin, so much for our scenic boat trip into Smith Sound. Is he going to make us wait it out on this stinking floe until the ice breaks up? Or is he going to condemn us to man-hauling the smaller boats until we reach open water?"

"If he puts us to hauling, he'll have to abandon the launch," Connell pointed out.

"He'll hate to be parted from the *Lady Greely*," Bender said.

"Well, we can't haul her, dammit," Connell growled.

"Then he'll have us sit it out," Charlie said.

Sergeant Brainard was sitting nearby, sewing a patch on his heavy wool pants. He was wearing the pants, but as it was his knee, he could keep his pants on. Rice had kindly supplied him with patching material. They were beset eighty miles from Littleton Island on the Greenland side. Lieutenant Greely's original intent was to gain Littleton. The relief could be there. They were also within striking distance of Cape Sabine, where supplies could have been left as well. Now the swirl of unpredictable currents had their floe heading north, just when their goal seemed within their reach.

The talk moved to rations.

"Eskimo Jens keeps us pretty well supplied with seals," Bender offered.

"Except for every two he shoots one sinks before he can haul it out," Charlie complained.

"That seal's blood tasted like warm egg whites," Bender said. "Didn't you think the seal's blood tasted like warm egg whites, Charlie?"

"We've got over a thousand pounds of bread, we might as well sit here and eat it down," Whisler stated, passing over Bender's remark, already thoroughly talked over.

"If you relish moldy bread," Connell said.

They fell silent, and Brainard wondered if they were thinking back to that morning at breakfast when Lieutenant Lockwood said, "I wonder what they are doing at home?" His family seemed to be more on his mind than ever. Then he blurted out, "This life is worse than anything. The daily inaction is more trying to me than any amount of risks. Look at this bread." He displayed his ration in his palm for everyone to see. "It's turned to powder." The lieutenant closed his fingers around the bread. He continued, as if talking to himself. "My hands are so extremely sensitive. This feels like crushing a handful of tacks." He poured the crumbs into his mouth. Brainard had to look away. As second-in-command, Lockwood should have better control of himself in front of the men.

"Lieutenant Kislingbury and the doctor want to move," Charlie said. "We have twelve hundred pounds of meat, but most of it's pemmican and all of it's old. I heard Sergeant Brainard tell the C.O. that."

"Sergeant Rice wants to wait until the ice opens." Bender attempted to draw this conversation to some sort of hopeful conclusion. "Then we'll set off in the launch."

"I don't argue with George Rice," Charlie assured Bender. "The bloody hauling takes energy. I hate hauling. I have nightmares about dragging that dead weight. When I wake up and find I'm reclining on a pile of rocks in a soggy bag, I'm glad. At least I'm not attached to that goddamned sledge."

"You're so big, Charlie," Schneider piped up. "You should pull as well as my dogs."

"Connell was our best sledge man, weren't you, Connell?" Bender said, slapping the Irishman on the knee.

"That's what the C.O. called me." He gave them his most self-satisfied smirk.

"I hated it," Charlie said again.

"Shorty, he's one of our best haulers, too," Whisler added. "I think sledging has more to do with wanting to, than anything else."

"Why did you want to lug that goddamn sledge, Connell?" Charlie asked him.

"I don't know. It made me feel good."

"You're a crazy Irishman." Charlie's voice turned serious. "When Sir John Franklin's men were reduced to man-hauling, it was nothing but a miserable walk toward their graves."

"Sergeant Davy," Bender shouted to Sergeant Brainard, "why did Lieutenant Greely take us off coffee?"

"You heard why, Private Bender. We're running out of coffee."

"But the green tea is bitter and the sugar is nearly gone." Bender's voice ended in a pitiful wail. They all stared at him as tears slid down his face.

At that moment, Lieutenant Lockwood strode into the scene. He went down on one knee next to Sergeant Brainard. Not attempting to keep his voice down, he said, "I see nothing but starvation and death ahead."

"Yet," Brainard replied, looking toward the little group of privates, "the men's spirits are good." Shorty Frederick, walking up to catch the last of this conversation, said, "Keeping up spirits will get us through. Lieutenant Greely sent me to tell you he's ready to serve out our daily rum ration."

Charlie Henry shouted, "More spirituous liquors! That's what we need to carry us out of this frigid hellhole."

✷

The earth turned on its axis. In the sky the light grew faint at midnight. A few bright stars appeared for the first time since spring as the globe tilted away from the sun. The temperature fell to zero, causing the ice to freeze solid on open pools of water. This sudden freezing ignited a roar in the midst of the constantly moving pack, a grinding and grating mixing with reports like rifle fire. Even the bravest could not tamp down his fear. The tide-driven floes pushed up flat cakes, one upon the other, great heaping towers—fifty tons of ice—until with a startling ear-splitting crash the towers toppled, and the men hung on as their floe rocked and the seawater rushed over them.

＊

Our 12th day adrift in the Kane Basin

7 September 1883

My Dearest Wife,

It has been impossible to write, as it is so very difficult to keep my ink thawed. It is not only the ink but the pages I write on. If the surface of the paper is below freezing, the ink congeals. I don't know how Lieutenant Lockwood does it, but I hear him scribbling into his journal by the light of one candle in the cramped conditions of the *Lady Greely* nearly every night. I've spoken to him about not wasting the candle on journal writing, but he continues nonetheless. I suppose it gives him comfort. He writes in shorthand and is rather vain of this accomplishment.

The men are well, generally speaking. We've had a bout of diarrhea. Our engineer, Cross, frostbit one foot, then frostbit his other, a negligence I cannot countenance. He has made himself useless for the work. Was this his intent?

Yesterday afternoon, while resting in our sleeping bags, I heard Lieutenant Kislingbury say to the doctor, "He doesn't know what he wants to do and he wouldn't tell us if he did." It was obvious he was speaking of me. We have been inactive of late, letting the drift take us, and inaction can cause grumbling and discontent. "If you criticize my actions to the men," I called out to the lieutenant, "your conduct is but one step from mutiny." Kislingbury immediately denied having said anything that could be so construed.

The incident caused me to think I might do well to break precedent and consult with my lieutenants, as well as with Sergeants Brainard and Rice. I could not very well leave out the doctor, but as he can be argumentative, I asked Lockwood to keep notes in shorthand. I invited them to withdraw with me into the *Lady Greely*. They know our situation is grave, I wanted each of them to state his opinion as to the best course of action, and I asked Lieutenant Kislingbury to begin. The Englishman recommended abandoning the heavy launch and making for the coast of Sabine with one or two boats. The doctor echoed this, except, he said, we should keep only one boat. Then Lieutenant Lockwood, our man of action—I watch him walk our floe until I fear he will split the ice with his pacing—recommended starting in a day or two. But Rice and Brainard spoke to leave matters as they are, drifting. This had been in my mind all along, and as we were divided evenly, I could cast the deciding vote. "For the present," I told them, "we cannot do better than to remain status quo." As we broke up, Sergeant Brainard, in particular, expressed his hopes for a continuation of such discussions. I suppose there is no reason not to, if it eases their minds since, as Lieutenant Lockwood stressed, "dangers and uncertainties lie ahead."

If we are forced to land at Sabine, I will do all I can to get us back to the Greenland side as soon as the young ice forms and cements the floes together. My darling, I feel less alone, less burdened when penning my thoughts to you. For the half hour the pen was in my hand it was as if you were at my side and we were talking.

Your adoring husband,
Adolphus

✳

On September 10, thirty-one days after leaving Fort Conger, Lieutenant Greely gave the order to strip and abandon the *Lady Greely* and the *Valorous* and load the three sledges with the smaller boats, *Narwhal* and *Beaumont*. Officers and men bent their backs to the drag ropes in the effort to move some sixty-five hundred pounds over a semifrozen ocean of jammed ice chunks, separated by open water. Brainard and Rice went ahead to scout the route, followed by men with axes to clear a path through the rubble ice. For weak ice, the sledges were broken down, and they made many trips to transfer the loads to a stronger floe. When they encountered ice heaved and weirdly stacked by the pressure, the men pushed, pulled, and lifted each boat up the irregularly angled incline, controlling the steep descent with ropes. Dangerous work that could cost fingers and toes. They were reeling off fewer than three miles a day. When the weight of the *Narwhal* began cracking the sledge, Lieutenant Greely abandoned the whaleboat. They couldn't move without the sledges.

A day later, Lieutenant Greely gave the men the opportunity to ditch the one-hundred-pound pendulum. "We will put this to the vote, and if you *all* agree we will off-load the pendulum," he told them. "Though," he cautioned, "keep in mind that if you leave it the measurements of magnetism our observers took at Fort Conger will be useless since they depend on observations made at home *with the same instrument.*"

"If we die on the floes, men," Private Henry shouted, "all our records sink to the bottom, so what's the point of hauling the goddamn pendulum a yard further?"

Lieutenant Greely gathered himself up to reprimand this private for his blasphemy when Private Bender squeaked, his voice unnaturally high, "But, Charlie, we're not going to die, and how can you vote to waste all those records that our observers worked so hard for? It's only one hundred pounds. I vote for the pendulum." Bender wildly waved his arms in the air.

The others' arms shot up with shouts of "Keep the pendulum! Hooray for the observers!" And the vote was carried. It was not unanimous. Private Henry stood with his arms tightly folded against his barrel chest. But there was no need for unanimity. They would carry the pendulum, and Brainard caught the look of relief on his commander's face.

On the night of September 15, within striking distance of Cape Sabine, a vicious gale swept them northeastward, back up into the Kane Basin. The temperature sank to zero. Their floe began to break and shift. Water rushed beneath them as the pack roared and ground in the solid dark. No one could sleep and when dawn arrived Israel's observations with the sextant showed they had lost fifteen miles and the pack was too splintered for sledging.

They were closer to the Greenland side, and Lieutenant Greely called another council of his officers. Dr. Pavy argued for Cape Sabine. There would be caches there. Sergeant Brainard pointed out that until the strong tides abated, they had little choice but to drift. Lieutenant Kislingbury, who always took the doctor's side, this time backed Sergeant Brainard, and one glance at the rotating pack settled the question.

It was a relief to do nothing. Days spent in their dampened bags were better than the brutal hauling, though the C.O. cut their rations by a third. They were eating seal blubber mostly, assured by Jens and Eskimo Fred that seal blubber would keep them warm. But this diet had Dr. Pavy busy handing out medicine against the cramping pain of diarrhea.

Two days later, their floe spun around in the night and they awoke heading south. Toward Cape Sabine. Lieutenant Greely ordered the sledges loaded. They were hauling over the broken ice again, in danger of becoming separated in the grinding mass. But the worst that happened was Rice missed his footing and took a header into the sea. He popped up puffing and snorting. They hoisted him out, Rice sputtering, "Sorry to put you chaps to the inconvenience," and on they went. Lieutenant Greely assured them they would reach Sabine tomorrow.

At midnight the men awoke in the dark to feel their floe moving under them at great speed, and by morning the southwesterly gale had beaten them twenty miles back into the Kane Basin. Gloom descended and they consumed their meager half-cooked breakfast in silence. Despite the occasional seal, they were not getting enough to eat.

Again Lieutenant Greely called a council of his officers, Dr. Pavy, George Rice, and Sergeant Brainard. They were standing near the sledges. "I propose," he stated, "we strike out for Littleton Island. I have always preferred the Greenland side, and now it is within my reach. We'll take twenty days' rations, our records, one boat, and one sledge. Abandon everything else."

Dr. Pavy and Kislingbury exchanged a look. "Very well," said the doctor, "Lieutenant Kislingbury and I will take nine men and the other boat and make for the Sabine shore."

Sergeant Brainard caught his breath. Greely's plan cut a narrow margin for error. The doctor's plan was a ruse to strike out on his own.

"You stay here," the doctor went on, thrusting his gloved fingers at Greely. "We'll return for you."

"Your boat will be overloaded with nine men, Doctor. You will swamp."

"So will you," said Kislingbury. He was leaning with an elbow on the rail of a sledge.

He always makes rude remarks, Brainard thought. He looked at Rice, and Rice winked at him as Lieutenant Greely said, "I won't stand for splitting the party, Doctor. I veto your plan."

The doctor was a victim of his own desires. He had wanted to reach the North Pole. He had failed, and now he wanted like hell to get out of the Arctic. If he and Lieutenant Kislingbury made it to Sabine, they would not return. Lieutenant Greely's plan was ill-conceived, but it was built on his desperation to save his whole party. It disturbed Brainard, the perverse pleasure these two took in antagonizing each other, and it was the men themselves who were the victims of this dogfight between the C.O. and Dr. Pavy.

But no one went anywhere. Another heavy snowfall condemned them to the floe and their sodden bags.

Private Henry's True & Accurate Account of the LFB Expedition

25 September 1883

O joy! I've found a way to supplement my diet. My opportunity comes when we're unloading and loading stores, a period of disorganization. Sergeant Davy is too preoccupied to notice my light-fingered raids on a fistful of raisins or a wedge of cheese. Ha! Ha! Ha!

✳

On the night of September 25, the wind veered around, setting up a churning in the cross currents of Smith Sound that propelled their floe west at a terrifying speed. The men, aroused out of sleep, stood huddled in the darkness, certain their floe would disintegrate at any moment. But it slowed, blocked by debris ice. Ned Israel estimated they were only six miles from the Ellesmere coast, again off Cape Sabine. But no way to get there. A loaded boat would be ground to splinters in the froth of seething ice. As the men stared into the darkness of Smith Sound, what felt like a stampede of bison rumbling across the Plains shook their floe. A crack like a lightning strike split their snowhouse down the middle. "Load the sledges," Lieutenant Greely boomed out. "Prepare the boats for emergency evacuation."

Sergeant Brainard prayed it wouldn't come to that, and no sooner had he thought it than a larger floe, careening down from the north, shoved theirs back together, and Lieutenant Greely shouted orders that had them as coordinated as his old post commander Colonel Miles on an Indian raid, moving boats, sledges, men, and supplies across the gap. The pressure held until everyone had splashed through the rotten ice, Lieutenant Greely the last to make the leap.

Brainard found himself standing next to George Rice, watching as the broken bits of what had been their home churned off into the blackness. "The doctor couldn't have managed that," Rice said, and the two men exchanged a look that spoke to their renewed confidence in Lieutenant Greely's leadership. Lieutenant Greely put the cooks to work setting up the stove, heating hot grog. As the day began to lighten, the men sat on the upturned sledges, cold hands wrapped around warm cups.

This respite was short-lived. On the 26th their floe began to come apart in a violent storm, and Brainard realized they were sweeping by Cape Sabine, about to be carried into Baffin Bay. That would be the end of them. They could not miss this last landing point.

The coast was not more than a few miles off, but the storm made it impossible to locate. By evening, when the gale eased, Brainard asked Eskimo Fred to accompany him. He was determined to find a way out of this imprisonment. He had a sense their floe had stopped, and he found it lodged against a grounded iceberg. "Very lucky for us," he said to Fred, whose sharp eyes spotted a lane of water about a half-mile wide stretching toward the coast. They reported this to Lieutenant Greely, who ordered the men to load the sledge and haul it to the lane, then directed Rice to launch the boat. They began to ferry loads to a floe about a mile broad, and spent what was left of the night at its edge.

Early on September 29, Greely asked Sergeant Brainard to scout out a route toward the land. They figured they were just north of Baird Inlet, with Cape Sabine thirty miles up the coast. Brainard spotted two lanes of water that allowed them to continue with the tiresome sledging and ferrying. Dangerous work since it meant separating the party during the transfer from floe to floe.

By six o'clock that evening the last load reached the coast and all twenty-five men, exhausted but safe, were on solid ground after fifty-one days at sea.

✳

Their food tins, the boats, the sledges, the buffalo-hide bags, and all their records in metal cases lay strewn among the barren, snow-covered rocks beneath a high, cone-shaped hill they had used as a landmark when they were in the Kane Basin. Lieutenant Greely named their landfall Eskimo Point, for the remains of three ancient Eskimo structures they found there. He located a sheltered spot, their building site, bounded by the conical hill on one side and glacier on the other two. The Eskimos, out hunting, found nothing. Winter coming on. Game gone south. This first day on land was spent in a light snowfall and a high wind that kept them uncomfortably chilled and raw-tempered.

The next day George Rice volunteered to travel the thirty miles up the coast to Sabine to find if there were caches there with food and messages. He left with Jens, a light sledge, a large one-man bag they could both squeeze into, and rations for four days.

"I hate to see them head off into the white void," Lieutenant Kislingbury said. It was snowing and Rice and Jens had quickly disappeared. "Rice is the toughest and best man I ever saw."

"Rice is brave," the C.O. said, "but to a fault. I fear for his bravery."

"I don't!" Kislingbury snapped, causing Brainard to look around. *The man can't forget he's a nonentity. That's the only way to explain his rudeness.*

Later, when the C.O. served out hot drinks, Lieutenant Lockwood remarked, "This tea tastes like rusty warm water. Today is my thirty-first birthday. I was hoping to be home to celebrate it." This remark caught their attention. Lieutenant Lockwood looked miserable. He had the beaten look of a cuffed dog. But as an officer, he should not be complaining about the tea.

Rice and Jens were overdue by nearly a week. But they had almost finished three huts. They pried rocks out of the frozen ground to build the walls. Chinked with ice, snow, and moss ripped up with their fingernails. Poured seawater to freeze and seal the cracks. Canvas, ropes, oars, and poles were used for roofing. They even managed to achieve some degree of comfort.

Lieutenant Greely was pacing back and forth, rubbing his hand down his beard, when he called the men to assemble.

"We have thirty-five days of rations left," he announced. "There seems to be very little game. I would like to cut our rations to make what we have last for fifty days."

Dr. Pavy stepped forward. "Lieutenant Greely, you will expose the men to greater suffering. Already you have cut their ration. Every day gets colder. A man needs more food to fight this cold."

"Fifty days, Doctor, will bring us to mid-November, with ten days of food left. With that we will sledge across to the Greenland side."

"You think the ice will be frozen?" Lieutenant Kislingbury asked.

"Goddamn it to hell, Lieutenant Greely, you'll starve us to death before then," Connell shouted.

"See? See? What I tell you?" Dr. Pavy insisted, his fingers curving like claws. "Why don't you listen to your men!"

Brainard wanted to stop this arguing. He wanted Rice to show up and tell them the cairns were packed with food. Private Henry's bellow thundered, drowning every other voice. "If we couldn't reach Littleton Island when we were halfway there, we haven't a rat's ass chance to get over from here on half rations. Goddamnit, we're already slimmed down to fence rails."

The C.O. took a giant step forward, forcing these men to fall back. He pointed at Connell and Dr. Pavy. "I will prefer charges against you for mutiny, for intemperate language, and for ill-spirited complaints about the leadership of this party. It's the two of you, and you"—the C.O. swung toward Kislingbury—"who are the source of criticism against me." His fingers rushed to his jaw, resuming the desperate massaging, as Whisler yelled out, "Here comes Sergeant Rice and Jens!" Everyone let out a cheer as their comrades emerged from the mist. Rice, stone-faced, halted before Lieutenant Greely, reached into his coat, extracted a packet of papers, and handed them to the C.O. The men stood in silence, fists balled in pockets, watching as their leader ran his eyes over the contents. Without looking up, Lieutenant Greely read aloud: "Cape Sabine, 24 July 1883."

"We were at Conger then," Sergeant Brainard stated. "And they were *here*. My God!"

Lieutenant Greely looked up. "Lieutenant Garlington has sunk the *Proteus*," he said. "Most of the rations and supplies meant for us went to the bottom."

The men stared at their commander with hollow eyes.

Lieutenant Greely drew himself up. His voice rang out into the solid white landscape. "Everything within the power of man will be done to rescue the brave men at Fort Conger from their perilous position. . . . It is not within my power to express one tithe of my sorrow . . ."

"Poor fellow!" Kislingbury blurted out. "His anguish over us must be extreme. God bless my friend Garlington!"

"You know him?" questioned Lieutenant Greely.

"To the devil with his friend Garlington," Private Charlie Henry growled.

"I firmly believe he's now at Littleton Island," Kislingbury went on, "and will be over to meet us as soon as it's possible for him to cross."

"His note confirms he'll save us," Bender squeaked.

"The *Proteus* has sunk!" Connell barked.

"I have faith in Garlington," affirmed Lieutenant Lockwood.

"But," Connell boomed, "he *sunk* his goddamn *ship*."

"Stop it," Whisler bit out, "you're such a fault-finding bastard, Connell."

Lieutenant Greely gave the order to abandon the huts. They must move up the coast to Sabine. Rice's discovery of three caches—one left by the English of 240 rations, the one left by the relief ship *Neptune* in 1882, and now this small one left by Lieutenant Garlington—gave him little choice. He had twenty-four half-starved men to feed.

✳

The next day, they left Eskimo Point. George Rice had convinced Lieutenant Greely to let him take Eskimo Fred and travel south down the coast to Cape Isabella. Captain Nares had left a cache there of 144 pounds of meat. Rice meant to retrieve this and follow their tracks up to Cape Sabine. They were within ten miles of the Nares cache; at Sabine they would be forty miles away from this meat. The C.O. let him go.

The rest of them began the thirty-mile trudge up the coast in the gray light of the approaching winter darkness, harnessed to the sledges, every step costing them in energy and spirit. The news of Lieutenant Garlington's shipwreck had them in despair as they maneuvered the sledges up and over the haphazard and irregular frozen landscape of ice. But when the sledging eased and they easily covered a few hundred yards of smoother ice, they were all convinced that Lieutenant Garlington must be on the Greenland side, at Littleton Island. Lieutenant Kislingbury knew Lieutenant Garlington. He had said one hundred times that Garlington would sledge across and save them.

After a certain number of hours of struggle, the C.O. called a halt. The men unlashed the buffalo-hide bags and spent an untold length of time thawing their way in. They were two, even three, to a bag. The wind blew in spindrift swirls. Their insufficient rations gave them little reserve to fight the cold. *How would Dana have handled this misery?* Brainard wondered. The book was in his pocket. Shorty, in the bag with him, was humming "Buffalo Gals." "You sound so cheerful, Shorty," Brainard said.

"It's the most cheerful song I know." Shorty gave a lopsided grin. "Let's sing it together. It will make the thawing go so much better."

And their voices rang out into the gelid air filled with squall.

> Buffalo gals, won't you come out tonight?
> Come out tonight, come out tonight?
> Buffalo gals, won't you come out tonight,
> And dance by the light of the moon.

The snow beat upon the heads and shoulders of the two men—companions from the Plains—sitting close together. When they came to the end of the song, they began again, in unison, and did not stop until their feet hit the bottom of the bag.

Interlude

Henrietta Rolls Up Her Sleeves
San Diego, California

13 September 1883–End of April 1884

The adventure had affected him deeply and would not let him
rest. The polar virus was in his blood to stay.

Emma De Long (1938)

Henrietta Greely knew her husband had rations for only forty days.
That was all that had been left by the two previous relief attempts. But
she had no assurance he had reached them. She knew he had left Fort
Conger, though, as he would have followed orders he had himself drawn
up. It distressed her when Todd Lincoln, whose father had been so remarkable, gave out in his fiscal report for 1883, which stated that her
husband had sufficient food and clothing to last to next summer. "If," as
the war secretary had phrased it, "it were known that they had remained
at Lady Franklin Bay." But Robert Todd Lincoln did not know. He
went on to say that even if her husband had left the fort, "It would not
be impossible for him to retrace his steps and reach the supplies left at
Lady Franklin Bay." Well, it *would* be impossible! The men couldn't
easily reverse their course once in the boats. If they took to the shore,
she knew about the danger of traveling along the ice foot from her own
Arctic reading of Kane, Isaac Hayes, and Charles Francis Hall. Her

Dolph had supplied her with the books of these great explorers when she had made clear she wanted to learn as much as she could about where he was going.

When on September 13 the news reached her that the *Proteus* had sunk, there was no word at all about the expedition's whereabouts. Since they had not been been reported dead, she would assume they were alive. Though it caused her anguish to think how cold and hungry her Dolph was, they all were. If they had reached Cape Sabine, they would be assuring themselves that Lieutenant Garlington was watching out for them from Littleton Island. Oh! It only upset her more to know that those poor men had no idea that they had been deserted. Lieutenant Garlington's letter to her was full of bravado. "If the ship does not get through," he had written from St. John's, "I most assuredly will." He would go by sledge and dogs, which indicated an alarming ignorance of Arctic travel. Why, the young man wanted to make a hero of himself. A competent navy officer should have been in charge, not this West Point graduate. The communication from the Signal Corps office informing her of Garlington's mishap wasn't even sent by General Hazen, Dolph's friend, but by the acting chief, Captain Mills. It was a stroke of bad timing that General Hazen was far away inspecting signal posts in Washington Territory.

Well, she could handle this second disappointment. Poor, sad Private Beebe, so inadequate to the job in '82, was dead by his own hand. And now this upstart Lieutenant Garlington! The government's incompetence was astonishing. She hated to think this about her country's leaders. The U.S. government had sent her husband up there. They had a moral responsibility to these men at Lady Franklin Bay, just as she had to her own family, her two daughters and her own father, who was not in good health. If one took on the duty, one shouldered the responsibility as well and should be proud, even honored, to bear the burden.

From San Diego she had immediately sent a telegram to the signal corps asking that an expedition be sent out posthaste. There was still time, if they acted fast. Public reaction was on her side. The *Proteus* fiasco was headline news, practically topping the shooting of President Garfield. Dolph's mother in Newburyport was reading these stories, and when Henrietta thought of that—the two women had become dear to each other through correspondence—she was more determined than ever to get her husband home before winter. *She wanted him home!*

At St. John's there were four sealers ready to sail. But Garlington, when approached to head back north, had equivocated. Too late in the season, he said, but, yes, he would be honored, though he might not get through. On September 15, Mills broke the news to her by telegram that "nothing further can be done this year." She felt it as a slap, and that night told her babies, as she tucked them in, "Daddy will be home soon." "Tomorrow?" piped Antoinette. "Not *quite* so soon, my darling." She shouldn't have said anything. But she was determined to keep "Daddy" alive in Antoinette's mind. She was two when he had left. Henrietta had promised that Antoinette would hear all about the adventures of the sledge Daddy had named for her when Daddy was safe home again. Little Adola could have no memory of the father she had been named for, but she meant for both her daughters to know what kind of man their father was. She kissed them "sweet dreams" and walked down the stairs, through the living room with the tall windows fronting the San Diego Bay, and found her father on the terrace in the soft evening light.

"I'm going to send a telegram to General Lockwood," she said. Mr. Nesmith smiled at his daughter. He had been a bank president and it pleased him that Henrietta had inherited his executive ability. "A good choice," he replied. Henrietta and Dolph were good friends with young James Lockwood's parents in Washington. The general had contacts in the government and in Washington society. "I'm going to telegraph as well Lieutenant Caziarc." Mr. Nesmith reached across the space between father and daughter and squeezed her arm, a firm grip that gave her strength. Next to General Hazen, this was her husband's closest friend in the signal corps. "I want a ship to leave at once," she said.

But it didn't happen. Despite General Lockwood's conversation with Secretary Lincoln, despite Caziarc's sympathetic agreement, she received a telegram from Mills on September 18: "The secretaries of navy and war concur . . . nothing can be done this season to reach Mr. Greely." All the Arctic experts were in accord, too full of hazard. Too risky. Did she want to lose more ships and, possibly, men, by sending them up too late in the season? Of course she didn't! But if a ship had been sent out immediately . . . She stopped herself. She must accept she had lost this round. Now she would throw her heart and mind into making sure a ship left at the earliest possible date next season. She didn't know how this could be done. But she knew that she would do it.

What upset her most was that, as General Lockwood wrote, Lincoln would not admit her husband was in peril. Oh, my heavens! Couldn't the war secretary see that these men weren't just names on a roster? They were *young* men. They had homes and sweethearts and families. They had a future.

✶

When Garlington reached Washington by train, he had brought his enormous shaggy Newfoundland along with him. The young army lieutenant had taken it in the neck from the press for sinking his ship, and now reporters were after him about how much Rover ate. "None of the food meant for the brave and noble men of Lady Franklin Bay," the brash lieutenant assured the press. Garlington was taking up too much space. As she scanned the newspapers for signs that the government was setting rescue plans for her husband, all she turned up, she wrote General Hazen—now blessedly back in the capital—was about Lieutenant Garlington, currently facing the Court of Inquiry. The questions were not about his inability to reach her husband. The court seemed only interested in what had gone down with the ship. They kept Garlington on the stand for ten weeks to conclude that the young man had only "erred" in not remaining on Littleton Island. He had been right to take all the food he could. Henrietta told her father, "That young man should have been court-martialed. He deserted those men and gets off with a slap on the wrist."

Her mother-in-law in far-off Newburyport, in the white clapboard house behind the picket fence, had the same reaction. She wrote to her "Rettie," "There is quite a long piece in the paper today about Court of Inquiry. . . . But what good does all this talk amount to? It don't help them poor fellows out there." Henrietta knew that "Mother F. D. Greely," as she signed herself, had not wanted her son to go on such a long journey to such a dangerous place, and Henrietta read an echo of her own thoughts when Mother Greely wrote, "What worries me most is that Adolphus has left his station and is now suffering with cold and perhaps sickness and hunger. 'Tis dredful to think of. . . . They ought to have sent out another expedition as soon as the loss of the *Proteus* was known. They don't send the right kind of men. Do you suppose that Adolphus would have acted in the way that Garlington did? I say no." Henrietta had quickly found the class difference counted for nothing with her mother-in-law, who had turned to factory work when her husband was too ill to work as a shoemaker. The two women understood each other at a deep level. Dolph's mother would have given much to send him to college. Dolph carried much of his mother's goodness, Henrietta was sure of that, coupled with a sense of responsibility to those in his care.

General Hazen, meanwhile, was working hard for her husband, and had let her know that on December 17, President Arthur designated him head of a four-man board, divided equally between navy and army officers, to come up with a new relief plan. The relief would be in the navy's hands, Hazen had said—she had been hoping for that—with two or three ships to be purchased at government expense. Pushing through the appropriation would be slow. It could put in jeopardy Hazen's last point—the one dearest of all to her—that the fleet reach Upernavik on the Greenland coast by May 15, poised to push into Smith Sound as soon as the ice permitted. She wrote him what was obvious to her: "It seems to me that no expense or pains should be spared this year as it is the last that can hope to see the party brought home alive."

Meanwhile, General Lockwood was working on President Arthur, but with disappointing results, the general writing that as the president had referred the matter to the secretaries of war and navy, he had done all he could. Or was going to do, was how Henrietta interpreted this. It was already the third week in January, the year turned to 1884. As General Lockwood put it in his reply: "My fears are not that the party will not be found and brought back, but that their hardships and suffering will have proved fatal to many of them. I feel sure that they are this day enduring all that mortal man can endure and live." These words could make her weep, if she let them. They shared the common cause as no others in Washington could. James was the general's beloved son. He

was doted on, and the family expected great things of him. Mrs. Lockwood was distraught by Garlington's failure. If James did not come
back, Henrietta feared for his family.

On January 31, the vote went into the Senate. How much money was
the government willing to spend to rescue Greely? The bill had passed
easily through the House but stalled in the Senate, and all Henrietta
could do was read the arguments in the papers. She read them aloud to
her father, the two of them seated on the spacious terrace that gave
them the view of bay, sea, and sky. An untroubled sky. Here she could
regain some calm from her distress of reading how Ingalls of Massa-
chusetts declared public money was wasted on these expeditions that
achieved nothing. How several indignant senators had to be assured that
no more such expeditions would be sent out, that this rescue bill would
be the last. Senator Eugene Hale of Maine, Henrietta quickly learned,
was Greely's champion. He argued that there should be no restrictions
in funds to rescue her husband, and his fellow senator Samuel Randall
backed him by saying, "This appropriation is in obedience to humanity,
and to the agreement made with Lieutenant Greely," which raised Henrietta's hopes, until Frye, also of Maine, proclaimed: Why use foreign-
built ships when Maine can build them, ready to sail in two months?
Because, Senator Hale countered, the work can be delayed for many reasons. A fire in the shipyard could seal the death warrant for those men.
Saulsbury of Delaware argued that relief be composed of navy volunteers
only. "I will not grant to the president the power to assign whom he may
please to this dreadful service!" the senator screamed.

So it went from day to day, worthy senators, each with his own
agenda, arguing for the sake of arguing, when men's lives were at stake.
"I cannot imagine," she said to her father, "how cold they are. I have
read the books Dolph gave me, but I cannot put myself in the Arctic. I
can't imagine their hunger, but I know that hunger can drive decent
men to act in ways our minds shy away from. Listen to how these senators argue about the cost." She picked up the paper. "McPherson of
New Jersey says the whole resolution 'confers upon the secretary of the
navy practically unlimited discretion as to the cost of the expedition . . .
and the Senate of the United States supinely submits.' All they are concerned about is topping each other in debate. They are consumed with

parliamentary procedure. These young men have spent their lives serving their country. No one speaks to that, Father."

A few days later, her father, who had taken to scanning the morning paper when his daughter was carrying out some domestic duty, called her out to their terrace seat. "Here's good news, my dear." She rushed out into the sun, her apron on. "Chandler knows how to act," he continued. "With no authority from Congress, the navy secretary has already begun negotiations in secret with England to purchase a ship."

"Oh, the brave man," she crowed. "But how did Congress react?"

Her father laughed. "It seems they could hardly believe it! They questioned him and his answer was that if a ship is not secured now among the Newfoundland and Scottish whalers and sealers, Greely's men will be in greater peril as these ships will leave their home ports and we'll lose the chance to purchase them."

Henrietta clapped her hands. "I will write and thank him." But she was still on tenterhooks. The bill was due to come up for vote on February 11.

When the post arrived on the morning of the 12th carrying that news, father and daughter took the paper out to the terrace. Best to face this together. Under placid skies and in the mild sea air, Henrietta read how Senator Hale of Maine made one last attempt to influence the outcome by saying, "I do not know how I should feel if the expedition should go up there and it should be found that those unfortunate men had perished within a fortnight of the time when the relief reached them, and that delay had been caused by our delay here." Delaware's Saulsbury, in a last attempt to do his worst, declared that the passage of this bill to rescue Greely gave the navy secretary power "to enter the vaults of the Treasury of the United States and take *ad libitum* any amount of money that he may see proper." "I hope," he intoned, "that this bill will fail."

But despite Saulsbury's effort to drive the last nail into her Dolph's coffin, the bill passed. Henrietta reached for her father's hand as she read the tally: twenty-nine votes for, twenty-two against, and twenty-five senators absent. A close vote, with the cruel irony that despite all the arguing, the bill had been approved in the same form in which it had passed in the House *twenty days before*. "Oh, my father," she said, "what a waste of precious time."

✶

The ship Chandler had purchased arrived in New York four days after the vote had carried. "What if," some wag had asked Chandler, "the vote had not carried?" "Well, I would have become the part owner of a good ship," the navy secretary replied. Henrietta could laugh with relief over that. The news from the house behind the picket fence was cheering too. "I think now the government has done everything that they could in fitting out the last expedition," Mother Greely penned. In response to the gift of the ship given by Queen Victoria, she wrote, "How nice it was in the Queen to give the *Alert*. I shall always love her." And Henrietta's mother-in-law went on to describe that she was "taking the best care of Adolphus clothes. I hung them out the other day, gave them a good airing." She was, she wrote her daughter-in-law, sending all the letters she had written to him over the last three years to Commander Schley, who would not only lead the expedition but sail the ship. The best news possible in Henrietta's opinion. Just gazing on his etching in the paper — a craggy face, eyes deep set, nose slide-rule straight, not unlike Stonewall Jackson — her confidence grew. Here was an experienced professional seaman. Commander Winfield Scott Schley would be writing her no last-minute letters of bravado about sledging up with dogs to save her husband.

✶

A wide ocean view. From her terrace seat she gazed upon the serene Pacific. Was her Dolph doing the same? A different sea, certainly, but, roiling or calm, he would witness the play of light as she did. Did it give him strength too? Did it calm him? How could it! If he had taken to the boats, and she was sure he had, he was fighting for his life on some frigid Arctic sea. But where? Where, in God's name, was he? On what part of the coastline? In what cove or harbor? She *must* do more. This three-ship squadron was a valiant effort, but the Arctic coast covered thousands of miles. It was famous for its numberless indentations. Her husband could be anywhere.

"Father" — her voice was urgent — "I've just had an idea." Mr. Nesmith's old eyes found hers. "We will offer a bounty, sizable, twenty-five thousand dollars, to the first ship to find them. Lady Franklin did this for her husband out of her personal fortune. I don't intend it for the navy, but for the fishing fleets as they go about their summer work. That sum will have them checking every bay, every wrinkle in the coastline that might suggest a harbor. There are hundreds and I want them to penetrate every one." She frowned and shook her head. "But I have not Lady Franklin's wealth. This money would need to be approved by Congress. And we have so little time! I'll write General Lockwood. The more ships searching the better."

Her father gazed on her with sparkling eyes. "Work with Otto on this," he said. "Your brother knows the editors of every daily paper in Boston. Involve our friend Douglas Glenn of the *San Diego Union*. Launch a press campaign, my daughter."

"Oh dear!" she said, but her face was beaming, "I know Secretary Chandler won't be pleased. He wants the navy to get credit for finding the lost men."

"The spirit of competition, my darling. This bounty will fix it that Chandler will not leave a stone unturned, or a cove in this case."

"It *is* a good idea, isn't it, Father? Secretary Chandler wants the navy to rescue the men. To build up their lost credit since the Civil War. He doesn't want some 'foreign' ship to bring home the men of Lady Franklin Bay." She laughed outright. Then covered her face with her hands. "Oh! He had assured me he would never go if he thought he'd be putting me through what happened to Lady Franklin."

"You are strong, my daughter. I see your strength increase every day." She brushed away her tears with the back of her hand. Her father's words had brought her to herself again. "You will see," he continued, "how competition will work to bring your Dolph home."

General Lockwood sprang to action and found that Senator Joseph Hawley of Connecticut was enthusiastic to introduce the bounty bill in Congress. The press campaign was crucial, he agreed, to generate pressure on Congress to vote the bill through as quickly as could be done. Those in opposition to the bill assumed a very grave responsibility if the expedition failed because of an inadequate search.

With this encouragement Henrietta, got to work. Unladylike she might appear by thrusting herself into this world of men, but she did not care. She was fighting for her husband's life and the lives of those with him. Even if she were to learn the worst, she must find out what had befallen these men. Emma De Long had heard what had happened to her husband because some on that polar expedition had lived to tell about it. It was far better to know.

Henrietta sat at her desk and wrote to far-flung family and friends, some of them women friends she hadn't seen in years, and she began to get results. A cousin in Atlanta stirred up the interest of the editor of the paper there; a cousin in Chicago called on the editor of the *Chicago Tribune*. Friends in Denver, New Orleans, and Philadelphia encouraged editors they knew to write strong editorials in support of the Hawley Bounty Bill. John Benton, assistant editor of the *New York Journal of Commerce*, encouraged his wife to write to Henrietta urging her to write President Arthur himself, and Mrs. Benton wrote. Send him a "strong letter, with your heart in it," she advised, "appealing to him as a woman to his manhood & trying to arouse his sympathies. Never mind whether it is dignified or not! . . . The President has full power & control over any amount of money. All the responsibility rests with him, and to appeal to him is to do more good than anything else." Henrietta wrote the letter and mailed it to General Lockwood to put directly into the hands of President Arthur at his regular Saturday open house. But in this task the elderly general was defeated by that weekly crowd of congressmen, and was forced to leave Henrietta's letter with the president's secretary.

The general had done his best, but this was a blow. She knew the Bounty Bill was not favored by either Secretary of War Lincoln or the navy secretary. President Arthur had shown himself indifferent to her husband's plight all along. She had written a letter that could have moved a Mongol lord to mercy, her father said. The president might have seen it, or he might not have. That was a shut door now. But she was confident about her press campaign. She was glad for this useful work that occupied her mind. It amazed her how one woman, sitting at her desk as far from the nation's capital as was possible to be, had stirred up interest, more important, sympathy, for the plight of the men of the Lady Franklin Bay Expedition, now carried by newspapers across the nation. She was counting on this to win the day.

The Senate easily passed the Hawley Bounty Bill on March 28. Then, as before, the bill stalled, but this time in the House. Not for long, but enough of a sputter to cause more delay, though this was soothed somewhat when Henrietta and her father read the vote in favor was unanimous. By now it was the second week in April. Commander Schley was set to depart on the 24th from New York. Henrietta felt she could breathe again. At least there was nothing more she could do. Except wait. She had received a letter from Dr. Pavy's wife, written as all was set for departure. Henrietta debated showing it to her father— Lilla Mae Pavy's approach to life was so different from her own, certainly more ladylike—but Henrietta brought the letter with her to the terrace seats that evening nonetheless. "Trusting in the God of all destinies," Mr. Nesmith read, "we have passed through days of gloom with their accompaniments of sighs and tears until this hour's arrival, which finds us on the eve of that longed-for month in which the departing vessels sail toward the North . . . There was a wise purpose in the mind of the Designer of events. . . . I trust that your heart has already become submissive and that you heard . . . the voice of the Comforter speaking even as the blow fell upon you."

"Ah, my dear," her father said as he returned the letter to her hand. "I would say our Dolph was a lucky man to have married you. The Lord, after all, helps those who help themselves."

"Well," she smiled, "I hope her husband comes back to her."

That night, as she tucked them in bed, she told her children, "Very soon. You will hear about your sled, Antoinette."

"From Daddy?" the child asked as she gazed up into her mother's eyes. "Yes," Henrietta promised. "From your father, my love, very soon."

Part Two

Camp Clay

6

"Most of Us Are Out of Our Right Minds"

Camp Clay, Cape Sabine

15 October 1883–Early June 1884

1

I believe that no man can retain the use of his faculties during one
long [Arctic] night to such a degree as to be morally responsible.

Noah Hayes, seaman on C. F. Hall's expedition (1871–72)

The sky was white with snow. The snow clotted the air and blotted out
the dark cliff faces. Wind whipped the snow from the ground and
swirled it off the steep-sided hills in hard-driving gusts that could lift
gravel. The wind scrubbed away footsteps and absorbed voices. The
wind was continuous and it was easy to see why. Cape Sabine stuck out
like a fist at the point where the Kane Basin merged into Smith Sound.
The men of the Lady Franklin Bay Expedition had been thrown upon
their own resources eight hundred miles north of the Arctic Circle on a
blizzard-scourged land of rock and ice.

The temperature, twenty below zero, coupled with their prolonged
exertion and meager rations, was visibly weakening the men. They staggered just carrying out ordinary chores around their camp. Their camp,
on a neck of land about halfway between Cape Sabine and a small island,
resembled a cocked hat and was so called. The location was dictated by
a freshwater lake, fed by the glacier that rose in the rounded and gullied

hills and crested to a thousand feet. This formed the camp's backdrop. They were sheltered in a slight depression that, it was desperately hoped, would give them some protection from the unceasing wind. They faced Payer Harbor, though their view of it was blocked by hills, steep and composed of a red granite that ascended to one hundred feet, leveling to a long crest. The harbor itself was overseen by two islands—Brevoort and Stalknecht—near the entrance to Smith Sound.

The sun had disappeared below the horizon, not to reappear until the latter part of February. Sergeant Brainard, going about his work of making their camp habitable, wondered how many of them would look on the sun's face again. Their situation could hardly be more desperate. Every hope of rescue had failed them. Starvation lay ahead. *No one at home knows where we are.* This thought staggered him. Yet their commander appeared confident that Lieutenant Garlington was on Littleton Island, and the men took from their leader's assurance that Garlington was there. *Perhaps he's seen that we've arrived,* Brainard heard the men say, *and he's waiting to cross by sledge on the firmer ice of winter.* It was as well they believe this. He knew they were dead men if they lost hope.

When they arrived at the place where the Beebe and Garlington caches were located on October 15, 1883, Lieutenant Greely had the men build one hut this time, where all twenty-five would be under one roof. He paced out a rectangle twenty-five feet long by eighteen feet wide with a narrow crawlway entrance like an igloo and room for Sergeant Brainard's commissary on either side. He located it about three hundred yards back from the shoreline, behind some jagged rocks to give them protection from the wind. The wind really did seem to be incessant. He had the men pry out chunks of the red rock for a wall and directed them to build it up to four feet. They were still sleeping in the open, spindrift blowing into their bags, a good incentive to be at work by nine when it was light enough. He kept them at it until two thirty when it got dark. Working hours were short, but it was all they could take on their short rations. "Very disagreeable," Lieutenant Lockwood called it. It didn't help that game was scarce. Long and the two Eskimos hunted every day, but found nothing.

The men poured seawater over the stones, freezing them in place. They heaped snow up against the sides and constructed a snow-block wall about a foot away. The hardest labor was lugging the heavy box of gravel two hundred yards, the wind scouring their faces, their noses running into their beards. They dumped this between the two walls. "Very severe," Lieutenant Lockwood pronounced. They had to make this hut as windproof as they could. Every man was needed to hoist the inverted whaleboat onto the stone walls, resting it on oars laid crosswise. This was the *Narwhal* that Greely had abandoned out on the pack ice. The sturdy New Bedford boat had broken free and arrived intact to beach up at Brevoort Island. The men had hauled her in, amazed at their good fortune, a true gift from the sea. They threw a sailcloth canvas over the boat and covered that with snow. Then they moved inside.

They pried out the rocks in the floor, lugged in lumps of snow and gravel, and did their best to smooth it out. Everyone except Private Henry could stand upright under the center of the boat. But no one could sit in his bag without grazing his head on the sloping roof, not even Shorty Frederick. The men faced each other in two rows. Lieutenant Greely placed himself in the center of one of the rows, Dr. Pavy was across from him. Both were in single bags, as was George Rice, at the end of a row. The rest were tripled up. They could keep warmer this way, though they were bumping shoulders. Their legs stuck into the aisle, and there were complaints of getting kicked when anyone crawled out to take care of "the minor office of nature," as the C.O. called these excursions. Private Henry, returning after such a mission, raised a laugh when he said, "Best to plant yourself downwind, boys, or you'll get a faceful of your own piss." For nighttime, the men used a tin, a large one that had contained roast pork, as a urinal. It sat by their entrance and Greely set up a rotational duty to empty it in the morning.

By the C.O.'s order they sat in the dark. They had only enough fuel for one lamp that Bender made from a tomato can. Rope or pieces of old sock served for a wick. It hung in the center, tied to the upright oar that supported the whaleboat-roof. Greely permitted the lamp to be lit *only* when the cooks served their messes. The stove fuel was a mix of alcohol, blubber, stearine, barrel staves or other wood they found in the caches, even tarred rope. Bender made the sheet-iron stove from a large tin that had contained roast beef. He fitted it to emerge through a small hole in their roof, but this chimney leaked, causing their living quarters to fill with smoke and the nasty greasy smell of the fuel that had all of them coughing and hacking and wiping their streaming eyes.

"Comfort," said Sergeant Brainard, who shared a bag with Shorty and Whisler, "is something of the past." He feared the truth of this, and its consequences. He was well aware it was the annoying trials of smoke at meals, bumping shoulders, and cold feet breaking up their sleep that would grind them down. At below zero outside, the temperature inside ranged from fourteen to twenty-five degrees, due to their massed body heat. Everyone was constantly thirsty. They were too short of fuel to turn snow and ice into water more than twice a day. Because of this fuel problem, Greely directed the cooks to barely thaw the ice crystals. They ate their food cold and they complained. "There are tribes of Eskimos," the doctor told them, "who have never heard of fires and consume their food raw and frozen. They dissolve the ice in their mouths until the morsel is thawed enough to masticate. Then they experience a sudden warmth as digestion takes place."

"Jesus Christ, Doctor," Connell snarled, "that's hogwash."

"Private Connell," the C.O. stepped in, "there is no need for your blasphemous opinion. Dr. Pavy lived in Greenland. I expect he knows what he is talking about."

Connell snorted. "The C.O. takes the doctor's side," he said in his bag-mate Charlie Henry's ear. "Write that in your diary for the *Chicago Times* editor." Everyone heard this, but no one commented. They were living so closely packed as to be eavesdropping on each other's thoughts. Privacy could only be gained by ignoring overheard remarks.

Their encampment in place with everyone under one roof, Brainard allowed himself to slip away. An hour's walk would do him good. He would put this time to use by climbing the hill with the level crest that rose out of Smith Sound and blocked their view. They could erect a signal flag up here. It was only about one hundred feet high, but steep and rocky. The exertion tired him. The C.O. had them on half rations, and this lack of food had cut into his stamina.

He sat down on a rock, breathing hard, when he reached the crest. He rested his elbows on his knees and gazed out into Smith Sound. It was too overcast to see all the way to Greenland, and too windy to stay long. He kept blinking. Facing the wind made his eyes tear. The sound was a froth of churning ice, battered by wind and waves. Watching this maelstrom, he wondered how they had survived it.

Army men in open boats. A crazy plan. A plan based on the government's ignorance of the terrain, the climate, and everything else. He frowned, thinking of Lieutenant Greely. *He's a different leader from what he was at Conger.* He looked out at the sound again. In the short time he had been here, the late-October light had dimmed. *The boat trip forced him to drop the martinet stance.* He caught a brightness on the horizon where the sun was sinking through the overcast. *He's gaining confidence in himself and his own abilities to lead.*

He stopped thinking and began working with his fingers in the gravel. *It's just loose gravel. Just stones. There is no dirt. Nothing can grow here. This is not a nourishing place.* He shivered. A thick bank of fog came flying toward him on the wind. *Dammit, even a good leader is capable of a bad decision.* Davy Brainard picked up a handful of gravel. *I can help Lieutenant Greely best by keeping him on the track he's on now. I will assert myself if I have to.*

Sergeant Brainard stood up. He raised his arm and let the gravel fly. The small stones spun out in the wind and scattered in a senseless manner, many of them landing only a little way from his boots. He wiped the grit off his face and shook his head at his own stupidity of throwing light objects into a strong wind. *You'd better watch yourself*, he said into the fog bank. He turned then and headed down the rubbly slope, back to Lieutenant Greely, the men, and their camp.

✳

Six days after they arrived, Lieutenant Greely sent out Sergeant Brainard with a detail to overhaul the cache left by Garlington. The "wreck cache," as the men were already calling it. Private Henry avoided this duty. He had frosted one of his feet. But he was not so handicapped that Brainard had caught sight of the private poking around the pile of offal, picking at the raw seal intestines. Smacking his lips over them, was Brainard's impression, and he despaired as to how he was going to protect their scant food supply from this private's prowling hands. They were stuck with Private Henry now.

The men, dismantling the wreck cache, turned out a profuse supply of canned vegetables, raisins, and lemons, but little in the way of canned meat, dried potatoes, or hard bread, the food items they craved. The thirty pounds of tobacco cheered them, and Sergeant Brainard, on the spot, issued this to the smokers. To the nonsmokers he handed around an equal amount of raisins.

Connell unpacked some looking glasses. "We can't eat these," he said in disgust. All too fresh in their minds was that Rice and Eskimo Fred had failed to bring back that 144 pounds of meat at Cape Isabella. Captain Nares had, for some unfathomable reason, placed it on a thousand-foot rise. Rice wanted to return with more men. "While we have the strength," he begged. But the C.O. vetoed this. That meat was forty miles away now.

They had nearly finished pulling apart the wreck cache when Sergeant Linn removed an old brass ship's lantern. About to tear away the frozen sheet of newspaper it was wrapped in, Linn was struck by a headline. "They're writing about us!" Linn shouted. Rice ran over. They carried it to camp to thaw it, and after supper carefully unfolded the newspaper to discover a page from the *Louisville Courier-Journal* dated May 20, 1883.

"Only five months ago," Sergeant Brainard pointed out.

Rice read the headline: "LIEUT. GREELEY'S SAFETY." Rice interrupted himself. "They spelled your name wrong, Lieutenant." The C.O. just said, "Continue, Sergeant Rice." So Rice went on: "NECESSITY OF SENDING A RELIEF EXPEDITION IMMEDIATELY. It's an article by our old friend Henry Clay," he said.

"At least Clay hasn't forgotten us," Lieutenant Kislingbury shouted. There was some cheering. But the C.O. cut it off with, "Silence, men, let Sergeant Rice continue."

Clay was critical of the relief plan that would head north on the Greenland side when Lieutenant Greely and his men would be retreating down the opposite shore. "'They cannot return to Fort Conger,'" Rice read, "'and there will be no shelter for them at Cape Sabine. The cache of 240 rations, if it can be found, will prolong their misery for a few days. When that is exhausted they will be past all earthly succor. Like poor De Long, they will then lie down on the cold ground, under the quiet stars, to die.'"

"My poor friend De Long," the C.O. sighed. "He is dead then. I carry the letter his wife gave me." He patted his breast pocket. They all sat staring into each other's blackened and bearded faces. So De Long really had died up here. "'It will be expensive,'" Rice kept reading, "'but the question of expense ought not to be taken into consideration. It is a matter of life and death to a brave band of officers and men, who are acting in the service and under the orders of their government.'"

"Hooray for Henry Clay!" Lieutenant Lockwood sang out.

"I propose to name our winter quarters Camp Clay," Lieutenant Greely said.

"What a Christly mess," Private Henry shouted and shook Bender's arm, cutting his bag-mate off in mid-cheer. "Our own government's fouled up our relief. We're going to die on this godforsaken coastline."

"No we're not, Charlie," Bender wailed.

"The lemons! All the lemons!" Linn was howling. "All are wrapped in newspaper too!"

For the next several weeks, their commander warmed up each lemon, unwrapped and smoothed out the scraps of newsprint, and read to them at bedtime in the dim light of the blubber lamp, down to the advertisements. They learned President Garfield had died. He had been shot a few days before they had embarked from St. John's. The new president was Chester A. Arthur, who had nothing to do with the Lady Franklin Bay Expedition. The only cabinet member left from Garfield's administration was Robert Todd Lincoln, and they knew the war secretary regarded Arctic explorations as a waste of time, manpower, and money. They hadn't thought much about this at Fort Conger, but now that the C.O. had set their daily ration at fourteen ounces—under a pound of food a day—it made them desperate to think they might have been forgotten. Lieutenant Greely's plan was to stretch their food—one thousand rations—enough for forty days, to March 10. By then either Garlington would have come to them, or, somehow, they would be on the Greenland side. It hadn't helped when Eskimo Fred shot two seals and both sank before he could squeeze himself into his kayak to secure them. It was horrible to watch that food disappear before their eyes. Now, Fred said, the seals were leaving. A fox had been nosing around their stores. They were trying to catch him. A raven had flown overhead, but too high up to waste a shot on. No musk oxen.

There were other surprises in Garlington's cache. The latest edition of the *Army Register* revealed that Lieutenant Lockwood had been advanced to first lieutenant. "My father will be proud of me," he said, running his fingers through his tangled mustache.

Brainard had concerns about Lieutenant Lockwood. Just that morning he had found him down on his hands and knees, clawing up the crumbs where the C.O. had the men dump the moldy dog biscuits. "Anything to fill me up, Davy," he said, his jaw working. "I have such a constant longing for food." He held up a morsel between thumb and forefinger, green with moldy slime. "There's a pungency that puts me in mind of my mother's ribs of pickled pork. She cooks them in cornmeal. Do try it." He held out a redolent green crumb. Brainard took it and forced himself to try it, for Lockwood's sake.

"Do you taste it?"

"What?"

"The cornmeal."

Lockwood wanted him to, so Brainard said he did, and watched in a certain amount of horror as the lieutenant's once-handsome face assumed a death's head grin, the eyes strikingly hollowed out. "I'm so glad," he breathed.

Brainard, as their stores sergeant and in his own sense of fairness, was carrying out their daily ration to the hundredth of an ounce. Bender had fashioned a pair of scales for this. "It's not possible," Private Charlie Henry said.

"Oh, it is, Charlie," Bender assured him. "You counterweight the ration with these cartridges."

"Well, dammit," the private said. "I'm not getting enough to eat. I can hold *my* entire daily ration in the palm of one hand."

The next day Sergeant Brainard had detected a good handful of the hard bread missing from his storehouse. He found that the marauder had loosened a snow block to gain access and he reported this to Lieutenant Greely. At their next mealtime, the lieutenant announced, "Sergeant Brainard tells me food was stolen from his commissary." His eye sought the eye of every man in their stone hut. "While all of us can sympathize with the hunger that drove a member of our party to commit such a despicable act," he went on, his voice stern and strong, "I promise you the culprit will be brought to light and punished." Sergeant Brainard kept his eye on Private Henry. It was hard to see in the smoky fug even though he was right across the aisle from this private. *I wonder if the men suspect me?* He was the one who had access to all their food. The blubber lamp flickered. It gave only half the light of an ordinary tallow candle. Its greasy smell seemed to thicken the silence. Spoons clanking on their tins—a scanty mix of the blue fox Long had shot and pemmican, flavored with lime juice as scurvy prevention.

"St. John's biscuits," Lieutenant Lockwood suddenly said. The men were aware of the lieutenant's partiality for this biscuit, served in the restaurants at St. John's. "Canton ginger root, cut oranges, and grated coconut," he continued.

"Are you starting with the appetizers, Lieutenant Lockwood?" Bender inquired.

"Pie of orange and coconut," he went on. "My mother serves a blanc-mange of blue color, but no one could tell why it was blue." He laughed quietly, seeming to savor this vision.

"Lieutenant Lockwood," Ellis, their eldest, prompted, "you skipped from the appetizers to dessert. What is the main course?"

"Good of you to ask." Lockwood peered into his tin, a can that had once contained stewed tomatoes. He lifted his head and his eyes wandered over to Sergeant Ellis. "The main course, you say? I was thinking of those St. John's biscuits and how, when we pull into that blessed harbor again, I'll take you to celebrate with a mutton-pie party at Topsail's, then we'll march down to Fitzpatrick's for their excellent ham and eggs. I'm so happy Long shot a blue fox this morning." He made a gracious gesture toward Private Long. "You've given us three and a half pounds to add to dinner. I'm taking so little exercise now, but I swear it gives me an increased appetite." He spread his mouth in an attempt to smile, stretching the skin over his emaciated lips. "Don't you find it so?"

Everyone in the hut stared at Lieutenant Lockwood. What he said was illogical. The wind was making its lonesome whining sound. The hut shook. Drafts caused the lamp to weirdly flicker and the greasy blubbery smell seemed to solidify, causing the boat ceiling to bear down. Already the grease had soaked into their bags and clothing, turning their hands and faces black. Ellis broke the silence. "Would you describe your mother's blancmange — the blue color — again, Lieutenant Lockwood?"

✳

A few walruses were spotted afar out in the water and Long killed one, but it sank before Eskimo Jens in the kayak could reach it. A solitary snow bunting, lost from its mate, hopped about their camp in search of crumbs. It chirped so mournfully that Long could not bear to kill it. "It's as miserable as we are," he said.

Rice, taking advantage of this scarcity of game, persuaded Lieutenant Greely to let him leave for Cape Isabella. This English meat, 144 pounds, Rice argued, would increase each man's daily ration by three-quarters of an ounce. He would take Shorty Frederick for his willing spirit, and Sergeant Linn and Corporal Elison, both still regarded as husky. The C.O. issued a few more ounces above the daily norm to prepare them for the ordeal of an eighty-mile round trip.

Lieutenant Greely could not refuse Rice's request. Their storehouse had been broken into several times. Lieutenant Lockwood discovered a can of milk, with the scratches made corresponding with the nicks on Schneider's knife blade. Schneider claimed he had loaned the knife to Private Henry. "You're trying to frame me," Schneider protested. And with that, Brainard saw that every man was set to suspect his neighbor, even his own bag-mate. If this expedition degenerated into a scramble for food, that would be very bad. Lieutenant Greely informed them that stealing expedition stores was mutiny and could be punished by execution. Brainard desperately hoped it would not come to that.

✳

2

A survival situation brings out the true, underlying personality. Our survival kit is inside us: But unless it's there before the accident, it is not going to appear magically at the moment it's needed.
Laurence Gonzales, *Deep Survival: Who Lives, Who Dies, and Why* (2003)

Rice's party of four left at eight o'clock on November 2. Everyone gathered around outside the hut to see them off. Rice and Linn were harnessed to the sledge, loaded with two sleeping bags, rations for the better part of a week, the cooking lamp, and a small amount of fuel. This lamp gave a more direct heat and so thawed food faster. No tent. Nearly every man had given them some item of his own—a pair of socks, mittens, a scarf—to add to their warmth and safety. Sergeant Linn complained of a headache. Most of them had achy heads from the constant smoke. Something had to be done about the ventilation, Brainard told himself, and soon. His gnawing hunger made it hard to think straight, hard to act. He thought about what Rice had said to him back at Conger, after the first relief had failed. "I see very clearly I've made a great mistake in leaving civilization." He had counted on one full year to document the Arctic landscape through his photography, but two years was costing him. Yet, here was Rice, hitched to the sledge beside Sergeant Linn. He had offered to make this risky journey for meat that would last a bare ten days at full rations. The temperatures sat on twenty below zero now. Their strength was not up to the rigors of this journey.

Brainard remembered when they had traversed from Eskimo Point to Sabine how the landscape appeared without features, how he couldn't be sure of what he saw. Partly because the light was dim, not quite black dark, but gray. Bergs, hills, and hillocks, individual rocks and outcroppings showed themselves in tones of gray. These objects didn't appear solid. It had to do with the light—the lack of it—and the immensity of the space. Pulling the sledge, leaning into the harness, he was looking down so that when he looked up he was in a different spot and the object he was passing showed a different aspect. Was it the same object? It was easy to become confused. He had found himself fighting down panic.

Eight days later, the C.O. had the cooks hold off dinner in expectation of Rice's team bringing in the English meat. All day the men were saying, tonight we dine like kings. He delayed dinner an hour, then had Long serve up an amount that looked more pitiful than ever: tea and a few ounces of meat from a tin containing pork. "A dog could down this in half a gulp," Private Henry commented. "And this bit of hard bread," he held it toward them in his palm, "wouldn't fill the paw of a mouse."

As they stared at the morsel, Lieutenant Lockwood began to talk. "I will tell you the things I will keep in my room at home for midnight eating," he said in his soft southern tones. He began to tick them off on his fingers. "Sardines, potted ham, smoked beef, smoked goose and eel, shrimps, anchovy paste, spiced oysters, stuffed olives, Boston pilot bread, buttered crackers . . ."

"Does your mother butter the crackers?" Bender inquired. "I've never had a *buttered* cracker." The others pounced on him to shut up, but the lieutenant continued, unaware of interruption, caressing each word.

". . . Albert and Arundel crackers, soda and water, ditto ginger, nuts and cakes, can of butter and condensed milk, preserved peaches, strawberries, and blackberry jam, *fromage de Brie*, and Schwitzerkäse—you Germans would like that—sugar, beer, ale and porter, and cider, and liqueurs, and Virginia seedling wine, mustard, vinegar, pepper, salt, and Maryland biscuit, black cake . . ."

"Lieutenant Lockwood, that will be enough." The C.O.'s voice crashed down like a sledgehammer. Lockwood focused sorrowful eyes on his commanding officer but broke off his recitation. The C.O. picked up the *Pickwick Papers* from the wreck cache, and began to read. He read aloud to them after supper and before sleep, a mournful time when thoughts of home most oppressed those who had homes. It had proved a welcomed change in reading matter. Otherwise they were restricted to Gardiner's Bible that the meteorologist had brought from Conger in exchange for an equal weight of clothes. When Charlie had tried to make a joke of this, Connell, of all people, said, "You have to understand, Charlie, Sergeant Gardiner's a very religious man. He hopes all this pain and suffering is good for his soul and will make him a better person."

After the reading, they sat up in their bags waiting for the arrival of Rice, Shorty, Linn, and Elison with the meat, even though they were best off if they could slide into sleep right after the reading when they retained a remnant of food in their stomachs and so of warmth. The C.O. had left on the seal blubber lamp, and some of them were writing in their journals. Lieutenant Lockwood kept his in shorthand. "That mark there." Charlie, diagonally across the aisle, pointed to it with a greasy finger. "It's in all your entries. Does it concern the weather? That's how I can begin my entries."

"That mark, as you call it, Private Henry, means memorandum." He looked around at this inquisitive private from where he was lying on his side in his buffalo bag, one mittened hand encircling his ink bottle in an attempt to keep it thawed.

"What do you make a memorandum of?" Charlie asked. This question aroused Brainard's attention. The men discussed Lieutenant Lockwood. He came from a world most of them could not imagine. A refined world. A happy family home. "He has no secrets," Private Henry said once. "He was kind to me when we were working on our little newspaper." And he went on to describe how Lieutenant Lockwood had drawn the masthead. A pen-and-ink sketch of Fort Conger looking small and snug in the snowy landscape, the ridgeline in back and one of the dogs in front, howling up at a crescent moon. "He liked my idea to call it the *Arctic Moon*," Private Henry had said.

"I'll read you one," the lieutenant replied and turned back a few pages. "'Memorandum: Vienna Coffee House, Broadway and Fourteenth Street, New York. Large assortment of cakes, bread, and pastry; fine chocolate, omelets, and *biscuit glac*é.'" He flipped forward a few pages. "Here's another one from the Vienna Café: 'Roulades, charlotte russe, tortes, roast suckling pig, Irish stew.'" He looked up. Every pair of eyes, sockets hollowed for lack of food, were fixed on him as if held by magnetic attraction. "We've discussed every dish under the sun," the lieutenant said, "all forms of vegetables and desserts. Tonight we ate"—he was not talking to them, he was talking to himself—"a morsel of meat, I think it was pork. It is hard to distinguish taste now. And a little bread. A very, very little. It couldn't have satisfied a child. Tomorrow we will have the same, or, if not precisely, it will taste the same." He made a waxing movement with his fingers toward his overgrown mustache that the men's eyes followed like obedient puppies. The C.O. stirred, about to cut him off, when every ear picked up the crunch of footsteps—a single pair of feet—and Rice fell through the canvas covering of their doorway.

He lay stretched across the bottom of their bags, breathing hard, too exhausted to speak. Biederbick reached out and touched his face, dislodging bits of ice that shattered on their sleeping bags. Rice's face was encrusted in frost from beard to eyebrows. He pulled himself to his knees, raked a mitten across his mouth, scattering more ice, and gasped out, "Joe Elison is dying at Rosse Bay."

"Heat rum for Sergeant Rice," the C.O. directed Long. Then he turned to Sergeant Brainard. "Take Eskimo Fred and proceed with all speed to Rosse Bay. Take only food and brandy with you." Next he put his hand on Lieutenant Lockwood's arm. "You will take six men and drag the sledge." This eased the tension. Brainard was relieved to see the C.O.'s semistarved mind worked well in the midst of an emergency.

"You'll be bringing back his corpse," Rice said.

"Then what the hell's the rush?" Charlie's growl filled the hovel. Bender, beside him in the bag, drew away.

Rice stared at him. "Private Frederick and Sergeant Linn need our help," he said. There was no judgment in his tone. But Charlie made no move to take back what he said. Long handed Rice the warmed rum and Rice bent over the can that had once contained pickled onions.

Brainard began assembling the food, and Eskimo Fred slipped on his outer coat, his *timiak*. Lieutenant Lockwood began calling out the names of his chosen six and when he called out Private Henry's name, the man cried out, "Oh, no. Not me!" Swerving toward his commanding officer, he said in a strange pleading voice, "I beg you, sir, to excuse me from this duty."

"Excuse?" The C.O.'s voice was sharp.

"My frostbitten foot." Charlie pulled his leg out of the bag and pointed at his foot the doctor had wrapped in a ragged shirt.

"You coward," Connell sneered.

"Oh, your frostbite, Private Henry," Lieutenant Greely said. "Private Schneider will go in your place." Schneider sprang to action. This was their first serious accident and everyone but Private Charlie Henry was clamoring to go rescue Elison.

"Linn and Shorty are in the sleeping bag with Joe," Rice said. "We managed to erect the small canvas fly." His lips were cracked and it was hard for him to speak.

"Fix Sergeant Rice some hot tea now, and beef stew and a few ounces of hard bread," the C.O. ordered. "I don't imagine you've had much to eat today, Sergeant Rice."

"Plenty," he said. "I took a chunk of frozen beef. We all had tea this morning." The blood was breaking on his lips.

"You must eat, Rice," Lieutenant Lockwood said.

"I'll take nothing more. On account of failing to bring in the meat."

"Come now, Sergeant Rice," the C.O. urged. "You've traveled hard with no thought for your own safety. You knew that if you failed, those you left behind would die. You are a bold man, George Rice, and now you must eat. There is no need to be so self-sacrificing."

"I know that, sir," said Rice. "So I'll take my weekly allowance of dog biscuit. I cannot digest more. I've been on the gridiron so long now I seem to have lost my appetite. And now you must let me go back for them."

"I will concede to the dog biscuit, Sergeant Rice, but your request to return to Rosse Bay is out of the question."

Brainard had his eye on Private Henry. The man couldn't take his eyes off George Rice, a look of fawning admiration. What's wrong with him? Brainard thought. He had given out on the Farthest North, not from weakness, and not from cowardice. Something else. The man needed to be near the food supply. This trip for Joe Elison would take several days. But it was shocking to Brainard. Private Henry's refusal to save—if they could—Joe's life spoke to something deep in his character. The man had committed murder: a Chinese in that bar in Deadwood. And Brainard felt a surge of fear in his throat at the strange forces their situation was unleashing.

Outside the darkness was intense. The surface snow, scuffed by the wind, blotted out the stars and their sense of direction. Brainard and Eskimo Fred marched all night—though the division of night and day made little difference in terms of how dark it was. Brainard tried to keep track of the time by counting off the miles—seventeen—in his head. But his mind would drift off. The landmarks were nearly invisible; only the tallest rock outcroppings stood out against the sky. He didn't look up often. He had to concentrate on his footing. The snow, hissing around his moccasined feet, began to disturb him. If it hadn't been so cold, he could swear he had stumbled into a pit of vipers. They nearly walked into the tent. Suddenly there was this darker object set off by the lighter darkness behind it. Brainard reached out his mittened hand and felt the surface give. Inside they could hear movement and Brainard, striking a match, knelt down to peer in. "I heard your footsteps," Shorty said. He was lying on his back. He seemed unable to turn his head.

They were lying on the icy ground in the buffalo-hide bag. The surface of the bag was frosted, the men's body heat emerging to condense and freeze on the outside. A viscous fluid oozed from Joe's eyes and nose. His nose was deadly white. He was going to lose his nose. That he was alive at all, Brainard saw, was due to the care of Linn and Shorty, positioned on either side of him in the bag. Shorty had Joe's hands on his bare chest. But in the process of thawing out Joe with the heat of their own bodies, they had made themselves desperately cold, their own hands, feet, and even faces blistered with frostbite.

Where they were was desolate to an inhuman degree, and the uncaring landscape propelled Brainard into the work of making a fire, anything to push back the rawness of their bleak surroundings.

The C.O. had left the wooden iceboat *Beaumont* at Eskimo Point and Rice had brought along some of that wood. In the stiff wind, Brainard had a tough time getting a blaze going sufficient to heat up the seal meat he had brought. He made it hot and their tea hot too. Eskimo Fred, in an effort to help the men sit up, found they were frozen in the bag, a solid mass of three, unable to free their arms, compelling Brainard and Fred to feed them by hand. As the warmth of the food reacted on their sluggish circulation, Joe began to moan. "Please kill me. I'm no good to anyone now."

All they could do was assure him he would be all right. Lieutenant Lockwood was coming with the sledge and they would be back at Camp Clay soon. Fred kept smiling at Joe, patting him on his head.

"We're awfully glad to see you fellows," Shorty said. "We were concerned about Rice making it back."

"All my fault," Joe moaned again. His face was so frosted it was hard for him to talk.

"He ate snow," Linn said. "I tried to stop him. We were hauling back the meat."

"I was so thirsty," Joe mumbled. His body shook, convulsed with shivering.

"Well, you shouldn't have eaten snow," Linn said.

"We've had a bad night." Shorty spoke up in an attempt, Brainard felt, to explain Linn's carping comments.

"Elison kept screaming about his hands," Linn went on. "I couldn't stand it."

"We'd thawed out his hands, got the blood circulating. It's a painful process, you know," Shorty explained.

"I tried to leave. I had to get out of the bag," Linn went on. "But Shorty grabbed me, wrestled me back in. I was freezing with Elison's great mitts on my chest. Joe kept screaming, the bag felt wet, and, dammit, Joe had pissed in the goddamn bag."

"That's why you find us frozen in," Shorty Frederick explained in his mild voice.

"I had to breathe so hard hauling that sledge," Joe said. "My throat felt like it was worked over by a cheese grater."

"The C.O. told us back at Conger that ingested snow would freeze your core. He couldn't walk. You should have seen his feet," Linn said. "Dead white, hard as wooden blocks. You'd really done a job on yourself." Linn kept glaring at Joe.

Shorty tried to intervene. "Don't be so hard on him."

"Sergeant Rice was very good to me." Joe attempted a smile that brought the blood beading on his cracked lips.

Shorty took over. "When Rice saw what kind of shape Joe was in, he called a halt—"

"We unlaced his goddamn boots and—" Linn interrupted.

"Please, Sergeant Linn," Brainard said, laying a hand on Linn's arm, let Shorty speak." He was surprised by Linn. The sergeant had never abused the men at Conger. What was this life doing to them?

"Nothing much more to say," Shorty continued. "We massaged Joe's feet and set him back on his pins. We'd gotten the meat off that thousand-foot rise and made it back to Eskimo Point. Spent the night in the stone huts we'd built, glad to be out of the wind."

"They had to haul me on the sledge," Joe said. His eyes were running, tears or the viscous fluid, probably both.

"Goddamn it," Linn said. Linn had never sworn at Conger either, not to speak of. The poor man, Brainard thought, he must be terrified at what is happening to us all. "We had to off-load the meat," Linn went on. "There were four cases of that *food*, and we had to leave it."

Brainard looked at Shorty to explain. "That was the next morning," he said. "It was stormy. But Joe could walk. Rice sent him off with Linn while he and I stacked the meat cases and covered them with stones. Rice stuck his Springfield rifle upright in the center to mark the spot. 'We'll return for this, Shorty, and soon,' he said to me. He meant while we still had the strength."

"Joe was a mess," Linn started up again. "He was stumbling around like a drunk. Couldn't see worth a damn with his eyes frozen shut. Why, his goddamn lashes were glued by frost to his cheeks."

"That will do, Sergeant Linn," Brainard broke in.

"Three-inch icicles hanging from his nose. His lips turned blue." Linn ignored Sergeant Brainard. "His hands were froze. I could tell because his fur mitts had gone white at the tips. We'd got his circulation going, but, dammit, Joe"—Linn turned on Joe—"you got yourself froze up again. Lurched like a man on stilts. Couldn't see. Had no idea where in hell he was, did you, Joe?"

"I'm sorry. I'm sorry." Joe was sobbing.

"I think you all did very well to reach this point." Brainard wanted to sound encouraging. In point of fact, they were all worse off because of this trip. The English meat was nearly as inaccessible, and Joe Elison, one of their stronger men, was now useless. Linn could be losing his mind. Shorty, though, was his same calm, helpful self. He could count on Shorty, his friend from the Indian Wars.

"They had to haul me," Joe said. "Leave me, I told them, I'm good for nothing now. Leave me and take the meat."

"Well, we did leave you. We couldn't drag you over the long hill," Linn snapped.

"You all did wonderfully well," Brainard said again. "Lieutenant Lockwood will be along soon with men and the sledge. But right now"—he gave them an encouraging look—"I'm going to chop you out of this frozen bag." And David Brainard picked up the ax.

✳

The C.O. did justice to Rice's effort and the rescue of Elison by saying when they were all back at Camp Clay, "For half-starved and en-
feebled men to make such a journey in temperatures ranging between
minus 19 and minus 34 degrees in near total darkness, without mishap or
disaster—"

"I would say there was plenty of mishap and disaster, Lieutenant
Greely," Private Henry broke in. "And no meat."

The metallic scraping of spoons on tins followed this statement.
Brainard started to speak to what Henry had just said, put the best face
possible on the last week, but, looking at the situation coldly, Private
Henry was right. The one thing that struck him, though, was Lieutenant Lockwood's performance. The man who had scraped up moldy dog
biscuits with his fingernails had vanished, to be replaced by the man of
action.

When Lockwood arrived, they placed Elison in a dogskin bag and
wrapped him in canvas for the sledge. Alternating haulers, they made
one stop at the northern entrance to Rice Strait, where they set up a
sheltering canvas for Elison, got tea into him and some encouraging
words that seemed to restore his natural cheerfulness. No more talk
about wanting them to kill him.

They were at the drag ropes again when the moon rose, and the
light it shed was so soft over the barren ice fields that a feeling close to
awe took possession of everyone. Brainard noted how they all moved
forward slowly, carefully, and in silence with Elison, their burden. It
was a weird scene, still the sense of desolation, with the chaotic masses
of pulverized bergs fringing the coast. But the moonlight gave it a
beauty that somehow lifted their hearts. Brainard hoped this working
together to save a comrade would pull them closer.

They reached Camp Clay at 2:10 a.m. Everyone swarmed out to
welcome them and carry Elison into the hut.

✴

A few days later, Lockwood sank back into lethargy. At dinner—a
meal, if it could be called that, of two dog biscuits and a mouthful of
English beef, followed by tea—the lieutenant told them how he was
thinking of eating his meat and biscuits together while waiting for his

tea. Then he changed his mind. He would keep his dog biscuits and meat until his tea was ready. Finally, he concluded in a melancholy tone, "No expedient makes much difference. There is never enough." He passed his fingers through his mustache, unwaxed and sadly overgrown. "How tiresome it is, this roar from the moving ice in the straits today."

"I'm as ravenous as a weasel, and I just finished my dinner," Private Henry said. "Did you know"—he said as he waved his spoon and addressed everyone—"a weasel must eat one-half its body weight a day? I learned this from my father. It's the only useful piece of information he ever taught me. What I mean is, knowing this fact about weasels is very useful to me in our present situation. Weasels are perpetually hungry. Did you know that, Bender?" Bender shook his head. His eyes were large. He looked scared. "Well, I'm telling you, that animal—it's a very small animal—is perpetually hungry. It's what keeps them vicious." He leaned over Bender and bellowed, "Vicious!"

"I'm just glad I'm alive," Joe Elison said. The doctor was feeding him now as his hands were useless. His hands and feet, and nose, too, were swollen up with blisters and turning black. The doctor said he lacked the instruments and clean dressings to amputate. Lieutenant Greely expressed his concern about blood poisoning, having witnessed this during the Civil War. The cold would keep away the infection, the doctor assured everyone. Joe would lose his hands and feet, and nose, too. These body parts would just turn black and fall off. But they were to keep this from him. He was in pain, but it was amazing how he had regained his good temper. When he needed to attend to nature's office, they took turns holding a pan. When Joe must "relieve his bowels"—the C.O.'s term—two men carried him outside and set him in a kneeling position. Squatting was out of the question. Joe suffered all these indignities in good grace. And no voices were raised in objection when the C.O. ordered up a few extra ounces of food daily to help him gain strength. The men were calling Joe Elison their "Baby Joe." Perhaps because the doctor spoon-fed him. Brainard was concerned about the doctor handling Joe's food. He knew how much willpower it took to handle food and not snitch small bits.

Their bags froze to the gravel floor. The hair inside, filled with frost, came off in clumps and found its way into the cook pot. They had on the same clothing from the day they left Fort Conger. Brainard, returning to their hovel from being in the fresh air, was knocked back by the smell: a mix of putrid food and the body stench of unwashed men, with an acrid underlying layer of urine.

A few days later, at supper, the C.O. thanked everyone who had volunteered to dig the waterhole again. "With the temperatures constantly below zero, our waterhole will continue to ice over," he said, "but it is not frozen to the bottom yet, and because of the excellent turnout, we have fresh water with our supper." Kislingbury and Brainard had taken charge. Lieutenant Lockwood had begged to be excused. "I feel a great apathy, a cloudiness almost impossible to shake off," he had said. It was storming at the time. No one had wanted to go out. Cross, too, had refused to budge. Private Henry used his frostbitten foot as an excuse.

But despite Lockwood's apathy, he became talkative over dinner. Food was his subject. "I would like to invite," he intoned in his soft southern voice, bowing from the waist in Sergeant Brainard's direction, "our faithful stores sergeant to come to supper at my home, where I promise to serve him Sally Lunn, stewed oysters, smearcase, slip, and preserved strawberries with cake. After supper we will smoke. Then will come more wine and cake and we'll listen to some singing by my dear Mary Murray." He sighed, as if flooded by the memory of her voice. "I invite Shorty Frederick and Long to come eat black cake served with hot porter mixed with nutmeg and sugar." Those invited expressed their thanks. But the possibility of the evening Lockwood had outlined seemed, to Brainard, horribly remote.

It was Lieutenant Kislingbury who, in Brainard's eyes, had of late become a real contributor. He and the fallen lieutenant regularly climbed the hill behind their hut to see what could be seen toward the Greenland coast. The C.O. seemed dead set on crossing Smith Sound when it froze. But, Brainard wondered, how could we transport Elison? It didn't seem possible to sledge him over an upheaved surface, hard enough when they were strong. They were not strong anymore.

The weakest were Jewell, Ellis, Israel, and now Linn and Elison. It was the weakest who clung to the notion that Lieutenant Garlington would come sledging across the horizon. Corporal Salor, who had remained in the background for the past two and a half years, was of the same mind. Hope, Brainard concluded, was hard to quash. He knew hope was necessary for survival, *but we cannot rely on hope alone. Why,* he asked himself, *do men need to believe in impossible things?* Emerson had written: "Trust thyself." His parents had the great philosopher's *Essays* on the parlor shelf. They didn't have many books, but as a boy he had been drawn to that shelf. The Bible was kept there, as was the *Enchiridion* of the Greek philosopher Epictetus. He suddenly found himself wanting to laugh at a line someone—perhaps his father—had underlined in Epictetus. "Why, then, do you walk as if you had swallowed a ramrod?" His thoughts flew to Greely. That ramrod was growing thinner, here, at Camp Clay, a process that had begun on the ice floes. Another line, not so amusing, but as true, from Epictetus: "The good or ill of man lies within his own will." And this, Brainard thought, connects with Emerson's great words in his "Self-Reliance." That none of us knows what we can do until we try. Rice must agree with that. Lockwood, too—that is, the Lockwood of the Farthest North. Dana, he was sure, would agree with Emerson, though he couldn't have read his work, at least not as a young man. Another Emersonian gem sprang into his mind: "What I must do is all that concerns me, not what the people think." *I know not what lies in store for us, but I still have my mind, I still have control over my own thoughts.*

"I ate two fox paws last night." Lieutenant Lockwood's voice broke into Sergeant Brainard's musings. "They are little more than bone. But as I chewed up the bones—cranberry jelly revolved through my mind. It is there still." Lockwood looked up, suddenly to find they were all staring at him. "Is everything cranberry jelly for you fellows?" No one replied. The C.O. ahemed, and that caused Lockwood to lift a hand to his mustache, his nails ragged and blackened from the greasy smoke. Brainard looked at his own nails, similarly encrusted. *Where are we headed? How is this going to end?*

✻

3

The psychology of people exposed to "natural starvation" is as much a psychology of fear and desperation as a psychology of hunger and food deprivation.

Ancel Keys, *The Biology of Human Starvation* (1950)

Nothing seemed to change. The wind was always howling. Because it was continually dark, time didn't move forward in the regular way of night separated by day. The darkness on moonless cloudy nights had a subterranean quality that sucked away hope. They were stuck here. Stuck like flies in amber. They were waiting. Outside, the black rocks high above loomed, but gave little protection. Inside, the boat-roof and walls were heavily coated with hoarfrost, moisture frozen from their own respiration. When the men brushed against this, they rained down on themselves their own breath. As much as they chinked their fortress, the wind found them, sending spindrift that covered their bags and their unprotected faces. The wind kept them from sleep. They were denned up like foxes. Just lying next to a fellow human brought a degree of comfort. Someone you could complain to about how damn cold your feet were. Those in the single bags were colder and lonelier, but all were kept damp from their body heat melting the spindrift and the hoarfrost. When they crawled in from being outside, they were nearly overcome by their own stink, by the urine smell in their fetid clothes. But they had grown used to this. In the extremity of their isolation, this smell meant home.

Sergeant Brainard tried to remember what normal life felt like but checked himself. He was better off just forgetting about being clean, wearing freshly laundered clothes, a pair of pants and a shirt, crisp and dry from hanging on his mother's clothesline. Clean hands were in a different life. *Cleanliness is next to godliness, David.* He could hear his mother's voice. His hands were encrusted with filth, rough as an unplaned board, small cuts that never healed in the cold, nails torn, fingers blistered from frostbite, and always there was the grease from their oily, smoky fires. He would not want his mother to see his hands.

This soot turned the snow outside a dirty gray and spread among the empty tins, the bent and twisted barrel hoops, shreds of canvas, a boot with the sole ripped off. No clothing. Those discarded rags were used for chinking. The snow near their entrance was urine-stained, and a few paces off, the piles of excrement began. Wild animals kept themselves cleaner, David Brainard thought. *But I hardly see this filth now. I'm used to it.* They were living in a way that was almost impossible to express in human terms, causing Brainard to marvel over the adaptability of man.

Their stores sergeant had managed to turn their Thanksgiving into a real feast with a bill of fare that started with a soup of seal meat and fox feet. Since nothing resembling food was wasted, the sergeant instructed the cooks to add the fox's intestines, an experiment that turned out to be highly prized by those fortunate to find them in their bowls. This was followed by seven ounces of hard bread to each man *and* butter that was got by cutting into rations of the next three mornings. When the rice pudding was served out, Sergeant Brainard related that this was made with six pounds of rice, five pounds of raisins, and three cans of milk—all heated not on the sheet-iron stove but over the alcohol lamp, making it warmer. As they licked their fingers over this incomparable rice pudding, Lieutenant Lockwood began to speak. "At home they are eating oysters, turkey, squash, pies, cakes, indeed all the delicacies of the day. My father is at the head of the table. He is carving . . ." The lieutenant's voice cracked and a silence descended, broken only by the men's pocketknives scraping the frozen bits off the sides of their tins.

Finally Ned Israel said, "When I'm home next Thanksgiving, I shall tell them that at Camp Clay we celebrated with an actual pound of food per man. I wonder if they'll believe me?"

"I'll tell you what." Lieutenant Lockwood had recovered himself. "Let's each of us dictate his favorite dish. I'll write it down in shorthand in my diary. Then when we're home again we can choose from these menus, and on our next birthdays invite any of the others who might be nearby." Any talk about food had the power to draw them together. The acrimony and petty squabbles fell away. They sat up straighter in their bags, eyes brighter, faces more alert. Even Dr. Pavy, Brainard noticed, joined in this game.

"Let's go around the circle," Lockwood instructed. "I'll start. My favorite dish is cold roast turkey stuffed with oysters and eaten with cranberries." He had his inkwell in his mittened hand; he unscrewed the cap and dipped in his pen. Lieutenant Lockwood was the only one who continued to write in ink. "Now you, Lieutenant Greely," he said.

"My wife makes the best Parker House rolls in the world," the C.O. said, "and the best coffee. Write down, as well, cheese omelet, chicken curry with rice, and preserved strawberries. Henrietta and I picked strawberries together only a few weeks before I left." He sighed heavily and drew his hand down his black beard, thick with frost.

Dr. Pavy spoke up for pâté de foie gras. "My wife is not French," he said, "but I have taught her the secrets of how to make this pâté."

The German boys—Schneider, Bender, Shorty Frederick, Long, Biederbick—requested heavy meat dishes of pork or sausage or spareribs, roasts, tenderloin, and schnitzels. Charlie insisted upon hamburg beefsteak. "It's my favorite dish," he said, "and I want it smothered in onions." Ned Israel allowed he would eat anything as long as it came from the German Jewish butcher his mother frequented.

Lockwood wrote down all the dishes in shorthand, then said, "I'll add roast oysters, peaches and cream. Any of my childhood dishes at home."

"Please name some of them, Lieutenant Lockwood," Whisler demanded.

"Rice pudding, not like what we just ate, though I know the cooks did their best, but the way my dear mother cooks it, very thick, milky, and rich." A dreamy look spread across the lieutenant's face. "My mother's doughnuts and flaky scones," he sighed. "I'm determined to have a good day's allowance for tomorrow so I will save a little of my bread." They watched as he tucked a morsel into his pocket. "I wonder," he went on, "if the dear ones at home are thinking of me as I am thinking of them." He slipped his ink and his pen, wrapped in a handkerchief, back into his bag. The wind buffeted their hovel and the loneliness descended. There was audible snuffling, prompting Lieutenant Greely to say, "Well, men, we will finish off this Thanksgiving feast with a milk punch, made with the lemons from the wreck cache. Sergeant Brainard, please fetch the rum from the storeroom." This raised a weak cheer, and Lieutenant Lockwood remarked, "Perhaps with the stimulation of the rum, my feet will warm. I don't like to complain, but they've been cold all day."

✷

Camp Clay

1 December 1883

Dearest Henrietta,

I miss you so much. At Conger I wanted you until my body ached. It is strange how that yearning has eased, due, I imagine, to the privation we are undergoing now. But the missing has strengthened. I miss your voice; I miss the sight of your calm face. You knew what I was thinking before I'd thought it myself, and I wish now, more than anything, for your words as I try to think beyond my own miseries to my moral responsibility to these men. We are ravenous and irritable, and in that "we" I include myself. One of our scientific observers, Sergeant Gardiner, confided that while he realized the fairness of the cooks in allowing a cup of tea or a plate of stew to pass through his hands, he could not prevent himself from mentally weighing the dish and comparing it to the portion that came to himself. My dear, I understand his feeling. I myself have avoided handling another man's portion.

If the others possessed such a conscience all would be well in the narrow confines of our camp. But our commissary has been broken into more than once. My duty is to nip this thievery before the disease infects us all. Stealing food from starving men is a despicable act. It is a form of mutiny, punishable by death. I only pray to God I am not driven to this. The tribunal here are the men themselves who have had their food stolen. My concern is heightened by Rice's failure to bring in the English meat from Cape Isabella. Perhaps I should have let him return for it as he wanted. But I refuse to second-guess myself, and will stretch our food until April 1, if I have to. Dr. Pavy continues to object to any reduction in rations. I am the commander here and he is compelled to abide by my decisions. That he knows this does not improve the state of things between him and me.

I gave Lieutenant Lockwood the assignment of caching our records—the pressed plants, the animal skins, all the scientific equipment brought with us from Fort Conger—because the lieutenant is a man of action and susceptible to losing heart when not in active pursuit of a goal. He erected a large cairn on Stalknecht Island, a spot more certain to be visited by a relief expedition. Our camp here is not visible to ships arriving from the south. I am determined that our work at Conger shall not perish with us. Lieutenant Lockwood stuck the pendulum upright in the top of the cairn, assuring me it will be seen by any ship approaching the Sabine coast.

Forgive me, my dear wife, I cannot go on. My fingers holding my pencil are numb and my candle flickering. I kiss you good night, and the children,

Dolph

✻

High, high up in the sky above Camp Clay the stars scintillated and sparkled, stabs of light in a slate-black setting. "Imagine being encased in an iceberg," Ned Israel said, "and that doesn't come close to how cold you'd be in the upper atmosphere. That kind of cold could shrivel you. Like holding a burning match to a sheet of paper. It's drier, too," he assured them. This Arctic air they were breathing was dry enough, yet despite the dryness, pinpricks of moisture filled the atmosphere like diamonds. The temperatures, taking note of the sun's distance from Earth as the winter solstice came on, held steady readings of below the thirty below mark.

When the moon rose on such clear, frigid nights, illuminating the icebergs in the sound, these ill-clothed, half-starved men were drawn out of their hovel by the imperative of the intense white light. The icebergs were lit as if by a thousand candles, their shaft-like shapes reflecting, absorbing, shifting, expanding, even dancing like prisms in the terrible cold. The men stood, held in a kind of frozen awe as the cold drilled into their bones, then like a flock of birds, wheeled for cover, and under their tread the supercooled snow squeaked and squealed like small animals in pain. Yet even on these coldest nights came the unwelcomed sound of the grinding pack, meaning that Smith Sound remained unfrozen.

✻

21 December 1883

Dearest Lilla Mae,

I write you on the solstice. The glorious sun has commenced its return, though we will not see his face until the end of February. While I write "we," I disassociate myself from these men. I, too, am affected by the hunger but choose to keep my distance from daily life at Camp Clay. By way of illustration, Lieutenant Greely asked if I would participate in a history discussion he was starting up. He laid it out for me. "We'll begin,

Doctor, with the construction of the pyramids in Egypt, move forward to the Roman conquest in England, then to Charlemagne in France. I would be much obliged if you would take us through the line of French kings up to the present day." *Naturellement* this interested me, but I remained silent. I wanted him to beg. "My aim, Doctor, is to give the men something to think about other than their hunger and discomforts." I assumed a preoccupied look. "I hope you can enlighten us, Doctor," he finally said. "It would be a boon to the men as well as to myself." This was more to my liking. I told him I would give him my answer in a day or two. He looked annoyed, but maintained enough control to say, "I'd be much obliged, Doctor."

I made him wait a suitable time and would have drawn it out longer except Christmas was fast approaching. I didn't want to put off our conversation so long it would get lost in this much-anticipated event, a feast day, the menu of which was the men's current topic of discussion. So, I sent him a message by way of a man I have been cultivating, one Private Henry, requesting that Lieutenant Greely pay me a visit. Certain occasions demand such formality. The lieutenant crawled over to my bag, positioned next to Elison, my patient, whom I feed by hand.

"Lieutenant Greely," I began, "I am inclined to accept your proposal." He looked suitably relieved. "However, I suggest you extend your discussion series to embrace American history. Many of these men come from immigrant families, and I dare say know little about the country in which they have found themselves."

"A good suggestion, Doctor."

He knew he had to agree if he were to get my help. "You yourself," I said, condescendingly, "could discourse on the American Civil War."

"I would be glad to," he said. "I was seventeen when I enlisted. I saw action at Ball's Bluff. I was twice wounded at Antietam and was commissioned a second lieutenant. Several here can talk about the recent Indian warfare. Sergeant Brainard was wounded in the face. Did you know that, Doctor?" I watched Greely's fingers flutter to his chin where, at Antietam, the ball had penetrated. I assured him I did, though, in truth, I did not.

"The battle with the Sioux, at Muddy Creek. He took a bullet to his right hand and another to his right cheek. His eye was affected, but, really, I believe he sees better than I."

"I am sure of it," I could not resist saying, and from his startled look saw he was piqued. Well, my dear wife, I live for such moments that allow me to gain superiority over this man who styles himself our leader. He is not mine! I shall report my dialogue to Private Henry. He despises Lieutenant Greely as much as I. Why, just this morning this private was forced to work on the waterhole—we're having the devil's own time keeping it open. He pleaded his frostbitten foot, but this time the commander would not listen. Private Henry is a man who is quite adept at preserving his life. He is determined to return so he can be hailed a hero. When Sergeant Brainard reports a break-in to his commissary, it is Private Henry who is blamed. He is not always in the wrong, though wrongdoing on his part means food in his stomach. I, too, know how to feed myself. Take comfort from this, my dear. It means your Octave will return to you.

Je t'embrasse,
Octave

✳

Christmas Day was clear and calm; Ned Israel reported a temperature of -35 degrees. It was Lieutenant Kislingbury's birthday. He turned thirty-eight. At breakfast Sergeant Brainard expressed the hope that nothing should be said to mar the pleasure of the day. And, indeed, the men did their best, with Lieutenant Kislingbury outdoing everyone by rolling cigarettes for all the smokers from his own scant store of tobacco. "In honor of my birthday," he told them. Since they had been cutting their tobacco with thrice-used tea leaves, Kislingbury's gift was generous indeed. The smokers immediately lit up and the soft glow from the ends of their cigarettes illuminated the dark interior of the hut in a way that, Sergeant Brainard felt, was almost festive. Little dancing points of light flickered on and off like fireflies, briefly illuminating each man's face.

The bill of fare was much the same as their Thanksgiving feast and closed with a similar rum punch, the only objection, expressed in a joking manner, that there was not more of it. Someone started a song and someone else suggested they go around the circle and sing songs in the languages of the countries they represented: France, Luxembourg, Germany, England, Canada, the United States of course, with the two

Eskimos contributing their native melodies. To top everything, Lieutenant Greely surprised his men by having the cooks prepare a few ounces of hot chocolate, after which Lieutenant Lockwood announced he was "too full for utterance."

"Really, Lieutenant," Private Charlie Henry broke out in his loudest, most sarcastic voice, "I don't see how that's possible." And there, right at the end, rang the sour note Sergeant Brainard had hoped to avoid. To counter it, everyone raised a great clamor in praise of the cooks and the feast they had turned out. "What I want to say," Charlie's roar downed them all, "is that if I could feel my hunger appeased by our Christmas dinner that would be all I would ask from the day."

"And have you?" Rice inquired. He was not smiling.

Bender piped up in his squeaky voice. "Have you, Charlie? Have you?"

"You little . . ." Charlie swung around toward Bender. He wanted to hit him but knew Bender was only asking a simple innocent question. He got control of himself and answered Rice. "This morning, when the C.O. gave the order to light up the stove, Sergeant Rice, I will tell you that I prayed, I actually *prayed* with my eyes shut: *Dear God let this meal fill me.*"

There was a small round of laughter at this, Charlie being more inclined to take the Lord's name in vain than otherwise.

"And did it?" asked Rice.

"Did it, Charlie? Did our Christmas dinner fill you?" squealed Bender.

"What's wrong with you, you little prick," Charlie shouted at Bender.

"If the Christmas dinner filled you, then you won't be forced to steal our food," Bender said.

Charlie's face, dark with the greasy smoke, turned several shades darker. He raised his hands and for a moment Brainard thought he was going to strangle poor Bender. But he changed his posture and one arm reached around his bag-mate's shoulders. "I would never steal food, Bender. You know that. Only a nasty thief would steal food from starving men."

Bender stared up into Charlie's face, his mouth agape. Time stood still inside their hovel and Brainard was quite sure that if they weren't half-sedated from Christmas dinner, these men would have picked up on Bender's remark. But on the other hand, some of the others steal, and so might be reluctant to accuse Private Henry for fear of being accused themselves. This pause, however, gave Charlie the opportunity he needed, and turning to Rice, he said, "I have had enough. Or nearly enough," he couldn't help but add.

"In honor of our Christmas," Sergeant Brainard said, "I've been reading *A Christmas Carol* by Charles Dickens. This story is filled with food. Lieutenant Lockwood"—he turned to his friend—"you of all people must remember the horn of plenty at the feet of Christmas Present. Even you would be hard-pressed to rival this description. Let me read it." And Brainard picked up the book that had to come to them along with the *Pickwick Papers* in Garlington's cache. "'Heaped up on the floor, to form a kind of throne, were turkeys, geese, game, poultry, brawn, great joints of meat, suckling pigs, long wreaths of sausages, mince-pies, plum puddings, barrels of oysters, red-hot chestnuts, cherry-cheeked apples, juicy oranges, luscious pears, immense twelfth-cakes, and seething bowls of punch, that made the chamber dim with their delicious steam.'"

"Oh my God," Lockwood breathed, and he covered his face with his hands.

"Then, my friend," Brainard went on, "do you remember what the Cratchit family ate? They were poor as church mice, you know."

"Bob Cratchit," Private Henry broke in. "He was a clerk for Mr. Scrooge." He reached for the book. "Mrs. Cratchit cooked the Christmas goose." He thumbed through the pages. "Here's my favorite part, 'Mrs. Cratchit, Looking slowly all along the carving knife, prepared to plunge it in the breast; but when she did, and when the long expected gush of stuffing issued forth . . .'" He stopped. He let out a sigh of pleasure and said, "I can smell it. Can't you all smell it?"

"Read more. Read more," Bender urged. He was wriggling with excitement.

Brainard reclaimed the book. "It was a small goose, 'eked out with apple-sauce and mashed potatoes.' The Cratchits were a large family and they ate that goose right down to the bones. And Mrs. Cratchit had baked a pudding, too, very small and round as a cannon ball. I imagine no one got more than a sliver . . ."

"With a green holly branch stuck into the top," Charlie chimed in.

"Plenty of brandy, I hope," said Lockwood. "My mother always makes sure of the brandy and she herself carries in the Christmas pudding blazing to the table."

"Mrs. Cratchit carried in her pudding blazing too," said Brainard, and he gazed around at their gaunt faces. "No one was so rude to comment," he said, "that it was too small a pudding for such a large family."

"Tiny Tim," took up Private Henry, "he said God bless us every one."

Brainard looked over to where this private slouched in his grimy bag, but his words were spoken in earnest; absent was the sarcastic bite. Was it too much to hope that his Christmas message had sunk in? If we continue as now, Brainard said to himself, there will be little danger of losing our minds.

✳

A day or two later Private Henry told Bender he no longer wanted him as a bag-mate.

"How come, Charlie? Do I snore?" inquired poor Bender.

This sounded so pathetic to Sergeant Brainard that he kept alert to what would happen next. He was quite sure Private Henry was ridding himself of Bender for his remark about Henry's stealing food. Sure enough, Charlie asked Connell to move in. Connell would, but wanted to bring along Ralston, his present bag-mate. "He sleeps most of the time," Connell added, "very useful for imparting his body heat." Ralston, Brainard knew, was one of the malingerers. Ralston, as an observer, was supposed to be helping Israel with the outside weather readings, but Israel was so conscientious, Ralston got away with contributing little. This was the man who had run through his wife's inheritance from her first husband. Ralston's true nature—preying on those weaker than himself—seemed to be coming to the fore. Brainard was quite sure Ralston had lifted cans off the shelves at Conger. The man didn't seem troubled by his conscience.

Bender moved into a bag with Schneider and Cross. Schneider was holding up well, helping with the camp chores of working up firewood from the barrels and fetching water. Cross, however, was nearly silent now. He used their urine tub during the day, not troubling to go out, and Brainard, if asked who would be the first to die, would have put his money on Cross. The man, after all, had led a dissipated life, and that left him ill-prepared to resist their present hardship.

That afternoon Lieutenant Greely, in an effort to stimulate discussion, talked about Kentucky, raising horses there. Sergeant Jewell contributed by talking about a relative who bred horses in that state. Salor surprised everyone by saying he knew someone who raised horses somewhere, he couldn't remember where, but possibly Kentucky. Schneider tried to draw out Salor, but that was all that could be pried. Private Henry indulged himself in a monologue. "Information," he said, "that sifts to you third- or fourth-hand is no better than hearsay. This ridiculous discussion has put me in a loathsome frame of mind, and here's why. I see field after field of green. I smell the grass. It has a freshness that is the exact counter to the offal smell inside our hovel. I see glossy-coated thoroughbreds, against the green, munching, munching, munching. I hear their horsy molars grinding. I *hear* them, I tell you." The private put his own hands over his ears in an effort to block out the sound. "Grinding as they stuff their bellies to a roundness that plunges me into a rage of envy." He began a frantic search in his bag, twitching and turning.

"What the devil are you doing?" Connell grumbled. "Get your stinking hands away from me."

"Food, food, food," Henry's voice was muffled, coming from inside the bag.

"You won't get at mine," Connell growled.

This roused Ralston, who began checking his pockets to make sure he still had the few morsels saved from their last meal, but since protecting his secreted tidbits was so automatic with him, he settled back down as soon as they were located.

"I'll send to California for the recipe of the Chinese way of making curry and rice with chicken." Lockwood was addressing his commanding officer. He nodded to Cross. "I promise to eat Welsh rarebit, black cake, and drink eggnog with you."

Cross came alive at that and caught everyone's attention by saying, "That will give me enormous pleasure, Lieutenant. I will introduce you to my wife."

"The honor is mine," Lockwood graciously said. "I will bring the cake."

"And my wife and I will furnish the other articles. She makes a Welsh rarebit that is acclaimed in our county. She makes it with quantities of beer." Cross gave Lockwood a sly wink.

Private Henry, who had by now righted himself, said noisily, "Why Lieutenant Lockwood would want to eat anything with that surly fellow I can't imagine." Then he laughed. "Ha! Ha! Welsh rarebit with beer. I'd eat that with Cross, I'd eat anything with anyone."

At supper that night, Brainard noticed how Henry kept his eye on Shorty, who was cook that day, dishing out the mess. As did Connell. Ralston had come alive at the sight of food, and the three of them sat up in their bag, holding their tins, resembling three peas in a pod, to use a favorite aphorism of his mother's. But these three, winking and smirking, exchanging covetous glances as Shorty began passing around the plates, filled Brainard with some degree of horror. Why, he thought, they're eyeing our food like predators. They would eat it all if they could. They could watch us starve without turning a hair. He looked over then at Lieutenant Greely. Their C.O. sat ramrod straight against the sloping wall. He was wearing his spectacles, customary when the mess was being served, and the soft glow from the stove played over the frames. He had the afghan that his wife had made for him around his shoulders. Mrs. Greely had knitted in their initials, and that must be such a comfort to him, Brainard thought. It's a comfort to me, to see him sitting there so calm. I'm sure his orderly demeanor serves to hold some of them in check. Sergeant Brainard's glance swung back to the three, who, now that they had received their portions, wasted no time in shoving it into their mouths, smacking their lips over the pitifully small portion of tonight's glop: a can of beef stew seasoned with two dog biscuits. *But how long can the chaos be held at bay?* Brainard wondered.

✳

Private Henry's True & Accurate Account of the LFB Expedition

26 December 1883

I am in a foul mood because all this month there's been no opportunity to visit Sergeant Davy's food larder. There is so much waking up at night with the need to piss, I have not had an undisturbed moment. I shed that twenty-five pounds I'd put on at Conger on the boat trip. But if I had not gained it in the first place, I'd be as bad off as the rest of them. Here's good news: our mess has taken it in hand to appoint someone other than the cook, in our case Shorty Frederick, to pass around the plates. Shorty is fair and square, playing favorites would go against his nature, but this job will rotate on a daily basis and I hope to benefit from the rotation. The other mess trusts to Long, who cooks and also passes around the tins. Do I wish I were in that mess? It includes Lieutenant Lockwood. Even so, I say no. As I trust no one.

✸

The sound had not iced over. At 20 to 40 degrees below zero, it was certainly cold enough. It was the first week of January and what these men were counting on had not happened. Lieutenant Greely's opinion was that the unusually strong currents as well as the tides must have defeated any attempt of the ice to remain firm for long. The incessant wind, too. He reminded them how defenseless they were against this turbulence in their open boats. Smith Sound would start to ice over— they could tell because of the silence. In absence of the usual din, they would lie in their bags imagining they could hear the sledges clattering over the ice. Dogs yelping. Shouts. Footsteps tramping toward their hut. It was Garlington. He had arrived! They were so sure, they scrambled out. But nothing. No one was there. Only the ice grinding and shifting of the pack. They hated that sound.

Lieutenant Greely was a very different man from the martinet of Conger who prevented daytime napping and restricted their walks. "I am proud of all of you," he told them, "for how calmly we can discuss our almost certain fate if no assistance comes from Littleton Island." *They would die.* But, as Sergeant Brainard thought to himself, just being able to say that left them more peaceful in their minds. It was like the kind of talk he had shared with Shorty or Long at Fort Ellis, on the eve of a battle against the Sioux or the Nez Perce. You were confiding to a buddy that you might not survive. Not that you said those words, but it helped to know that the other fellow understood. Yet no one could dismiss from his mind that *Garlington could be over there.* They needed to say that, too. Sergeant Brainard knew that. They needed to sustain that hope to keep themselves alive.

Right around New Year's, for no obvious reason, or perhaps the reason was that no matter how much of their own ragged clothing they stuffed to chink their "mansion," as Private Henry called it, the drafts could not be stopped, a gaming element took over the men at Camp Clay. Or maybe it was the stifling darkness, or that each man was sick of every other man, or that nothing they could do made any impression on the fetid smells of confined living, or the sounds—each man could be identified by his snore, by his cough, by the distinctive way he turned in his sleeping bag, by the way his knees scraped along the aisle when he went to relieve himself. But most of all what set off the gaming was their obsession with food itself, ignited by their own raging hunger.

"I'll trade you that piece of hard bread for my dog biscuit." Charlie waved the biscuit under Schneider's nose. He grabbed it. The trick was to hit at a man's weak spot, the dogs in Schneider's case, or, as Connell put it, "You keep an eye on what a man saves because he saves what he craves."

Bread for butter, meat for bread, bread for soup. Lieutenant Lockwood traded half of his son-of-a-gun—a bread pudding made with milk and raisins—their most prized breakfast because it best filled the hunger hole—for eight ounces of Biederbick's bread. But as the hospital steward wolfed down the son-of-a-gun, along with his ordinary breakfast, he ended up with an overfilled and aching stomach.

Sergeant Brainard, on the other hand, had secured a hard bread pudding from Jewell. He spooned it down at breakfast along with his own allowance and spent the rest of the morning lying in his bag in a dreamy state. He was amazed at how comfortable he was and announced to no one in particular, "I feel on better terms with myself."

"I, too, am perfectly warm," Lieutenant Lockwood responded. "I slept through the night." Then he added, "But I don't like this marketing. It resembles gambling. I know my father would think the less of me for it. In our hunger, we are taking advantage of the cravings of those about us."

"That's exactly the point," Charlie sneered.

This stirred up Connell, who said, "Lieutenant Lockwood, I'll swap you that bread for the next fox shot by Sergeant Brainard."

"That's speculation!" cried Kislingbury. "What if the sergeant never shoots another fox?"

"He will," remarked Connell. And with that both Linn and Elison offered to take Connell up on the deal.

Elison's remaining foot had dropped off that morning, but per the doctor's instructions, no one had told him. Elison should be told, but did Elison really need to know he was never going to walk again? If Garlington showed up, there would be some point in telling Joe Elison about the state of his feet. Otherwise, why give him this disagreeable news?

Charlie began laughing harder than he had in a long time. "You men would turn over your food to Connell when the fox isn't bagged and might never be bagged? Goddamn! You are a pack of fools."

Everyone began offering an opinion of whether Sergeant Brainard would shoot a fox, when the C.O. stepped in. "Men," he intoned, "I find this market-day atmosphere offensive and unworthy of army men. I will not allow Camp Clay to turn into an Arab bazaar."

"Really, men," Rice said in his quiet steady voice, "how can we maintain a spirit of helpful cooperation if we engage in this competitive trading?"

"What a killjoy the C.O. is," Charlie said to Connell. "Can't he see we're just passing the time? But Rice is right, you know."

"I don't care a damn about what Rice thinks," Connell smirked. "Listen, Charlie, let's you and me continue to carry out a little high-level trading."

"But you don't hoard food."

"That doesn't matter."

"Forget it, Connell. It's no fun, anyway, after what Rice said. Just shut up, will you?"

"You're telling me to shut up? Well, damn you!" Connell heaved himself upright, clenched fists in the air.

"Back off, you blasphemous hot-tempered Irishman. My stomach is at ease right now. All I want is to lie flat and enjoy the feeling of it. It never lasts long, and when it goes the hunger returns stronger than ever. And listen"—Charlie put his hand on Connell's upraised arm— "Lockwood's talking."

"Cracked wheat with honey and milk," Lieutenant Lockwood murmured. He was lying on his back, addressing the overturned boat above his head. "Summer strawberries. Beef à la mode."

"What could beef à la mode possibly be, Connell? No, no, don't ask him now. Don't cut off his lovely words. Not when I'm as comfortable as a cow chewing her cud in a grassy green pasture."

Over the next two mornings, Sergeant Brainard reported that food had been lifted from his commissary. A hole had been cut in the canvas, then carefully covered by snow blocks. Sergeant Brainard had his eye on two men. He set a spring gun and told everyone that anyone who tampered with the provisions did so at risk to his life. The gun was there; they could see the metallic gleam of the barrel. "I can't believe Sergeant Brainard would mean to kill a man," Private Henry said to Connell. The Irishman, lying on his back with his hands behind his head, looked Charlie in the eye and winked. The wink seemed to say: *You'd better watch yourself.* "I don't want to get shot," Charlie said. "I want to return a hero." What Charlie didn't know, what none of them knew except Lieutenant Greely because Sergeant Brainard had told him, was that the spring gun was not loaded.

Sergeant Brainard reported that a full barrel marked English Hard Bread in black letters had been cracked open and about five pounds of bread extracted. He knew Private Henry was out with the ax breaking up empty barrels for firewood, but he hadn't seen him in action. The evidence was circumstantial. No accusation could be made, but that didn't stop the uproar when he told the others of the stolen bread at supper.

"The dirty thief. He's eating our food."

"We'll die the sooner."

"Arrest him."

"Who is it?"

"He's killing us."

"We should kill him!"

"Make him confess."

"I'm willing to offer my bread," Rice said. He pulled his supper ration out of his own food can, "if the culprit will admit his thieving and promise to reform."

"I'll do the same." Lockwood dug into his own precious can and displayed a dog biscuit.

This had every man in the hut pulling out food—mostly bread since it was easiest to save—to draw a confession from the thief in their midst, Private Henry, Brainard took note, shouting the loudest, "Take mine, take *my* bread you thieving bastard!"

No one admitted to the crime and silence descended upon the hut. The men lay in their bags, exhausted by this outburst, while out in the sound the ice ground and thrashed in a turmoil of tide changes and the unrelenting wind.

✱

Camp Clay at Cape Sabine

8 January 1884

My Dearest Wife,

I have just spent a sleepless night. The doctor is stealing Elison's bread. I am sure of it. I heard the muffled scrabbling of his fingers against the tin, the same sound his hand makes when he is feeding his patient. I am directly across our narrow aisle from Dr. Pavy; I am quite certain I am right. The darkness in our hut is profound, but my hearing has grown acute to compensate. A few moments later, I heard him chewing. Much chewing goes on at night. The men hoard food and eat it then. A nibble of chocolate or a bite of bread can provide the bit of warmth needed to send us into a doze. And the masticating helps the time to pass. I speak from my own experience. Nonetheless, nighttime eating aside, the scrabbling in the can, followed by the grinding of the doctor's jaws, convinces me that Dr. Pavy is a thief. A thief of the vilest sort as he is preying upon his patient. You may be assured I will keep my eyes on him. And ears, too!

I spent several hours staring up into the darkness and came to the conclusion that I must remain silent. If I confront the doctor openly, this is sure to be the spark that will cause us to break. I, as the leader of this expedition, must not let this happen. There are those who would support the doctor. Our best chance of survival is to stay united. I owe it to the men to restrain myself and not to antagonize the doctor. Aside from preserving the party's unity, we are in need of his services, and will only come to need them more.

I am deeply shocked by the doctor's action. There are others here who could feed the doctor's patient without a thought to stealing his food. Sergeant Brainard, of course. He handles all our provisions, meal by meal. The men have never seriously questioned his honesty. I, too, could feed Elison because, if I were tempted, I would think of you, my dear. I could not return to you if I had on my conscience stealing a man's food. George Rice could feed Elison even though it was on his trip that Elison ate snow and froze himself. Rice abandoned the English meat to save Elison, yet it's clear that Rice holds no resentment toward the man. Dr. Pavy could have given the job to his hospital steward, Biederbick, if he did not trust himself. Biederbick is trustworthy. But he did not.

Most of the men steal food, crumbs dropped by others, and when apprehended they are sorry, some abjectly so. But one or two display no conscience, and our stores have been broken into more than once. The men fully grasp the seriousness of this and could take matters into their own hands. I cannot let this happen. A murder at Camp Clay would bring on mayhem.

I have mentioned my concerns about the doctor to Sergeant Brainard, as he is a check against my thinking. I admit, also, I told him for the relief. As writing you, my dearest Henrietta, gives relief and allows me to see the incident as you would and so be guided by your own sound thinking. But, ah, my dear, I fear for our future. It is not the cold or darkness or even our restricted diet that is the real enemy here at Camp Clay. The doctor's action has opened my eyes. It is ourselves I fear. What will happen to us as we become, day by day, more demoralized? More, I hesitate to use the word, degenerated? If you could see us with our wild matted hair and beards you would take us for beasts.

In the night I am taken over by the desperateness of our situation. It shines a strong light on aspects of our natures of which we are unaware. Take Lieutenant Lockwood, who at supper last night dropped his bread, and while leaning to pick it up spilt his tea. It was only the last drop, but it might as well have been the whole cup, he was so cast down by it. Immediately Long, Biederbick, and myself insisted Lockwood take the remainder of our tea. But he refused, saying it was his own fault. We prevailed, however, and the lieutenant graciously received our offering. Then Ellis, still in the marketing mood that I have attempted to discourage, offered to trade with Lieutenant Lockwood for half a cupful. The lieutenant, I was glad to see, turned him down. Ellis is not a bad man, but, clearly, he meant to take advantage of Lockwood's misfortune. You can see, my dear, how we, sorely tried men, are tested. How, in our desperation, aspects of ourselves, normally held in check, are revealed.

Your loving husband,
Adolphus

✳

4

You forget how the loss of a biscuit crumb left a sense of injury which lasted for a week; how the greatest friends were so much on each others' nerves that they did not speak for days for fear of quarreling; how angry we felt when the cooks ran short on the weekly bag.

Apsley Cherry-Gerrard, *The Worst Journey in the World* (1922)

Above Camp Clay an unfathomable mass of black clouds pulled apart, then clashed together in a rhythmic collision of storm. A frantic wind began to sweep the surface of Smith Sound, searching for weaknesses in the pack, prying open fissures until the solid ice was rent apart as efficiently as a seamstress tears cloth in strips. Vapor rose from the open water in dense clouds until a thick mist filled the air above the sound. The companionable trio of wind and tide and currents kept the water open and the floes fighting each other in a continual noisy booming that further maddened the men of Camp Clay.

Israel reported the mercury frozen in the bulb at minus 39 degrees. So they didn't really know how cold it was, but there was no doubt that it was *cold*. The ice had broken up again, the pack ice slapping and jabbing and careening about in the sound, like a bar fight gone mad. In the hut they listened to Lieutenant Lockwood talking to himself about his favorite dishes. Cross, who was losing hold, babbled about his wife and his birthday. He would be forty tomorrow. The sun would return tomorrow, too. Cross was wrong about the sun, but the darkness was less intense, and Lieutenant Greely named February 2 as the day Rice and Jens would begin their journey to Littleton Island in search of assistance. They were already making preparations by cutting off the extra dog skin on Dr. Pavy's sleeping bag to make warm stockings.

"The doctor," Whisler chose this moment to inform them, "is eating Elison's bread."

Eyes shifted toward their doctor. He stared back at them, lips compressed, gaze steady. His beard was overgrown, his mustache as tangled as the rest, yet when Dr. Pavy tilted back his head and looked down his very straight French nose, he could intimidate with his aristocratic bearing, even in their present desperate setting. A profound silence had settled over them. The doctor slept beside Elison and had charge of Elison's bread can. They had all heard the scrabblings.

"Didn't you hear what I just said?" Whisler addressed this remark to the C.O.

Lieutenant Greely ran his fingers through his beard, seeking out the indentation where he had taken the shot at Antietam Bridge.

"I'm upset myself with the doctor," Lieutenant Lockwood broke in. "He has shut down my smoking. I find it a great deprivation even though I'm mainly smoking used tea leaves. But the doctor objects. He claims it causes my diarrhea."

"Please, Lieutenant Lockwood," Greely said. "Please stop."

"Bannock cake. Pudding of green corn," Lockwood began. He could not stop. "Eel and anchovy paste. Fisk and Gould Cafés, New York, Chatham Street. Curry, pumpkin butter—"

"Look to Sergeant Cross," Rice interrupted. "He appears to be dying."

"Prepare some soup with brandy for Sergeant Cross," Lieutenant Greely directed the cooks, and Brainard breathed an inward sigh of relief. This crisis with Cross was well timed. A confrontation with the doctor over Elison's bread could only bring on trouble. Greely crawled to Cross's bag, and with the help of Israel, propped the engineer up, supporting him against his own body. "If the soup is ready, I'll take it," he said. Long passed the can and a spoon. "This will do you good, Sergeant Cross," the C.O. said, but the soup the C.O. attempted to spoon into Cross's clenched jaw ran down his chin and was absorbed by his collar.

Private Henry, who was watching this procedure with the studiousness of a cat over a mousehole, interjected, "Look! He's too far gone to open his damn mouth. He's dribbling that food! It's all going to waste." He hoisted himself up. "I can't watch this," he said, and went out. By the time he came back, Bender and Jewell were sewing up Cross's corpse in a coffee sack.

"The doctor said he died of dropsical effusions of the heart," Connell told Charlie as he slid into their bag.

"That's bullshit," Charlie said. "The poor bastard starved to death."

"One less mouth to feed," the Irishman offered. "They'll bury him tomorrow. On his birthday."

"Lemon butter," came from Lieutenant Lockwood. "I will not allow Cross's death to depress me. I suppose it doesn't help that I can say little in favor of our engineer. Nor can I join the burial party. I am no longer fit for the work of hauling and digging. I congratulate Sergeant Brainard's foresight to go through the deceased's pockets. He always spoke so warmly of his wife, and now she will have his pocket watch to remember him by. We were to eat Welsh rarebit together, with eggnog and black cake."

"It's my birthday tomorrow, too," Gardiner announced. "I'll be twenty-seven."

"You'll pull through, Gardiner," Lockwood said. "You're young. Your wife is waiting for you at home. Just keep up your spirits." He reached across the space between them and squeezed Gardiner's arm.

Biederbick turned twenty-five on January 25.

Eskimo Fred celebrated his thirty-seventh birthday on the 26th.

On February 2, right after breakfast, Rice and Jens set off for the Greenland coast. The C.O. had attempted to strengthen them for the ordeal over the last week by adding a few ounces to their rations. The doctor had checked them over and pronounced them as fit as it was possible for half-starved men to be. Sergeant Brainard prepared bread, meat, and chocolate with a little rum thrown in for medicinal purposes. Their packs weighed fifty pounds apiece. It was not the food; it was the two-man sleeping bag and the canvas they would use for a tent. They could not haul the kayak, so hoped to find spots where the open water was bridged by ice.

Sergeant Brainard and Eskimo Fred carried their packs down to the ice foot. The four men stood in a wind that blew steadily out of the northwest and listened to the terrible grinding of the moving pack until Sergeant Brainard said, "God bless you." They shook hands and Rice and Jens strode into the bewildering confusion of the upheaved ice of Smith Sound. Sergeant Brainard was sure these brave men would be turned back, but he kept this thought to himself. The wind was forcing moisture from his eyes that, he realized, were real tears. He was overcome with the heroism of these two men who, for their comrades' sakes, were about to endure more than should be asked of anyone. He wiped his eyes to clear his vision and searched for Rice and Jens. They had vanished among the towering bergs, the menacing glassy shapes, of Smith Sound.

✶

The sun returned on February 12. According to Israel's calculations, it was 10 degrees above the horizon at noon, but invisible because of the dark water clouds. They had not seen the sun in 115 days.

To counter that good news, their waterhole was frozen to the bottom. If it's not one thing, it's another, went through Brainard's head and nearly made him laugh, his mother's words were so apt. No one had the strength to dig another, so they melted snow and ice, using as little fuel as possible, and were plagued by thirst. Lieutenant Lockwood became so pitifully persistent in his pleas for water that Lieutenant Greely melted ice for him with his body heat in his sleeping bag. This took hours and Lockwood was so grateful he wept, causing Israel and Bender to sniffle, until Private Henry cut it off with a bout of swearing that roused the C.O. to reprimand him for his blasphemy.

This seemed to settle them and raise spirits at the same time, causing Brainard to meditate on how predictable they were: Henry's swearing followed by the C.O.'s attempt to discourage it. He never will succeed, Brainard thought. Private Henry knows he can't be severely punished. He likes to swear, he likes to annoy Lieutenant Greely, and so he will keep on swearing. Our reactions to our life here are determined by our own mental makeup. Even our own health. Brainard remembered Private Biederbick, who, when they left Fort Conger, could hardly walk for his rheumatism. Now the hospital steward was working hard to help the weakest. In the face of cold and hunger, discomfort and despair, Biederbick had steadily improved in health and spirits. Why, Brainard wondered, do some men rise in adversity and others fall?

These daily trials were nothing compared to the sufferings of Rice and Jens. After just four days out, their trip to cross Smith Sound ended in near disaster. "We were forced to turn south," Rice explained, "to get around the open water." What I had feared, Brainard thought. Then a gale sprang up, their stove broke down, and they had to eat their food frozen, and Jens froze his fingers in the bag. "Sergeant Rice, he . . ." Jens demonstrated by inserting his hand between the buttons of his shirt to show how Rice had thawed out his fingers. "Then we run," Jens said. "I thought we might both freeze in that bag," Rice said. "We were best off running around in circles until it got light enough to move."

"Goddamn," Private Henry growled.

"I estimate that we traveled about fifty miles," Rice concluded, "but we never got more than a couple of miles away from the Sabine coast."

"Could you see over to the Greenland side?" Lieutenant Greely asked.

"Too stormy," Rice said.

"I propose that we set the date of March 6 for a crossing of the whole party," announced the C.O.

"Goddamn," Private Henry said, louder.

"Offensive language, Private. I could break you for that."

"He'll never get me pulling a sledge," Charlie said. His face was stony and he was lying on his back with his arms crossed, staring up at the boat-roof above their heads.

"I know that if it was you over on the Greenland side, Lieutenant Greely," Whisler said, "you'd come looking for us."

"If Lieutenant Garlington is not there himself, he would have left a competent officer," the C.O. said. "I can't believe that Littleton is empty of the army presence." He turned to Private Henry. "You will haul a sledge, Private. We will all bend our backs to the sledges. I owe it to all of you to get you safely to the Greenland side. If rescue will not come to us, we will seek it out ourselves."

"You hear that?" Connell said to his friend. "You're stronger than any one of us. You're stronger than me, dammit. You'll pull a sledge or, or I'll smash your face." The Irishman was close to sobbing.

"I'll be your sledging partner," Bender's squeak floated upward. "You can count on me, Charlie."

But Charlie Henry had burrowed into his bag, shutting out their begging and their pleas.

✱

Day followed day, and in each there was always the wind. Yet the wind in reality was many winds. Far above the smudged small dot of a camp on Cape Sabine was a great mass of moving air flowing from the west and southwest, air originally warm in its origin but now chilled when joined by Arctic tributaries. Coming up against this current was another high stream swirling clockwise around the pole and westward across Greenland and Baffin Bay. When the two giant rivers of air collided, they sprayed currents to the south and east, some high in the sky and some falling to earth. But all the while there were the constant shore winds coming from the sound, buffeting the barren rocks, the solitary camp, and its human inhabitants, clinging with frozen fingers to stay alive.

Sergeant Brainard was out on a walk. He needed time away from them. He needed to breathe clean air. He wanted to keep his legs in good working order. He had lost much of his strength. Their camp chores—chopping ice for water, breaking up barrels, and searching for other fuel—kept them active to some degree. But he was aware how long it took to perform even the simplest task. They all moved in a seeming slow motion, like automatons. David Brainard was determined to keep up his strength as long as he could. He had always liked to walk.

The waning moon lay low in the sky directly before him as he crested Cemetery Ridge. On this midmorning of February 19, he felt the sharp wind only on that part of his face not covered by his helmetlike cap above and scarf below, the wool beaded with frost from his own respiration. From inside the shell of the cinched hood, he peered out as though looking through the aperture of a camera.

A pinkish hue colored the horizon to the northeast, over Smith Sound, and in that faint light he could see whitecaps dotting the entire expanse of water. No ice of any description was visible, and the waves pounding the ice foot sounded to the sergeant's ears like the knell of their certain doom. He stopped when he made out an oblong of stones and stared down at his feet where the remains of Cross lay beneath a slight heap of gravel. The burial party had attempted to set off this first grave from the empty landscape by giving it a border of small stones. But to Brainard their pathetic effort seemed only to further emphasize the bleakness of their situation. A passing shadow made him look up to spot a raven. He reached his arms upward to this black bird.

Why, it's so beautiful. But how strange I can still see beauty here. How glad I am for that. If he had his gun, he would be forced to aim and fire at this creature for the few extra ounces it would give to their next meal. He issued that morning the last of their frozen bread, and yesterday they had finished off the English beef. He would issue the last of their tea tonight. But he was without his gun. He stood in the buffeting wind with his arms flung up to the raven, who rode wild and free through this empty land. *This raven can fly across Smith Sound, but we, I am very sure, will never cross to Greenland.* And his mind reeled back to their first week, when they were building Fort Conger, and he had taken that walk up Cairn Hill. *Could it be the same raven? We had been eye to eye. I felt such hope then, when I was young and strong.*

A few days later, George Rice reported that the ice had bridged the sound to the south. Spirits rose like a sunburst; escape seemed a certainty. All they needed was an intense cold calm spell to cement this newly formed bridge of drift ice. Two days later, under the influence of the destructive wind, the ice bridge vanished. Their mercurial spirits plummeted, and Lieutenant Kislingbury wrote Lieutenant Greely a letter. He was willing, he wrote in ink he had gone to the trouble to thaw, to conduct a small party of the strongest to Littleton Island as soon as the sound solidly froze. He employed Bender to carry the mail across the aisle and everyone watched as Lieutenant Greely unfolded the missive and read, first in silence, then aloud, to all of them. "Lieutenant Kislingbury," the C.O. addressed this man who had disappointed him, "getting all of my men to the Greenland side is foremost on my mind. But, I can tell you this, I will never divide the command or the party."

"Then," announced Kislingbury, "I hope you will not increase our meat ration until we have augmented our supply."

The C.O. remained silent. Brainard hoped he would stay silent and not get into an argument. What the fallen lieutenant had just said made little sense. There was very little meat left. The chances of augmenting their supply was nearly hopeless. Lieutenant Greely could be thinking, as Brainard was right now, that the doctor probably put Kislingbury up to this. In the open boats, it was Dr. Pavy and Kislingbury who proposed striking out on their own. The doctor, however, had vetoed every effort Greely made to cut rations, while at the same time urged that Elison's rations be increased. This, Lieutenant Greely had done, with the support of every man at Camp Clay, though they all knew this mainly benefited the doctor. But there was nothing to be done about it. They could not risk their doctor refusing to treat them. It was Pavy who held trumps in his match with Greely.

Kislingbury plunged on. "Lieutenant Greely, are you aware that Lieutenant Lockwood is using tobacco despite your orders, and Dr. Pavy's orders, too?"

"I never used tobacco," Lockwood defended himself.

"You did," said Private Henry. "We all saw you."

"I deny it. The doctor never issued such an order. If he had, or if Lieutenant Greely had, I would have followed orders."

"You smoked," Charlie persisted. He was lying on his side, leaning on an elbow. He looked relaxed. He was grinning.

"We all saw you," Connell chimed in.

Sergeant Brainard expected Lieutenant Greely to cut this off. It smacked of bullying. Poor Lockwood didn't seem to remember either the order or breaking it. He looked very put upon as he tried to bring some degree of management to his mustaches with shaking fingers. Brainard hated to witness the mental breakdown of this man who had led them to success on the Farthest North.

"Today's my birthday," Charlie asserted in a change of subject. "You bloody bastards forgot it. Not that the day of my birth is memorable. Nor is it a happy day at Camp Clay because Sergeant Brainard told us he issued the last of the blubber, the pickled onions, the dog biscuits, the coffee, and the beef extract." He ticked these items off on his grimy fingers. "Yet the sergeant says our stores will last until the first week of April. Though, by God, to pull that off, Lieutenant Greely will have to slash our daily rations further. And the doctor won't like that." Private Henry stared at Dr. Pavy, who was unresponsive.

On March 5, Sergeant Brainard issued the last of the corn, soup, tomatoes, and the English evaporated potatoes. The last can of lard went to the cooks on March 6, with a small portion retained for the treating of Elison's wounds.

On March 7, the men enjoyed what was left of the chocolate extract and the cloudberries.

On March 8, they all watched as the debris in the bottom of the rice bag was shaken into the morning's soup.

At each of these "lasts," Sergeant Brainard watched Private Henry for his reaction, but he showed no more than a glum resignation. Yet Brainard knew what Private Henry's hunger felt like because he felt the same. All these men felt a hunger beyond their imaginings: the gnawing in their guts made their chests burn with an evil sort of smarting that sent sudden shoots and hurtful pinpricks. Brainard knew they never ceased to think about food and how to get it, because that's what he thought about and dreamt about too: his mother's oatmeal sweetened with their own maple syrup. He would awake smelling it. What made their situation worse was that they received enough in their daily rations to stimulate their appetites, but not ever enough to satisfy. *We'd be better off if we had no food at all and could die quickly. Yet, all I can think about is how to get more food for them and so preserve our lives a little longer.* He needed to find some sort of food source fast. Already some of the men were having difficulty crawling to the urinal. On the Plains he had heard the story of the Frémont expedition, caught deep in the mountains by early snows, the game gone. When they began to starve, they ate their boots, then they chewed the leather on their knife scabbards and belts. It was well known that cannibalism was practiced by the mountain men. He just couldn't let that happen here. A stitch in time saves nine, he thought, and smiled at the homey aphorism, so in contrast to the horrible images that filled his mind.

✶

9 March 1884

My Dearest Lilla Mae,

There are too many Germans. German food is their favorite topic. You should hear them jabber about a dish they call hash. I am sick of hearing about how many ways there are to prepare this hash, a dish of the common people, consisting mainly of ground-up meat and potatoes. Each man has his favorite. Private Henry, whose nature interests me, describes his favorite dish, hamburg steak smothered in onions, which has him wiping the drool off his chin. I'm sure he's tasting it.

I will be frank with you, we are obsessed with food. My contribution to the discussion is pâté de foie gras. I could kill for it. The fat. I long to eat fat. Lieutenant Lockwood is mentally deranged by hunger. The men listen in a kind of exquisite pain as he talks about his mother's roasts, her scones and rolls, her hearty soups, her blancmange of a blue color. The men are fascinated by the color of this dessert that I have eaten a million times in France. The correct way, the French way, to prepare blancmange is with almonds and gelatin. "Is that how your mother prepares it?" I asked Lieutenant Lockwood. "I hope she doesn't substitute cornstarch." He assured me his mother prepared her blancmange with gelatin, but I am quite sure, Lilla Mae, that he had no idea what I was talking about. He was merely defending his mother's cooking. I will teach you to prepare blancmange in the French manner, but God forbid it should come out blue!

I talk about food, too, but not with such desperation. I will tell you why, my darling wife. Your clever Octave has found a way to supplement his diet. The man who frostbit his hands, and his feet, even his nose—he would be hideous to look at if it were not so dark in our hut. But I get off my subject. Your Octave suggested to Lieutenant Greely that this man be given more ounces than the rest of us to help him build his strength. I had a ruse behind this generous gesture. Private Elison has no hands. He cannot feed himself. I, the doctor, feed this man. I feed him faithfully. But as payment I take those extra ounces of his bread at night. He gets what he needs, I am not cheating him. I leave him no hungrier than the rest. But I get what I need to make sure I return to you, my beloved Lilla Mae. This Private Henry I have spoken of has a similar attitude. He doesn't hesitate to take what he can get. In his case, the thieving is more serious as he has broken into our stores. So far his assaults are circumstantial. The same is true in my case. I am suspected in lifting Elison's bread, but my position as doctor here protects me. Ha! Ha! I have the whole camp over a barrel, to use your quaint American expression!

I write you these things, Lilla Mae, not to terrify you, but to show you the odds I am up against. I write to assure: *I will return*. The day is not far off when your Octave will sweep you up in his enfolding arms and imprint his kiss on your trembling lips.

Your loving husband,
Octave

✴

The sun gained in strength and length each day. It had warmth and when Sergeant Brainard was out upon the rocks near the hut, laying a tempting bait of fox skins for crows he hoped would come and get shot, he lingered to enjoy the warmth. This sunlight, the sergeant said to himself, was like bathing in perfumed water—Dr. Kane's words, the explorer from Philadelphia, who, though unsuccessful in his search for Sir John Franklin, gave his name to the Kane Basin. Brainard understood what Dr. Kane meant, but would have chosen a different phrase. Bathing in perfumed water didn't appeal to him. His heart went out to a woodland pool he knew from boyhood, fringed with cooling ferns. He imagined his young self approaching this pool in an overheated, sweaty state from farm work, shedding his clothes and slipping in. How often he had done this! In reality his pool, fed by a mountain stream, was too cold for lingering, but Brainard in his imagination changed the temperature so that he could remain in this lovely longed-for spot all the rest of a peaceful afternoon. As he stood lost in this meditation, a lashing wind sprung up from the southeast, knocking him to his knees. The day had darkened, black and storm-swept, and Sergeant Brainard turned for home.

By the third week of March, as the Eskimos had assured them, the birds returned, and since the sound remained open, Long and Fred took out the kayak. They brought back four dovekies. The birds were small but plump, and each contributed a pound of meat to their dinner, discounting bones and feathers. White feathers tipped in black, meaning, the Eskimos said, the birds were still dressed in their winter clothing.

Over breakfast, a mouthful of bread and a cup of weak tea, Lieutenant Lockwood said, "I am glad as each day draws to an end. It puts us nearer to the end of this life—whatever that end is to be." The day was overcast and the wind was blowing up such drifts it was clear to Sergeant Brainard that in their present mood, little outside work would get done that day. He took up the new fishnet he had made from a burlap sack, and a dovekie skin for bait, and crawled out. He wanted to bring them food. He wanted to do something that would supplement their daily diet, and this fishing idea had come from George Rice, who had spotted crustaceans at the point of land where Private Beebe of the *Neptune* had left his cache in the summer of 1882. Brainard called them shrimp since they looked like shrimp, and there were thousands, though very small. Beebe Point, as they called it, was a mile walk from their hut. That evening at dinner, the cooks added Brainard's catch to their mess: six happy ounces of shrimp.

"Why, the damn things are two-thirds shell," Connell blurted out, jabbing at his teeth with a filthy, ragged nail.

"Private Connell." The C.O.'s raspy voice filled the hut. "You could show a little gratitude. Sergeant Brainard stood for five hours in the wind, dipping and dipping his net for the shrimp you just ate."

Connell whipped a hand across his mouth, staring upward at the boat thwarts.

"One can fix one's mind on nothing else," Lieutenant Lockwood said in a hopeless voice, "but food."

"Why don't we eat our sealskin pants," Connell said. "We've talked about that."

"How often," Lockwood continued, "I think of the dear ones at home and what they are eating right now."

Brainard looked at this friend. It was clear poor Lockwood had little idea of what was presently being discussed at Camp Clay.

"Connell," Bender piped up. "I made a fish hook today."

"Well, aren't you the industrious little chappy." Connell reached across the aisle and patted Bender on the head. "Give it to me. I'll try it out tomorrow. Used to be quite the fisherman in my boyhood."

Charlie started to laugh. "You'll not use that fish hook tomorrow or any other day. You haven't been out except to piss in the last forty-eight hours."

"Why, you bastard!" Connell drew back his fist and Charlie ducked down into their bag. But the blow never came. Instead Connell was laughing. "Right you are. And so it will be. I'm not wasting my energy tramping back and forth for anyone. But, hell, I can tell you a few grand fish stories."

"Tell us, Connell," Elison said. "I'd love to hear a good fish story."

"Well, my river, the Blackwater, the river of my boyhood, was the place I loved best in all the world," Connell started. The men exchanged glances. This was a side of Connell they had never seen. "The hills around, my Irish hills, were so green." He stopped. "So green." His voice caught. "So *damn* g-g-green," he stuttered. "Oh fuck!" and he buried his hairy face in his grime-encrusted hands.

Finding food from the sea had taken over Camp Clay. Gardiner worked on a dredge for seaweed. Schneider made baits by sewing seal-skins over large stones. He placed them in the bottom of a net. "See?" he said. "The stones weigh down the nets and the skins act as baits." Rice and Brainard set the traps and checked them two or three times a day. While the crustaceans added bulk to their diet, the doctor assured them they gained little in nutritional value. Still, this addition to their meals cheered the men. It gave them a new food to talk about and the cooks to experiment with. All agreed that shrimps combined with tallow made an excellent stew. Israel, their numbers man, set himself the task of counting the crustaceans and ascertained that it took thirteen hundred to fill a quarter of a cup. "Impossible," Connell shouted. "That means they're microscopic. How is eating what I can't see going to do me any good?"

This received no comment. It was clear that the Irishman's touching boyhood memory left no permanent effect on his general temperament.

Deaths

1. William H. Cross, 18 January 1884.

✳

5

> Hungry people will not endure reason, they will not listen to justice, nor will they bend to any prayer for mercy.
>
> Seneca, Minor Dialogues (ca. 4 BC–AD 65)

It was never silent at Camp Clay. And the wind held prominence over all other sounds. The wind came in rushes and in spurts. It came to punish in heartless manic gusts. It came as a bully. It came to flatten on his face any man who staggered out to check the temperature. The wind came without warning, without preamble. It struck to injure and to humiliate. The worst wind came driving out of the southeast in terrifying, prolonged storms that kept them confined in the hut, in this gritty, grimy, greasy world of their own making. Here each man lived in a space no bigger than that occupied by his own body. Here, urged into bad temper by the wind, he could detest his bag-fellow for taking up more than his share of the bag. Burrowed in their bags, they heard the wind in their sleep. It woke them, and, as they lay awake, they cursed it. When the wind roared to a siren pitch that hijacked their minds, these men knew, if they knew anything at all, that they could not have built the snow-block walls thick enough to keep out the insane sound of this wind.

✳

The day of March 24, 1884, dawned clear and cold, with -23 degrees reported by Israel. Every morning, Ned Israel dragged himself out on hands and knees to perform this duty. His outer trousers were worn through at the knees. Smooth-shaven back at Conger, he now kept his beard tucked into his jacket to keep from tripping himself. How often Brainard had thought as he watched Ned at this painful task: *Does he wish he had never come?* There was not a word of complaint out of him. Ned never went on about missing his family the way Lockwood did, yet Brainard saw when Ned spoke of his mother's cooking—the beef sausage purchased from the German Jewish butcher—how clearly he missed them.

Ned struggled back in to wait with the others for Biederbick, today's cook, to thaw the tea water over the alcohol lamp. Biederbick was in the act of reaching up for the bacon—a full half pound that Sergeant Brainard issued for their breakfast sat on the boat's thwart—when he keeled sideways, landing on poor Elison. Pavy and the C.O. started up to help. Gardiner shouted, "It's the stove, the alcohol fumes, we're killing ourselves!" and quick as thought, Shorty reached up to tear away the ragged cloth the cooks used to plug the ventilation hole when the stove was not lit. They began crawling over themselves to get through the narrow passage and into the fresh air.

Those who fainted inside were better off, since the poisonous air soon cleared. But when those who crawled out began to breathe in the frigid air, all strength left them and they fell to the ground in a dead faint. Brainard regained consciousness, scrambled to his feet, and collapsed again. He heard himself crying out, "Oh, my poor fingers. I'm going to lose them." Gardiner and Dr. Pavy, less affected, came rushing over to shove mittens on his hands. Those on the inside tossed out coats and hats. But Brainard, along with Lieutenant Greely and Connell, were repeatedly helped up, only to keep falling a good half-dozen times. Finally everyone was shepherded inside, and Lieutenant Greely had the cooks pass out two and a half ounces of bread and a special round of rum. Connell, back in the bag next to Charlie, said, "Christ! I thought I was a goner," to which Charlie replied, "You're too mean to die."

Biederbick, back to preparing their breakfast, shouted, "Where's the bacon!"

"It was on the thwart," Sergeant Brainard answered.

"Must have got knocked off in the melee," Lieutenant Lockwood said in his old take-charge voice. "Let's find it, men."

But that half pound of bacon couldn't be found, and Rice said, "Charlie, you're some tough guy. You didn't keel over."

"Yes, I did."

"I didn't see you."

Ellis said, "Who helped you up, Charlie? It was Schneider who helped me."

Schneider said, "Dr. Pavy helped me." They went around telling their stories and a kind of camaraderie emerged in the telling of who had helped whom that had Brainard recalling similar times on the Plains when, after the thick of battle, they sat around the campfire and recounted close calls and who had helped out in a pinch. If only we could continue like this, he thought, and he remembered how Dr. Pavy had come to Lieutenant Greely's rescue with a jacket and mittens.

They dozed most of the day. When the dinner stew was served out—mostly bacon to make up for the absence at breakfast—Private Henry said, "I'll set my portion aside for later." Sergeant Brainard, becoming alert, cast a glance at Rice, who was sitting upright, his eyes on Private Henry. They watched as the private stowed his dinner ration in the depth of his bag. He had turned deathly pale, his forehead sweaty. Suddenly he threw himself out of his bag and lurched toward the entrance, hand covering his mouth, and vomited into the urine tub. Shorty Frederick sprang up and, examining the mess, turned on Private Henry. "So you're the bloody thief. Look at this, men," and he tipped the contents so they could peer in. "Here's our bacon, half-chewed and as raw as the day the poor hog died."

"You devil!"

"You brute!"

"You lying son-of-a-bitch!"

"God, what a stink."

"You goddamn bloody blockhead" and other accusatory comments filled the fetid air before the C.O. clamped down and enforced order.

"Take it easy, boys," Private Henry said. He had regained his color. "That was our dinner's bacon."

"Like hell it was, Charlie," Connell said with a grim laugh.

"Private Connell!" the C.O. thundered, or tried to. His voice was reduced to a fragment of its old commanding sound. "We will proceed in an orderly fashion. What do you have to say in your defense, Private Henry?"

"I have this to say, sir. I'm wrongly accused. What I disgorged was the bacon issued for supper."

"But you didn't eat your ration," Shorty Frederick snapped, and Biederbick added, "You told us you were setting it aside."

Connell started pawing around in the bag. "Here it is!" he shouted in triumph, holding aloft Charlie's dinner.

"Get that damn bacon away from me!" Charlie began to gag.

"He overloaded his stomach," Biederbick explained. "He must have bolted that whole half pound when we were near dying from the stove fumes." Private Henry glared at the hospital steward and slumped over, pulling the bag over his head.

"Here what Private Henry do," Eskimo Jens cut in with his broken English. Brainard caught Private Henry peeling back his bag as Jens jumped up to extend his right arm toward the thwart. "Bacon! You all on hands and knees, but Jens see."

"I object," Henry growled, "to the testimony of an Eskimo being used against me."

No one paid much attention to this comment, and Long, giving Charlie a suspicious look, said, "I'd swear you came through the rum line twice." Then, addressing everyone, he added, "Why, I ladled out rum to him twice!"

"And last fall," Connell picked up, "I watched him walk off with a can of beef when we were dismantling the caches. You didn't see me, Charlie, but I saw you. You're a goddamn thief, that's what you are."

"Private Connell, watch your language," the C.O. snapped.

"You marauder," Charlie shouted, "you never overlook an opportunity to lift a morsel."

"Private Henry," the C.O. broke in. "You are the one on trial, not Private Connell."

"Charlie stoled canned food back at Conger," Bender squeaked.

"*You* stole the canned milk, Charlie," said Schneider. "You said the knife marks were mine, but it was your knife. You'd lent it to me—a plant—to make it look like I'd—"

"Thank you, Private Schneider. That's enough."

"Lieutenant Greely," said Rice, "I propose we take extreme measures. When Captain McClure of the British Royal Navy was looking for Sir John Franklin and they became hard-pressed, he ordered three men flogged for stealing food. *For stealing the dogs' food.*"

"You're all against me," Charlie said. He turned to Connell. "I thought you were my friend." Connell looked away.

There was dead silence until the C.O. said, "If anyone has the right to ask that Private Henry be put to death, it is you, George Rice. You contracted yourself to this expedition as our photographer and you have risked your life for us many times."

Why doesn't the doctor speak up, Brainard wondered? In the dim light, it was hard to see how the doctor was reacting, but he was aware that some sort of companionable feeling existed between the doctor and Private Henry. Then it came to him. The doctor would not want any attention drawn to himself during a discussion of stealing food. And it flooded into Brainard's mind that if Lieutenant Greely ordered Private Henry's execution, he risked being cornered into formally accusing the doctor of stealing Elison's food. While Brainard understood why the C.O. hesitated to take this step—Dr. Pavy could refuse to treat the men—he could not help feeling that Lieutenant Greely's inability to confront the doctor was cowardly. Far easier to threaten Private Henry's life, yet, Brainard reminded himself, it was Rice who proposed taking extreme measures. And Brainard knew why Rice had suggested this. Private Charles Henry was a thoroughly rotten apple. It takes only one rotten apple to rot all the other apples in the barrel. It was a harsh measure, but, by God, Henry was a murderer. Rice didn't know this. Only Brainard carried this weight, and it grew, like Sisyphus's load, more burdensome every day.

"You will be placed, Private Henry, under close arrest." The C.O.'s words interrupted Brainard's thoughts. His attention flew to Private Henry, who was sitting soldier-straight in his sleeping bag. "You will not be permitted to perform expedition duties," Lieutenant Greely continued. "Furthermore, you cannot leave your sleeping bag without permission or our hut unaccompanied." Henry made no response. "Do you understand?" Greely said.

"I understand," the private muttered, and Brainard watched as he tossed his head, an insolent gesture that spoke of indifference. Why, the man is cutting himself off, Brainard thought as Henry slid back into the bag, and Connell scrunched as far away from his bag-mate as he could get. With that rebuff, Private Henry drew a grimy snot-encrusted sleeve across his face, and Brainard saw him sneak a look at Rice.

George Rice was admired by all of them. His words carried weight. Brainard wondered if Private Henry was, somehow, ashamed. Brainard knew that Rice understood the danger when a man was driven by the obsessive cravings of his stomach. At Camp Clay, if any man topped that list, it was this man without a conscience, Private Charles B. Henry.

✳

If the day was clear, the thermometer could crest zero if exposed to the sun. But the sun was not often seen at Camp Clay. Still, it was light more than it was dark, and this daylight penetrated into their hut, giving more of itself every day. As the month of March closed down, a gale blew in, marauding the men for three days, and storms always brought on a general gloom. Private Henry's theft of the bacon—more than that—the private's cold-blooded, uncaring attitude as his companions were passing out from the deadly fumes, though not openly discussed, was on their minds. Sergeant Brainard had written in his diary: *To think that in our midst was a man with a nature so devoid of humanity as to steal food from his starving companions when they might be dying.*

Lieutenant Greely had stopped talking about crossing to Greenland, though no one knew, and no one asked, if that trip was now out of the question. The mere fact that it could not be proved that Garlington wasn't there fixed it as a hope to cling to, a hope that grew fainter with every passing day, yet who among them could speak out and deny that Garlington was there? That would mean they had lost hope in the U.S. government, which had pledged to rescue them. But Rice's upcoming excursion for the English meat shed a solid ray of hope. Rice was giving all of them a chance to hope for something that might really happen, as Brainard heard in the general conversation: *It won't be long before we'll be eating that English meat!*

They were all, as Lieutenant Lockwood put it, "agreeably disappointed" in the shrimp. Lieutenant Greely maintained that three pounds of shrimp was equal to two pounds of meat. But the C.O. was just trying to put, Brainard said to himself, the best face on a ready food source that was, he was the first to admit, disagreeably shelly.

On the morning of March 26, Sergeant Brainard reported that the chocolate ration set aside for Elison was missing. As this was only two days after Private Henry had stolen the bacon, the finger pointed straight at him. The private, protesting his innocence, turned to Lieutenant Greely, "Please, sir, allow me to perform some share of our daily duties."

The C.O. didn't even look at him.

"You are killing me with injustice," Charlie continued, and his eyes filled with tears.

"My God!" Connell exploded. "What a crocodile you are."

"Ha! Ha!" Bender laughed. "Crocodile tears! Charlie's a big blubbering baby crocodile."

"You could have cared less if we'd asphyxiated ourselves," Connell sneered. "'There would have been more food for the rest of us if some of them had died.' That's what you said."

"Well, dammit, it's the truth, isn't it?" Charlie snarled. "You had to be thinking the same thing."

"Crocodile tears," Bender shouted again. "Charlie's crying crocodile tears!"

"That's enough," the C.O. cut in. He was hoping that this day, his fortieth birthday, might have ended without acrimony, when, through a master stroke of good timing, Long, Jens, and Salor burst through the canvas flap.

"In honor of your birthday," Long said as he spread the dovekies out in an overflowing heap beside Lieutenant Greely in his bag.

"*This*"—the C.O. waved a hand over the meat as if blessing it—"marks a turning point in our fortunes. Private Long, you are the hero of the hour."

Long smiled, a great toothy smile, as if this were the proudest moment of his life. "The sound was covered with birds," he said. "They crested every wave. As I shot, Jens, out there in his kayak, bagged them, and Salor grabbed the ones that floated to the shore. There are twenty-three birds here, Lieutenant. I'd hoped to make it an even forty for your birthday."

"You've brought us nearly twenty-three pounds of meat, Long," Sergeant Brainard said, and Long got a rousing cheer.

Lockwood took charge. "Let's pluck these birds, men. We'll set the wings, heads, and feet aside for Sergeant Brainard's shrimp bait."

"Sergeant Davy." The frenzy of preparation gave Ned Israel an opportunity to whisper in the sergeant's ear that the doctor was definitely stealing from Elison's food can. "I saw him," Ned went on. "I saw his hand in the can. It's light enough now. I watched him chew. What can we do?"

David Brainard shook his head, and Ned knew there was nothing they could do.

They were living on shrimp and dovekies and the occasional ptarmigan. They could see seals in the harbor, returned with the spring. All that meat! It was driving them crazy. Long shot at one, but missed. Despite the slight increase of ounces, Sergeant Brainard was upset with himself. He could feel his will weakening. And his body too. As the daylight grew stronger, he was growing weaker. The men's faces were pinched and hollow-eyed, and he knew his was too. It took all his grit to make himself trudge down to the shrimping ground and stay there. It took hours to catch enough shrimp for their supper, and he made sure they had some for breakfast, too. He carried back ten to twenty pounds of shrimp. It exhausted him. He stumbled over the stones. He reeled like a drunkard.

But it gave him a chance to be off by himself, to be away from their hovel, as Private Henry called it, with its bickering and stink. Piles of empty tins, consumed months ago and thrown outside the hut, were beginning to rust. He was glad to get away from this shambles and breathe clean air. He feared for Lockwood, who rarely went out now. Lieutenant Greely was sinking. He could help these men best by getting food for them. He would keep up the shrimping as long as he had the strength for it. The physical strength, but even more important, the mental strength.

Davy Brainard smiled to himself. He was a farm boy, from a dairy farm. When you milk cows twice a day, you learn what hard work means. Those cows had to be milked, and at regular times that could not be put off. You didn't get thanked for it, either. As a young boy, he had hated it. He had seen milking as only drudgery. But when he turned fifteen, something changed. And the cows were somehow responsible for this. They were the ones who gave of their milk, and he, as the farmer, could offer this good milk to a market, to people. He was happy to be this person. It made him feel proud of their cows and of his own work. The shrimping had turned from drudgery to a task full of meaning. And he knew he could keep going. He would bring these men food until he dropped.

Everyone was concerned about Eskimo Fred. "I will never see my family again," he moaned. Brainard was concerned Fred's despondency would infect the others. Fred knew he was starving to death—Brainard was sure of that. He was very vocal about needing more food. Lieutenant Greely increased the Eskimo's ration to what the hunters received even though Fred hadn't hunted for them in days. The Eskimo did not improve. He was no longer cheerful, helpful, and friendly. He was sulky and angry and demanding. This upset them all. "You're getting an extra portion, damn it," Connell pointed out, "and you're doing nothing to earn it, so shut up your bloody mouth."

"Don't be hard on him," Brainard said to Connell. "We all know it's not the man who speaks. It's the hunger."

"Doctor," said Elison, "my toes are burning and the sides of my feet itch. Can't you do something for me?" Pavy went through the motions of relieving Elison's feet, though Joe had no feet. They had kept him in ignorance, and now, in early April, Brainard was not sure why.

On the morning of April 5, at breakfast, Lieutenant Lockwood began, "These shrimp, they do not take the place of meat. I will not be convinced of that. They are so very small, about the size of canned corn and look like canned corn, too. My mother would never have allowed *canned* corn at *our* table."

As Lockwood wandered on, the doctor slid over to check on Eskimo Fred, who appeared to have sunk into a doze. "He's dead," Dr. Pavy said.

"Are you sure, Doctor?" Lieutenant Lockwood asked. "I didn't think he was in any danger of dying."

"Of course I'm sure."

"Well, if Eskimo Fred is dead, his death makes me feel very sorrowful," Lockwood went on. "He was very strong on the Farthest North with me. Check again, Doctor. He just finished his breakfast. I imagine he's suffering from indigestion. These shrimp stews give me diarrhea. Perhaps this is the case with the Eskimo."

"It is not the case," Pavy snorted.

That afternoon they sledged the body of Frederik Christiansen up to Cemetery Ridge. The Greenlander was laid to rest next to Cross, and a salute was fired over his shallow grave.

Brainard had never seen life pass more easily from anyone. Fred had a family waiting for him at home in Greenland. It was wrong that they wouldn't be bringing Eskimo Fred back to his family. Brainard was afraid that Lieutenant Lockwood would be next. Or Linn. Neither was able to tolerate the shrimp. Lieutenant Greely made sure they received an extra allowance of dovekie, but Sergeant Brainard knew this was not sufficient. Their strength was too depleted. Heaven help them, he said to himself. Heaven help us all.

✗

Sergeant Brainard was right about Linn. He died the next day. His death didn't bring forth much emotion, even among the Germans, of whom Linn was one. He was the first German to die. At Fort Conger, Linn was well liked. He was strong and a hard worker, but his ordeal in the bag with Elison had changed him into a petulant and irritable man. But that wasn't why no one appeared grieved over Linn's death. They were all at the edge of life now. They had been half-starved for too long and indifferent to everything but food. The night Linn died, Rice was sharing his bag. His own sleeping bag was on the sledge, ready for the trip to Baird Inlet. He was going to bring them back the 144 pounds of meat. Rice needed the sleep. He went right on sleeping next to Linn's corpse.

The C.O. asked Sergeant Brainard to go through Linn's pockets. He extracted a folding knife, a notebook, and a gold pen. Ralston laid claim, saying Linn had asked him to see these items went to his eldest brother, in Philadelphia. Lieutenant Greely was about to impound them—Ralston was not regarded as trustworthy—but the meteorologist confirmed his claim by producing the brother's address written in

Linn's hand on a tiny scrap of paper. Sergeant Brainard knew the C.O. could have ordered Ralston to turn these items over, but he didn't. Instead, Lieutenant Greely asked Gardiner for his Bible, and pulling himself into an upright position, holding the open Bible in his ungloved hands, his black beard white with frost falling over the page, he intoned:

> I am the resurrection and the life, saith the Lord,
> He that believeth in me, though he were dead, yet shall he live,
> And whosoever liveth and believeth in me shall never die.

It was a solemn moment. Private Henry, who as a result of his crimes had been cut out of the general conversation, coughed noisily, drawing attention. His eyes were unusually bright. "Those words," he said, "so full of poetry. By God, I'd give my right arm to have them sounded over me." He fell back in his bag, spreading his fingers across his face. And Brainard remembered coming across this private standing before a black-faced cliff at Fort Conger, his arms raised, shouting out Tennyson's lines:

> And there they lay till all their bones were bleached,
> And lichened into color with the crags . . .

He remembered, when he tried to make a bond with this private over these lines, that Private Henry had turned from him. This man loves words, Brainard thought. He has perhaps a poet's feel for poetry, yet the character he has shown to us, and from what I know of his past, reveals he is nothing but a blackguard. Perhaps Rice can do something with him. When George returns, I'll talk with him about Private Henry.

Kislingbury interrupted these thoughts by volunteering to dig Linn's grave while a detail sledged up the corpse. "Aren't you joining us?" Connell barked at Charlie, who was still lying on his back, hands hiding his face. "What's wrong with you, anyway?"

Charlie righted himself with a grin that displayed all his crooked teeth. "I'm confined to quarters. I get to lie right here. You can tell me all about it when you get back. And I can tell you right now what you'll say. You'll say this: 'Brutal work, it was, hauling that cortege. Stinking soul-crushing work. We hadn't enough gravel to cover the poor sod's boots.' And I'll say, 'Stop your complaining, you bloody Irishman. You know, and every man at Clay knows, too, that Linn's absence gives us a little more elbow room. And one less hungry mouth to feed.'"

"So now it's said, and I don't need to say it. It's nasty words and nasty thoughts," Connell said. "You're right, though. That's the trouble with you."

"As a rule," Charlie said, eyeing his bag-mate, "I can stand you, Connell, but right now I hate your bloody guts."

"Not as much as I hate yours." Connell tossed his head as he gave his companion-in-crime a friendly push.

After breakfast, Brainard and Ellis hauled Rice and Shorty's traveling gear up over the height of land to save them a mile. He so much wanted to go. He tried to persuade the C.O. to send him in Rice's place. He would go with Shorty. It made sense. He and Shorty had been on so many Indian raids together. They responded to each other in helpful ways in so many tough situations. But Rice's argument won out: Shorty had been with him last November. He and Shorty had left that meat cached in a cairn with the Springfield rifle sticking up to mark it. They knew the lay of the land, the shapes of the hillocks and grounded bergs that marked the spot. So Sergeant Davy had given in. He put together their rations: nearly a pound of food apiece for six days: pemmican and bread. He felt awful about the state of their bread, rock hard. They would have to soak it when they melted ice for their water. Rum and spirits of ammonia, he made sure of an ample supply. They had a two-man buffalo sleeping bag, a rifle, an ax, an alcohol lamp, and a cooking pot. No tent, to save weight, and to make room for the 144 pounds of promised meat.

When the four men reached the height of land, Smith Sound spread itself out below them: a jumble of ice moving in a froth that made Brainard remember the large Western rivers—the Yellowstone, for instance—he had seen at breakup, the ice tearing and pounding like a horse race, defying a man in a boat to attempt the crossing.

There was no possibility of reaching Greenland now. They were trapped here. This hit him as he watched Rice and Shorty step into the sledge harness. The four men grasped hands. They faced each other with wet eyes. Brainard wanted to ask Rice to call it off. Yet he was desperate for him to go through with it. There was a chance they would bring the meat home. But, by God, Rice and Shorty were in for ferocious cold, unrelenting hunger, and a bleak time alone in this mind-numbing wasteland. It was already swirling snow, the clouds black and heavy. Rice grabbed Brainard's shoulders, as though he could read the sergeant's unmentioned thoughts. And Brainard said, "Lieutenant Greely himself could not have stopped you, but for all our sakes be careful, George Rice."

Later that day, Whisler cut two windows in their boat-roof. It made a cheerful change. They had constant daylight now and why not make the most of it. But they were not a cheerful sight. Now were revealed the sunken eyes, hands and faces black from the greasy sooty smoke, clothing and bags greasy too. Always the complaints about how unpleasant to have everything they handled slick and gritty from the grease. Some of them were too weak to stand. Jewell was unable to cut ice today. But the C.O. had Biederbick issue a stimulating drink composed of one part alcohol, two parts water, and flavored with a dash of ammonia. They called it their moonshine, and the C.O. promised to serve it out once a day.

✷

After the wind, the most prominent sound at Camp Clay was the pack ice. Tides, currents, and wind affected the pack. The pattern was simple. Frigid temperatures froze the ocean's surface. This surface could freeze solid to a depth of a dozen feet, even twenty feet. This pack ice could crush ships as easily as a child cracks a nut with a nutcracker. The trio of wind, tide, and current could split the pack apart, opening up leads through walls of ice with seemingly as little trouble as a man splits cordwood with an ax. This splitting apart was a noisy process. And as the pack was constantly undergoing the effects of tides, winds, and currents, the men at Camp Clay were never unaware of the grinding, this shoving and bumping, the splitting and tearing and rending, the squealing and crashing, booming and growling that went on in the pack. Trapped in their hut, the men had a constant ear on the pack. The noise, or diminution of noise, told them when the sea was opening and when it was closing up. On their minds was Garlington. Could he get to them? Or them to him? It all depended on the wind, tides, and currents. Yet these men must have known that if they ventured out with loaded sledges, hauling their invalid Elison on this semifrozen ocean, their chance of making that thirty-mile passage to the Greenland coast was as hopeless as any one of them going against a polar bear with a penknife. Yet they could not let this hope that defied reason go.

✳

Lieutenant Lockwood was under the C.O.'s care. He was receiving four ounces of raw dovekie a day, about equal to the amount on a scrawny undersized chicken leg his mother would have turned up her nose at.

"It's more that we can spare, Lieutenant Greely," Dr. Pavy argued.

"I know that."

"You will starve the others in your misguided attempt to save Lieutenant Lockwood, who is going to die."

Brainard knew the doctor said this to annoy the C.O., but Lieutenant Lockwood was lying right there on his back staring up toward the sky visible through their new window. Good God!

After supper the C.O. had Biederbick pass around their moonshine drink. They found it marvelously reviving. They looked forward to it all day. Lieutenant Lockwood asked for seconds, but was refused. "I'm afraid not, Lieutenant," was how the C.O. put it. Lieutenant Lockwood began to disentangle himself from his sleeping bag. He struggled to stand, his legs shaking like a newborn calf's. He managed one step, then another step in the direction of the doctor, saying, in a shaky voice, "Then I will go to the fountainhead. May I have a second helping, Dr. Pavy?" He held out his tin with both hands. The doctor looked him in the eye and shook his head, and Lieutenant Lockwood fell, full-length across their feet.

"Oh, God!" choked their commander.

Biederbick and the doctor took over and wedged the lieutenant back into his bag. They succeeded somewhat in bringing him around. But he said not a word, and by the time they awoke on the morning of April 9, the news was passed around that Lieutenant Lockwood was no longer breathing.

"It was Eskimo Fred's death that got him," Charlie muttered to Connell. "The Farthest North and all that. I'd really been looking forward to a meal with him, after we got back. He knew more damn restaurants."

"He'd invited us to his home in Maryland," Connell said. "No one could talk about food better. Remember his coconut pudding with alternate layers of crackers and coconut?"

"Apricot paste," Charlie said. "Pear cider."

"English plum pudding," added Connell. "He wanted to serve us his Maryland dishes. His mother's preserved peaches. Goddamnit, he wanted us to meet his family."

"His sweetheart, Mary Murray," Charlie continued. "I would have given my right arm to have met her."

"She's a widow, before they were married," Connell said. "But she doesn't know it."

Charlie let out a bark of a laugh. But turned it to a cough as the others' eyes were on him. Biederbick and Sergeant Brainard were already at work straightening poor Lieutenant Lockwood, first his arms, then his legs, as narrow as fence rails. More like pipe cleaners. Any one of them could have circled his thigh with one hand. The doctor crawled over. He was touching Lieutenant Lockwood's face and hands with an index finger. "You will note the marble coloring," he said.

"We're not your students, Doctor," Charlie growled.

"The veins are much shrunken, all but disappeared," he went on, picking up poor Lockwood's arm. "The deceased's pulse, as I have monitored it lately, was much diminished." He had his grimy fingers on the lieutenant's unresponsive pulse. "His heart these last days exhibited only a fluttery action."

Why doesn't the C.O. stop him, Brainard wondered? He looked over toward the commander, who seemed mesmerized by what the doctor was saying. Pavy waved poor dead Lockwood's arm in the air, then dropped it. "Please, Doctor, please stop," Brainard said.

But Doctor Pavy was in his own private world. "You will recall," he continueed, "how he complained of the painful passage of his bowels, like expelling little stones, he said. I am in the unique position here to observe the human body in its final stages of starvation. My findings will be a contribution to science. You may take me at my word when I say my report will reach the proper hands when I return." Brainard could feel his own hands clench with the desire to close them around Pavy's scrawny neck. Instead he smoothed a large protective hand over the brass buttons of poor Lieutenant Lockwood's jacket. Back at Fort Conger, the lieutenant kept those buttons polished.

"We'd worked on the *Arctic Moon* together. He was kind to me then," Private Henry said.

"My feelings toward him were those of a brother," Brainard said more to himself than to anyone else.

"This will be a sad blow to his family," the C.O. added. "He was a good man."

"Well, damn," Henry broke in, "everyone knew that."

Whenever this private allows himself to show his softer side, he quickly blots it out, Brainard thought, with a cruel or unnecessary remark. I wish I could have talked his case over with Rice before he left.

✻

The storm that started on the day Rice and Shorty left raged for four days. Not a man doubted those two were in for it. You couldn't see or even think in a pounding storm that battered your ear drums in a water-fall of sound. You couldn't stand. You could hardly crawl. You entered a disintegrating world. To face such a wind was like going against a battery of razors.

Jewell couldn't eat his shrimp. He was sinking. Biederbick was ill, but kept up his spirits. He encouraged the others. Gardiner, Ellis, and Salor; even Connell were losing ground too. No one was getting enough to eat. Ned Israel couldn't crawl out for the temperatures. But most worrisome was Jens. They were counting on him and his kayak to bring them seals. Sergeant Brainard did not dare venture out today, but his own private concern was that he would use the last of his birdskin baits the next time he went shrimping. After that, he could get them no shrimp.

Because of the storm, they had been unable to bury Lieutenant Lockwood, but now that the blow had diminished, they managed to drag his emaciated remains the 375 yards uphill to Cemetery Ridge. It took eight of them to haul the large sledge. Sergeant Brainard elected to dig the grave for his friend, though he could only scratch a shallow

depression, hardly six inches deep, in the stones and gravel. It was inadequate, but Sergeant Brainard was forced to give in to Cape Sabine's
stony soil. They laid in poor Lockwood, their fourth interment, his
wool hat pulled down over his face, wrapped in a canvas, his arms folded
across his chest.

Lieutenant Greely ordered Sergeant Brainard to issue himself two
extra ounces of pemmican daily. Sergeant Davy protested, but Greely
insisted. They depended on him to bring them shrimp. The C.O. increased Israel's and Jewell's ration by four ounces. Brainard was aware
that Lieutenant Greely was particularly concerned about Ned Israel. He
had invited this young man, their gifted astronomer from the University
of Michigan. It was marvelous how Ned had fit in. He had his whole
life ahead of him. Losing Lockwood was bad enough. But not returning
Ned Israel to his family would be calamitous.

The day after digging Lockwood's grave, Sergeant Brainard managed to stagger the mile down to the shrimping spot. He paced up and
down to keep from freezing while waiting for the little crustaceans to
collect. His thoughts were occupied by the dishes he would eat if he
made it out of here and how much ground they had lost since Rice and
Shorty left. If those two didn't show up with the meat, it looked like
they would all be dead in the next few weeks. Why, they had lost three
men in the last five days. Who would be the last? Left to die alone? He
hoped to God it wouldn't be him. Yet he didn't want it to be Lieutenant
Greely. He went through their names and decided they would be best
off if it was him. There was no one he would want to give that job to.
Not even that thief Private Henry. "When Johnny comes marching
home again, Hurrah! Hurrah!" began to play in his head. "Hurrah!
Hurrah!" he sang and made his feet go *tramptramptramp* to keep them
warm. *Tramptramptramp.* "Hurrah! Hurrah!" That's what his eldest
brother, Henry, sang when he came back from the war. Henry was a
hero. He had come back to them. Brainard sang the words of this Civil
War song over and over:

> When Johnny comes marching home again,
> Hurrah! Hurrah!
> We'll give him a hearty welcome then

Hurrah! Hurrah!
The men will cheer and the boys will shout
The ladies they will all turn out
And we'll all feel gay when Johnny comes marching home.

He was going to make it home. He had to do it for his family, just as his brother Henry had.

He looked up from his nets to see a medium-sized polar bear two hundred yards away, moving toward him at a shambling gait. He grabbed the hatchet and ran behind a hummock. This bear was moving fast, faster than he could move. He braced himself for the attack, holding the hatchet across his chest. He stared at its dull blade. Then dropped it. He must be crazy. A hatchet was not a weapon with which to fight a bear! He grabbed the five pounds of shrimp. That was their dinner. He was not about to leave *that* for the bear. And he started running. He was not really running. He was incapable of running and this bear was going to catch him. But something must have detained the bear because Brainard made it over Cemetery Ridge. Coming down the other side with the hut in sight, he dropped his heavy mittens and sacrificed the shrimp to move faster. Pushed through the canvas doorway on hands and knees, shouting, "Bear!" He was too exhausted to say more. Lieutenant Greely ordered Biederbick to portion out diluted alcohol. Brainard swallowed this and told the hunters, Long and Jens, where he had met the bear. They crawled out with guns, followed by Kislingbury, who was soon back, gasping, unable to keep up, too weak to surmount Cemetery Ridge.

For those inside, there was nothing to do but wait. There was little talk. Each man knew his life was hanging in the balance. "You'll be eating bear meat soon," Biederbick said to Jewell. But the man who had learned about wind from being an observer on the summit of Mt. Washington was unresponsive. Three hours crept by before they heard gunshots. Now the waiting was excruciating. Was the bear dead? Or were their hunters?

Connell, who never looked on the cheery side, said, "Even if they wounded him, that bear would run into the ocean and swim off."

"Not long now," Biederbick said to Jewell, "you'll be eating bear."

And suddenly they heard footsteps crunching, running or nearly running. They exchanged looks with glittering eyes. Long and Jens would not be running to bring bad news.

The hunters burst in. "Place your bets, gentlemen," Long panted, and told them the bear was lying dead within a few feet of open water about three miles from their doorstep.

Biederbick leaned over Sergeant Jewell to let him know, but the words were never spoken. "He's dead," the hospital steward said, though no one was listening. They were putting on jackets, lacing boots in an uproar of high spirits. Gardiner shouted, "It's Good Friday!" Two or three shouted back, "Then we'll call him the Good Friday Bear." They wanted the story. "Tell us. Tell us what happened. We heard the shots."

"Lieutenant Greely," Biederbick addressed their C.O. "Sergeant Jewell is dead."

Greely stared at Jewell, who was certainly plainly dead. He was the only one not moving in the hut. He coughed. He passed his hand through his beard, scattering frost. They were all listening to Long, who was telling the tale. Greely said nothing. And Biederbick, Brainard was relieved to see, backed off. It was more important for these men to hear about this successful hunt, the first to bring them enough meat to keep them alive, than it was, at this moment, to acknowledge Sergeant Jewell's death. "We had the dusk on our side," Long started. "We used the hummocks to hide behind. He was running away from us, headed for the water."

"See?" Connell stepped in. "What did I tell you."

"Shut up, Connell," Charlie yelped.

"Jens winged him in the forepaw." Long clapped the Eskimo on the shoulder.

"But he limp along pretty good," Jens said, and hopped down the length of the aisle, making everyone laugh. "Then Long shoot. Good shot." And the Eskimo fell on his back, waving arms and legs in the air. The men hooted, and Long, grinning as broad a grin as had ever been grinned at Camp Clay, continued, "I threw my hat and mittens down on the snow to get off the best shot I could. I knew I wasn't going to get a second chance." Everyone was shouting. Jens slid over to Joe Elison and took Joe's stumps in his hand. "Joe," he said, "you be all right."

Brainard stared at Jewell. His body had stiffened up, his face white as a plaster mask. The Jewell they had known was gone. This was a corpse. Lieutenant Greely addressed the hospital steward, "Private Biederbick, put together a few men. We'll remove the remains." And Charlie Henry shouted, "You bet, Lieutenant, we need to make room for this bear."

They reached the hut with the carcass at 2:20 a.m., the sky still holding light. Bender and Biederbick began the skinning and dressing. Sergeant Brainard asked for the liver, windpipe, feet, and stomach. He breathed a great sigh of thanks. Now he could replenish his baits. "Look at his stomach," he said, "nearly empty. The poor fellow was as hungry as us. He would have eaten me if he'd caught me." All the meat was hauled into Sergeant Davy's storeroom, including intestines, lungs, heart, and head. "We will use the blood to thicken our stews," Sergeant Brainard assured them. "We will reach our homes because of this bear." Lieutenant Greely had Long start up the alcohol stove. Bender handed him strips of meat and the wonderful smell of fresh meat cooking filled the hut. They kept reaching out their hands for more, the juice running down their beards. On the spot, Lieutenant Greely told them he was increasing everyone's ration to eight ounces of meat per day. But the hunters, Long and Jens, and the shrimper, Sergeant Brainard, would receive eight ounces above that. Elison too. Joe had become their mascot, a pet to take care of. The doctor siphoned off most of it, they were aware of this, but keeping Joe healthy was the one thing they all agreed on. They liked watching him smile when someone did something for him. He was like their dog that way, wagging his tail to show happiness. It made them feel good. It pulled them together.

Deaths

2. Frederik Thorlip Christiansen, 5 April 1884.
3. David Linn, 6 April 1884.
4. James B. Lockwood, 9 April 1884.
5. Winfield S. Jewell, 12 April 1884 (the day Long and Jens shot the Good Friday Bear).

⚹

6

This is the Hour of Lead—
Remembered, if outlived,
As Freezing persons, recollect the Snow—
First—Chill—then Stupor—then the letting go—

Emily Dickinson (ca. 1862)

The storm started as snow in the air, circling in an aimless, harmless manner. As Sergeant Brainard made his way down to his shrimping spot, he watched the cloud mass grow darker and more menacing, and by the time he reached the shore he was seized in a senseless upheaval of squall and shrieking wind. White and dense and pitiless. Landmarks vanished in a blast of storm-driven madness. Snow filled his nostrils, plugged his ears. Snow stung his eyes. He should go back to their hut, but he couldn't. Rice and Shorty were out in this. They weren't going to return to Camp Clay without the English meat. The least he could do was collect a few shrimp.

He set his baits, the bear's skin wrapped around the stones that served as weights to sink the burlap net. This took longer with the wind buffeting him. At last he was satisfied, and he watched, from his crouched position, as the shrimp began to collect. When he stood, black spots filled his vision. He held himself steady, trying to breathe evenly, his legs spread to keep his balance until his sight cleared. He looked around. Nothing to see but the inside of the storm, thickened into an intense whiteness, nearly blinding, and swirling in a way that made his empty stomach churn. It was very unpleasant. He crouched again, too dizzy to stand. It felt like this storm was taking place in his own head. He could fix on no landmarks; all were blotted out in the great churning whiteness. It seemed an evil color. It was no color at all. It was the color of the great white whale that had driven Captain Ahab mad. He was on the verge of madness now himself. He forced himself to break out of whatever it was that had a grip on his mind. Rice and Shorty, he thought. What if they don't come back?

One of his weights had shifted. The small crustaceans were floating away. He crawled over, tossing off a glove to make the needed adjustment bare-handed. He stood, reaching for his glove, but it had vanished. "You stupid!" he told himself, his voice flying off in the wind. He pawed around and there was the glove, a dark spot blown back to him in a swirl of snow that eddied around his wrists. "Christ," he said, and grabbed it. The fingertips on his right hand had already turned bone white. He took the glove off again, stowed it in his pocket this time, and tucked his fingers under his armpit.

If I were a little animal, he thought, if I were a fox, one of the beautiful foxes we see here, I would never need to think about going inside to get warm. I would know how to live in this cold. I would know how to find food and keep warm. I wonder if the foxes are ever frightened in the cold and wind? I almost lost my glove from being careless. He frowned and shook his head. I'm so stupid. A fox wouldn't be out in this weather. He's in his den, keeping safe and warm. And it came to him how like a den their hut was, and how being denned up like foxes gave them some degree of comfort.

Thinking about how the foxes lived gave him the courage to go on collecting the shrimp he needed for their supper, and for their breakfast, too. But when David Brainard trudged back to the stone hut, he couldn't keep his mind off Rice and Shorty. They had no fox holes to take shelter in.

This storm of snow and wind raged all the next day. The temperature rose, melting the frost from their roof, and the moisture rained down on their heads and bags. When the temperature dropped, this wetness turned to ice. They were all wretched in their cold and frozen clothing. Dr. Pavy, however, who contributed little in the way of chores, went out in the storm to chop ice for them. Since there were few now with the strength for this duty, he got thanked by Lieutenant Greely. This raised Brainard's spirits, both the doctor's help and Greely's genuine acknowledgement of it.

The next afternoon, when Brainard was coming back from shrimping, he passed Private Henry breaking up the last of their barrels for firewood with his buddy Connell. It had stopped snowing but a wild wind had them shouting back and forth in the effort to be heard as they worked. "The doctor's never volunteered for anything," Connell was saying. "That pond lies not that far from our cemetery."

Brainard stopped. It was not his nature to eavesdrop, but he backed away to keep out of their line of sight. He was quite sure they hadn't seen him.

"He's a regular weasel, our doctor." Charlie laughed. "Pavy knows how to take care of himself."

"You and me, Charlie," Connell said, tearing apart the barrel staves with a grating sound, "we're the meanest weasels here."

"You're the meanest"—Charlie pointed at his friend with the ax—"*I'm* the hungriest." They broke into a screaming fit of laughter that evidently left them exhausted, as they stopped their work and sprawled on the rocks.

Brainard, picking up his shrimp bucket, walked on by. If they saw him, they paid no attention. *So they don't know I overheard. I promised myself to keep the firearms out of the hands of those two. I pass over Cemetery Ridge every day. I've noticed no disturbance to the graves. I'm so worn out by the climb up to the ridge I don't stop to look around. It's such a sad place anyway.* Lockwood's boots had come uncovered. It was so windy there and the bodies so shallowly buried. He must stop and replace the gravel over Lockwood's boots. He must be more attentive, he told himself, now that I have been warned.

✗

Expedition Diary of David Brainard

14 April 1884

Will anyone ever be able to decipher this writing? It is in great part illegible, the sentences incoherent, and all written in a hurry and with great rapidity and under the most trying circumstances of our miserable conditions. My notebook is, however, well suited to the job, being long and narrow, 10 inches by 4 inches. It opens like a ledger, from the top, though it is not lined. It's got a firm leather binding and slips easily into the deep pocket of my wool coat. The color was once a lively red but is now worn and dulled by my own greasy fingers and our grimy living. I write in pencil as it is too difficult to keep my ink thawed.

✗

Jens had caught a seal for them and they had just eaten what the men were calling the dining event of the entire winter — trimmings of bear and seal heads, their hearts, lungs, and kidneys. The cooks had made good use of the bear's blood they chopped from the ice, the secret ingredient that enriched the stew, making the gravy thick and imparting a delicacy of flavor that would have left diners at Delmonico's with upturned noses, but here at Camp Clay threw them into ecstasies of epicurean delight.

"How Lieutenant Lockwood would have enjoyed this feast," Ned Israel said.

"I miss his recitation of dishes from the best restaurants," Schneider added.

"What would his mother have thought of our bear's blood gravy?" Bender squealed, making them laugh.

Their spirits were high. Lieutenant Greely had raised their ration to a pound of meat a day. They could feel their strength returning with this meat.

"Rice and Shorty. They're on their way with *more* meat!" Henry bellowed.

"When do you expect them, Lieutenant Greely?" Whisler asked.

The C.O. sighed. "Soon," he said. "I imagine the storm delayed them."

They were quiet after that because every man in the hut knew that Rice and Shorty were overdue. "I'll go out for the evening temperature," Ned said. They had managed to maintain this observation largely because of Ned's commitment. He began pulling on his coat when every head looked toward the entrance. Footsteps crunching, coming toward the hut. A single pair, and Shorty Frederick was in their midst.

Private Henry began to scream like a wild beast in pain. He rocked back and forth, his hands covering his face.

"Stop that, Private Henry," Greely ordered, but his voice had lost its old power.

Charlie Henry could not stop. Connell grabbed his bag-mate by the shoulders and shook him. "You're upsetting everyone, Charlie. What's wrong with you?" Charlie stopped. His hands dropped.

"It's all up with me then," he said. His cheeks appeared more sunken, more deeply lined, as if Shorty's news had aged him beyond his young years. Not that the private had told them Rice had perished. Those words didn't need to be spoken. Rice was dead. And this cold fact pushed their own deaths closer.

Shorty lay panting across their feet. His outer garments were frozen into a stiff armor. Ice was in his beard and icicles hung from his mustache. He struggled to raise himself, helped by Brainard and Biederbick working to get Shorty out of his coat and heavy pants, the ice cracking and snapping and landing on the others.

"Private Long," Lieutenant Greely said, "prepare Private Frederick some bear meat and tea, as much as he can eat." Long had already set up the stove. He lit it and a small amount of heat filled the hut. Shorty pulled a grimy parcel out of his pocket. He handed it to Lieutenant Greely.

The C.O. took the packet wrapped in oil cloth. He stared at it as though he hadn't grasped its meaning.

"That's Sergeant Rice's ration," Shorty explained.

"You didn't eat it?" Private Henry croaked. "You fool!"

Everyone stared at Shorty with a kind of amazement. "Well, it didn't belong to me," he stammered.

"Can you tell us what happened?" Lieutenant Greely asked. He seemed to have regained control over his thoughts.

"It's hot," Long said, and passed over the tea. "Drink that first, it will help the bear meat slide down."

"Rice was a goddamn reckless idiot," Private Henry lashed out.

"Blasphemy, Private," the C.O. said. And this reaction, so typical of Lieutenant Greely, served to lessen the tension.

"The bastard overdrove himself," Charlie went on. "Goddamn him to hell for that, is what I say."

Brainard seized the private's arm. "You've said enough." Private Henry wrenched away. But Sergeant Brainard hung on. "You will stop," he said between his teeth, "or I will break your arm." His intent was to meet Private Henry's force with his own and that seemed to work. The private fell back into his bag. He lay there staring up at their boat-roof with unblinking eyes.

Brainard glanced at Shorty, beside him in the sleeping bag. He had finished his tea and was forking in the bear meat. It was doubtful,

Brainard thought, whether he had taken in much of what Private Henry said. Brainard knew that Private Henry admired George Rice, that Rice's innate kindness, his exertions for their welfare, carried out in such an unassuming manner, made a deep impression on this private. Rice might even have provided an anchor for Henry in some moral sense. And now Rice was gone, and Private Henry was left adrift. *And I cannot help him. I cannot do for him what Rice had done.*

Shorty scraped his tin and the C.O. said, "Would you like more meat, Private Frederick?"

"Thank you, sir, I've had plenty." He scrubbed his fist through his mustache, breaking off the remaining icicles. "But I would take another cup of tea. I'm awfully thirsty." He breathed in deeply and looked around, his eyes coming alive as if, Brainard thought, he's seeing he really is back with us. Shorty looked over at Private Henry. "His great flaw," he said, as if trying to explain, "it grew out of his great heart. I tried to stop him. Oh God!" He gave a gasp; very close to tears. "He promised. We promised to tell the other when we were weakening."

"Here's your tea, Shorty," Long said, and smiled at him in a way that reminded Brainard that those two had been at Fort Ellis together, through the Plains wars together, as he had.

Shorty took the warm tin and held it between his bare hands. Brainard felt he wanted to say more, but couldn't. We must not push him, he thought. He must have lived through an ordeal beyond expressing. Private Henry had sat up. Shorty was facing him across the aisle. "I was angry at him too," Shorty said to Private Henry. "It came to me on the walk back how angry I was and I hated myself for it." He swallowed the remainder of his tea and tucked the tin into the folds of his bag. He sat stooped forward between his friend from the Plains and Private Whisler. His mouth was open, his mustache and beard clear of ice now. Brainard watched Shorty's eyes close. He jerked, and his eyelids flew open, and Brainard said, "Easy, easy now," and helped Shorty slide down into the center of the buffalo-hide bag.

I hope he can tell his story. It's not good for a man to hold on to such pain. And this spun Brainard off into his very first battle. He was not much past twenty and he was fighting the Sioux. He was riding with a hundred other men at a terrific pounding speed. The ground sprayed out from under the horses' hooves. It was impossible to see. He breathed in dust. He was going to choke on it. The thunder of the cavalry charge set up a vibration like an earthquake. He was packed in, carried along by the unstoppable forward momentum, out of control, on the verge of panic. He was sure he would be dead in the next few minutes. He heard a whirring, an ominous throbbing hum as the storm of arrows hit, and the man beside him, Dick Kelly—they played cards together—took an arrow through his neck, the blood from the burst artery erupting like a geyser on Brainard's uniform coat. His hands were sticky from the fresh blood. By the close of that day, he wondered why he was still alive.

He became aware of the soft sounds the men were making as they positioned themselves for sleep. Brainard lowered himself down next to Shorty. When he told Shorty about that first battle, the nightmares eased. He came to realize that what he had experienced was no more or less than any other soldier's initiation into a bloody war. But Shorty's inability to bring Rice back, that was something different. He turned toward his friend to see if he were awake and might want to talk, but Shorty was solidly asleep. He was snoring. As Brainard listened to Shorty's snores, he heard a chorus of snorts and wheezes and muffled sounds that indicated that every man at Camp Clay was asleep. And Davy Brainard took comfort from this homelike sound, the same sounds of sleep his brothers made in the bedroom of their family's farmhouse.

✱

Nineteen left now.

Lieutenant Greely was not feeling well. Dr. Pavy diagnosed his ailment as an irritated heart and urged the C.O. to issue himself a few extra ounces of bread and pemmican daily. "Take it as a kind of lunch," the doctor advised. They had been eating only two meals a day, break-fast and supper, the latter of which the cooks began preparing around three. It could take forty-five minutes to thaw out most of the ice crystals. Sergeant Brainard was grateful that Greely agreed to this extra food. *We need our leader more than ever to keep order around here.* He was thinking of a moral order that would keep them this side of the line of each man for himself. He knew who had little regard for that line, and if they crossed it, life at Camp Clay would end in bloodshed.

Shorty Frederick slept the whole day after his return. Then, as though the incident with Rice had never happened, he took up his daily chores—carrying water or canvassing the camp for anything that would burn. One afternoon Brainard found him collecting the old tin cans and carrying them off behind some boulders. "I'm sick of stumbling over them," Shorty said. He was back to his old cheerful, helpful self. But he hadn't offered a word about his ordeal and Rice's death, and Brainard knew better than to ask.

Deaths

6. George W. Rice, 9 April 1884, of exposure.

✕

7

> Behold, how good and pleasant it is
> For brethren to dwell together in unity!
> **Psalm 133**

A clear, bright, beautiful mid-April day came in on a westerly wind and Whisler cut another trap door in the boat-roof. This opened the hut to the first really strong light in six months. He and Bender tore out the lining of the boat for fuel. Without fuel they would be eating their rations frozen and sucking on ice for water. In the sun the temperature could rise from 5 degrees to 45, if the sun was shining directly on the thermometer. The downside was that the frost melted on the inside of the roof, dripped on their heads, soaked into their bags and clothing, then froze when the sun dipped or a cloud passed over. Then, even Sergeant Brainard commented, they were left "very wretched."

But Sergeant Davy Brainard spent little time in their hut. His hardest duty was cutting up their bear meat, frozen into a solid block. He used the hand saw, standing with his feet planted, working the saw endlessly back and forth. It felt like he was sawing through granite. He stopped to recover his breath after twenty strokes. He was too weak for this, but he urged himself to a full twenty because Sergeant Brainard knew that if anything would get them through it was this bear meat; full of fat, and being fresh, it went a long way to fighting scurvy. They were terrified of scurvy. Connell's gums were blackening and spongy. He wiggled his teeth with grimy fingers to demonstrate, insisting his meat ration be increased.

Shrimping was on Sergeant Brainard's mind as well. He doubted his toil provided much nourishment. The crustaceans were three-quarters shell and only one-quarter meat. But there *were* a lot of them. His legs felt rubbery and unstable, his feet were swollen—a sign of scurvy—and too tight in his boots, exposing him to frostbite. Some days he was so without ambition all he wanted was to lie in his bag like the malingerers, Henry or Connell or Ralston. But Sergeant Brainard couldn't pass off his shrimping job. He had tried. Even Dr. Pavy bungled it.

Pavy's mind seemed not very clear. The doctor complained to Lieutenant Greely that the extra ounces of meat that Brainard issued to the hunters was almost wholly without bone. "Of course Sergeant Brainard wouldn't include bone in the ration, Dr. Pavy," the C.O. explained. "That's absurd. Our hunters are working hard to obtain food for us. They need all the *meat* we can spare. What are you talking about?" But Pavy would not explain. Then, when the doctor offered his help with the shrimping, Brainard couldn't refuse. He wondered, however, if this was because the route to the shrimping spot took him conveniently past the cemetery. But Pavy's help didn't last long. When Sergeant Davy trudged to the shrimping grounds next, he saw that the doctor had tossed away the bait and weighted the burlap down with rocks. "Why did you do that, Doctor?" Sergeant Brainard asked. What the doctor was doing to his shrimping effort felt like sabotage. Pavy hiked his shoulders to his ears and displayed his palms, fingers spread. Sergeant Brainard thought he was going to maintain his inscrutable silence, but he said, "I was thinking of something else," which was inscrutable in itself. Then he announced, "I have spoken to Lieutenant Greely. He will remove your extra ounces, Sergeant. All who are strong enough will take turns at the fishing. No one gets extras. It's more fair."

"But, Doctor, no one wants to do this job. Ellis, Whisler, Bender, Salor, Schneider have helped, but none stick with it. Biederbick has his hands full taking care of the sick and weak. Long and Shorty are hunting for us round the clock, splitting the twenty-four hours. Lieutenant Greely is ill, and not strong enough anyway, nor is Lieutenant Kislingbury."

"You eat too much," Pavy said, and drifted off.

Sergeant Davy's ration *was* cut. The C.O., he thought, must have given in to avoid a fight. He was surprised, and hurt, too. It was not right to cut his food allowance. He could have helped himself when he was portioning out their daily rations. It was strange he didn't. But he didn't. The men, it seemed, had grown to trust him, or were used to him, or saw they were best off with him. After all, he had been their stores sergeant since Conger. They were used to the routine. That might have meant everything. If even the worst, like Henry, suspected him of stealing from their food supply, why, all restraint would fly away with the next zephyr and they would be tearing at each other's throats like wolves.

When the men found out Sergeant Davy's ration was cut, Israel offered a portion of his. So did Elison. "Please take it, Sergeant Brainard," Joe said, "I'm not contributing in any way, and you are doing so much for me." But Brainard could not accept. He was greatly touched, moved by Elison's generosity and told him so, but, really, he could not accept.

Near the end of April, Private Henry got his hands on the diluted alcohol and drank enough to become obstreperously drunk. Reclining in his bag, he entertained himself by calling the C.O. a "bloody coward," a "goddamn bastardly bloody coward," in a singsong voice. Everyone clamored for him to shut up but he wouldn't, and finally Gardiner, who took the C.O.'s side when it came to blasphemous language, crawled over, threw himself on Charlie's chest, wrapping his fingers around Charlie's still-beefy neck. Connell pushed him off; Charlie hooted with laughter when he had got his breath back. But even Connell was disgusted with his bag-mate. "Shut up," he yelled. "You stink. You're nothing but a born stinking thief."

"It's *such* a horrible life," Charlie chortled. "We all may go mad. I aim to enjoy myself before it happens."

"By God, you scoundrel, you have a point." Connell let loose a salvo of laughter. He cut it off and hissed in his bag-mate's face, "So why didn't you give me some?"

Dr. Pavy, who was sorting through his medicines, the little vials of essence of clove or those in the narcotic lineup, said, "Private Henry is, of course, right. But *I* shall not go mad." He pulled out a bottle filled with an inky black substance the viscosity of tar, smelled it, wrinkled his nose, and brought it to his lips.

"What are you doing, Doctor? What was that?" Lieutenant Greely, who had appeared asleep, was now awake.

"Ah," replied their doctor. "Something that is good for me, that is all." And quick as the guilty hiding the evidence, the doctor's medicine chest vanished into the shadows.

That night Sergeant Brainard wrote in his diary about Private Henry's drunken spree. Recording the theft of the alcohol, he added, *He is a born thief as his 7th Cavalry name will show—a perfect fiend.* There, he thought to himself, if I die, my journal at least will let others know that I knew of this private's past.

✱

Shorty Frederick, one of their quietest sleepers, was waking them all now.

A few weeks after Shorty's return, Brainard was awakened by Shorty thrashing in their bag, making horrible sounds. There were words, but Brainard, in the shock of being woken, couldn't make them out. He shook Shorty. "Quiet down, friend," he said. And Shorty did quiet down. To Brainard's surprise, he rolled over on his stomach and fell back asleep. Brainard, now thoroughly awake, stayed sitting up. He looked around the hut. Most of the men had woken up, and most had settled down again. Private Henry's dark form loomed against the slight light that penetrated their hut during the nighttime hours now. He was leaning on his elbow, staring at Brainard. "Shorty said, 'Come back with me, old fellow.'"

"What do you mean?" Brainard asked.

"Rice collapsed. Shorty couldn't get him going."

"How do you know what went on?"

"He talks in his sleep." Charlie paused, as if deciding how much he would reveal. "You sleep through it. But I'm a light sleeper. I've got the whole story now." The private rubbed his hand across his face. "Shorty is the real hero. It's not Rice. I used to think he was, but it's Shorty." Private Henry threw off his bag and crawled over to crouch next to Sergeant Brainard. "I've got it written down," he whispered, "Shorty's story. I'm going to make that *Chicago Times* editor pay me good money for it."

"You know what happened?" Brainard asked. "I can't believe that."

"Well, I do." Charlie said. "Shorty knows. I've checked the facts with him, like any good reporter."

"I'd like to read your story, Private Henry."

Charlie spread his teeth in a kind of grin. "I'll read it to all of you bastards."

"You'd better make sure of that with Shorty."

"I already have." He bared his teeth again. "I've written it like a real story, the kind in the best adventure books. This is no Horatio Alger stuff. Shorty's no Horatio Alger, he's the real thing. He doesn't see himself as a hero, which makes my story even better." The private passed a hand over his face again. "Shorty's just a simple man who did what he had to do. His inner workings left him no choice. That's true for all of us, but for those who are truly good, well, they, when the hard test comes, can turn out heroes. You see what I mean?" He stopped talking and crawled back across the aisle and into his bag.

Sergeant Davy Brainard lay back, his arms under his head. *He seems to relish his badness. He doesn't want to become good, yet he's fascinated by goodness and what makes heroes. Perhaps he sees what it takes so clearly because it's so in contrast to himself.*

The light grew stronger, slowly filling the hut. At seven o'clock Lieutenant Greely had Long start the stove for breakfast. The men stirred. Some crawled outside to relieve themselves; those too weak used the urine can. Biederbick assisted Joe Elison. Long and Shorty served out a tea of thrice-used tea leaves to accompany the shrimp Brainard had caught the day before. There was little talk. The hut at Camp Clay was filled with the sound of crunching as they chewed the shells, mingled with the slurp of the watery broth. Breakfast passed quickly, and as the men tucked their tins and spoons into their sleeping bags or pockets, Sergeant Brainard said, "Private Henry has written up Shorty's story.

He'd like to read it to all of us. How do you feel, Shorty, about the private reading it?"

"I feel kind of sorry about not telling you myself. It was a pretty bad time." He looked around at the men, his friends. "You have a right to know what happened to Rice, so if Charlie wants to read it, that's as good a way as any." He ducked his head in a nod to Private Henry, who pulled his journal out of his coat pocket. "I'm calling it," he said, his eyes meeting the eyes of every man around the circle, "'The Making of a Hero.' It doesn't need much introduction as to who we are and what we're doing because my readers will be familiar with our story. Well, here goes."

The Making of a Hero

The men on Lieutenant Greely's expedition were in a tough spot. We had run seriously low on food, so two of our number, George Rice and Private Frederick, whom we called Shorty, had agreed to travel forty miles down the Arctic coast to where the British had left 144 pounds of meat. The meat was in tins and they planned to sledge it back. On the morning they left, the weather turned and a blizzard sprang up. We, back at our camp, knew Shorty and Rice were in for it. What you are reading here I got straight from Private Frederick.

They made a poor camp the first night, unable to light the alcohol lamp in the wind, so they had no warm drink. They chewed frozen pemmican while thawing their way into their buffalo-hide bag. There they remained for twenty-two hours, until the storm let up enough for them to travel. In the next march, they reached Eskimo Point and spent the night poorly sheltered in one of the old stone huts we built seven months ago. The morning of April 9, the day Lieutenant Lockwood died—though they couldn't have known this—they set off but left their sleeping bag to keep the sledge weight light. They felt sure they could locate the meat and return to Eskimo Point that night. They crossed Baird Inlet, which separated the point from Cape Isabella, where Rice had sacrificed the meat for saving Elison last November. Here the wind caught them with spindrift so thick their sightline was cut off. They couldn't penetrate more than forty feet ahead. None of the bergs that Rice and Shorty had set in their minds as location points looked the same. "Something happened here," Rice yelled into Shorty's ear to make himself heard over the wind, "and rearranged our landmarks. What do you make of it, Shorty?"

"The ice I remember as smooth is hummocked," he yelled, "and what was hummocked is smooth. Then, bears could have pulled apart the cairn we built." It was a wretched piece of bad luck.

"But the Springfield rifle," Rice shouted. "We should see it. A bear wouldn't have walked off with *that*." They had rammed the rifle into the top of the stone pile where they had stowed the meat. Rice's eyes darted about in a desperate way. Not like Rice at all. The wind shrieked, buffeting them, swirling spindrift around their boots, piling it up to their ankles. Shorty watched his friend apply his mittened hand to his nose and cheeks in an attempt to draw out the frost. But when Rice took his hand away, his nose was still white. This was bad. Rice couldn't thaw his face; he was too cold. Shorty shouted against the wind, "Let's return to Eskimo Point." Rice's eyes turned steely, so Shorty added, "We'll come back tomorrow."

"We can't return and come back. That's a fourteen-mile round trip. A little more searching, Shorty. Just a little more. We owe it to them."

"But, George"—Shorty rested his gloved hand on Rice's sleeve—"we agreed. If either of us felt ourselves to be weakening, we'd tell the other."

"Oh. I'm only a little tired," Rice told him. "I'll walk a little slower and recover in no time."

What Rice had just said made no sense to Shorty. But Rice started off. In twenty paces he was staggering. This was no good. Shorty rushed to catch up, dragging the empty sledge behind him. He nudged Rice and pointed toward a berg that rose like a ship's prow. "Let's head for it and rest there." To get Rice to do this he added, "I need a rest even if you don't," and managed a smile through his cracked lips.

The berg was farther off than it looked and by the time they reached it, Shorty had Rice's arm across his shoulder. They crawled to the lee side of the berg and Shorty helped Rice to settle on the sledge and sat beside him. Rice slumped down, his back against the icy berg. "Time for a pick-me-up," Shorty said. He pulled the rum and spirits of ammonia

out of their pack. Poured some out for Rice. Got out the spirit lamp
and started heating pemmican. They sat side by side on the sledge,
passing the can and spoon back and forth. Shorty heated tea, a cup for
each. He let it get warm enough so the tin between their hands felt
warm. He had done all he could for his mate. "We're fed and warmed
up, old fellow," he said. "Let's get going. Race you back to Eskimo
Point!" Their buffalo-hide bag was there, waiting for them in one of
the old stone huts.

Rice spread his lips, the attempt of a smile to show his willingness.
But the bravado was gone. His eyes were vacant. A tangled knowledge
of fear settled in Shorty's stomach. He stood. "We need to move now,
George." He made his voice stern: a parent encouraging a child. Rice
looked up into his face. But he wasn't moving. Shorty stayed standing
next to his friend. "Listen to me, George, we have to get out of here.
We'll freeze otherwise."

Rice gritted his teeth. He tried to get up. He gave it his best shot.
Shorty could see that. Then sank back against the berg. "I'll feel better.
Don't worry about me. I'll sit for a spell. Sit and keep me company."
Rice reached up for Shorty's arm and gave a tug. "I don't want you
standing out there in the cold."

Shorty sat.

Rice said, "You start. I'll catch up."

"I'm not going anywhere without you, George. Here, sit right up
close to me. We'll keep warm together. I need you to help me keep
warm." Shorty stripped off his coat, his *temiak*, as Eskimo Jens called it,
and wrapped it around Rice's feet and legs. He helped to position Rice
so his head was on Shorty's lap. They were quiet, each occupied with
his own thoughts. Then Shorty asked, "Do you have a girl waiting for
you, George?" He knew there was one. He hoped it might ease his
friend's mind to talk about her.

"Helen and I have an understanding," he said. "We came to that
before I left. I carry her letters here." He touched his chest. "Shorty,"
Rice said, "you know what I'm going to eat when I get home?"

"Tell me, George."

"Cod and herring. My mother makes the best white sauce from our
own grapes. You must come and visit me." He fell quiet. The two
friends sat in this barren spot devoid of any life except their own. The

landscape gave off varying shades of whiteness in a merciless way that wormed itself into the mind and ran neck and neck with an intense loneliness. "If I should die here, Shorty," Rice finally said, "I'm asking you to see my manuscripts reach the *New York Herald*. They're expecting stories from me." Shorty leaned over his friend's face and Rice looked up. Their eyes met and Shorty knew that Rice was dying and that Rice knew this. "Make sure Lieutenant Greely brings home my photographic plates. There's a cold beauty here. That's what I tried to capture." Shorty nodded. He didn't trust himself to speak. He folded his arms around his friend and in a little while Rice lost consciousness.

Shorty sat there on the sledge, his back against the berg, his arms holding Rice, for two more hours, until he could feel Rice's body had grown cold. Then he relaxed his grip. It would be so easy to lie down beside his friend and follow him. The snow swirled around in empty drifts. He was utterly alone. He shook himself and forced that thought out of his mind. If he stayed much longer, he would die. He stood up. He felt as stiff as an old man. He reclaimed his *temiak* and tied his pack on the sledge. For Rice's sake he would make it back to tell what happened. He knelt down beside his friend and kissed his cheek. Already it was as hard and white as marble.

Shorty set off, traveling north. In seven hours he reached Eskimo Point. His bag was frozen iron-rod stiff. He tried to unroll it and couldn't. He feared he might die, sitting beside the sleeping bag. For some insane reason this made him giggle and that started him searching his pockets for food scraps. His fingers landed on a small vial. His heart leapt with a sense of reprieve, and he downed the few drops of ammonia, then he went to work on the bag. Wedged his way in and lay there, drifting in and out of consciousness.

At 8:00 a.m. by his pocket watch, Shorty struggled out. The winds had eased. He was as exhausted as when he crawled in, but he was filled with purpose. He fired up the stove, forced down a little warmed pemmican. Repacked and set off south, back toward Rice. The air had cleared and he spotted the dark shape of his friend long before he reached him. The body was as rigid as cordwood. There was a waxy, blue-tinged pallor on the skin of Rice's face. A crust of frost outlined his eyes and lips. Shorty pulled his gaze away from this corpse that no longer bore his friend's features. He steeled himself to search Rice's pockets and found his watch and the letters. He would make sure Rice's family got the watch and Helen her letters. Then he began hacking at the ice, loosening and removing it with his hands. He would be damned if he would allow his friend's body to be pulled apart by bears, or his eyes pecked by ravens. A thousand years from now, the movements of the ice would send George Rice's body to the bottom of Smith Sound. But Shorty viewed this natural absorption into the world of ice and sea, even as food for fishes, a fitting end for the photographer who had made it his work to render this fearsome yet indifferent beauty on his glass plates.

He felt better after he covered Rice. He stepped back and gazed up. The iceberg made a fitting tombstone. He marched the seven miles back to his sleeping bag for another cold night and set off the next morning for Camp Clay. He was so weakened he had to haul in stages, first the empty sledge and then the bag, with a rope tied around it. It took him three days to reach home. Plenty of time to think about Rice.

He couldn't help feeling—he hated to think it—angry. Rice had promised. Rice was famous for pushing himself to the very edge. That was why Shorty had exacted that promise. Shorty gave a fierce kick to the ice hummocks and cried a little, moaning to himself. But he broke this off. He was working himself into a state and his tears were freezing on his face. He had George Rice's ration in his pocket. He was not going to touch that. It was not his. This food belonged to the general stores now, and he would hand it over to the C.O. when he got back.

These men would survive and return to their homes, and remember George Rice's sacrifice.

The men had been lying or sitting in various attitudes in their bags. There was very little squirming or fidgeting, little movement of any kind. Outside, the wind increased and this had the effect of making them lean forward, elbows on knees, so they could better hear. Shorty sat in his bag next to Brainard. He kept his head down, nearly sunk upon his chest. It was hard to tell just how much he was listening, Brainard thought. He felt protective of his friend. Henry's story certainly did bring out what looked like heroism: returning to bury Rice, bringing back his ration. But Brainard was sure Shorty didn't want to be elevated like that. He had never acted to draw attention to himself. Shorty

Frederick was a thoroughly modest man. Now the hut was filled with a kind of reverential silence that seemed to compel Shorty to keep his head down. Brainard wanted to break this silence, but wasn't sure how to manage it.

Lieutenant Greely shifted his position and spoke. "Thank you, Private Henry," he said. "Your story speaks well of two fine men. While we have lost George Rice, I will see to it that his photographic work is brought home and receives the commendation it deserves."

Then Connell clapped Shorty on the back. "You're a brave laddie," the Irishman said. "Glad you made it back. We need you to keep things steady around here."

This was followed by a chorus of "well dones" and similar compliments, and Shorty raised his head. "Gosh, fellows," he said. "I didn't bring you meat." His gaze wandered off up toward the boat-roof, and his eyes got a watery look. "Dammit all," he said, and smote his knee with his fist. "I'd as soon it was Rice sitting here in my place." He glanced quickly at the C.O. "Apologies for the profanity, Lieutenant, but that's just the way I feel about it."

✳

The weather remained fine. The wind was in a tractable mood. The constant daylight came with its own drawbacks, one being the danger of snow blindness, the other the adjustment to daily living in a world that never fully darkened. The night sky revealed stars of only the strongest magnitude. The men were living in an Arctic spring again, one they had hoped not to see. They should have been back home with their families or at their army posts. Because of this, the mood at Camp Clay was not reflective of this spell of good weather. Six of them would never see their homes again and despite Eskimo Jens's hope for seals and birds, the region remained desperately empty of game.

It was in a cheerful frame of mind that on April 29, Long and Jens went down to the ice foot with the kayak and the Springfield rifle. Almost at once they spotted a seal on a drifting cake. Jens slid the kayak over the ice to reach open water, then wedged himself in. He had the rifle. This seal was large. Long, on the shore, gave a start as the kayak's bow tilted sharply downward and the stern sprang up, pitching Jens, still paddling furiously, into the icy water. Jens made no sound, no cry for aid. His body hung on the surface, like some new aquatic species, propelling Long to sprint onto the ice, slipping and sliding, risking his life jumping from cake to tilting cake, the turbulence lashing his boots. He was within a few feet of Jens, his hand reaching for his *temiak*, when the body sank as if weighted. Long looked around for the kayak and watched as Jens and his kayak rolled over each other until he lost them in the depth. He looked around for the rifle, but it had gone down with the kayak. This was bad. The loss of the Springfield left them with only one working rifle, the Remington. Long could not keep himself from scanning the waves. Jens was so strong. He might just free himself from the kayak and come swimming toward him, his dark head cresting the chop like a seal's.

Long's ears were full of the ocean's roar, the lifting and breaking, monotonous and dreadful and never to be bridged to the Greenland coast by them. Lieutenant Garlington was not waiting for them on the other side. This hit Long with the finality of death. And, now, with their Eskimo hunter gone, without the kayak and the best rifle, they had as much chance of catching a seal as catching a star. The sealskin of Jens's kayak must have ripped on a projection of ice. Jens had told them back at Conger that his father had drowned in his own kayak while out hunting. Long turned away, tears freezing on his face. He regained the shore without thinking where he was leaping, not careful where his foot landed. If he had fallen in the water, he later confided to his friend Brainard, he wouldn't have been glad, but it would be easier to die there than return to tell the others what had happened.

✳

Camp Clay

30 April 1884

Dearest Wife,

After a great deal of mental worry, I agreed to an extra issue—a small quantity of pemmican and hard bread that Sergeant Brainard gives me at noon. I do not want to take away from the men, but Dr. Pavy pointed out the weakened condition of Lieutenant Kislingbury and led me to see I must keep myself strong for the well-being of the party. I venture from the tent but little. The doctor is concerned about the action of my heart. I have secured Dr. Pavy's word of honor that he will inform me when my own survival is in question. I tell you to let you know I am trying to keep as good care of myself as possible. My duty centers on our consumption of fuel and food. I oversee the details of the barometer and temperature readings that Ned Israel collects three times a day. But my overriding concern is with morale and discipline. This takes all my energy.

It is with great effort that I manage to think clearly. In fact, rereading the above I see I have not told you that my reason for accepting the increase in my ration is that Lieutenant Kislingbury is failing. Well, I did tell you that, but the point is that I restored him to duty after Lieutenant Lockwood's passing. That was on April 9. Then Private Long shot the bear on Good Friday, April 11, and poor Lieutenant Kislingbury, in the effort to join in the hunt, collapsed in a faint after running only a few dozen yards from our hut. He is often now disoriented, unaware of what is passing around him. He has lucid periods, but he is not in a position to succeed me.

Lieutenant Kislingbury's illness is a blow to Dr. Pavy. The doctor knew that if I should die, the lieutenant would take over. The doctor himself, being a civilian, could not command, but if Lieutenant Kislingbury had succeeded me, Pavy could have influenced command. As this will not happen, the doctor's long-held hopes are dashed. He had hoped to command and he had hoped to reach the pole. As he has attained neither goal, both of which clashed with those of this expedition, I imagine the doctor is a disappointed man. For this reason I keep a close eye on him and have advised Sergeant Brainard to as well. A disappointed man can be a dangerous man, capable of anything that will ease his burdened mind.

I will end by telling you about my recent conversation with Private Biederbick, our hospital steward. His words have put new heart in me. He asked to talk to me in private and I made room for him in my bag. He said that if he didn't make it through, he wanted me to know he had done me an injustice in his thoughts at Conger and on the retreat coming here. "You have done everything for us that one man could do to keep us up and alive," he said. I thanked him and told him I would keep trying to do so.

"Lieutenant Greely," he went on, "I think it better that you and our records be saved than all of us together." At this point I assured him I meant for all of us who were still alive to come through. "And I will do my best for you, sir," he said. "You can count on that." I have not been especially popular with the men, so I hold his words the closer to me. I wanted you to know them too.

Lovingly,
Adolphus

✷

Everyone witnessed Kislingbury acting like a baby when they were out uprooting the saxifrage plants for fuel. The lieutenant, with no apparent provocation, threw himself on the sledge, scattering the plants, beating his chest, actually weeping, carrying on about how he would never see his four poor motherless boys again. "I cannot fight any longer," he wailed. Sergeant Brainard watched the men draw away. They had been listening to Kislingbury's rant ever since he had missed the ship. Now he was on the brink of hysterics. The lieutenant was not fit to command, and the next morning as Brainard was gathering his baits, about to leave for his shrimping duty, Lieutenant Greely put his hand on his arm and said in a low voice, "Here, I've written it out. If I die, you are to take command." The C.O. showed his sergeant the paper. Showed him where he inserted it in his journal. He kept his journal in his bag, wrapped in a shirt that had belonged to Sergeant Cross.

Sergeant Brainard did not want this command. But since he could not tell his commander this, he said as hopefully as he could, "We've made it to May first, Lieutenant Greely. Eighteen of us have. The men seem cheerful enough. They talk of little else but food. Yet what else is there? It's all I think about. We have provisions—that is, bacon and pemmican and tallow—for nine days more."

"You are the only man capable of holding them together," Greely said. "My obligation is to prepare for our future."

"I understand," Brainard said, smiling. He wanted Lieutenant Greely to know he would accept this responsibility.

"Don't overstrain yourself with the shrimping," his C.O. advised in a fatherly manner. "You can't feed us all single-handedly, so I beg of you, don't even try."

"I know you're thinking of Rice, but I'm fairly confident I can keep us going on the shrimp and the kelp." This sea vegetation they were calling kelp was something new. Brainard used an iron rake he had manufactured from barrel hoops. It was heavy. It exhausted him to carry it down. It exhausted him to use it. It exhausted him to carry it back, along with the twenty pounds of shrimp and six or seven pounds of the kelp he could catch on most days. Truthfully, he didn't see how he could keep this up. He wasn't about to let on to Lieutenant Greely. Nor about his other worry. There was little of the bear left for baits. Just bits of skin. He wouldn't allow himself to rob the men of the good meat. The shrimp, he discovered, were particular about what they would feed on. They wouldn't touch old leather. He tried them on strips cut from a worn pair of gloves. These shrimp wanted fresh meat. Same as them. The dovekies had migrated through.

They were fighting bravely for life, how bravely the world might never know since none were likely to live to tell their tale. Brainard wrote in his journal but no words of his could do justice to the horrors of their situation. Just as well. He wouldn't want his family to know about the constant gnawing hunger that awoke them in the night and kept them weak and short-tempered. They jumped at noises. They could barely speak above a whisper. They fixed each other with vacant stares. They stooped; they wobbled and shook like feeble old men. Their clothing hung on their emaciated forms.

Brainard was glad to get away from them to go shrimping. Their hut was a foul place. Those too weak to move around outside — Lieutenant Greely was in this state now — appeared to be rotting in their bags. With the warming temperatures came the armpit stench of decomposition, the dizzy-making smell of alcohol, urine — fresh and old — along with the reek of vomit that once in your nose was hard to get rid of. Around their camp, the piles of excrement crept closer, thawing in the sun, fouling the air. He was glad to get away and breathe in the salty smell of the sea. But when the shrimp wouldn't attack his bait, he was overcome with helplessness. He had the sense of his own flesh being consumed, as if he were pursued by an unseen predator that compelled him to search for food more out of fear than the hunger itself.

When he crossed over Cemetery Ridge, he forced himself to see that all was in order. If the wind caused the brass buttons on Lieutenant Lockwood's coat to show through the gravel, he went down on one knee to cover them, and remembering how his friend had kept them shined back at Conger, was flooded with an appalling loneliness. He was only twenty-seven but he felt used up, their Conger life a lifetime ago. He would give his right arm to see a tree again, he thought as he descended slowly from the ridge. He would never live to see another tree. He would die, like those who had already died. His body would be eaten. His mind recoiled, stopping him in his tracks. He looked back up toward the cemetery where Lockwood lay. Cannibalism could not happen here. These were honorable men. Shorty and Long, his boon companions. Whisler, Schneider, and Biederbick, all hard workers. The observer Gardiner had a sterling moral character. Joe Elison, always cheerful. Ned Israel, who made a friend of everyone. Brainard could not imagine them turning cannibal. A heavy cloud blotted out the sun and a raw wind scoured his face. He quickly buttoned up the topmost button on his coat, thinking of Connell and that strange man Private Henry. And the doctor.

✶

On May 3, as Sergeant Brainard walked into camp with his load from the sea, shouts caused him to look quickly around. Some disturbance was taking place around his storehouse. Private Bender was waving his arms and shouting. They had seized poor Whisler's arms like city constables and were marching him toward the hut.

As Brainard slipped in, Bender squeaked, "Sergeant Davy, Whisler stole our bacon!"

Whisler was on his knees before these men, the ones too weak to work or too indifferent, and the ones who had been working with every ounce of their remaining strength. All were crouched in the dim interior light, staring at Whisler. "I'm sorry, *I'm sorry!*" Whisler blubbered.

"I'm . . ." He covered his face with his hands. Brainard looked around at these stony forms, like statues in a wasteland, their sunken eyes, their grime-encrusted faces, primitive, bestial, so hairy as to appear hardly human. Ready to cast judgment, ready to tear this man, their comrade, apart for his crime. "My mother," Whisler moaned, "she would be so ashamed. Of me." He was crying now, hands pasted to his eyes. As Brainard watched, these judges shifted position, an embarrassed rustling. They were well aware of Whisler's tears. Bender pulled Whisler's hands away to reveal his dirty face, furrowed and streaked. "I saw you," he squealed. "You broke Sergeant Davy's lock."

"No!" Whisler came alive in his own defense. "The door was ajar. The wood was splintered. I was just walking by. I bet it was you, Bender. *You* broke Sergeant Davy's lock."

"Not me!" Bender's features assumed the look of the wrongly accused. "I saw you," he went on. "I saw your hand stuff that bacon in your shirt. I saw it all!" Bender screamed these last words.

The meat was sitting in front of Lieutenant Greely, as if it itself were on trial. A pitifully small amount. A child could have wrapped his hand around that bacon.

Whisler raised his face to his accusers. "I couldn't help myself," he said. "I saw that bacon on the shelf, our last two pounds. My God, the smell." He stared down at his right hand—the broken nails, the ground-in grime—that lay inert by his side. "I couldn't stop it. If you put me before the firing squad . . ." Whisler began to blubber again. "I say to you as a starving man, I couldn't have stopped myself. You can kill me if you want," he concluded in a choking voice. He looked around; each man dropped his eyes.

The C.O. cleared his throat. "I see you are repentant, Private Whisler. But if you offend again, it will be necessary to take those extreme measures you speak of." The C.O.'s eyes scoured all their eyes, and there was not a soul in the hut who didn't doubt that if *he* were caught, the firing squad would be his fate.

"I didn't force the lock," Whisler said again and swung to point at Bender.

"Don't look at me! It wasn't me!" Bender squealed.

"Damn you, Bender, you tried to frame me!" Whisler's voice rose.

The C.O. straightened himself to his old ramrod position. "That's enough!" There was silence. "Who forced Sergeant Brainard's lock?" His voice was hardly more than a whisper, a breath of air. Its strength was gone, but it held them. No one answered, though heads turned toward Private Henry.

"Don't lay this one on me." The private laughed, putting up his palms, fending them off. "I've got witnesses. I've been sitting here the whole time."

"You have not," Joe Elison said. "You just came in."

"I've been here, here in the bag," Charlie snapped. "It was Connell who just came in. You saw Connell, Joe."

"Well, fuck you," Connell said, but without much heat. They lacked the energy now to keep the inquisition going, though they were eyeing one another like suspicious dogs. Who jimmied Sergeant Davy's lock? It could have been any of them.

Private Henry was still a prisoner, though the C.O. allowed him outside in a work party. He was their strongest. He could carry the heaviest load and work longer. He had more energy. Where did he get this from? Brainard had been asking himself this question. From what food source? Not the cemetery, he was pretty sure of that. The graves appeared untouched and Henry was watched too closely. Brainard sometimes felt like kicking himself for not telling Lieutenant Greely about Private Henry's past history of crime. Yet he didn't see how he could have come to any other decision. By the time he had learned about Henry's past, it was too late. The last thing he wanted to do, at the beginning of their expedition, was appear to be questioning his commanding officer's decision to take this man.

✶

Schneider had scurvy, that was what the doctor said. He made out his will. So had most of the others. They wrote farewell letters to friends and relatives, or dictated them. Death was a matter of business now.

Private Henry wrote a postcard to his old commander, Captain Price.

Only six more days' provisions are left us. Starvation looks us in the face. Seven of our party are dead and the rest of us are resigned to follow. The expedition has been a success but I have unfortunately not been. Thanking you for past favors. I am yours, living in feeble hopes of succor.

C. B. Henry

He tucked it in his journal. Some of it he had written in German, some in English. Most of it was water-stained and unreadable. This should upset him, but it didn't. He had intended it for the editor of the *Chicago Times*. But the only thing he cared about now was food. He sat in his bag, biting his pencil. When he looked up, Sergeant Brainard had his eye on him. The private withdrew his knife from his pocket and scraped at the lead. He ripped out the least-grimy page from his journal and started writing again.

Dear parents and siblings:

Probably this small slip of paper will be the last one you will receive from me. There is only a small ration left for the next six days (not more than half a pound of meat), and we are not hopeful to get help. If we are not getting birds or seals, we are all going to die. We are all faint and hardly can stand up and I can't outline my thoughts in a reasonable letter.

Dear parents and siblings, don't grieve about me. I'm not worth it. Don't worry about me. I hope that you are alive and healthy.

I'll stay your son and brother,

Charls Buck or Charles B. Henry

✗

The light was constant. And because of that, unwelcomed. Cloudy days were the worst because the sun should cast a gentle light. But nothing about this diffused light was gentle. The ink-black rocks appeared more malevolent, the snow a stinging white, more cruel. The waves out in the sound, flashing signals to the bergs, turned them into implacable pillars of glass. This light reflected off of everything and everywhere at once.

The wind kept the light in motion. When the wind came in unsteady, unpredictable bursts, it put a man on edge. He might be resting his eyes on a safe spot of shade when a boisterous bouncy wind shoved away the clouds and the blinding glare had him tugging down his hood, cursing this soul-exposing light. Filtered or unfiltered there was no escaping this raw Arctic illumination. When the sun lowered, a man cast a long, emaciated shadow.

It was important in the hut, though, to let in light, and Schneider helped Whisler cut another large section from the side of the boat-roof and cover it with canvas to keep out the snow. They needed wood for fuel, but their timing was poor as this southeast gale hit with ramming speed, dropped the temperature, and stuffed their igloo entrance with snow, making it hard to draw a decent breath. They lay in various attitudes of wretchedness. Connell was sprawled on his back, eyes staring, mouth open. He looked dead. To find out, Charlie kicked him in the leg and Connell let out a reassuring groan. Sergeant Brainard crawled out. Catching shrimp was imperative, and he craved fresh air. When he crawled back in, three hours later, with twelve pounds of shrimp and two of kelp, an argument between the doctor and Lieutenant Greely appeared to match the storm outside.

"You give yourself extra food," the doctor shouted. "You think you save yourself by taking lime juice pemmican. But, I, the doctor, tell you, the lime juice is old. It cannot protect you from scurvy."

"Dr. Pavy," the C.O. said, "it was at your suggestion I am taking these few extra ounces."

"You steal food from starving men," the doctor raved. "Yesterday, I recommend extending the fresh bear meat but today you order men have bacon and pemmican *instead* of fresh meat."

"Dr. Pavy"—the C.O.'s voice rose in his frustration—"can't you see? By ordering the bacon and pemmican, *I am extending the fresh meat.*"

"I see everything! I am the doctor!" Pavy clawed his way out of his bag and toward the commanding officer. "You never listen. You cut Private Elison's ration by four ounces. Private Elison is our sickest man.

You are crazy! You are stupid!" Pavy was crouched in front of Lieutenant Greely. "Look at me!" he shouted in his face.

"Dr. Pavy, stand off." Lieutenant Greely shrank back against the icy wall, his face chalk white under the grime.

"By God, our doctor knows how to hate." Charlie Henry made no effort to keep his voice down.

"Our doctor's a bloody hypocrite!" Connell shouted. "Pavy's living off Elison." There were nods and a few snickers. "Doctor Pavy." Connell's voice had turned dead serious. "What you just said about the lime juice. Is that right?" He began to root around with his fingers in his mouth. "Dammit it, my teeth."

Charlie laughed. "You blustering Irishman, I'd swear you're more afraid of scurvy than you are of dying."

The doctor paid attention to none of this. He shook his fist under Lieutenant Greely's nose. "You issue Sergeant Brainard rations without bone in it," he screamed.

More snickers and Ned Israel, who avoided disputes, broke in with, "Think of issuing a diet of bones to the very man who is working so hard to put food in our mouths."

"Shut up! Shut up! Shut up!" The C.O.'s voice popped like rifle fire.

"Never!" bellowed the doctor. "You cannot make me."

"If you were not the surgeon of this expedition, I would shoot you!"

"The doctor's right," squeaked Bender. "Everybody listen to our doctor."

"Private Bender"—the C.O. turned on this new threat—"you will preserve silence or I will shoot you as well."

"I'm for the doctor. He should be commander. Who's for Dr. Pavy!" squealed Bender, throwing off his sleeping bag and crawling on hands and knees toward the C.O.

Lieutenant Greely seized the Remington, leveling the barrel at Bender, who, seeing he was about to be shot at point-blank range, screamed as though the shot had been fired.

"Showdown at Camp Clay," Connell yelled. "The strong will get through by shooting the weak. *This is it!*" He beat his chest in a fit of lunatic laughter.

Charlie slapped him in the face. "Stop it!" His voice was hard as iron. "You're mad." Connell stopped. His face was red from the slap and his eyes ran.

Sergeant Brainard, who had been waiting for the right moment, lifted the weapon from his commanding officer's hands. "Private Bender," he directed, "you will return to your sleeping bag at once."

And, as though the switch had been flicked off, they were overcome by a lassitude. Connell fell back in the bag, eyes fixed on nothing. Bender, too, crumpled into a comatose state. The doctor, back in his bag, held his head in his hands, muttering to himself in French. Sergeant Brainard saw to Lieutenant Greely. "Easy, easy," he said, helping his superior officer slide down into his bag.

"The C.O. is a bastardly coward, just like I've always said," Charlie muttered to the air.

Sergeant Brainard heard this and half-agreed. Lieutenant Greely should never have lost his temper. The doctor was a very ugly customer, but David Brainard hated to think what might have happened if his commanding officer had pulled the trigger. Lieutenant Greely was unable to deliver a clear order that addressed the situation. Any leader was capable of making a bad decision, and Brainard had promised to assert himself if his leader showed signs of doing so. He was glad he returned from his shrimping when he did. He could have found somebody dead if he had been a few minutes later.

In the lull, Whisler began, "Tomato butter. Use the wild grape jelly in a pie. Save some for tarts, though." And so they went on in the only way that gave them comfort.

"Fry the dumplings left over from chicken pot pie and scramble eggs over them," Elison responded.

"I'll have my mother send each one of you her recipe for champagne cider," offered Israel, words he had said many times before.

Whisler sat up. "Last night," he told them, "the meal before me, the aroma of the mashed potatoes swimming in the gravy from the pork roast . . ."

"Did you say pork or pot?" queried Bender.

"Pork."

"Ah," Bender sighed and licked his lips.

"Shut up, Bender," Connell barked. "Go on, Whisler."

Whisler seemed unaware of the interruption. "The baked beans, hot and sizzling in the bacon fat . . ." He stopped. He burst into tears.

"The bacon fat," Charlie said. "Don't cry now. For God's sake, go on!"

"I picked up my fork," Whisler wheezed between gulping breaths. "I picked up my fork to devour this feast when the smell of it, *the overpowering smell of it*, woke me up."

✴

On May 12, at breakfast Sergeant Brainard passed out twelve and a half ounces of bacon and tallow to each man. It was a two-day ration, he told them; it was the last of their provisions. They might as well have all of it now. "You can each decide how you want to portion it out," he said.

Private Henry weighed it in his hand. "Pocket change," he said.

"What did Charlie say?" Bender asked.

"Doesn't weigh any more than pocket change, Bender," Charlie explained. "I'm going to eat mine now." Charlie opened his mouth and stuffed in all of the bacon and tallow. He had stopped using the forks brought from Conger long ago. His mouth was crammed so full he could hardly chew.

"You're disgusting," Connell said. Charlie attempted a smirk, forcing the food to spurt between his teeth. He shoved it back with his fingers. "You stink like garbage." Connell held his nose, though he couldn't help laughing.

"From now on," Sergeant Brainard broke in, ignoring these privates, "we'll be living on the shrimp. Shrimp and kelp soups. Elison has turned over the last bit of lard the doctor uses as ointment on his stumps to the commissary and the cooks can add that to the soups. There are green buds on the saxifrage now. We'll see how these taste. Well, it's not taste I'm concerned about, it's nutrition. The lichens upset some of the fellows' stomachs, and, Ned, I know you have trouble with the shrimp. We need food that is digestible." He gave them a quick smile. "So let's see how these attractive green buds work out."

Sergeant Brainard kept his concerns about his baits to himself. Also his strength. He crawled out nonetheless and fished in the current storm for the rest of the morning. The Greenland coast was blotted out, but no one was over there anyway. He was soaked and chilled. But he could drive his discomfort out of his mind *if* the shrimping went well. He stuck it out until he had twenty-six pounds he could split between two large buckets and sling—yoke-like—across his shoulders with a strap.

His load was too heavy. He staggered across the hummocks until blood was gushing from his nose. He was forced to sit. His vision darkened, and he hung his head down between his knees, wondering who would assume his duties when he was used up. He thought about death: the easy way out at this point. He didn't want to lose his mind like Kislingbury was doing now. Or like poor Lockwood. To stop this line of thinking, he got to his feet.

The sun came out. It was shining as strong as it had ever shone at Camp Clay. Davy Brainard found all of them lying on tattered clothing they had pulled from the hut, spreading themselves like seals on an ice floe. Private Henry had his shirt off. He was flat on his back, his ribs protruding like bars on a xylophone. His stomach was so sunken, such a livid white, it was hard to believe this man was still alive. But he was; he was their strongest. Back at Conger, Brainard told Henry that he had never seen a man of such strength with less work in him. "Watch out you don't sunburn yourself, Private," Sergeant Brainard said as he passed by. He was looking for the doctor, to fill him in on his nosebleed. "That kind of hemorrhage, Sergeant," Pavy informed him in a knowing tone of voice, "is caused by overexertion." Well, *he* could have told the doctor that.

✱

Camp Clay

16 May 1884

Darling Rettie,

I have always endeavored, in my letters, to give you a fair appraisal of our situation, and now, as the chances of our returning grow thinner by the day, I will write my thoughts for your future as clearly as I can apprehend them under the circumstances. Of course I think very much of you all. The whole party are prepared to die, and I feel certain that they will face death quietly and decently when it comes as have those who have already passed. My will is as strong as ever but the doctor fears for my heart and has let me know my chances are slim.

As regards to your future, I trust to your own good judgment. I wish, however, that one of the girls, or perhaps both, be educated as analytical chemists. Such would enable them to support themselves. I would neglect music & singing but cultivate painting if either has the talent. Instruct them in useful branches only—including German even if French is neglected.

No game now in twenty-seven days.

I have cut off some hair for you. I would like a set of plants to go to the Newburyport Public Library, where also I would wish my private journal to go when you or our daughters have no further interest in keeping them as family records. I send you a complete set of unmounted photographs. These (plates and negatives) were taken by George Rice and cannot be duplicated. Lieutenant Lockwood brought you a stone from his Farthest North and it will come to you with your napkin ring and the silver monogrammed fork that I keep with me at all times.

I give and bequeath to my beloved wife, Henrietta Nesmith Greely (whom may God bless and keep in the hollow of his hand), all my property, real and personal . . .

A. W. G.

Deaths

7. Jens Edward, 29 April 1884, drowned.

✕

8

Fortitude is necessary, and patience and courtesy and modesty and decorum, and a will, in what may for the moment seem to be the worst of worlds, to do one's best.

Marcus Aurelius, *Meditations* (ca. AD 161–180)

The sun, now positioned above the North American Arctic, effected its seasonal change at Camp Clay. The temperatures seldom went below zero. When the sun was out and the breeze light, the men went about their chores in a world that had heat. The temperatures remained low, around ten degrees. But when the sun shone forth, its heat penetrated their bones. Lying in a sheltered sunny alcove was like lying in an oven. The sun put heart into the men; they swore it strengthened them. But this life-giving orb was their enemy, too. The sun had the power to thaw the ground and the ground in their hovel was wet, condemning its inhabitants to lie in puddles. At night—or what they called night— when the temperature dropped, the ground froze, freezing the bags and ensuring a wakeful miserable time. The C.O. ordered the large wall tent to be hauled to higher ground, up near Cemetery Ridge. But since this took the combined strength of four or five men, the task remained undone, though Connell pointed out the advantage: "Shorter distance to lug them when they die," he said, getting a mix of chuckles and glares.

Most of them had nearly reached this point, including the Irishman. Whisler broke down while sawing one of the sledges for wood. Bender, to everyone's surprise, took over. "You came to the fore, Private," Sergeant Brainard told him with a clap on the shoulder, and Bender puffed up his chest as much as his starving state allowed.

Long shot a raven. Brainard seized it for shrimp bait against a storm of opposition. Though all knew shrimp bait was the highest purpose for this scrawny bird. Biederbick had explained that they only stimulated their appetites by eating such small amounts. They were worse off than if they had eaten no food and could die quickly.

Ellis died of starvation on the 19th. Sergeant Brainard had difficulty finding enough men with the strength—or willpower—to haul the corpse to the cemetery, and voiced his outrage to his diary: *If the U.S. does not send a vessel with the whalers when they pass Melville Bay during the first days of June, it will be criminal on their part or the most inexcusable ignorance.*

On May 22, Lieutenant Greely hand-fed Ralston a portion of his own shrimp stew. The observer sang a song, fell into a state of delirium, and drifted into death sometime in the night. The corpse was dragged out of the hut. It sat outside their door for two days, until there was manpower willing to transport the remains on the sledge. By the time they returned, Whisler was gone and some of the men were openly weeping. Brainard directed an inquiring look toward Lieutenant

Greely. They were all pretty indifferent to death now. Apathy, provoked by their constant hunger, had driven out their more human feelings. "Whisler begged for forgiveness for stealing that bacon," the C.O. explained.

"That was two weeks ago," Brainard answered, "and we did forgive him."

All these deaths seemed painless and that was a large comfort. The victim slid into an unconscious state and sailed away. If this happened at night, it was not noticed until the cooks started the stove in the morning. Sergeant Brainard's job was to go through the man's pockets for personal items the family would want. Photographs of loved ones, a watch or a clasp knife, letters unfolded and refolded until falling apart. He went through Whisler's pockets and pulled out tea leaves. Tea leaves so used they couldn't have colored water. "He must have been smoking them," Connell growled, "the dirty thief. He could have offered them around."

By late morning of May 25, Brainard put together a team to haul Whisler's corpse up to the cemetery. No sooner had they struggled the well-trod 375 yards than the sun was blotted out and a storm hit, snow stinging their faces as they fought to get the gravel over poor Whisler's corpse. An inadequate job, but Sergeant Brainard couldn't hold the men longer and they fled down the hill like Napoleon's army retreating from Moscow. As Bender passed the wall tent—they had managed to set it up—he came to a dead halt. "Look!" he shouted and pointed to a caterpillar crawling around in a bare spot. Charlie, who was with him, stopped. The others streamed on past. "It can hardly crawl," Bender said.

"Too cold, you numbskull."

"There's another!" cried Bender. He snatched it up and popped it in his mouth. "Too much meat to lose, Charlie," he said with his mouth full.

Charlie watched him swallow it. He couldn't figure it out. Normally he would have demanded Bender give him half. Why, he would have broken Bender's arm if he refused. But this caterpillar wiggled as Bender dropped it into his mouth. It was alive! And the idea of having a live wriggling thing in his mouth revolted him. "What did it taste like, Bender?"

"Not bad."

"That's no answer. Was it furry? It looked furry."

"Don't know. Hardly chewed." Bender licked his cracked lips. "Try one." Charlie looked around, spotted several more lured out by the sun, now frozen in place by the quick drop in temperature. "I've seen you eat seal intestines," Bender urged. "This is only a caterpillar."

But Charlie had turned downhill. He was waving his arms to attract the others. "Bender ate a caterpillar," he shouted. "Hey, you fellows. Fresh meat!" But no one stopped. "See that, Bender? They didn't want to eat live crawly things either."

When Sergeant Brainard reached the hut, he grabbed his shrimping gear and took off again. He was exhausted from hauling up Whisler's corpse, he felt weak, and he had a throbbing headache, but they had lost three men in the last four days. When he reached the shore, he set his baits and began to pace up and down the stony beach. Waiting for his nets to fill, he lectured himself on the importance of sticking it out. "We've lost three men in the last four days," he sang, the words revolving in his head like an organ grinder's tune. "Glory, glory hallelujah!" he added. "We've lost three men in the last four days. Glory, glory hallelujah!" He couldn't seem to stop himself. "But the troops go marching on." He smiled at this addition that made him think of his brother Henry and that made his feet march. He forgot his shrimp. The marching warmed him and for some unaccountable reason, he felt a rush of joy that had him swinging his arms, all in time to the song in his aching head, until he found himself lying facedown on the stones.

He lay there awhile, the wind blowing over his back, until he noticed the song was gone. His headache had about disappeared. He turned over and sat up. Then he remembered his nets. They held very few shrimp and Davy Brainard blamed himself for that. *I neglected them. What happened to me? I was marching with my brother. I was out of my mind, I think.* He shook his head, filled his buckets (not enough for their dinner despite their depleted numbers), and began the trudge home, to Camp Clay.

Back in the hut, desperate to add to their dinner, he picked up a sealskin thong and started cutting it into small pieces. "Here," he said as he handed them to Shorty, whose stubby form was bent over the cook pot. "Add these. We'll eat the leather now," he told everyone. "We've got boots and sleeping bag covers. It will be our substitute for meat."

"Like Franklin's men," Charlie muttered. "When you're down to the leather on your knife sheath, it's the beginning of the end."

"The end of the end, I'd say," Connell growled. "It's a short march to the grave. I've got scurvy," he informed everyone. "My mouth is sore and my teeth are loose and my gums feel spongy. Sergeant Brainard, I can't chew the damn leather!" Connell's complaint ended in a pitiful wail.

"Well, do your best, Private." Brainard went on, "We'll try the black lichens. Plenty of them around. We'll send out parties and scrape it off the rocks."

"*Tripe de roche*," Doctor Pavy said. "You give the men diarrhea."

"I approve of Sergeant Brainard's proposal, Doctor," Lieutenant Greely countered. The C.O. had Ned Israel in his bag with him now. He had increased the young man's ration by a few ounces and was feeding him himself. No one begrudged Ned the extra food. He was their mascot as much as Elison. His handsome, serious face was wasted, eye sockets hollowed out, the flesh gone from his cheeks. Ned Israel had a bright future. He was too young to die.

"I *dis*approve," the doctor bit out, coming alive when he argued with the C.O. over food. "You want to kill them? They are too dehydrated to withstand diarrhea now."

Brainard shrugged. "You're talking about the water loss, I understand that doctor. But I have experimented with these lichens on myself and have had no trouble digesting them. We must take advantage of any food source."

"Foolish! Stupid! You commit murder!" Pavy raved. But he got no support. It took too much energy to pay attention to Pavy now.

Ned Israel fell into a delirious state, babbling about the beef sausage his mother purchased from the German butcher. They had heard this many times but never tired of hearing it. He died in the C.O.'s arms. Sergeant Brainard went through Ned's pockets and pulled out paper money, enough of it to fulfill Ned's last wish that he and Lieutenant Greely visit his parents in Kalamazoo, Michigan. He wanted them to take the train and stay in the hotel. Brainard stared at the bills, mostly fives and tens, but there was one twenty with its image of Alexander Hamilton, meaningless here in their isolation: no streets, no houses, no restaurants, surely no hotels, no buildings of any kind, no people other than themselves, no human sounds other than those made by them. He tucked the money away for safekeeping.

They lugged poor Ned's corpse up to the cemetery the next day, May 28, and covered him with the gravel. It was noon. They stood in the wind, encircling the small mound—Charlie, Bender, Connell, Schneider, Shorty. Long was out with the one working rifle, the Remington. The others—the remaining observer Gardiner, Corporal Salor, Kislingbury, and Lieutenant Greely—were too weak to do more than crawl a few feet away from the hut now. Elison couldn't crawl anywhere, and the doctor rarely assisted on these strenuous uphill hauls. Sergeant Brainard spoke. "Ned Israel, we will remember you for your frankness, your honesty, and your generosity. Your gentle spirit won all our hearts." He wiped a hand across his face as his voice broke.

There was another task, since they were up here: to erect a small shelter in front of the tent. The hut, with its soaked floor and its boat-roof gone to firewood, was uninhabitable now, though some of them were still sleeping there since the wall tent couldn't hold everyone. Hence the need for a smaller shelter: a canvas and two poles. Nine had been laid to rest in the cemetery on the ridge. Rice froze. Jens drowned. Fourteen were still alive.

✻

Camp Clay

29 May 1884

Dear Henrietta,

I want you to know why I decided not to remain at Conger. We had plenty of supplies, food, and clothing. The men were reluctant to take to the boats. I was myself. But to remain had me going against orders, orders that

I myself was a party to. If no relief appeared, my orders were to start out along the coast. We would provision ourselves from the caches we'd laid down on the way up. I hoped to run into the relief.

I believe in following orders. Yet, I was free to make up my own mind. That is, I was free to disregard these orders. Many times I was on the verge of talking my thinking over with Lieutenant Lockwood. But he was often out exploring. I could not talk with Lieutenant Kislingbury, no longer part of the expedition. I thought about turning to Sergeant Brainard, a most reliable man and a clear thinker, but it did not seem right to involve him in a decision that was mine alone to make. I must admit, I felt my isolation. The doctor was against leaving Conger. I would not like to say my nerve failed me, but if we had stayed at Conger and I had begun to lose men, that would have ended my career. I chose the safer course, not only for my future, but in terms of what was expected of me in Washington.

The men were not happy in the boats, but within a month we could see Cape Sabine only fifty miles south. My plan had always been to gain the Greenland side, land at Littleton Island, where the Eskimos there could help us, as they had Elisha Kent Kane. It was at this point the little luck we'd had ran out. We became buffeted about by crosscurrents, by wind and ice so cruel we took to the floes to prevent the boats from being crushed. We drifted in the cold and the wet. We lay in our makeshift shelters in misery and idleness. This was the situation when Sergeant Brainard came to me. "What a fine spring retreat we could have made," he said, "from Fort Conger with the sledges." He meant if we had wintered over we could have traveled on land down the coast. I had suspected that he was not in favor of leaving Conger. He went on. "Our sufferings would have been so much less." I looked him in the eye. "You surprise me," was all I said. I had followed orders. I was not going to defend my decision, even to him.

We landed at Eskimo Point, just south of Cape Sabine, at the end of September. No one was more aware than I that to survive the winter on this desolate cape, where the black cliffs rise straight from the sea and all was utterly lifeless, would test us severely. It was at that point I realized I was beyond the reach and censure of those issuing orders in Washington. It was entirely up to me to keep my men alive. This, Henrietta, is what I have dedicated myself to. It is from this I draw my strength. I have ceased to second-guess myself about the decision I had made that brought us here.

My dear wife, it eases me to write you my most hidden thoughts.

Your loving husband,
Adolphus

P.S. I don't know if I've told you that the men have been willing to supply our frostbitten invalid, Corporal Elison, whose hands and feet are useless, with a few ounces more of food a day. This began last November. As these extra ounces come from their own rations, I regard this effort to care for Elison—and the world should regard it too—as a supremely generous act.

✱

On the last days of May, a gale blew up from the southeast. Storms from that direction delivered a merciless pounding that left a heavy drift. This gale, Sergeant Brainard felt, regarded them as its personal enemy, keeping up a steady attack for forty-eight hours, delivering a barrage of wind intent on mowing them down like a cavalry charge. It left them weakened, bone-chilled, and nearly senseless under a fresh accumulation of snow that melted into their bags. Any man pursued by the Furies of such a storm was so brutalized by wind as to be left barely human, a victim of the cacophony of noise.

Sergeant Brainard was in the recently erected shelter with Dr. Pavy and Salor, the three of them sharing one bag. They couldn't keep out the drift or the flying gravel, and the poles that supported the canvas twisted and jumped in their hands until the whole shelter collapsed around their heads. Finally the storm let up enough to let them scrape their way out and pitch the shelter again. Then Sergeant Brainard set off for the fishery. He managed to catch eight pounds of shrimp before the wind and snow blasted him again. He had a fearful struggle to regain the shelter. Dropping to his knees to crawl in, he encountered Dr. Pavy. "You're too wet." The doctor stuck out his face. "We don't want you." He raised his arm and pushed Sergeant Brainard out.

"Don't want me? What are you saying!" Brainard called out, "Salor, let me in."

"Sleep in one of the bags out there. Plenty around." Salor's response came so easily Brainard wondered if he and the doctor hadn't planned this.

"Let me in!" he shouted and tugged at the flap.

"Get away," the doctor snarled, and Brainard realized they were holding it closed from the inside. He was exhausted. He had no energy to fight them, so he stood up, staggering around, inspecting the bags. All were frozen and full of snow. He picked up one and tried to shake it out but the frost clung to the inside. Nevertheless Brainard forced his way in. These bags had been abandoned for good reason. The closures were broken, and he spent the night fighting to keep out the spindrift, freezing his hands in the process. His whole body shook from the cold. He could not relax. Sleep would not come. The discomfort was intolerable, yet he knew he *could* bear it.

Worse was the storm raging in his mind. He was seething over the wrong done to him by the doctor and Salor. Corporal Salor had not distinguished himself on their expedition. Brainard knew little about him other than his father lived in Luxembourg and was the beneficiary in Salor's will, a document Brainard had in his own safekeeping. But Salor was not by nature a bad man. He must have been influenced by the doctor. He wondered if Doctor Pavy wanted to get rid of him, and, in his misery, Brainard got to dwelling upon their hopeless state, their abandonment by the government who had sent them up, their extreme suffering with no end in sight. It would be a relief, he thought, if he did die in the night. But then his mind turned to the courage of Rice, who died for them, and Jens, their lost hunter, and of Elison, who was always cheerful, and how important it was to keep Lieutenant Greely alive. He couldn't die now. He was needed. There was no one to take over the shrimping. There was no one to divide their food, no one as trustworthy. So David Brainard spent the rest of the night fighting to stay alive, and puzzling over how they managed to be alive on six pounds of shrimp a day. Well, he reminded himself, this meager intake was reflected in their bowels. And for some reason that made him laugh. Though it was no laughing matter that their bowels functioned no oftener than every twelve to eighteen days. They dreaded the act. It was accomplished with great pain and left them exhausted. It was worst of all for Elison, who had to be carried out, propped up, and held in place by two men since he was too weak to support himself.

Morning came and Sergeant Brainard was still breathing. He struggled out from under a foot of snow and limped over to the wall tent. Here he found a welcome. "You're terribly swollen in the face, Sergeant Brainard," the C.O. said. "And look at your hands! Did you have a bad night?" He nodded and came in for his breakfast. He remained silent about his trials. The doctor and Salor had shown up, and he had no wish to confront them since it was sure to bring in Lieutenant Greely and only add to his antagonism of the doctor. As it turned out, they ate no breakfast. The gale was still in full force, shaking the tent and blowing out the stove. They were prisoners. Not even a swallow of water passed their lips.

It was clear that Lieutenant Kislingbury was losing ground. He kept begging for water. Lieutenant Greely melted some snow for him in a bottle he held against his chest, but the doctor kept insisting, "No! I prohibit it. I will not allow. I am the doctor saying this. Water will make Lieutenant Kislingbury worse. Lieutenant Kislingbury does not want water now."

"He's your friend, Doctor, give him water," Private Henry said. This drew attention. Private Henry was not noted for his humanitarian ways.

"What?" Pavy looked around. "Who said that?"

This was strange. They knew each other's voices, aurally speaking, as distinctive as fingerprints.

"I did," Private Henry growled.

"Oh. You," said the doctor. His eyes revolved around, focusing on nothing. "Lieutenant Kislingbury is not my friend," he finally said. "He might have been, once. But . . ." Pavy's voice trailed off and they were left listening to poor Kislingbury pleading for water. The doctor is not very sane, Brainard thought, but still he has us cowed.

Lieutenant Kislingbury lurched bolt upright.

"Praise God from whom all blessings flow," he sang. "Praise Him all creatures here below . . ."

Each word was as clear as sunlight in his clipped English accent. He fell back and drifted into an unconscious state. When Biederbick checked on him a few hours later, Lieutenant Kislingbury was no longer breathing. It was June 1 and the storm had passed.

✶

Pools of water were forming now in the depressions of the rocks and around their tent. Whoever was doing the cooking gathered enough for two days, most fortunate as their fuel was nearly used up.

Sergeant Brainard put together a party to drag Lieutenant Kislingbury's corpse up to the ridge, exhausting themselves, even though the haul was only seventy-five yards. When they returned, Brainard knelt by Lieutenant Greely's bag. "I cannot ask these men to make another trip. I came close to blacking out myself. And once up there, we have to dig through that gravel." He didn't tell the C.O. that Linn's feet were fully exposed, his feet bare. The men were buried with their boots on, except, somehow, for Linn. "Mummy's feet," Connell said, drawing everyone's attention to Linn's feet. "Feet of a bird of prey," he added. Indeed, with the blackened toes, elongated and distinctly jointed, there was a similarity. Sergeant Brainard wanted to cover them but did not ask that of the men, as this meant additional work. In fact that trip seemed to finish off Connell. His joints were so swollen he could barely hobble. His spongy gums were bleeding and his teeth so loose he couldn't chew. "I need fresh meat," he told them at supper, his eyes on Sergeant Brainard. "I have scurvy." And Brainard saw his rotting body terrified him.

Salor died in the night. Brainard, lying beside him in the bag, sensed that Salor was gone—the man was so utterly still. He didn't have the strength to roll this dead body out, so went back to sleep and slept soundly until the cooks announced breakfast.

Private Henry, who had maintained his strength better than anyone, came to the fore. He assisted Shorty, who was doing all the work about camp—cooking, gathering saxifrage for fuel, and cutting up wood from the boat-roof. Long continued to hunt, though with very little success.

Biederbick was diligent in his care of the invalids, who now included the meteorologist Gardiner and Lieutenant Greely. Both could do little more than lie in their bags and keep Elison company. The doctor did not neglect his medical duties, but took direction from no one. Schneider managed to bring in water, but could do nothing more. Bender and Connell were about used up, but Sergeant Brainard prodded them to crawl around and scrape the black lichens off the rocks. They managed this on hands and knees. These lichens went into the shrimp pot, and Sergeant Brainard was relieved to find that most of the men could digest them. Doctor Pavy was not eating anything. He just took a little weak tea. "Why aren't you eating, Doctor?" the C.O. asked him at their supper that evening.

But Pavy being Pavy did not answer. "I've noticed," Lieutenant Greely went on, "that you have been sorting through your medicines lately. Are you treating yourself? Do you have an ailment we should be concerned about, Doctor?" As the C.O. spoke, Pavy reached for his medicine chest, clutching it with both hands. "Doctor," said Greely, "I am not going to take your medicines away from you."

The doctor gave Lieutenant Greely a wild look. "You will kill these men. You will all die like Franklin. I will live. I eat no *tripe de roche*. I write my wife that her Octave will return to her."

"Doctor!" Bender cried out. "What's wrong with my hand? My hand is bleeding!"

He shook it, splattering everyone with drops of blood.

"Stop that, Private Bender." The C.O.'s voice was sharp.

The doctor crawled over. "Unbutton your shirt," he ordered, the crazed look gone. "Take it off." Bender did this. Little drops of blood dotted his chest. The men gasped. Blood seemed to be seeping out of Bender's pores, pooling in the great hollows of his collar bones, oozing from around his protruding ribs. "Look at him." Connell waved his arm. "Bender, you could be a skeleton in an anatomy class."

No one laughed. Not even Private Henry. Bender leaking blood was too horrifying to be funny. "What's wrong with me?" Bender squealed.

"It's the scurvy," Pavy announced. "I have never seen this. Very interesting, Bender. Let me examine your head." Bender lowered his head; he was starting to blubber. "Ah! As I thought!" The doctor was excited. "The mucous membranes. They break down." He displayed his fingers, still long and slender, covered in blood from Bender's scalp. The men began tearing off their shirts. Connell forced himself to run a hand over his chest. He licked his fingers. No blood. He pawed through his scalp. Licked his fingers. Again, no blood. "I'm clean," he told everyone. "Charlie." He poked his bag-mate. "I'm going to pull through."

Meanwhile, the doctor had Biederbick dig out the discarded clothing and other rags they used for padding on the tent floor. They wrapped Bender up. Schneider said, "Wrap him up good, Doctor. I don't want him leaking all over me in the bag. He'll give me scurvy."

"Impossible!" Pavy said in a singing voice. He sounds happy, Brainard thought. "Old wounds can unknit," the doctor sang. "They just come apart. I have heard this. Now I will see."

The C.O.'s hand flew to his jaw, where the bullet had passed through at Antietam. Sergeant Brainard's eyes flicked from the C.O. to the doctor to the rest of them. There wasn't anything he could do.

Deaths

8. William A. Ellis, 19 May 1884.
9. David C. Ralston, 22 May 1884.
10. William Whisler, 23 May 1884.
11. Edward (Ned) Israel, 27 May 1884.
12. Frederick F. Kislingbury, 1 June 1884.
13. Nicholas Salor, 2 June 1884.

9

There are few acts so basically revolting as cannibalism. However, to eat the bodies of the dead may not seem an unreasonable last resort to save the living.

Ancel Keys, *The Biology of Human Starvation* (1950)

The power drained from the wind as if from a spent bullet. High above the cliffs of Cape Sabine, up in the atmosphere where storms breed, the wind sputtered and blustered in a never-ceasing attempt to reach earth. But for this day, at least, Aeolus kept the drawstrings on his bag of demonic winds pulled tight. Even Smith Sound remained unaffected by the wind, the surface unruffled, glassy smooth. A deep calm had followed this storm.

✳

Private Henry's True and Accurate Account of the LFB Expedition

4 June 1884, midmorning.

A beautiful day. You can't say that very often around here. We sledged Salor's carcass downhill and slid him into the tidal crack. That's what the C.O. and Sergeant Brainard decided on, since the uphill haul for starving men is out of the question. We stood around—Shorty and Long, the sergeant and me, that's who we're down to for the able-bodied—and looked out over Smith Sound. The surface was smooth as a mirror, not a bucket of ice in sight, not a thimbleful. We silently scanned the horizon for a relief vessel. No one said anything, but that was the obvious reason for our intense concentration: to pick up a smokestack or sail. How nice that would be! But there was nothing. Not that I was expecting such an outrageous piece of good fortune. Still, I'd be glad not to die young.

✳

They performed their tasks mechanically now. Primary was collecting wood for the cook's fire. They scavenged barrel staves strewn around the camp, broke up the sledges, useless now since they were too weak to pull them, cut the woody stems of the saxifrage. There was always water to be fetched, an easier chore if they could place a pot under a ledge where the snow was melting and catch the drip. Shorty Frederick set himself the task of removing the piles of excrement from around the hut. "You've taken on the worst job of all, Shorty," Sergeant Brainard said. "I wouldn't have assigned what you're doing to anyone."

"Oh, I just like to keep busy," Shorty replied. He was using an old cook pot as a shovel, one with holes in it, and Brainard watched as Shorty trudged off, his short and still-stocky figure bending to the rhythm of working his improvised shovel to remove their shit.

All they thought about was food.

⚞

Private Henry's True and Accurate Account of the LFB Expedition
4 June 1884, noon.

The C.O. has been taking a light luncheon per doctor's orders, and I've been doing the same. There is a quantity of sealskin down at our old winter quarters and that's where I go for a snack. We've been ordered to keep away from there. The sealskin—sleeping bag covers, the thongs, mismatched boots—is off bounds. They've become expedition stores to be shared communally. The C.O.'s been very clear about this. Only Sergeant Brainard is allowed down at our old hut. So I'm up to my dirty tricks, and the C.O. is going to be hard on me if I'm caught. But being a sneak spices up my existence and gives me something to think about other than food. Well, that's not true! I'm obsessed with how to steal food. So the joke's on me. Ha! Ha! I keep what I make off with under little piles of rocks. My caches, and I visit them daily. I cut off tidbits and fill my pockets—a comfort beyond the telling. There is nothing like my outrageous relief when I sink in a hand and paw food. I'm like a burrowing animal that way, making sure of my underground food supplies.

Today I am determined to make it up to the ridge, with or without the doctor. Connell's legs have gone bad, so he's not in my way. Sometimes I give him a morsel, though if either the doctor or Connell finds out I've been up there without them they'll be angry. The doctor acts as if it's his own private hoard and he's in charge. But they won't find out. Concealment is my specialty. Why, no one here knows who I am! If Sergeant Brainard did, he would have said something to the C.O. long ago. It all would have come out, my whole inglorious past.

The temperature, as I write, is 32 degrees, but in the sun it registers 62 degrees. I find this difference between sun and shade as incomprehensible as I do the plain fact that more than half of us are dead. Does anyone back home remember their names? My name? Does anyone in Washington think about them? About me? What about the C.O.'s friend, General Hazen?

Well! Any astute reader of my diary will see that I have a difficult decision to make every day. My two food sources lie in opposite directions. Oh, the irony! I have to choose one. I am too weak to make a trip to our old winter quarters and then climb up to the cemetery on the same day. Today, before I do either, I want to record one more story for the *Chicago Times* editor. Perhaps the C.O. will let me read it to everyone after our supper. I hope so. Here goes:

Dear Readers: This is a story about how Private Bender blotted his copybook.

The doctor lets him sit outside. He tries to keep him wrapped. He's not a very pleasant sight, is our Bender. Long shot a dovekie. He shot and killed a king duck and an auk, but they fell into the sea and could not be retrieved. Hearing of this loss of food must have gotten to Bender. He knows the hunter and the shrimper get to split the trophy dovekie. The C.O. never lets us forget those two have to keep up their strength if they are going to hunt and shrimp for us. But Bender walks over and stands, wrapped in his blood rags like Banquo's bloody ghost, in front of Sergeant Davy and Long where they were crouched on a rock cutting up the bird. "I want my twelfth," he demanded. "There are twelve of us here and a twelfth of that bird belongs to me." He was screaming, or trying to. No one can voice much more than a hollow croak.

"Shut up, you bloody idiot," Connell weighed in. That made me laugh. Bender was the living personification of a very bloody idiot.

"I will not! I want to eat!"

"*Well, fuck you,*" Connell snarled.

"Private Connell"—the C.O. ratcheted up his voice above a whisper from where he was lying in the doorway of the tent—"you will cease your abusive language." But this phrase, so commonly employed by our C.O., had long ago lost its force. At this point Biederbick walked up and took Bender by his bloody arm. "Come with me, Bender," he said, "let them alone. They have to eat if we're to eat, too. You understand that, don't you?" Biederbick went on, *explaining*. He put his arm around Bender's bloody shoulder as if Bender were his kid brother. "I just want to eat," Bender blubbered.

Of course! He would get no argument there, but that's typical of life around Camp Clay these days.

✳

On June 4, when Sergeant Brainard passed over Cemetery Ridge to go shrimping, he cast his usual glance at their graves. Ten scrapes in the earth that make ten small mounds. He took in Linn's mummified feet and the brass buttons on Lieutenant Lockwood's coat, as bright as when cared for by the lieutenant at Conger, though now it was not tarnish remover rubbed on by Lockwood's hand, but the gravel that scoured those buttons.

A bit of fluttering cloth caught Brainard's eye. He walked toward it. Saw the canvas wrapping Kislingbury was cut, as were Kislingbury's trousers up to the thighs, the thighs exposed, the flesh pared down to the bone. "Oh, Christ," he muttered and wiped a hand across his eyes. Scanned the ground. Spotted Whisler's mound. Cloth showed beneath a thin sprinkling of grit. As he brushed this grit away and the cloth came with it, his fingers grazed bone. *Whoever made these cuts took pains to arrange the trouser legs to hide what was going on here. If I hadn't seen the fluttering cloth I never would have spotted the harm done to the remains of these men.* His stomach heaved. A wrenching attack of nausea brought him to his knees, levering up his breakfast of liquid shrimp. His body went clammy. He shook with cold. *So it's come to this. What Rice had foreseen.* Brainard remembered their conversation before Rice and Shorty had left for the English meat. "I hope," Rice had said, "that if the worst comes, I may retain my mental strength even after my physical has failed." If George Rice had lived, they might have avoided this. The men respected him—even Private Henry. If Rice had returned with the meat, his heroism, demonstrated by his selflessness, could have carried them through. But Rice was dead. Two months dead.

Brainard stood up. His head had cleared. He would put a stop to this. He would get them on a moral footing he could live with. He turned over in his mind whether to go back to the tent now and talk this out with Greely. No. He would catch their supper first and think this through while he was waiting for the crustaceans to find his traps.

Now I know where I can get something fresher than the old and cracked seal skins the shrimps turn up their noses at. But the thought of cutting into any of these men, even for shrimp bait, horrified him. He spent seven hours at the shrimping and trudged back with only two and a half pounds. This sea contained as many shrimp as there were stars above their camp, yet he was held back from feeding these men by his un-appetizing baits.

Long fared no better. He shot two dovekies but they landed in the water and drifted away. So the men spooned down a soup of the meager shrimp augmented with bits of leather that turned it gluey and with lichens that yielded a dark tar-like sauce to this mess.

All partook but the doctor, who drank weak tea alone. He set aside his tin and started rummaging through his medicines, pulling out one vial and then another, scrutinizing each with gestures and shrugs. "Ah! This is what I want," he announced. "This is for *you*," He thrust a tiny bottle at Elison. "It will make your feet grow. Drink it. Drink all of it!"

Biederbick intercepted the vial. "This is mercury. You want to kill him? Only a few drops takes care of syphilis."

"Not our problem at Camp Clay, eh boys?" Connell's crack elicited a round of snickers, but the doctor wasn't listening. He selected another vial, and as they stared, he emptied the contents down his throat.

"What was that you just took?" queried the C.O. in a raspy voice. But the doctor did not answer. He licked his lips, leaving a viscous black smear around his mouth. He proceeded to replace his little bottles, few of which found their proper homes.

"Here, Doctor," Biederbick said, "let me help you get them in the right slots."

"Get away!" Pavy pushed at Biederbick's hand.

"Was that the ergot you took, Doctor?" Biederbick would not be put off.

Pavy's eyes roved around. He seemed not to know his own hospital steward.

"I think it was," said Biederbick. "You took it for the iron, didn't you, Doctor Pavy?"

The black-rimmed mouth spread in a ghastly way, and Pavy rocked back and forth, clutching his medicines in a fierce grip.

"Well, be careful," Biederbick cautioned. "That's strong stuff to take with only a cup of weak tea in your stomach."

"What's wrong with you, Doctor?" Connell blurted out. "I don't think I trust you to doctor me anymore."

Schneider said, "Fry the dumplings left over from the chicken pot pie and scramble eggs over them." This was Elison's contribution from months ago, and had been ruminated upon so often, it had lost its ability to generate food talk.

"Listen to me." Lieutenant Greely struggled to rise. "Sergeant Brainard has brought to my attention the body cutting that has been going on in our cemetery." His voice was as clear as it had ever been at Conger. The men seemed to stiffen in place, but their eyes moved, each eyeing his neighbor. "I am not asking for confessions here," Lieutenant Greely went on, as if he were going over their daily assignments at Conger. "Instead I have a proposal. I have already consulted with a few of you and we conclude we have reached the point where we could add human flesh to our diet."

"So, it's official!" Connell shouted out. "Cannibalism at Camp Clay!"

"You Irish fool!" Charlie Henry growled. "I would like to go on record that I disagree with the C.O.'s decision."

"This is not an order, Private, I hope you understand that," Greely said.

"You'll find there is little flesh on starving men," Charlie continued in a menacing voice.

"Charlie," squeaked Bender, "Lieutenant Greely is giving us a chance for life. Don't you see?"

"It won't help."

"Of course it will," Biederbick said. "Dr. Pavy." The hospital steward turned toward the doctor. "Please give us your opinion."

"What I think?" The doctor had taken out all his vials and was once again attempting to replace them. "It will make us ill. I told Lieutenant Greely. I said—"

"Right you are, Dr. Pavy," Charlie cut in. "A diet of human flesh can make us sick as dogs."

"It will help my scurvy," said Connell. "Fresh meat, that's what you said, Doctor. But those scoundrels, they just want it for themselves."

"Each of you may do as your conscience dictates," the C.O. went on, ignoring Connell. He had talked it over with Brainard. As a way of keeping peace, no one would be accused.

"Will you yourself, Lieutenant," Elison began, "eat the flesh from our dead comrades on the ridge?"

"I will, Corporal Elison."

"Then I will, too."

"And so will I," Schneider said.

"Me, too," squeaked Bender.

"Well, damn. It's about time," growled Connell.

"Sergeant Brainard," the C.O. continued, "has agreed to be in charge, as he has been of all our edible stores. All will be carried out in a seemly and organized manner. Sergeant Brainard will bring the meat here and the cooks will serve it in our stews, mixed with the shrimp." He broke off. He raked his shaking fingers through his beard. "Please help me," he moaned, and Biederbick supported his commanding officer as he sank back into his bag.

"He's taking care of us, Charlie," Bender said, and put his arm around his friend's shoulder. "Can't you see?"

"You're so dumb, Bender. Get your bloody arm off me."

"You've been going up there, haven't you, Charlie?"

"None of your damn business, Bender. Now, get away from me." He gave Bender a shove.

"You're strong, Charlie. That hurt. I bet you're getting stronger. From what you're eating." Bender looked up at his friend from where he was sprawled across his soggy bag. "Charlie, bring me some. Next time you go. Help me get strong, Charlie."

Private Henry's True and Accurate Account of the LFB Expedition
5 June 1884, Thursday morning.

I can't keep myself from staring at the sound, but there is no ship in sight. We are running out of time. The time is running away and I am running out.

I need to resupply my pockets. I need to check on my caches. Dr. Pavy is waiting for me on Cemetery Ridge. No, he is not waiting. He needs my help; he needs me to lean on to make that walk now. I'm snared in a tangle of desperate needing. Slow down, Charlie. Don't forget. You're the weasel. A weasel sticks to his prey. He pursues it down holes. He is single-minded. He never lets up. Be a weasel. And it comes to me that despair itself is a kind of hope.

✳

The temperature had reached 34 degrees by afternoon and the wind from the west was light: a pleasant spring day at Cape Sabine when it was calm enough to hear the water dripping off the icebergs and the larger cakes cracking apart, out in the sound. On warm days, the men could drink the clear meltwater from the little pools. What luxury to scoop up a handful of water when the sun was shining and melting the snowbanks! But it made Sergeant Brainard think of Lieutenant Kislingbury. He died asking for water.

The doctor continued to take only tea. It was not really tea, just tepid water with a pinch of the used tea leaves extracted from Whisler's pockets, supplemented with saxifrage buds. These, unfortunately, imparted a bitter taste, and there were complaints.

When Long came shuffling back with a dovekie and Brainard limped in with a few pounds of shrimp, the C.O., seeing how exhausted they were, appointed Private Henry as cook. Shorty was still out foraging and those in camp were too ill for this duty now.

Private Henry set up the stove outside and when Bender tottered by, he said, "My, that smells good," and leaned to look in the pot where the dovekie was slowly simmering in its own juices.

Charlie glanced up, his jaws working.

"My God!" Bender squealed. "You're eating it!" His voice rose to alert the camp. "Charlie's eating our dinner!"

Private Henry stuck his fingers in the pot for another fragment, and, stuffing it in his mouth, began to chew in the rhythm of his stirring. Chunks of dovekie revolved around, the meat falling off the delicate bones and mingling with the shelly shrimp.

"Stop that!" Bender wailed. He was the only one at Camp Clay who could express himself with any force. "Lieutenant Greely, make Charlie stop!"

Private Henry wiped his mouth and rounded on Bender. "Goddamn you, Bender, you blackhearted, gutless, sniveling bloody bastard. I thought you were my friend!"

The C.O. crawled out on hands and knees. His elongated fingers, splayed on the gravel, appeared fleshless, the bones held together by the tendons alone, and his face was as drained of color as a dead man's. He inched toward Private Henry, and with great exertion that caused his breath to come in rapid bursts, pulled himself to his feet. He stood, swaying like a sapling in a high wind. "Private Henry," their commander said in a voice that had no more force than a kitten's. "Your offense is criminal. You are taking food out of the mouths of the only ones who are still able to feed us." He stopped to catch his breath and gestured to Long and Brainard, who had come out.

Private Henry's eyes were on the dovekie and he kept the spoon moving in gentle sweeps around the pot. Finally he looked up at Lieutenant Greely. "Do you smell it?" He lifted his hand—the one not holding the metal spoon—as if about to seize another morsel of their dinner. This propelled Sergeant Brainard forward. He stopped, but he was damned if this thieving man would eat more of Long's dovekie. "I asked, do you smell it?" Private Henry said again, addressing Lieutenant Greely, and Brainard stared as a generous rivulet of drool coursed down the private's chin and splashed into the pot.

"It was reported to me this morning," the C.O. went on, "that you were seen eating sealskin lashing and sealskin boots. You stole from the public stock. You violated my orders. What do you have to say for yourself, Private?"

Private Henry kept stirring. His eyes were fastened on the dovekie, now dissolved to skin, bones, and the smallest particles of meat. He scratched the back of his neck with his free hand. At last he said, "It was this way, Lieutenant Greely. I volunteered for the Lady Franklin Bay Expedition because I wanted to make my stake. We'd fenced in the Indians. Fighting them had played itself out. I needed to ensure myself a square meal, you know?" He flashed his teeth at Lieutenant Greely from where he knelt before the pot placed on the small flame of saxifrage twigs.

"I don't understand you, Private," Greely said. His face had turned a greenish gray with the strain of standing. "Your offense"—he took a deep breath—"is mutinous." He staggered and put out a hand. Brainard moved to intercept his commander before he fell, but Private Henry reached his C.O.'s hand first. "Why," he said, "your wrist is as thin as a chicken leg." From his kneeling position he helped the C.O. right himself, causing Brainard to see just how strong Private Henry still was, and how quick his reactions. "For the sake of us who are still alive," Lieutenant Greely continued speaking, his voice hardly above a whisper, "and in memory of those whom we have lost, can you promise not to steal food again, Private Henry?"

Shorty had returned and stood, shoulder to shoulder, with Brainard and Long, listening to the C.O.'s final sentences that sounded like a prayer.

Private Henry's metal spoon had never ceased to revolve. Occasionally it grazed the sides of the pot with a musical clink. Staring at the pulverized dovekie, he intoned, "I promise."

"I hope you are sincere. We are coming to the end and I cannot go on forgiving you." Sergeant Brainard stepped forward and took his commander by the elbow. Long assisted on the other side, and Shorty held back the flaps of the tent's opening, these three friends who had been through the Plains wars together. "Let me sit in the doorway," Greely said. They lowered him carefully, to let him sit in the sun.

✱

Private Henry's True and Accurate Account of the LFB Expedition

6 June 1884, Friday, early a.m.

I woke up feeling no better than a mouse or a shrew, some small rodent driven to ground.

The day was clear, like yesterday, the wind was out of the west. Shorty and Long and Brainard, too, were out looking for some sort of food, so the C.O. was stuck with me as cook again. Without a thought, and in front of everyone, I dipped my dirty hand into the cook pot.

"Look! Look! Stop him! Charlie's eating our breakfast!" screamed my friend Bender.

"You are relieved, Private," ordered the C.O. "Private Biederbick will cook."

I fell back in my sleeping bag. "You're done for now, you bastard," Connell mouthed in my ear. I didn't react, I just lay there, my hands behind my head staring at the tent fabric, nearly faded to white, moving gently in and out with the pleasant morning breeze.

I prepared myself for the C.O. to pronounce my sentence. After all, I had broken my promise. He beckoned to Sergeant Brainard, who had just crawled in. They began a conversation in inaudible tones. I was fairly confident they were conferring about me, but I cared not. In my mind a ship was in the sound. Close enough to see the men on the deck. An officer in a blue navy cap was looking straight at me and smiling. Suddenly my stomach cramped. I needed to take a shit. But if I left now I'd miss my share of breakfast. The C.O. extracted his notebook and pencil. Brainard crouched beside him, staring at his boots. The C.O. wrote, tore out the bit of paper, and passed it to him. Sergeant Davy read it and nodded, looking pretty grim about the mouth.

Biederbick dished out the mess and I got my fair portion, though Bender *had* to say, "Charlie's already eaten his. Don't give him any breakfast." A nasty, unnecessary remark but it got my mind off my attack of diarrhea enough to spoon it down.

"Let's go out," I said to Connell. He wouldn't look at me. "I bet we'll see a ship." But Connell turned away. "Aw, Connell." I gave it one more try. "Let's go out to look for flies. I've seen them. They're active during the hottest part of the day. Big as dragonflies, Connell, and buzzing. Come out with me and we'll catch flies. Ha! Ha!" I stupidly started to laugh. "We'll catch flies for Bender. Bender!" I addressed our bloody apparition. "You ate a caterpillar. Now I want to see you eat a fly."

But they don't want anything to do with me. I picked up my journal, smearing words across the page: Bender's down bad with scurvy. Connell has scurvy, too. They're going to die. The C.O. and Sergeant Brainard are up to something and it has to do with me. The tent's gone dead quiet. There is a ship out there. No one knows this but me. The doctor wants me to bring my knife when we go up later. He's lost his dandy little scalpel. "You lost it?" I asked. "*Non, non.*" He pats himself down as if he were the criminal. "Eet's only meesplaced." Lost or misplaced, the point is he needs me. We'll sneak away for a private feast even though my knife's broken and leaves a ragged telltale edge. But first I have my own business down at the old hut. I'll take the lichen pail, useful to put them off when I go among the rocks to check my sealskins. They're lucky to have me still on my feet. I'm about the only one left able to negotiate the heavy work around here.

✳

The weather held. The great everlasting orb in the heavens was generous with its light and heat. The vegetation emerged from its winter confinement of ice, and the snowbanks shrank. Water ran in rivulets down the rocks. Mosses sprang loose from the damp ground, spreading carpets of green. The saxifrage leaves unfurled, their green hues blending with the coarse grasses and the flat-edged sedges. Most eye-catching were the poppies—yellow, silky blooms that unfolded in the sun and closed in the shade. They made a blast of color. All this vegetable life, responding to the melting snow and softening earth, gave heart to the men of Camp Clay. They were living in the glory of an Arctic spring, whose origins of seasonal progression were lost in time and defied comprehension. Yet, because of that, it cheered them, even though this thaw came with the price of wet footware as the snowbanks turned mushy and the gravel-strewn ground spongy.

June 6, a Friday, was a bright day. The C.O. was propped in the tent door with the flap up watching Private Charles Henry climb the hill from the old hut. His second trip this afternoon. Sergeant Brainard, since his conversation that morning with the C.O. and reading the words on the scrap of paper, had kept close to the camp. He was keeping a vigilant eye on Private Henry; he had sacrificed his afternoon shrimp excursion to this end.

"What have you got there?" the C.O. called out. Private Henry didn't answer. He couldn't have heard, their commander's voice was so broken down. But Brainard saw, as Lieutenant Greely must have seen, that Private Henry had something in his pockets. He inserted a hand and pulled out a tangle of strips, nodding his head, and—Brainard was quite sure Private Henry grinned at these strips—then jammed them back in the pocket of his wool pants. His pockets were bulging.

As Private Henry drew closer, Lieutenant Greely repeated himself, reclining there on his buffalo-hide bag, staring at this private whose thefts amounted to mutiny. Brainard took note of how grimy black was his commander's face. He glanced at his own hands, equally black, and concluded his own face must look the same. He breathed in deeply. He seemed to be doing that these days; somehow he needed to force air into his lungs. Seeing Lieutenant Greely out in the sun was kind of shocking. His C.O. was about buried in his own long hair, and his clothes appeared to be sloughing off his limbs, like bark off the trunk of a dead-yet-still-standing tree.

Private Henry, when he reached Lieutenant Greely, began talking, causing Brainard to reflect how verbal the man was. Brainard had never forgotten, at the beginning of their Conger days, coming upon this private reciting Tennyson to a black-faced cliff. He regretted again that he had been unable to reach this man who, Brainard felt sure, had a poet's soul, but buried fathoms deep. *Too inaccessible for me to reach.* Right now Private Henry was standing, looking down on poor Lieutenant Greely in a smirking, smiling way that must have made their commander very uncomfortable. "In the last nine months," Private Henry began, "we've been through enough to turn the best of us into monsters. I heard your question. I have sealskin thongs. I took them from the hut." Charlie pulled a heap out of his pocket and let them dangle a few inches from Lieutenant Greely's nose.

"I ordered the men to stay out of the hut, Private Henry. What is in there is army property." He made a swipe at the sealskins as if to bat them away. "Once again you have violated my order." His tone was so sepulchral Brainard thought he sounded more in wonder at Private Henry's disobedience than angry.

"I will conceal these sealskins to eat later." The private went on in an offhand way that convinced Brainard that this man was beyond the point of caring what he said.

"Private Henry, you are bold in your admissions," his commander said. "Don't you see you put us all at risk by your stealing? I have told you I will take extreme measures, if needful." He pulled himself to a more erect position. "Have you no conscience, man?" the C.O. rasped out. "If not, perhaps you might exercise a little common sense." He was forced to pause to catch his breath.

"I know, sir, if we are to survive, we must put the needs of the party above our own. You have emphasized this since we landed at Cape Sabine." Sergeant Brainard saw a movement draw the private's eyes down. Their C.O. seemed to be engaged in the unmilitary action of wringing his hands. Private Henry spread his lips across his teeth in the manner of a smile. "You see, I do understand, sir." And to Brainard's ears this statement sounded free of irony. The private went on in a conversational tone, "Isn't it a lovely day, Lieutenant Greely? We are deep in the days of constant light. It makes me feel good to be alive." A raven gave out a raucous croak high, high up, and far out of gunshot if Long were prowling about. "I wish I could fly as high," Private Henry said, gazing up at the raven.

"Private," the C.O. said. His voice seemed to come from a long distance off and he did not complete his sentence. Brainard looked up at that raven, too. He and Private Henry gazed skyward at the same moment. Then both looked down on Lieutenant Greely, who had not noticed the bird. Private Henry drew back his foot, as though, it seemed, to kick his commanding officer. Brainard had to restrain himself from leaping forward. But Private Henry slowly brought his right leg back in line with his left, his two feet in his broken-down boots remained at rest before Lieutenant Greely. Then the private turned quickly and, as he headed back down the hill, swirled to give the C.O. a jaunty wave. "Common sense, sir, I'll remember," he said as though they had just whiled away a happy moment in amiable chat, the lowly private appreciative of his commanding officer's efforts to set him right.

Private Charlie Henry continued down over the rocks, his step upon this uneven ground firm, speaking to the fact that his legs were still strong. Sergeant Brainard took this in. When the private was about halfway to their old winter quarters, he turned right into a heap of boulders. He did not emerge, and Sergeant Brainard began to descend.

✶

Private Henry's True and Accurate Account of the LFB Expedition

6 June, midday.

I'm sitting with my back against a boulder feeling content with myself. I'm out of that bastard of a sergeant's view. He has the eyes of a lynx, but I'm the wily weasel. The C.O. is a dastardly coward. He couldn't keep the doctor from preying on poor Elison, a man with neither hands nor feet nor face. And I have no more friends, even Bender and Connell want nothing to do with me now.

But what do I care. My mind is an agreeable blank. Nothing is going to happen to me. Though right now my gut churns from the diarrhea. They all have a touch of it from the lichens, just as the damn doctor had warned. I hate him for being right.

I almost kicked gravel on the C.O. Ha! Ha! His righteous talk put me in mind of my prison term for forging the signature of my commanding officer, Lieutenant George D. Wallace. Meat was my special interest. Oh! That was a good trick while it lasted. Old Charlie fixed it so he ate hamburg beefsteak every day! But what the C.O. was saying had me back carrying that ball and chain. I could feel its chafing on my ankles and that's what made me start to kick the gravel—to get rid of that everlasting chafing that had rubbed my legs raw. Better that I got control of myself then. I only would have made more trouble for myself.

I'm doing all right now. I've got my back against a secure boulder. I'm sitting beside twelve pounds of sealskins. I've cut myself off a nice tidbit that I'm in the act of masticating. The sun is strong. It warms me even though the wind is blowing; it ruffles these pages. But I'm going to sit here and write about everything that's happening to me because that editor at the *Chicago Times* is waiting to print it, and then the world will know about the life of one insignificant private. Me!

Brainard scribbles in his diary every evening. The bastard. I bet he's sneaking up on me right now, but I can't hear him because of the confounded constant wind. It's his fault and the C.O.'s too, that we didn't get to cut up Salor. Our doctor spoke for hanging on to Salor—fresh meat, you know—but the sergeant and our own Lieutenant Greely directed that Salor's carcass get dropped in the tidal crack. What a waste. Good-bye to a square meal.

But, my God, speaking of a square meal, let me tell my readers what I just ate! Don't be shocked, Gentle Readers, a starving man will eat anything. He is not fastidious. He doesn't require a china plate or silverware or a crystal goblet. He uses his fingers. Well, this starving man just spotted a curl of ptarmigan droppings—feces, to be exact. He was not so much driven by the scourge of hunger, as by the necessity of eating to prolong his life, so this minute feast went into the man's mouth. As he chewed— and picked out the grit that lodged between his teeth—he was flooded by the memory of Lieutenant Lockwood's recitations of his favorite dishes that had delighted us even as they drove us mad. You will recall, Reader, that Lieutenant Lockwood had a voice soft as a girl's, yet never was there a more manly man than Lieutenant Lockwood. Pumpkin butter, curry paste and chickens, guava jelly, pineapple. As I write the word "pineapple," a sharp burst of saliva floods my mouth and mingles agreeably with the droppings. Raw beef and onions minced. Mashed potato cakes, with a layer of sausage and a poached egg served on top with . . .

✳

Sergeant Brainard tracked Private Henry down only a little way. He didn't need to know where the private was or what he was doing. He was satisfied. He knew all he needed to justify this execution. As far as Sergeant Brainard was concerned, Henry's thieving had crossed into something coldblooded when he had filched the bacon as the rest of them were passing out from the stove fumes on that frigid morning of March 24. Rice wanted to put Private Henry before the firing squad right then, and though Brainard had not reached that point, he fully saw that Private Henry was as indifferent to the well-being of his fellows as were the lions let loose upon the Christians in Roman times.

When Lieutenant Greely had passed his written order to Sergeant Brainard that morning in the tent, he said, "I will not be present. In my weakened state I would only interfere with your ability to take Private Henry by surprise. And I advise a surprise capture. His strength is twice that of any other man. I suggest that Privates Long and Frederick assist you. That gives you two to carry the loaded guns, while one will bear the firearm with a blank cartridge."

Brainard went off to round up Shorty and Long and arrange to meet down at their old hut in the early afternoon. "The C.O.'s forgotten there's only one reliable rifle in camp, my Remington," Long said when they were gathered. Customarily, for a firing squad, guns were passed out with one blank, so no man could hold himself responsible for the fatal shot since he might be firing the blank. They were on the far side of the stone wall they had built up to four feet. Some of the stones had fallen in, but they remained screened.

"We'll draw lots," the sergeant said, but when the short stick fell to him, he realized this job was his responsibility, his alone. He dropped the small splinter of wood. "This will never do," he said. "I'm senior to you both in rank. The responsibility falls to me."

"I would like to think we all take responsibility," Shorty said.

"I go along with that," Long agreed.

"Very decent of you, men," said Sergeant Brainard, "but I'll shoot him. Lieutenant Greely advised we use a ruse. We'll tell him he's wanted on wood detail down at our winter quarters. When he bends over to pick up wood I'll pull the trigger."

That was when Shorty Frederick made it clear he would not be a party to taking Henry by stealth. "We must give him a chance for a last prayer," he said.

"It's too risky," put in Sergeant Brainard. He was not in the mood to take chances. Why, if Henry managed to harm either Long or Shorty, the sergeant knew he could never forgive himself.

"I don't care," Shorty said. "It's wrong to shoot any man in the back."

"I'd as soon shoot Private Henry in the back," Sergeant Brainard said between his teeth, "as kill a mad dog, and I'll tell you why." He cast a glance around. He didn't need anyone overhearing what he was about to reveal. "I'm only going to say this once, and I don't want you to press me as to how I know. Henry's thieving goes back to his days in the Seventh Cavalry. He forged his company commander's signature on orders for whisky and other supplies he took a fancy to. He was caught and sent to prison. He escaped. Turned up in Deadwood, where he killed a man over a gambling debt. I'm telling you this to impress upon you that our Private Henry is a dangerous man."

"He came to our expedition from the Fifth Cavalry," Long pointed out.

"That's right, Long. The man the private killed in Deadwood was a Chinese. The sheriff didn't put much effort into tracking him down. When Henry reenlisted in the Fifth, he changed his name to the one you know him by. The Fifth was Lieutenant Greely's old cavalry regiment, and this, I'm sure, is why the C.O.'s been so lenient. Also, Captain Price, who knew the C.O., wrote Henry a strong recommendation. Lieutenant Greely told me Henry sent several telegrams expressing his enthusiasm to join up. You can understand how leaving the country for a few years might have seemed like a wise idea to him."

"I take it," Long said, "that Lieutenant Greely doesn't know about Private Henry's past. That is, you haven't told him."

"I didn't find out until after the *Proteus* had left Discovery Harbor. I kept a close eye on our private at Conger. He'd be tried for his past crimes when we got back to Washington, and if he'd accounted well for himself on the expedition, that would count in his favor. I wanted to give him that chance. When we didn't get picked up, and landed in this mess, well, I was hoping Private Henry would see how essential it was for all of us to pull together. He's far from stupid. But instead I find out what I should have always known: the man's a born thief." Sergeant Brainard gave a loose stone a solid kick. "The C.O. knows now," he continued. "I told him after he'd written out the execution order."

"I suggest you tell the rest of them," Long said.

"I bet it was that photograph taken in George Rice's brother's studio," Shorty said. "Was in the papers. Somebody who knew his past saw it and—"

Sergeant Brainard cut him off. "Could have been." He looked both men in the eye but remained silent.

"George Rice never liked Henry," Shorty said. "Well, here's my final word on this matter. You say you want to shoot him." Shorty turned toward his sergeant. "You may have that honor, but I refuse to let you bear the guilt. We'll keep mum about who pulls the trigger. What do you think, Long?"

"I agree," Long said. He was leaning against the stone wall.

"I'll accept that," said Sergeant Brainard.

"Long," Shorty said, "pass the Remington around. We'll each hold it and swear: so help us God, never to reveal to a living soul who carried out the execution of Private Henry."

They looked each other in the eye as they spoke those words, and Shorty was sent off to find the private. Long began breaking up a barrel with the ax, snapping the staves to construct a pile of firewood. Sergeant Brainard held himself concealed behind a stone corner. The roof was gone, burnt for fuel. The clothing they had slept on had turned to a pile of sodden rags. He gripped the rifle across his chest. He was so weak, he hoped he could hold a steady aim. He picked up Henry's firm clump coming down the slope, and Shorty's limp behind. Brainard wished he could plug this man in the back. If something went wrong . . . He took a deep breath and told himself to concentrate, just concentrate on what he knew he had to do.

"You want me to break up barrels? There're only a few left." Private Henry gave a barrel a kick that made it roll until it hit a rock. He looked up, and a suspicious light filled his face. "One of you boys should be out hunting." His eyes flicked to Long, who was standing next to his barrel staves. "What's going on here. You don't need me for this job," he said, and then, his voice rising, asked, "Who's got the rifle?"

Sergeant Brainard took that as his cue and stepped from behind his cover. Henry's eyes widened at the Remington pointing at his chest. Why, the man's surprised, Brainard thought as he said, "You are to be put to death, Private Henry, by order of the commander."

"We have agreed," Shorty spoke up, "to give you the opportunity to kneel and make your peace with God."

"You're wrong," Henry cried. He raised his palms, putting them off in his customary gesture. "You've misjudged me . . ." His eyes fell on the ax that was lying on the ground near Long's foot and he lunged for it.

"Quick!" Shorty yelled and Long's ragged boot landed on the ax handle. *Exactly what I was afraid of.* And Brainard's heart went steely cold as he adjusted his aim to miss Long, and the rifle cracked. Henry reeled, righted himself grasping his chest, blood spurting between his fingers. He remained solid on his feet. "You bastards! You've tricked me!" He spun to face Brainard. The sergeant, gripped by his instinct to defend Long and Shorty, was thrown back into the Sioux Wars, and in

The execution of Private Henry as depicted by Charles Sarka in Frank Barclay Copley's "The Measure of Human Grit," *The American Magazine* (January 1911): 336.

a detached white heat of anger pulled the trigger a second time, opening a hole in the midpoint of the private's forehead. The man crashed down in an outpouring of blood that stained the dirty snow an ugly gluey brown that glistened like shoe polish.

The air ringing with the second shot, Sergeant Brainard dropped to his knees beside the dead man's body. "I'm going through his pockets," he said, looking up, his eyes asking them to bear witness as he inserted his hand into Henry's right trouser pocket. He pulled out a bulge of sealskin thongs. From the left trouser pocket came a folding knife with a broken blade, and from Henry's right coat pocket a small clump of tea leaves crammed inside a leather glove. Sergeant Brainard lined up each item in the mushy snow by his knees. He forced himself to unbutton Henry's jacket, soaked in blood, and retrieved a notebook from the inside pocket. "It's the man's journal," he said in a flat voice. "Lieutenant Greely will know what to do with this." He fastidiously wiped off the blood on his own pant leg and slid Private Henry's diary into his own back pocket.

"All his stories," Shorty said. His voice carried a note of awe.

The other two looked at him, and Long said, "You'll be in print soon, Shorty," easing the solemnity.

"What's this?" Brainard gave a snort as his hand, in the left coat pocket, closed on a round, flat, smooth, cold object. He pulled it out, displaying it on his palm. "So that's where it got to!"

"The chronograph! I'll be damned," barked Shorty.

Sergeant Brainard ran his sleeve over the instrument in a fruitless attempt to wipe away the tarnish. "Lieutenant Greely asked me if I remembered it getting into the boat. It was in the instrument box. Right on top. I'd placed it there myself that last morning at Conger. We both assumed it had fallen on the rocks in transport, or dropped into the sea. I felt stupid I hadn't done a better job of securing it." He stood up and the three men stared at the corpse at their feet. The head was blown apart, nearly separated from the body by the large caliber Remington Sergeant Brainard had fired at close range.

"A born thief." Long echoed the sergeant's words.

"A magpie can't help but pick up a thing that glitters," Sergeant Brainard pointed out.

✶

They returned to the tent. The men hoped the shots meant food, but Lieutenant Greely told them that was not the purpose of those shots. He wanted them to hear the execution order and directed Biederbick to read it out:

> Notwithstanding promises given by Private C. B. Henry yesterday, he has since, as acknowledged to me, tampered with seal thongs if not other food at the old camp. This pertinacity and audacity is the destruction of this party if not at once ended. Private Henry will be shot today, all care being taken to prevent his injuring anyone, as his physical strength is greater than that of any two men. Decide the manner of death by two balls and one blank cartridge. This order is *imperative* and *absolutely necessary* for *any chance* of life.

Biederbick gave emphasis to the C.O.'s stressed words. Brainard glanced at Bender. The private, wrapped in rags soaked with his own blood, had his head buried in the crook of his arm as if warding off a dreadful blow. They could hear him snuffling. If Henry had a friend these last three years, it was Bender.

"Last night Charlie was eating burned sealskins," Schneider felt called upon to point out. "I heard him chewing in his bag. 'Give me a morsel,' I asked him, 'just a bite.' 'Get your own goddamn sealskins,' he said. 'You'll get none of mine.'"

"That's enough, Private Schneider." The C.O. waved his hand as if to clear the air. "We don't need—"

"Charlie blamed me. He accused me of eating sealskins," Schneider interrupted. He crawled out of his bag on hands and knees and planted himself in the middle of the circle. "I deny this. Deny it, I tell you, as I'm a dying man. I only ate my own boots and part of an old pair of leather pants Lieutenant Kislingbury gave me. But you search Henry's pockets, you'll pull out sealskin." Schneider fell in a faint across their legs. Biederbick dragged him by his armpits out of the circle.

"Lieutenant Greely," Gardiner said in a hushed voice. "You did the right thing." Gardiner was in fearful pain from an inflammation in his bowels. He could not pass his stool. All of them were in this state, but Gardiner had irritated his rectum by working with his fingers in an attempt to dislodge his feces, small and round and hard as ball bearings. Biederbick was treating him with calomel. He had prepared suppositories for him, all to no effect. As Charlie put it a few nights earlier, if Biederbick was successful at loosening Gardiner's shit, they would be advised to clear the area as the effluvium from the explosion would blanket them like Vesuvius. No one laughed, not even Bender, who always laughed at his friend's jokes. This time he said in a rusty voice, "It's not nice to make fun of people's hardships, Charlie."

Everyone was expecting Dr. Pavy to say something. But the man seemed unaware that an execution had just taken place. The doctor opened his medicine chest, his long, dirty fingers among the vials. They watched as he raised a small glass container to his lips, tipped back his head, and swallowed. The same black viscous smear surrounded his lips.

Bender lifted his head from the shelter of his arm. "You should have read us the execution order before you killed him." His bloodshot eyes focused on the C.O.

Everyone became a little more alert and Connell growled, "Bender's right. We should have been told."

"This was my decision and mine alone," Lieutenant Greely said. His voice was firm.

"If I may," Sergeant Brainard spoke up. His eyes swung around the circle of half-starved, foul-smelling, hollow-eyed, long-haired men crowded together in the tent. "I'm going to fill you in on Private Henry's past in hopes that the reason for his execution might be better understood." He paused to let this preamble sink in. Then he went on to tell them what he had said to Shorty and Long, adding, "It was Lieutenant Greely's intent, by having Private Henry executed, to give us all a better chance for life."

"He was a thieving bastard. He deserved what he got," Connell growled, "but you should have told us all this months ago, Sergeant. If he'd shot that man in Deadwood, as you say, what was to stop him from shooting us as we lay in our bags? I don't care if the man was only a Chinaman."

"I want you to think, Private," Sergeant Brainard said, "if I had been told something like this about you, would you like it if I'd told everybody else?"

Connell stopped grumbling. The tent went dead quiet, except for the wind, the constant wind, beating the canvas. They sat, each man occupied with his own thoughts, and Sergeant Brainard became aware that Lieutenant Greely had not asked him for a written report. The only official paper was the execution order. The C.O. had not inquired how the three of them handled the problem of the rifle. From the way Lieutenant Greely phrased the execution order, it appeared he was unaware there was only one working rifle in camp. This filled Brainard with alarm. He wondered if the ordering of this execution had weakened his commander's mind. Lieutenant Greely had asked for no details, so Shorty's plea not to take the condemned unaware had not come out, nor had Private Henry's struggle that took two shots to bring him down. There was only the fact of the dead body. If we all die now, thought Brainard, Henry's death will have made little difference. If rescue comes too late, I'll have killed this man for nothing.

"He was my friend!" Bender's wail filled the tent in a way that seemed to underline their utter isolation. They all watched as poor Bender drew his greasy, bloody sleeve across his filthy face.

"I am aware of that, Private Bender. Don't think that I am not." The C.O. stretched out his hand toward Bender. "If I had been able, I would have shot Private Henry myself."

Bender fell back. He brought up his arm to blot the sounds coming out of his mouth.

Later Brainard said, "Private Schneider, give Bender a nudge, will you? He's been very quiet."

Schneider didn't move. "I think Private Bender is dead," he said.

Biederbick crawled over to have a look. He nodded.

"Bender," Schneider said, picking at a clot of dirt on the back of his hand, "was a cowardly man."

"You are speaking of the newly dead," the C.O. rasped. "Try to show some respect, Private Schneider."

"I don't care. He tried to pin the blame on me for his thieving. He called me the biggest thief in camp."

"When we are stronger," the C.O. went on, ignoring Schneider, "Sergeant Brainard will lead the burial party to inter Private Henry's remains in the ice foot."

"Cut him up first." Dr. Pavy's loud voice startled everyone.

"I think not, Doctor," the C.O. stepped in.

"You said we would cut up the bodies," Connell growled. "You said that two days ago. We haven't seen that flesh yet."

The doctor laughed, revealing his blackening gums. He dug through his vials, withdrew the one that contained the dark substance, and held it against his chest.

"What is that you've got, Dr. Pavy? You are dosing yourself?" the C.O. inquired.

The doctor clutched the bottle so tightly Brainard was afraid he would crack it. Pavy sent a wild look around the tent.

"It's the ergot, Lieutenant Greely," Biederbick reported.

"This little bottle"—the doctor shook it—"is keeping me alive for my darling Lilla Mae." Pavy's eyes rotated in their sockets. Brainard was sure he could not see them.

By evening Shorty was ready to serve up a stew composed of two boot soles, a few lichens, and a handful of reindeer moss, the latest addition to their diet. "Somebody wake up the doctor," he requested. Dr. Pavy had fallen into an uncharacteristic doze. Schneider administered a nudge. "By God," he choked, "the damn doctor's dead."

Biederbick pried the ergot vial out of the doctor's grip. "He drank it all," he reported. "There was three ounces in that bottle."

"Pavy killed himself, the bastard." Connell let out a snort.

"Abusive language, Private," the C.O. snapped. Sergeant Brainard found his commander's predictable reaction strangely comforting.

Connell rolled over on his face, his laughter exploding in muffled gasps.

"I believe," Biederbick continued, "the doctor thought this was iron."

Schneider was heaving with laughter too. Great unnerving baying sounds. "Three in one afternoon! Hooo! Hooo! Who's next? Who'll be next into the stewpot? Whoooo?"

"Private Schneider." The C.O. struggled to make himself heard. "Stop your noise. *No one will be put into the stewpot.*" Schneider came to a gasping stop. He looked surprised. Was it he making these inhuman sounds? "My dog Flipper. You must remember her, Lieutenant Greely? She, she drowned." Poor Schneider began to weep.

"There, there, Private Schneider." Lieutenant Greely threw off his bag and crawled on his knees over to Schneider. "Don't take on so. It will be all right. You'll see. Everything will be all right." The C.O. patted Schneider's back, soothing him, calming him. Calming them all.

Deaths

14. Charles B. Henry (Charles Henry Buck), executed, 6 June 1884.
15. Jacob Bender, 6 June 1884.
16. Dr. Octave Pavy, 6 June 1884.

✻

10

> Man is a creature who can get used to anything, and I believe that is the very best way of defining him.
>
> Fyodor Dostoevsky, *The House of the Dead* (1862)

The snow around the tent was gone from the rocks. Even in the shaded depressions, the snow was slushy and receding fast. Brainard, on his way to his shrimping grounds, spotted a bumblebee sampling the saxifrage blossoms. He *heard* it, this homey buzzing that sent his thoughts to the sun-drenched pastures of his family's farm. He sighed. His father and brothers would be bringing in the first cutting of hay. Summer must be here, he said to himself, looking toward Smith Sound. It was clear of ice. Too early to expect the relief, *but if it doesn't come soon, they'll find no one alive to rescue.* He felt somewhat strengthened from the dovekie Long had shot and they split yesterday. Only temporary, if Long didn't bring another to the table.

When he returned, Biederbick helped him dress the bodies of Dr. Pavy and Bender for burial. Bender's blood had dried and stuck his ragged shirt and trousers to his corpse, so they left them in place. They did this work in the tent, nearly suffocating them all with the smell. "It's coming from their mouths," Biederbick pointed out. "It's the scurvy. See their blackened gums?"

"Get those corpses out of here," Connell ordered. "They make me sick with their rot." The private covered his own blackening gums with both hands. "Death stinks," he choked out. He was beginning to gag. His eyes, enormous and sunken in their sockets, showed them his terror.

The next day, when they were out foraging for saxifrage to replenish their wood supply, Biederbick came walking toward Sergeant Brainard. "Look at this," the private said. "I just found it concealed under a stack of stones," Biederbick handed Brainard a stocking that, when the sergeant peeled it open, revealed a lump of flesh. "It's not bear meat," Biederbick said. "And it's not seal either."

"No, it's not," Brainard agreed. The flesh, partially thawed, glistened on his palm. Up until now, he had not yet begun to carry out Lieutenant Greely's plan that was so hard to name, yet which gave them the only chance for life. He slid the flesh back into the stocking and wiped his hand on his wool pants.

"Well," Biederbick went on, "if Private Henry cached this, he never got around to eating it."

"It's meat," Brainard replied. "We'll add it to the shrimp."

Later at supper, Connell, in the midst of chewing, said, "What am I eating? It's not bear meat. But it's as good as bear meat. Okay. *Who* is it?" He sent Sergeant Brainard a crooked smile.

Brainard's stomach gave a lurch and he set his tin aside. In truth he didn't know, and he wasn't about to get into a discussion with Connell, so he said nothing.

"Well," Connell snickered, "about time you began bringing it. Bring us more. The doctor said flesh was good for my scurvy." Connell swung around to address the C.O. "Lieutenant Greely, Sergeant Brainard goes over the ridge every day for the damn shrimp. Have him bring us more flesh."

Lieutenant Greely looked up, his face a blank. Did he really have no idea what Connell was talking about? Brainard wondered. "We've still got Bender," Connell went on. "Unwrap him and cut him up. Here"— he threw back his bag—"I'll do it myself."

"Don't be crude, Private," Lieutenant Greely said. And Brainard was relieved to see their C.O. had recovered himself. He went on, "Private Bender will join the doctor in the tidal crack as soon as we have the energy to carry out this duty."

"Then you're denying us fresh food," Connell snapped, moving toward Bender's corpse.

"Private Connell. Stay where you are," Lieutenant Greely said, struggling to push himself into a more erect position. "If we are forced to nourish ourselves in this manner, we will go about it in a civilized fashion and—"

"Ha!" Connell snorted. "There's nothing civilized about cannibalism."

"And with respect. Besides, you might want to consider what could happen if you consume a body riddled by scurvy."

This stopped Connell. Brainard was all too aware they didn't know. But they all had scurvy now and were up against the end. He had broken through the taboo with this pound of flesh, and he would bring them more. A pound a day. If he didn't, Lieutenant Greely would die. *I can turn off my mind when I am at it. I am their stores sergeant and I will carry out my duty.* But he would draw his own line. He would not touch Lockwood with the knife. Or Ned Israel. Or their faithful Eskimo, Fred Christiansen. He would take only from the bodies previously cut. But would what he was forced to do now be of any use? Biederbick said their own bodies were so depleted they could never replace the deficit.

✳

The next day, Sergeant Brainard erected a distress flag made of scraps of sailcloth and an old shirt worn by Dr. Pavy. He picked colors that would stand out and climbed the hill, a ridge with a level top, about one hundred feet high, that dropped off steeply down to the shoreline. The white of the sailcloth flashed in the sun, set off by the maroon of the doctor's shirt, visible to any ship passing Sabine.

He labored slowly back down the rocky slope, then up the hill, passing their tent. When he reached the cemetery, he was so winded he had to sit. They were in a spell of unusually fine weather and he let himself take in the view. He could make out the signal flag he had just erected, snapping in the wind. His eyes found their old winter hut, the roof burnt for fuel, about four hundred yards from where he was sitting. Their graveyard made the apex of the triangle, with the old hut below to his left and the signal flag to his right. The shrimping grounds were behind him, to the southeast. He felt rather proud of the distance he had just walked. It couldn't be measured in miles, yet the hills were steep, rocky, and hummocked. He hadn't stopped at their tent, only seventy-five yards below him at the bottom of Cemetery Ridge, but he had picked up the handsaw.

His heaviest knife was in its scabbard, attached to his belt. He gazed at the saw in his hand. He used it on the bear. The bear meat was frozen. "Bear meat," he said out loud and made himself focus on the ten bears laid out under the gravel. *It's probably a good idea to pick the freshest. But that bear's almost used up, the one who died on June 1.* He moved past the bear that died on May 27, knelt down by the one who had died on the twenty-fourth, and pawed away the gravel around a furry leg. He easily cut away the soft fur, but to get at the meat, he had to turn this bear over. All the bears were lying on their backs. He clawed away more gravel and edged his arms under the body of the bear. It was not heavy at all. They had needed six men to drag in the Good Friday Bear. His mouth filled with saliva, thinking of that bear's meat and how they had eaten until their stomachs ached. *My, that meat was good.*

Working with his knife, he cut away a portion of the bear's hind leg, the flesh around what on a man would be the calf. The meat was pulpy, partially thawed, and that made the job easier. He weighed the meat in his own paw and saw he had only cut a small chunk of the thawed meat. Not enough. He felt around with his claws where he had cut and knew he had to go at the rest of this calf—too frozen for the knife—with the saw.

He worked in a kneeling position, counting the strokes, stopping every twenty to rest. He was at Camp Clay, sawing up the Good Friday Bear for their supper. The saw hit the bone with a rasping, grating noise that startled him. But he knew what to do. He set aside the saw and began working again with his strong knife, digging around the tendons and sinews that held the meat to the bone. He worked and he rested, just as he had learned to do over the Good Friday Bear.

At last he had enough of this good bear's meat. The final job was to cut it in small strips so it would be ready for the cook's pot. All the cook had to do was slide this meat in with the shrimp and the lichens. And the reindeer moss, too, the new item they had added to their diet. Still on his knees, he pulled out his handkerchief, hemmed by his mother. Once a brilliant shade of blue, it was now a faded, filthy rag. He was placing the small strips on it, edging them carefully side by side with his claws, when his gut went into spasms. He had barely time to turn away from the corpse when he vomited a spray of bile that stung his nose and seared his throat. *Oh, God, Whisler. It's you.*

He stood up. Looked down on the strips of Whisler's flesh lying on his handkerchief. He shut his eyes, trying to control his breathing. When he opened them, the flesh was still there. He knelt again, carefully folding the handkerchief around this human flesh that was thawing in the sun. He leaned over it, sniffing. Already Whisler's flesh was giving off a smell of turned meat. He picked up the handkerchief with both hands and placed it in his coat pocket. He knelt a final time, inserted his arms under Whisler's body, and turned him on his back. He pulled down his wool pant leg and, with his bare hands, covered the corpse as well as he could with the gravel. His stomach had settled. He stood beside the small mound, his hands clasped, and said aloud, "Thank you, William Whisler." Then he turned and made his slow way back to their camp.

✳

Gardiner was dying. His bowels were inflamed; he was horribly constipated. Poor Gardiner lay in his sleeping bag clutching the ambrotypes of his wife, whom he married only a few months before he left, and his mother. With his two hands, he brought them up before his face. "Wife, mother," he said to them. He had been saying this for days. It was hard to watch and worse to listen to. But Gardiner was so uncomplaining. No one jumped to shut him up. Not even Connell. In the early afternoon, the young man fell unconscious. He would be in this state a few hours, then slide into death. They had witnessed this numerous times now: how easily death came.

They weren't talking about food much anymore. The restaurants and recitations of favorite dishes didn't bring comfort the way it used to. What they were eating now was so desperate. They knew their evening meals contained the flesh of their comrades. They knew that Sergeant Brainard was seeing to this.

For tonight's meal, the flesh was supplemented by strips of the sealskin sleeping bag covers donated by Long, Brainard, and the C.O. They were eating the covers of the living now, having devoured the covers of the dead. Shorty roasted or boiled the strips to suit each man's taste. But there was nothing to drink since no one had the energy to fetch water.

"Who are we eating tonight?" Connell demanded. He pointed to the pail of lichens and the handkerchief next to it, near the stove that Shorty had set out for their dinner. He got only stares in reply. "If Charlie were around he'd find that funny," he said. The silence in the tent thickened. "Goddamnit, you either laugh or cry in a situation like this. I prefer to laugh."

"I see your point, Private Connell," Sergeant Brainard finally said. "But to me the situation is not humorous."

Connell started to stand, then sank to a crouch as his knees buckled.

"Give me one-ninth of that there," he gestured toward their supper. "Now! Turn it over, Shorty." He lunged, nearly upsetting the cook pot.

"Private Connell." The C.O.'s voice still expressed authority.

"Damn it to hell! I don't have to listen to you anymore. I'm leaving."

"If you leave us, Private, where will you go? You can't survive out there on your own."

"You would abandon us *now*?" Sergeant Brainard asked. "After we've been living together so close to the line for the past nine months?" He could not believe this was how a man could think.

"It's every man for himself, is how I've seen it all along," growled Connell. "Give me the rifle. You can keep the damn lichens. They give me diarrhea just like Doctor Pavy said."

"Check on Gardiner, would you?" the C.O. broke in, and Biederbick crawled over.

"He's gone," the hospital steward reported and pried Gardiner's stiffening fingers back to free the ambrotypes. He held up Gardiner's hand. "His fingers," Biederbick rotated Gardiner's hand to catch the light. "I swear to God I can see the bones."

"We'll bury him in the ice foot," Sergeant Brainard said.

"He's fresh meat," Connell growled, glaring at Sergeant Brainard. "Cut him up now."

"I will bring you the flesh, Connell," Sergeant Brainard said between his teeth, "but no one will cut into the newly dead. We will bury Gardiner in the ice foot, when we can gather strength."

What they were eating was not capable of giving anyone strength, and diarrhea had them going in and out. Those who couldn't crawl, Elison and Schneider, used the urine pot, keeping Biederbick busy emptying it. It was a struggle to dump it away from the tent and out of the walking paths. "I hate the doctor," Connell snarled. "Why did he have to be right?"

"You don't need to eat the lichens or the shrimps, Private," the C.O. replied.

"I'm going off on my own. Just need to get a little strength back. I'm done with this stinking hog pen, all of you dropping your drawers."

No one paid attention to the Irishman's bluster.

Sergeant Brainard, however, checked to make sure the rifle was safe. It was always in his bag or Long's, if Long didn't have it in the field, or entrusted to Lieutenant Greely.

Eight of them left now.

✻

On June 13, the thermometer reached 40 degrees, the sun so pleasant that everyone who could work was out working. It lifted Sergeant Brainard's spirits to see them contributing to the common good. He wanted so much to think well of these men. Even Lieutenant Greely— Brainard had not thought he would see him out of the tent again— crawled among the rocks until he had collected two quarts of lichens. He was certain the C.O.'s renewed strength came from their change in diet, and that gave him the heart to go on with it. Biederbick was watching over the C.O. as he collected his own lichens. Shorty broke up barrels with the ax, then trotted off to get water. He was doing all the cooking now. Schneider was burning the hair from a pile of sealskin clothing to render it edible in tonight's stew. And Connell! Connell was positively putting himself out amassing a quantity of saxifrage. "Just smell these flowers," he said, and held them under Brainard's nose. "Aren't they as sweet as the breath of an Irish lassie? Now *taste* them!" He plucked off a blossom and dropped it in the sergeant's palm.

"Why, it tastes wonderfully fresh," Brainard exclaimed, astonished at Connell's generosity. He had given him food!

At their evening mess, Shorty served up the sealskin stew. Each man, as he received his portion, lost no time spooning it down. Brainard, wanting them to know how impressed he was with their willing help, held his bowl, untasted, and began, "This has been the most enjoyable day I've spent on these inhospitable shores. I want to thank . . ." But his words were drowned by a sudden fit of gagging as the others made a rush on hands and knees for the tent flap. Brainard crawled out behind them and found a vomit of half-chewed skins, the hair still on in matted clumps, and Schneider, the cause of it, retching along with the rest of them.

Private Connell, his eyes running, wiped the vomit off his chin. "Take my advice and cut up that bastard Lieutenant Greely had shot." He glared at Sergeant Brainard. "I'll go after him with my knife if you won't. He deserves to be eaten. He'd be feasting on us if it were the other way around."

Brainard moved away from Connell. *Private Henry will not be cut by me.* He saw the poetic justice in consuming Private Henry, but to shoot a man and then add him to the cook pot would only add to the horror of their cannibalism. The C.O. didn't want to know anything about any of it. "I've given my permission," he told Sergeant Brainard. "We eat to keep alive until the rescue comes." *My distress flag has blown over. I must climb up the hill and right it again. Right it again. Right it again.* The words made a song in Brainard's head.

Back in the tent, Connell sat upright, his arms folded across his shrunken chest, glaring at Schneider. "It's all your fault," the Irishman growled. Schneider coughed. He was coughing and crying at the same time.

"Leave him alone, Private Connell," Brainard said. He was so tired of Connell's constant carping and bullying. He reached inside his buffalo-hide bag and pulled out his diary and pencil. *June 13*, he wrote.

I have discovered a new shrimping spot that shortens my two-mile round trip by half. I'm using the human flesh for fish bait and this means I don't have to cut so much flesh. I can do it, but I vomit up bile, just like the first time. I tell myself that the mountain men, caught in winter, were known for eating their comrades. The story I heard at Fort Ellis was that Kit Carson said that in starving times, no man who knew Bill Williams ever walked in front of him. Making a joke of eating people, the way Connell does, doesn't help me do this job. What enables me to pick up the knife is knowing that I am keeping the few of us who are still alive, alive.

We have tea for only three meals more, and have Private Henry, Dr. Pavy, and Bender to thank since this tea came from their pockets.

I'm concerned about the men's mental vigor. I'm concerned about my own. All we want to do is sleep. We are groggy. We leave our chores undone, or shift the work to someone more willing, Biederbick or Shorty, or Long. Discussing topics of interest is a thing of the past. Arguments don't last for long since there is no energy to sustain them. A bewildered look crosses their faces as if what they were discussing has gone out of their heads. I'm afraid that Connell will get hold of the rifle. This wakes me in the night. I check my bag, and if it's not there, my fear forces me to check Long's bag or the C.O.'s. I try not to wake them, but no one sleeps well and they wake anyway.

The shrimping takes me away from camp and out of range of Connell's complaints and the smell. The whole place reeks of sewage. I can take care of my own problems with diarrhea better down by the shore's edge.

The great recent news at Camp Clay is that Private Elison can use the urine tub *by himself*. "No one needs to lift me anymore," he crowed. If all were as good-hearted as Joe Elison, our life here would be so much easier to bear. Elison did little to distinguish himself at Conger. His frostbite, it could be argued, led to the death of George Rice. Elison is young, though his face is old and lined by pain, yet he is not beaten like Connell. He's cheery. He's happy to be alive. This makes me ponder how suffering can bring out the best in men. Some men. Here, in our misery, is where we meet our truest selves.

✷

A light snow began to fall on the afternoon of June 15. Long walked around the rocks and hummocks with his rifle but killed no game. He had killed nothing since June 11, when he shot two guillemots. He shot dovekies on June 1, on the second, and also on the ninth, meager fare for the remaining eight men. Walruses dove and splashed in the small pool near the ice foot but were too far out to reach. Seals, too, but without the kayak, their chance of bringing in a seal was nearly hopeless. The dovekies were gone. Cape Sabine seemed unfavored by game.

"I don't feel hunger anymore," Sergeant Brainard said. "I'm only eating to keep my life going until the relief shows up." They were gathered in the tent for the evening mess of gluey lichens, their pound of flesh, and a handful of shelly shrimp. No one collected wood, so they ate all this raw.

"It's the same for me," Biederbick confirmed. "The extreme craving for food has left me."

✷

Monday morning, June 16. The wind blew hard from the north. Only Shorty cranked himself out of his sleeping bag. There was breakfast and he was the cook. "This is the last of our tea," he told them as he passed it around.

"We know this," Connell grumbled.

Biederbick decided this was the moment to issue the last of the iron in Dr. Pavy's medicine chest. Not enough to cause harm, but perhaps enough to counteract the lethargy. They seemed more done in than ever this morning. Well, the nights were never restful, with the urgency to pass water that had them scrambling for the urine tub disturbing the entire tent for nothing more than a dribble. A few of them—Brainard, Long, and Shorty, since they were able—continued to go outside, threading a maze through food tins melted out in the thaw, discarded sleeping bags, and ragged clothing.

After breakfast, Sergeant Brainard took himself down to the shrimping spot. He kept tripping on the stones. He told himself to pick up his feet, that he was shuffling like his grandfather when he was too old to milk cows. His grandfather came out to the barn anyway and one of his grandsons, often himself, helped him sit on the milking stool. No one complained about what a trouble this was; how looking after the old man slowed down the whole milking process. His grandfather had milked cows all his life. He couldn't stop.

Brainard went down on one knee to set his baits, a combination of the tanned leather and human flesh. When he stood, black spots flooded his vision and he sank to a crouch again. He stared at his baits. The crustaceans weren't biting. The flesh was too old, and he muttered "Dammit" out loud.

"Don't swear," a voice very close to his ear said. He nearly toppled over, putting out a hand to hold himself steady. He looked around and saw Lieutenant Lockwood sitting on a rock, looking like his old self.

"James," Brainard said. "You've come to help me collect shrimp." With one part of his mind, he knew it couldn't be Lockwood; his vision was off, but it made him happy to see Lockwood sitting there, brass buttons and braid gleaming in the sun.

"We had to resort to the body cutting." Brainard didn't think he spoke these words. He turned back to his baits. Lockwood's distinctive and southern voice replied, "It's what you had to do. My friend, you are handling it right." Brainard rubbed his hand across the back of his neck. He turned around so quickly his vision filled with black spots again, and he nearly pitched into the water. He felt Lockwood close, and the wonderful days they had spent together on the Farthest North. "My," he said, "that was grand." He smiled to himself. "I'll never forget that time with you, James." He began to cry a little, got ahold of himself, and hung over his baits. "The shrimp scorn my offering," he said out loud. He pulled out his pocket watch. He had stuck it out for five hours. He stood up slowly. He had caught no shrimp and saw no point in taking his nets back. He felt so weak he wasn't sure if he would make it back himself. I have to, he lectured himself, and began a slow shuffle, fastening his thoughts on his grandfather, milking cows until the last day of his life.

When Davy Brainard crawled into the tent, he was so out of breath he couldn't speak. His face was waxy with fatigue. "I've no more baits," he panted, "and the shrimp won't take the tanned leather. They won't take the flesh. It's not fresh enough. I can catch no more shrimp for us."

"It's your own damn fault," Connell grumbled. "You threw all the fresh meat in the tidal crack."

"We'll eat lichens," Biederbick said, and touched his sergeant's hand. A little while later, Long entered. With no birds. "The ice is bad and the wind too strong," he explained. "Plenty of walruses, but they won't climb up on the ice. They won't approach the shore to let me get a shot at them."

"Long," Connell informed everyone, "hasn't shot a bloody thing since the two guillemots five days ago."

Long gave Connell a level stare, though he didn't say anything. It was a statement of fact, if not a tactful one. "I shouldn't tell you fellows this, but I might not shoot anything again," he said. "The rifle wavers when I take aim, my arms are so weak."

No one went out for lichens. The winds were too strong. So there was nothing to eat for supper. Nothing. "I don't care," Connell growled. "My gums are too sore to chew anything that isn't boiled to mush." He threw a dark look at Shorty, who boiled nothing to mush, not having the fuel for it.

They awoke next morning to a day that turned clear and almost warm in the sun.

Shorty served a "decoction," as Sergeant Brainard called it, of saxifrage—a substitute for tea—at breakfast. After making a noble attempt to swallow, he gave it up. "I'm terribly sorry, Shorty. I cannot manage my tea. It's nauseating me." Brainard held out his cup. "Would any of you others care to divide it?"

"I thought it rather fine," Joe Elison said.

"Would you like it, Joe?" The sergeant held out his tin.

"I'll take that." Connell intercepted the cup. "It's the only thing my gums can tolerate." He downed the liquid in a gulp. Biederbick, Elison, and Schneider stared at him like beaten dogs. Though they said nothing. Nor did Brainard. He was sick of dealing with this man. He had rested enough. He had to get out into the air and do something useful. His days as a shrimper were done with, so he limped down to their old mansion, as Private Charlie Henry called it, tied a heap of barrel staves together with an old belt, slung this over his shoulder, and lugged it uphill. "I'll split it," he told Shorty, "but I have to rest first."

"You sit, I'll split," Shorty offered.

"What an iron will you have, Shorty. I admire you for it," Brainard said, sinking down on a rock in the sun. "You're as broken down as I am, yet you can keep going."

"Aw, Sergeant. You work harder than all of us combined." Shorty picked up the ax.

Schneider called from inside the tent for someone to help him sit up. "I want to sew a patch on Sergeant Brainard's boot," he told Biederbick, who ducked under the flap.

But that patch never got sewn on.

Biederbick came in later to find Schneider on his back, a piece of leather and a long sharp needle gripped between his fingers. "Careful there. You don't want to stab yourself." Biederbick rescued the needle. "If that patch is too hard to manage, Schneider, why don't you help me cut up the sealskin covers from Long's and the sergeant's sleeping bags. They're our last covers."

"You mean the last we can use as food?"

"Yes."

"We'll not survive long after these strips are eaten. Will we, Biederbick?"

"I wouldn't imagine we would."

"Do you think we'll all die around the same time?"

"Likely. Within a day or so."

"Then who will bury us?" Schneider's cry awakened the C.O.

"What. What?" His voice was thick and his eyes, crusted at the corners, darted about the tent. The C.O. abruptly sat up. "Private Schneider, have you picked lichens today? I'm going out to pick lichens." He shoved back his sleeping bag with surprising vigor and began to move on all fours toward the flap. As he passed Schneider, he said, "You look poorly, Private. Pale to a lurid degree. You need sun. Come out in the sun. Follow my example. I'm going into the sun."

"Lieutenant Greely," Schneider said, "I want you to know that Private Henry accused me of stealing sealskins. I never did. He gave me a fragment from time to time from what he stole. I'm sorry if I ate them. I wanted to tell you. I feel myself going fast."

"Now, now, Private Schneider," replied the C.O. "Come with me. You're a good man. Come out in the sun."

"I'll help Schneider out later, Lieutenant," Biederbick said.

"Where's Connell? Is Connell picking lichens?" Schneider asked the hospital steward.

"Yes, my friend, Connell's out picking lichens."

"He's still strong in the legs," Schneider pointed out. His words came out breathy, with many pauses. "He walks to pick lichens. He won't allow himself to crawl. He's determined to make his legs stronger. I know his plans. He tells me at night. 'I'm building myself up, Schneider,' he says. 'I'm going to come through.' He will do it. Connell is afraid of nothing. Do you think he will come through, Biederbick?"

"On one meal a day? Probably not."

"One meal?" asked Schneider. "What do you mean?"

"You heard. Shorty told us at breakfast he can only cook one meal a day. It's a good plan. This way we can draw the food out and not exhaust Shorty at the same time."

"You cook, Biederbick. You are strong. Biederbick, you will make it."

"You will too, Schneider. But you have to buck up."

✳

At breakfast on the 18th, Biederbick tied a spoon to Joe's stump. They all watched as the private transferred the boiled sealskins from his tin can to his mouth, *by himself.* Joe's eyes gleamed with the triumph of it. "What a marvel you are, Corporal Elison," Sergeant Brainard said.

"Schneider's lost consciousness." Biederbick cut in with this news.

No one reacted except Sergeant Brainard, who reached for Schneider's wrist. He detected a pulse, quick and fluttery, a moth beating against his fingers.

"Stop kicking me!" Connell raised a fist. "Biederbick, lay off or I'll flatten you."

The hospital steward, his legs twitching, reached into his bag and pulled out his long johns. "That's been on me since last August. Nearly eleven months ago."

"Damn!" sputtered Connell. "You stink. I'm living in a hog pen with you men. Get away from me you little piece of excrement." Connell gave Biederbick a push.

On his back, Biederbick managed to wrench his long john shirt over his head. He righted himself, crawled across Connell's legs, opened the tent flap and pitched his underwear, ragged and stained a dirty yellow at the crotch, out. He was naked now. "That's better. Snakes must feel good when they shed their skin."

"Snakes stink," Connell said.

"Private Biederbick," the C.O. rasped. "I beg you to clothe yourself."

"I can't wash, Lieutenant, but I can change my underwear. I want to look my military best when the relief comes."

"Ha! The relief," snorted Connell. "What's the rush?"

"Look at my legs." Biederbick rubbed his hands up and down his legs, flaking off dead skin.

"Like chicken legs," Connell sneered.

"This is what a starving body looks like, men," Biederbick went on. "Enlarged joints. No fat. Muscles dissolved. It hurts me to sit, my bones are so lightly covered."

"So cover yourself, Biederbick. You talk like the doctor. Put on your damn clothes," Connell grumbled. "No one wants to look at your shrunken gonads."

"I find it kind of fascinating. We're skeletons held together by tendons and skin. But we're still alive. *We're alive!*" Biederbick said, and reached for his trousers.

"Biederbick." Sergeant Brainard pulled up his own trouser legs, exhibiting his calves. "Look, my muscles have melted away like candle wax."

"When we lose half our body weight," Biederbick instructed, "death quickly follows. That's what Dr. Pavy told me."

✗

At four o'clock, Sergeant Brainard made himself crawl out of the tent. He staggered to the rocks a dozen yards away and started scraping lichens. Connell joined him. "My vision," the private said, rubbing his eyes, "it's dim, like night is falling." They scraped away in silence, Connell keeping to his feet as he moved from rock to rock. But something was wrong. He lurched and stumbled, his boots catching on little stones. He fell, landing hard and cutting his palms. "I can't seem to manage my legs," Connell said in a shaky voice. He put his hands to his swollen face. "Is it the scurvy? What is wrong with me?"

Sergeant Brainard heard his fear. "You're holding up well, Private," he said. He wanted to say more, something that might help. "My face is swollen, too, and my joints, especially my knees. We all have a touch of scurvy."

When they crawled back in the tent, Biederbick said, "Schneider is dead. Lieutenant Greely helped me straighten his limbs. Look at this crust around his eyes and at the corners of his mouth." The hospital steward pointed with his forefinger. But no one was eager to gaze on poor Schneider's dead face. It was the color of ivory, the skin stretched taut, bringing into relief the cheekbones, sinking the eyes further into their sockets, pulling the lips back around the teeth. A true death's head grin.

"What a stink," Connell said. "His damn body's rotting. Get it out of here."

"What you're smelling, Connell," Biederbick said, "is scurvy and it's coming from Schneider's mouth."

"Fuck." Connell sank onto his bag, covering his mouth with his hands. He looked up at the men, his eyes wild and pleading.

✳

During the night of June 19, the sky remained clear. The wind came from a westerly direction and Long, wanting to make use of the good spell, left the tent with his rifle for his nighttime shift. It was broad daylight, but the men still divided the twenty-four hours into night and day, in their minds and in their conversation. While he was out, the wind changed to the southeast and began to blow at a high velocity.

Long had reached the ice foot as the storm moved in. It was not terribly cold. The temperature was only a bit below the freezing mark. He stood in a snow squall and regarded the sound. The wind was playing havoc with the ice, breaking up the surface into a froth of cakes colliding and butting each other apart. He had watched this many times with the same grim fascination. Like watching warfare. But he was being buffeted himself by this wind, so he turned his back on the sea to trudge uphill to their shelter.

"I'm concerned about the tent," he said when he came in. "The canvas is so worn. If this blow turns into a gale, we could be flattened. I shot two dovekies," Long went on, reporting on his night's work. "But they were carried seaward by the ebbing tide." His voice had a hollow grave-yard sound.

"Goddamn you, Long," Connell said. But there was no heat behind his words.

"So I'm going to hunt in the daytime now," Long said. "I wasn't sure I could still shoot straight enough to bring down game." He smiled a thin smile at Connell.

"But what good does it do if you can't bring it to us?" Connell complained.

"Why don't you just keep your unhelpful thoughts to yourself," Biederbick said.

"Well, it's the truth, isn't it?" Connell snapped.

Sergeant Brainard looked toward his C.O. He was slumped on his side. He seemed barely conscious, so Sergeant Brainard said, "Men, men." But they had stopped. The words had stopped, but the unpleasant-ness remained, along with the bad air in the tent.

Schneider, whom they had meant to bury that day, was not buried. He was only dragged a little ways downhill, nearer to the ice foot. The terrible odor continued coming from Schneider. It permeated the tent. "It's the scurvy," Connell moaned. He knew it was scurvy, and he knew what this meant. He complained about his mouth. It was so damn sore. His face was puffy, his legs swollen at the joints. Connell did not leave the tent that day.

But Brainard went out in the high southeast wind to collect wood for Shorty. He staggered to the shore's edge and dipped up saltwater for

Shorty's cooking. He forced himself to collect lichen and a little reindeer moss. It was not enough. Not anywhere near enough. He couldn't
seem to push himself to amass more even though he knew Long was
out there hunting. What they needed was flesh. He had taken what he
could from Whisler. There were three bodies up on the ridge that had
previously been cut. Jewell, Ellis, and Ralston. The meteorologist had
died on May 23. His flesh was the freshest of the three. It took strength
to cut into human flesh. He started slowly up toward the cemetery. He
might make it up, but he was not sure he could make it back. There
was Schneider. That body was lying only a few dozen yards away from
their tent. But not even Connell was talking about butchering Schneider. Schneider had scurvy. The last time Brainard had visited their old
hut, he had seen that Henry's body had been sliced. It must have been
Connell, determined to carry out the irony of feasting on a man who
had made a meal of others. This gruesome thought so disturbed Davy
Brainard he turned around; he turned his back on the corpses in the
cemetery and collected lichens instead.

✳

It was still blowing when Shorty remarked, as he served up lichens and
reindeer moss for breakfast, "Today is the summer solstice." "I'm sorry,"
he added. "There is only enough for a few bites." He was feeding only
seven now, but merely a morsel could be doled out to each or there
would be nothing for tomorrow. No one complained about his meager
portion, not even Connell. Connell was worse. "My legs are useless below
the knees," he informed them. A statement of fact, such as Joe Elison
would make. Sergeant Davy wondered if the complaints had wormed
their way out of Connell, like the exorcising of evil spirits.

And Joe—why, Joe Elison wielded his spoon with the abandon of a
young child who has just learned to feed himself. It was wonderful to
watch. It put heart in them all.

No one went out. The gale would topple them. Besides, they needed
anyone who was mobile to keep the two poles upright. The wind hurled
itself in pounding gusts at the fabric, causing the snow to sift through
like sand, intent on burying them alive. It was hard to breathe, the air

was so filled with fine particles. Joe Elison was trying to tell them something, but his voice was too weak to overcome the shuddering, quaking, flapping that threatened to collapse the tent around their ears. Joe was encouraging them, they could tell that, so they hung on around the poles. Their bodies in a huddle, keeping each other warm.

When the evening mess hour rolled around, Shorty passed out a few pieces of sealskins he had kept safe from what he had boiled up the day before. There was no water to help it down. "Chew on this," he shouted in the ear of each one of them. "It will give you strength." To Connell he said, "Suck on it. Let it dissolve in your mouth."

"Like the wafer," Connell said, and spread his lips so Shorty could set the sealskin on his cracked and blackened tongue.

Lieutenant Greely picked up his journal to make an entry, but the volume fell from his hand. Sergeant Brainard, who had not missed the ritual of daily writing since July 7, 1881, did not record this fearsome day. This gale would finish them and, though he was on his legs clinging to the tentpole, he was filled with despair.

After midnight, as the wind screeched to a pitch that numbed their minds, one of the poles twisted and jumped from their grasp. It lay across the bags of Greely, Brainard, and Long. The other pole remained upright. The canvas came to rest, spreading itself out, and the dreadful flapping eased. They lay, half-smothered, aware of the sea. It was running high tonight, roaring out in the sound.

Deaths

17. Hampton S. Gardiner, 12 June 1884.
18. Roderick R. Schneider, 18 June 1884.

Part Three

The Rescue

7

"It Seems So Long to Wait"
Camp Clay, Cape Sabine

22 June 1884

It has been said that when the planning and organization is complete and the expedition begins, its fate is already determined.

Joe Wilcox, leader of the 1967 Mt. McKinley expedition
in which seven died

The wind out of the south blew all night, and on the morning of Sunday, June 22, it was still near gale force. This wind had broken up the ice for a long distance along the coast of Cape Sabine. The snow continued to swirl in squally gusts, a wet snow that indicated the temperature was near the freezing mark. Greely, the tentpole lying across his legs, turned his head toward his friend Brainard. "Today is my wedding anniversary," he said, and paused with a puzzled look. "Or was it yesterday?" Davy Brainard gave his commander a cracked-lipped smile. He was pinned as well, the pole across his body. "Our sixth," the C.O. continued. "I've spent nearly half my married life away from my beloved Henrietta."

Shorty Frederick, fussing over the fire, broke in, "I can't keep the darn thing lit in this wind." He had lichens and sealskins in the cook pot. "I'll let this mess soak," Shorty told them. "If they'll soften up, we can eat them cold." So they ate no breakfast.

Later in the morning, Shorty and Long managed to push the tent-pole off Lieutenant Greely's legs and Sergeant Brainard's chest. The remaining upright pole kept enough of the canvas off them so they could sit. Around noon, Shorty passed around the drinking water. Everyone took a swallow except Connell. The Irishman hadn't said a word since yesterday. He hadn't moved. His eyes were glassy and locked in a fixed stare. No one wanted to look at him. Connell was on his way out. They had seen enough of the final stages to know that. Now and then Biederbick laid his hand on the Irishman's chest and told them, "He's still breathing."

It was evening and the light had turned gray when Brainard suddenly sat up. "What's that sound?" The others looked at him. "By God," he said, his voice strong, "it sounded like a steam whistle."

"Not possible. No vessel has ever gotten through so soon," their commander reminded them.

"I heard three blasts," Long affirmed.

Greely turned to Long and Brainard. "Could you manage to walk up to the ridge and take a look?"

The two men stumbled out. Long kept in the lead as they ascended the steep, rocky hillside with the long, level crest that paralleled the sound. Brainard, who made the one-hundred-foot climb only a few days ago to check on his signal flag, couldn't keep up with Long. When he increased his pace, he became breathless and dizzy. He was pushing through a nightmare, his legs in hip-deep sand. His vision blurred. He thought he would black out and began stumbling over the rocks, starting them rolling downhill. This caused Long to look around. He slowed up, but when Brainard nearly caught him, Long started off and Brainard was left behind again, taking him back to the night he and Long were riding at breakneck speed across the Montana plains, trying to catch up with their cavalry troop. Long was ahead and Brainard's horse could not keep pace. Long looked around and slowed and the distance between them diminished until Long, aware of this, sped up. Long was right to push the pace. They *had* to catch the troop before the men left for the predawn charge against the Sioux. That night was dark, and his horse's hooves struck sparks from the stones. If they arrived in an empty camp, they would be charged with desertion. They could be shot. If the ship weren't in the harbor, they would die. *And our own government should be shot for deserting us.* At this thought, Brainard lowered his head and pushed himself forward over the rocks. He *would* catch up with Long. He *would* see that ship when they reached the crest. They had *heard* the steam whistle.

Long stopped walking and waited for him. He stood in the wind and let Brainard catch up. Brainard wanted to tell Long what had gone through his head—that night ride, they had laughed about it afterward—but he was too out of breath to speak. Long smiled. "Let's go on together," he said.

As they reached the crest, the wind's full strength hit them, bringing them to their knees. Together, kneeling, they gazed into the wide expanse of Smith Sound. Brainard could hear himself panting as they looked to the left and to the right. The glare coming off the surface hurt their eyes, but if a ship were out there, they would see it. They saw nothing. Nothing but the wide and wild storm-driven sea they had seen a thousand times before.

They looked at each other. Brainard signaled he was going back. Long nodded and cupped his hand to his sergeant's ear. "I'll go to the knoll," he said. Brainard knew Long was going up to raise the signal flag, sure to have blown down. He squeezed Long's arm, conveying his thanks as well as his apology for his inability to do more than get himself back to the tent. "Be careful," he mouthed, words that Long could not hear but Brainard knew he understood.

Long proceeded along the crest, but after ten yards turned to make sure his friend was all right. Brainard was on his feet, and Long watched as the sergeant, pushed by a sudden squally gust, staggered and disappeared below the crest. It happened so fast, it was as if Davy Brainard had vanished into thin air. Long, his legs spread to hold himself steady, stared into the space that Brainard had occupied seconds before. He shook his head and waited until he made out his friend's form farther down the slope before he started forward, doubled over to fight the wind. When he reached the signal flag, attached to its broken oar, he bent to pick it up, slowly righted himself, and saw a small boat round a

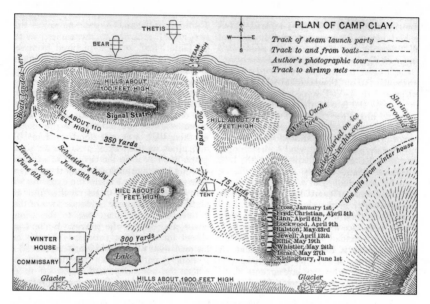

Plan of Camp Clay at the time of the rescue, 22 June 1884. (*Note*: distances do not correlate to one another.) Drawn by Charles Harlow, 1885. Published in *Century Magazine*, 1887.

tiny neck of land not far from their old wreck cache. He rubbed his palm across his eyes to clear his vision, in his exhaustion not trusting his eyes. But when he gazed again, the craft was still there. Men were in it, drawing closer. Long hoisted the broken oar and with all his strength waved the tattered bit of cloth back and forth. A man in the boat picked up a flag and waved back. Long dropped his own flag and began to descend the steep, stony slope. His legs shook. He stumbled. He fell. He picked himself up. He fell again. His heart was racing. He kept jerking up his head to make sure those men were really there. At last he reached the flat.

"Who is left?" A voice rode across the water toward Long.

"Seven," Long shouted. They couldn't have heard him. His voice had no force.

An officer leapt onto the ice foot as the boat touched it, running toward Long. Long threw off his glove and as the officer reached him held out his skeletal hand.

"I'm Lieutenant Colwell," the officer said. "John Colwell, with Commander Schley of the U.S. Navy. We're here in the *Thetis* to pull you off." The lieutenant closed his own ungloved hand around Long's.

Long winced.

"I've hurt you," Colwell said. "Your hand is wasted."

Long spread his lips. "Your voice is so loud." His hand went to his jaw that convulsively twitched.

Colwell stepped back. This man appeared more beast than human with his blackened greasy face, his eyes feral, sunk in their sockets, long hair tangled with the beard. But the smell! Colwell took a further step back. Body wastes and something worse. Hopelessness perhaps. Or the kind of dogged survival built on despair. Or whatever it was this man was eating. "Where are the others?" Colwell asked.

"In the tent." The lips pulled apart to show the blackened gums, and Colwell realized he was staring at a man with scurvy. "The tent is down," Long added and turned to point from where he had come.

"Is Lieutenant Greely alive?"

"Yes."

"The other officers?"

"Dead."

"Who are you?"

"Long. Private Francis Long."

Colwell signaled for two of the men to start up the hill. Long stared as they ran off. "They run so fast." Again he said, "The tent is down."

"Private Long," Colwell said. Long was staring right through him. Colwell wondered if this man knew that he had just been rescued. His motions were slow and jerky, like a clock running down. "Private Francis Long," Colwell said again. "My men will help you into the cutter." Then he took off up the ridge after the two men.

✶

At the crest, Colwell paused to digest the scene below. Rock-strewn. Barren of vegetation. As desolate as when he had made it to this same shore as a survivor of the *Proteus*, wrecked through the ineptitude of Lieutenant Garlington eleven months ago. He stood in the howling wind, enveloped in a driving, spitting squall. Great God! Colwell could not imagine keeping alive in such an awful place. Partway up the rise across from him sat the tent, half-collapsed, as Long had said. His two men, Norman and Lowe, had nearly reached it. Colwell dropped quickly off the ridge.

"We heard you. We heard footsteps *running*. So I came out." A ragged man was speaking as Colwell sprinted up.

"This is Sergeant Brainard." James Norman made the introduction, adding, for Colwell's benefit, "I was with these men in '81. When the *Proteus* dropped them off at Fort Conger." Colwell was well aware of Norman's connection to the men of the Lady Franklin Bay Expedition. Norman survived as well the Garlington fiasco. He seemed to think it gave him special privileges.

This man, Sergeant Brainard, was about to salute, but Colwell intercepted his hand. "I'm honored to meet you, Sergeant." He meant it. That anyone was alive bordered on the miraculous.

"The honor is mine, sir," Sergeant Brainard replied.

What a strange conversation—its correctness, its formality—to have while standing in this *squalor*. Colwell could find no other word to describe the scattered heaps of rusting tin cans, scraps of old clothing wildly flapping in the wind, discarded sleeping bags belonging, he imagined, to the dead men. What snow was left was dirty, much of it stained yellow. He had to watch where he stepped to avoid their excrement. But this soldierly man before him seemed unaware of his slovenly surroundings. There was little difference between Sergeant Brainard and the other man, Long—the filth, the wild growth of hair, the unwholesome greasy appearance, and the smell. This smell was strongest near the tent, and at that moment a frail voice coming from inside ordered, "Cut the tent."

And another voice followed with, "Who is out there?"

"It's Norman!" The ice pilot announced himself. Several voices from inside sent up a weak noise meant to be a cheer.

Lieutenant Colwell dropped on his hands and knees, forcing himself not to flinch at the reek of stale urine, the unwholesome stink of bodies stewing in their own odors for months. One pole still held the tent fabric off the inhabitants, but peering through the tunnel-like entrance was like trying to see into the menacing dark of a cave. As his eyes adjusted, Colwell made out figures, more beasts than men, the wild filthy growth of hair, outer garments more like hide than clothing. The man lying across the entrance, nearly touching Colwell's knee, appeared to be dead. His eyes fixed and glassy. His jaw had dropped, but that might be because his head was being held by another man who had just spooned liquid into the open mouth. A second man knelt beside them, holding a rubber bottle. Lieutenant Colwell smelled brandy. They must have been administering the last drops to this half-dead man.

Across from this trio was a poor fellow with a disfigured face, a spoon attached with a thong to his right wrist. From the look of those shriveled blackened stumps, Colwell was sure the man had been in this condition many months. Yet he seemed more alert than the others, his eyes gleaming with a more human light. The last man was wearing what might have been a nightshirt or dressing gown. Shiny with grease, it was the foulest garment Colwell had ever seen, and the man was buried in a thicket of black hair, held in partial check by a dull-red nightcap. His eyes darted about like a trapped beast, unable to focus.

"Who are you?" Colwell asked. But he knew. It had to be Greely. He watched as the commander, pawing his clothing, pulled forth a pair of spectacles, urging the wires around his ears.

Sergeant Brainard said, "That's the Major, sir. Major Greely."

Colwell crawled over a pile of rags—once army-issue clothing and sleeping bags—that made up the tent's floor, and took the skeletal hand. "Greely, is this you?" There was a long pause during which Colwell had time to think about this promotion to major. Greely was on the verge of it when he left three years ago. For this sergeant to call his commander major spoke to the attachment this subordinate must feel. Colwell reminded himself that these two men had scarcely been out of each other's reach for the last three years.

"Seven of us left." Greely's words came in broken, disjointed phrases. "Here we are—dying—like men. Did what I came to do—beat the best record." He fell back against his sleeping bag, exhausted by the effort of uttering what might have been his last words.

"Did you bring us food?" one of the ragged men asked.

Colwell pulled pemmican out of his jacket and began cutting it into small pieces. "What in God's name," he asked, "have you been living on?" He wanted to know, yet dreaded knowing.

One of the men tipped a can toward the lieutenant. "What is it?" he asked, fighting down the bile that rushed to his throat, confronted with this viscous, vile-looking jelly.

"It's sealskin, sir," Brainard answered. "Shorty, that is, Private Frederick cuts it in strips. He boils it for us. And lichen, too. Only this morning we couldn't eat since the wind blew out the fire."

"Does it blow all the time at Sabine?" Colwell asked. They nodded their heads.

He softened some pemmican in a can with a little water and turned to the nearly dead man, who revived with the brandy. Colwell forced himself to run his hands over this man's body. He had been big once. The heart was barely giving out a pulse. His whole frame felt cold, especially his legs. As if he were dying from the feet up. "Can you tell me your name, soldier?" Colwell asked. He received a blank stare back.

"That's Private Connell, sir," Sergeant Brainard said.

The rest introduced themselves, going around the circle: Corporal Elison was the man who lost his hands and feet, and also, Colwell realized to his horror, his nose. He raised his left stump, offering to shake hands. His lips were parted in a smile. Colwell took the stump in his hand and shook it. Private Biederbick had been spooning the brandy into Private Connell. Private Frederick, known as Shorty, indicating his popularity with these men, had assisted in this maneuver.

"Where is Private Long?" Sergeant Brainard spoke. "I went out with him. We thought we heard a steam whistle."

"Private Long is under the care of my men. They're taking him in the cutter out to the *Thetis*." He didn't say any more. He didn't think they could take it in. It was food they needed. He began to spoon the pemmican into Private Connell's mouth. But the man's teeth were so loose he couldn't chew. "Here," Colwell turned to Norman and Lowe. "Get out the biscuit and soak it in the condensed milk." He looked around at this circle of faces. The way they stared back unnerved him, as if he were surrounded by a pack of hungry wolves, yellow eyes gleaming out of the darkness, a predatory stare. Colwell adjusted his position so his back touched the tent wall.

Norman passed around the sweetened biscuit and they snatched at it with skeletal fingers, stuffing the morsels in their mouths like starving monkeys. Their appetites activated, they crowded toward Norman. "More. Give us more!" The words were clear enough.

"Now, men," Colwell stepped in, "I'll not overfeed you. That can kill starving men." They were on their knees, pushing around him. They would have food, and they answered him with groans and pleas and pitiful sobbing cries. And threats.

"Goddamn, sir, give us that food. You brought it. You bloody well give it." Connell, the nearly dead man, had come alive.

"It's been a hard winter, sir," Sergeant Brainard said, as if to explain Connell's rudeness. "A very hard winter."

Lieutenant Greely had finished his biscuit and began exploring for dropped crumbs, his fingers like busy insects rustling in the folds of his clothing. As Colwell watched, Greely's hand landed on the can of uncooked sealskins. He picked it up, gripping it to his chest, and began pulling out the pieces, eating with his hands as he eyed Colwell over the rim.

"You must give it to me, sir," Colwell said in the kind of persuasive voice adults use on difficult children. He held out his hand, and Lieutenant Greely, like a child, turned over his prize.

These men were so nervous, so irritable and anxious. Colwell watched as they picked at crumbs, their emaciated fingers scuffling along the folds of their clothing, burrowing in their sleeping bags, with the rustling sound of cockroaches. "Let me tell you," he said, "what has happened at home since you've been away. President Garfield was shot."

"That happened before we left," Sergeant Brainard said.

"Well, he died. He held office only one hundred days," Lieutenant Colwell added.

"We know he died," Brainard said. "Chester A. Arthur is president now. We read that news in the papers the lemons came wrapped in."

Colwell smiled. "For castaways, you are amazingly current."

"I am so glad to see you," Lieutenant Greely broke in. "Are you English?" Then, taking in Colwell's surprised look, he covered his mouth with a grimy palm.

Colwell was about to explain when Sergeant Brainard straightened out the situation. "Lieutenant Colwell is with the American navy, sir."

"Ah. The navy? I see," Greely said. But Colwell was not sure he saw at all. "Those lemons that your dear wife so kindly put up for us . . ." Greely began and stopped, the clawlike hand fluttering to his mouth.

"We've been in sore distress, sir, sore distress, as you can see." This time it was the man with the blackened stumps who tried to explain his commander's wandering mind.

This rescue arrived in the nick of time. That was obvious. Colwell dismissed Lowe to return to the ship and report to Commander Schley that Greely and six men were alive. "Have the commander send more men," he ordered. "Both surgeons, more digestible food, and blankets. Stretchers, too, as I bet these fellows would prefer a ride to the shore." He smiled, and they smiled back, spreading their cracked lips and revealing blackened gums, a horrifying sight as the blood beaded up. He steeled himself to hold their gaze.

✳

Commander Schley was, quite frankly, surprised, to have found Lieutenant Greely at Cape Sabine. He had expected Greely to remain at Conger. Or, if he had left and reached this far south, to be at Littleton. But that got ruled out when Schley found the coal pile Greely had left there and Beebe's cache undisturbed. As Sabine had been established as a message depot, he was obliged to check here before steaming north. So Schley had crossed Smith Sound.

"Are you Englishmen?" Lieutenant Greely asked when Commander Schley took his hand.

When Sergeant Brainard again explained, Greely said, "You look like Stonewall Jackson." Schley smiled. Indeed, he was built as compact and strong as a rugged square rigger. He had a razor-straight nose and a hawk's eye. He had a bushy black beard. "I am so glad to see you," Greely said.

"I was stationed in Boston in '81, Lieutenant Greely, when you sailed from St. John's." Commander Schley's voice exploded like a cannon inside the tent. "I hope you don't mind if I say this, sir, but when I saw the item in the newspaper—your army expedition going so far north—I said to the fellows at the Charlestown Navy Yard, 'This means that some navy officer will have to go up there and bring them back.'" He grinned broadly. "I couldn't have guessed it would be me!"

"I am so glad to see you," Greely repeated, his voice shaking, his hands quivering like small defenseless animals against his chest. Commander Schley was sure Lieutenant Greely had little idea of what he had just said.

"Your families are well," the commander went on. "We inquired about all your families before we left. We have pictures of your wife and children, Lieutenant Greely, waiting for you on board the *Thetis*."

"It is so kind and thoughtful," Greely murmured.

Commander Schley sent a signal for Ensign Harlow to come with his photographic equipment. He put a man to work kindling a fire against a sheltering rock near the tent. The only wood seemed to be the charred bits left from former fires.

"You move so quickly," Shorty Frederick said as he watched this sailor. "You can keep it going in the wind. I couldn't keep mine lighted this morning." He was outside, sitting in his sleeping bag, his back propped against the sagging tent. Brainard and Biederbick were on either side of him, all three covered with blankets brought from the ship. Shorty kept stroking his blanket. "It's so clean and soft," he said. Elison, Connell, and Lieutenant Greely were inside. It was night but not dark and wouldn't become dark. But it was squally and there were no stars. "You're wet," Sergeant Brainard said to the man who was feeding the fire. "You're wet through."

"It was a rough passage, Sergeant, between ship and shore. None of us escaped a wetting," he explained, laughing.

The three survivors—they were survivors now—made a kind of laughing sound back, and Biederbick said, "You're wet and we're dry, as dry as we've been in months."

Sergeant Brainard patted his blanket. "This blanket," he said to the man, "is the softest thing I've ever felt."

"You've had a rough time of it," the sailor said. "Norman told us you ate your own boots like Sir John Franklin. And God knows what else. 'Watch you don't get downwind of them.' That's what Norman said." The sailor laughed again. "The smell. No disrespect. You can't smell yourselves, but we can."

But Brainard, Biederbick, and Shorty weren't listening. They were watching the doctors direct the placing of the pots the men carried up from the shore on the blaze.

"Milk punch. Beef extract." Dr. Green pointed to two pots. "We'll feed you at ten-minute intervals, until Dr. Ames and I feel you are strong enough to be carried to the cutter and out to the ship.

"Ah, Doctor." A sigh from Lieutenant Greely, who heard this from inside the tent. "It seems so long to wait."

✴

"I would say," Colwell remarked in a quiet voice to the doctors, "that these men are not able to take in their good fortune. They show little enough excitement."

"Bear in mind these were tough men to start with," Dr. Green said. "They are hardened now to privation beyond anything we can know. But this present storm has brought them down. If the days leading up to their rescue had been fair, we might have found them more alert. Less indifferent."

Colwell didn't think Lieutenant Greely had been out of his sleeping bag in days. Sergeant Brainard told him that in the last forty-eight hours, none of them had moved from the tent. They hadn't been able to feed themselves. The incessant pounding of this storm must have made it clear that their own deaths were at hand. They were as weak as fledglings. No wonder they appeared dazed.

"I'd say we snatched them from the very jaws of death," Dr. Ames said. "Even the sergeant could not have lasted more than a few days more."

"I'm impressed," Dr. Green said, "with how well they've cared for that helpless man, Elison. He was completely dependent on them."

"He told me they tied that spoon on his wrist only a few days ago,"

Colwell said, "so that if he were the only one left, at least he could feed himself."

"It's clear they didn't deprive him of his fair ration," said Dr. Ames. "He has more flesh on him and is more mentally alert than his mates, excepting possibly, the sergeant."

✳

Commander Schley ordered his men to scour the area. The snow had pulled back to the north sides of rocks and hillocks. The ground was spongy and though the rain let up, the wind continued to bear down. They found the graves, not seventy-five yards uphill from the tent. They counted ten mounds. Three of the graves were surrounded by neat rows of stones. The rest had no definition, little more than a scattering of the gravelly dust. Hands, boots, belt buckles, even heads, showed above the surface. Ensign Harlow photographed the grave site. Then Lieutenants Emory and Colwell began to exhume the bodies, the wind blowing gravel in their faces.

Commander Schley slipped into the tent. "Sir," he said to Lieutenant Greely, "I have been requested to bring home the bodies of the dead." Greely gave him a startled look.

"To their families, Lieutenant Greely," Schley added.

Greely drew himself up in his sleeping bag. "My men shall lie where they died." His fingers clawed at his beard. "Lieutenant Lockwood would want to remain in the ground consecrated by his great achievements. His family would want that." He slumped back, hands shaking, eyes staring.

"I understand your sentiment, sir," the commander said. He wanted to proceed carefully with this man, not add to his suffering. Yet he had his orders. "Our government will bear the expense, just as they did for the De Long expedition. I know you were friends with Commander De Long. If we leave the bodies of the Lady Franklin Bay Expedition here, our government would fail in its duty, sir."

"De Long. I have a letter for him. Entrusted to me by his wife." He spoke with his eyes closed. Schley waited, expecting the lieutenant to say more, but he appeared to have fallen into a doze. Suddenly his eyes sprang open. "Cross died in January." His voice gathered strength. He looked directly into Commander Schley's eyes.

"Cross was a drunkard," Connell barked.

"We were a full complement from when we landed—only down one," Greely went on, ignoring Connell's disparaging comment about Cross, "until Fred Christiansen died on April fifth."

"He'd just eaten his breakfast," Connell added. "A waste of good food, that death was. But what can you expect of an Eskimo."

"Jens drowned in his kayak when hunting for us. On April twenty-ninth. In those three weeks, we'd lost six," Greely went on.

"The other damn Eskimo," Connell made clear.

Schley was surprised at how lucid Lieutenant Greely's mind was for these details, yet he seemed incapable of checking his subordinate's ill-placed comments. As a commander himself, Schley realized the battle with Connell had been going on for months, probably since Fort Conger.

"Rice died in early April," Greely continued. "But he's not up there." He waved gnarled grimy fingers toward Cemetery Ridge.

"You couldn't say enough good about George Rice, Commander," Connell said. "Linn was with him on the first trip. He was never the same man after that. Linn, I mean. *He's* up there, what's left of him." Connell gave his commander a smirking glance. Schley was not surprised by Connell's dark hint. He doubted he would have found anyone alive without some body cutting. The story would come out. Schley wouldn't push it now.

"Joe Elison was with them," Connell went on. "Ask him how he got his stumps."

Corporal Elison looked down at the blackened skin where his hands used to be. "I'm sorry," Joe said in such a sorrowful voice it was clear to Commander Schley that Joe Elison felt no pity for himself, merely sorry to have put the others to such trouble over him.

"The bear was shot on Good Friday. Two days after we'd lost Lieutenant Lockwood." Lieutenant Greely was talking again. "Oh! Why could not dear Lockwood have held out just two more days?"

"It would have made no damn difference," Connell cut in. "If he hadn't died then, he'd have died before these men came." Connell turned to Schley. "Lieutenant Lockwood was not a man to stick it when the glory went out of the game."

"Lieutenant Lockwood," Elison said, sending a defiant glare at Connell, "was a soldier and a gentleman."

"Lieutenant Lockwood," snarled Connell, "lost hope. If you give up hope, hope gives up you. I'm alive because I never gave up hope." He spread his blackened lips at Commander Schley.

"I'd say you were alive, Private," the commander said, "because we got here in the nick of time."

"That's what I mean, sir," Connell smirked. "It's the luck of the Irish."

"I can't forgive myself for Ned Israel's death," Lieutenant Greely muttered.

"His mother's beef sausage got from the Jewish butcher," Connell said. "He was going to send us her sausage."

"Sergeant Brainard and I will tell his family how bravely he died," Lieutenant Greely went on. "He left money for our travel expenses." The lieutenant rummaged among the debris behind his sleeping bag and extracted a roll of bills, paper money.

It made a thick wad. Commander Schley had never seen anything quite so incongruous, so worthless in this setting, as this pile of American dollars in Lieutenant Greely's hands.

Norman stuck his head in the tent. "A word with you, Commander," he said, and Schley crawled out. "Sir." Norman made no effort to keep his voice down. "Some of the bodies are cut up bad."

Schley was expecting this.

"They've got their clothes on so you can tell the officers," Norman continued, "but we don't know who's who. The skin's tight and black as a mummy's on their hands, and each one's got his woolen hat pulled down or a handkerchief hiding his face. Each one's got his arms crossed on his chest and is lying on his back tied up in a blanket or a canvas. There's five with slices out of the fleshy parts—thighs, backs, buttocks, upper arms, across the shoulders. I can tell you, sir, there can't have been much meat on those bodies, even before the cutting began. Of the two lieutenants one is about et up. The other one's whole."

"Lieutenants Emory and Colwell are tagging the bodies in the order they are removed," Schley said. "Don't you concern yourself with who is who, Norman."

"I only meant to say, Commander, it's not all of them that's buried up there." Norman was put out that his news wasn't being received for the sensation it was. "The doctor, for one. The one they called Doctor Pavy. Ain't nobody up there who looks like a Frenchman."

"Your job, Norman, is to assist Lieutenants Emory and Colwell. Treat those bodies with utmost respect. Understand?"

"Yes, Commander."

"And another thing, Norman, whatever has happened here at Cape Sabine is not to be talked about when we get to St. John's. Now get back up there." Schley dismissed Norman. But Commander Schley knew that to stop Norman from talking—especially when newspaper reporters bought him drinks—would be like trying to stop the tides.

He walked over to the three men lying outside the tent—Brainard, Biederbick, and the one they called Shorty. "Norman tells me there are ten buried on the hill," he said. "Lieutenant Greely says your man Rice died of exposure and one of your two Eskimos drowned. How about the others? Where are they buried?"

"Salor, Bender, Gardiner, and Doctor Pavy are all in the tidal crack," Sergeant Brainard answered.

"We had not the strength to haul them up to the ridge, sir," explained Biederbick.

"You did right," the commander said. "There are two more to account for. As there are seven of you left and you were twenty-five to start with."

"Schneider lies near there," Shorty said.

"Near the crack?"

"He died only three days ago, or four," Brainard explained. "We dragged his body as far as we could."

"Thank you. One last man. The same?" But Schley knew whatever the story was for this one, it was not the same. The men's faces went blank.

"You must ask Lieutenant Greely," Sergeant Brainard finally said.

"The man's name?" Schley asked.

"Private Charles Henry."

Commander Schley put off that conversation. He wanted to locate the body first. He knew the story of Charles Henry Buck. Enlisted men as well as officers in the Montana Territory where Buck, alias Henry, had served identified him from the expedition photograph that appeared in *Harper's Weekly*. The forgery, the murder of the Chinese, the dishonorable discharge—all had come out. Schley imagined that having a proven thief along when the grub ran short would have its problems. But Schley was satisfied for now. Salor, Bender, Gardiner, and Dr. Pavy—those bodies would have disappeared and could not be recovered. It crossed his mind that they might not have reached the tidal crack whole. But Schley dismissed this. He did not believe those three men lied.

The survivors were now restored enough to be wrapped in blankets and placed on stretchers. Sergeant Brainard wanted to walk, but since he could barely stand, he allowed himself to be carried. Shorty, however, managed to hobble down to the cutter with the help of two sailors. Ensign Harlow, running up the hill with his tripod over his shoulder, passed the private. "How are you, old fellow?" he asked.

"Oh, I'm all right, I guess."

Harlow rushed on, then stopped dead in his tracks as the casual tone of this conversation sunk in. He could have been on a street corner at home, making this inquiry of an acquaintance who had missed a few days of work. Ensign Harlow shook his head at the oddness of it and marched on up to the hill, with his camera and tripod to photograph their grave site.

✳

Commander Schley sent a party off to collect the scientific records that lay in the cairn on Stalknecht Island, constructed under the leadership of Lieutenant Lockwood. The one-hundred-pound pendulum in its long narrow case was still stuck upright, a landmark to anyone sailing off the coast, a desperate message.

Lieutenant Emory, in charge of collecting all the property at the campsite, crawled into the empty canvas flapping in the wind. He stuffed a duffle with their ragged clothing. He rolled and tied their sleeping bags he could hardly bear to handle for the grime. He packed up their note-books and diaries. He found the Remington rifle, used to execute Private Henry though he did not know that yet. Under Lieutenant Greely's bag was ammunition, quite a lot of it, which, Emory imagined, only spoke to the scarcity of game. The tin can holding that disgusting coagulated mix that Shorty Frederick had meant for their breakfast Lieutenant Emory dumped out the door.

"The place smells like the stockyards," Norman said as he crawled in to assist. He ferreted around, collecting the little packets of personal items each man had wrapped, meant for relatives and friends at home. The ones he found by Sergeant Brainard's sleeping bag or Lieutenant Greely's belonged to the men who died. The living had made up their bundles as well, tied with leather thongs. "I was with them when they were dropped off in '81, you know." Norman juggled a small packet in his palm. "So. *This* is what a man's life comes down to!"

✱

Lieutenant Colwell found Schneider's body not far from the ice foot, stretched out on its back. A foul-smelling odor came from the mouth, but the corpse was intact—not a knife cut on it.

One man left. Lieutenant Colwell headed down toward their old hut, the men's winter quarters. It was near midnight, and a gray light filtered through the overcast. The wind kicked up a gravelly stinging dust. The whole scene, especially now that the men were safely got off, was taking on a strange significance for him. Twenty-five men had spent the winter here. He had arrived at the end of the story. It was their coming that brought it to a close. A miracle of timing. It was clear the story would have ended with the deaths of all of them in a day or two.

Colwell strode toward the western end of the cape, where the cove cut in. They had placed their hut, now broken through by water, in a hollow. This had given them shelter, but as the season turned, the melting ice drove them to higher ground. By the time of that relocation, only a month earlier, seventeen were still living.

"They moved some big rocks," said Norman, who had tagged along. He gave the wall a kick. "Still solid," he pronounced. They had chinked with snow that turned to ice, and with moss. These walls were three-feet thick. Raised to a height of four feet. The boat-roof was gone.

"They could barely have stood upright, even under the center of the boat," Colwell said.

"Shorty. He could have," Norman said. "Connell told me they cut it up for fuel when it was still their roof."

Colwell had the feeling the Lady Franklin Bay Expedition was turning into history before his eyes. He peered over the wall at confused heaps of disintegrating sleeping bags and helpless clothing. "By God!" he cried and ran around to the open end. "Here's my uniform coat!" The cloth was held fast by a thin covering of ice that splintered as he jerked it free.

"It must have made its way to shore after the *Proteus* went down," Norman said.

Colwell shook it off. His uniform coat! Become a relic! He'll take this home.

Norman paced off this stone structure. "Twenty-five feet in length and seventeen in width," he said. "Those men were wedged in as tight as penguins in a rookery. Well, it served to warm them."

"I don't think anything could have kept them warm," Colwell said.

He had circled around to the back of the hut when he spotted a dark object on a patch of dirty snow. He was halfway to it when Norman caught him up. "By Christ," Norman shouted, "it's a body."

The man was stretched out, face up. Except there was no face. There was hardly a head. The flesh on its hands and neck had mummified, sun and wind turning the skin nearly black. Insects had riddled the clothing and penetrated the flesh.

"Damn," Norman said, "look here. This one's pretty well et up." He dropped down on one knee. "The same kind of cuts into the thighs and upper arms. He was a big man too, though wasted. I wouldn't say they got more than a meal or two off him."

Colwell was examining the neck. "It looks like the head got ripped off," he said. "Perhaps shot off."

"Shot, then et, I bet." Norman sent Lieutenant Colwell a look.

"Watch what you're saying, Norman."

"It's got to be Henry. Charles Henry Buck," Norman said. "The thief. Got himself shot. Look. Here's where a bullet went into the chest." Norman pointed to bone fragments with his finger. "I remember him on the voyage up. A talker, a braggart, with a loud voice. Seemed friendly enough. But you can't know a fellow from casual acquaintance." Norman gave the corpse a shove with his boot.

Lieutenant Colwell crouched down and spread his uniform jacket over this man. He worked his arms under the body. Lifted and stood.

Norman watched as the lieutenant easily swung Henry's wasted and headless body into balance on his shoulders. "I see he's lost considerable weight." He laughed.

Colwell, sick of Norman's company, stepped out at a rapid pace. This man was not shot for food. That wasn't what happened here. Not with men like Sergeant Brainard, Shorty Frederick, and Greely himself, from what he could tell, though Colwell wasn't sure what to think about Greely's leadership. What happened at Cape Sabine might never be fathomed. Things done in the situation these men were in were better left unspoken.

Colwell reached the landing place at the ice foot. "Get a blanket," he said to the sailor in the waiting cutter, "so I can wrap this man up."

8

Under the Apple Tree

Portsmouth, New Hampshire, and
Newburyport, Massachusetts

August 1884

But then again, how can one who is in good health and well-fed
expect to understand the madness of starvation.

Knud Rasmussen, *Across Arctic America* (1927)

On the morning of August 12, a week after the homecoming festivities
in Portsmouth, New Hampshire, Adolphus Greely sat in his customary
spot under the apple tree at the residence provided for his family at the
Portsmouth Navy Yard. He watched the morning light dance on the
waters of the harbor. The air was mild and fresh, a soothing fountain of
breezes. He had grown up in this air but had never stopped to notice
it. The tall grasses in the nearby field waved in a slow kaleidoscope of
yellows and greens. Everything was soft; nothing was harsh here. He let
his mind drift back to the celebration the city of Portsmouth held in his
honor over the weekend of August 2 and 3. The honoring done his men
was all he could have asked for, or nearly. The governor of New Hampshire, Samuel W. Hale, attended. An array of senators came up from
Washington. His dear friend General Hazen was, of course, there.

Every town official was on the podium: the mayor, the sheriff, aldermen, and clergymen. Their rescuers, Commander Schley and his men, drew a great roar from the crowd as they marched down the aisle. Robert Todd Lincoln of the war department, the branch of the government that had sent the Lady Franklin Bay Expedition up to the Arctic, was conspicuously absent. Navy Secretary William Chandler filled in. He praised their Farthest North, their mapping of the Greenland coast carried out by Lieutenant Lockwood, as well as Greely's own exploration into the interior of Grinnell Land.

He stared out toward the sea, his mind in such a tangle of resentment over Todd Lincoln's affront, surprised to see his wife walking toward him, carrying the newspaper. He gave a tight gasp. She brought the paper out to him every morning. He had not tried to change this. It was better this way. He would know, he told himself, if she had seen the dreaded news. This morning he knew. He knew by her step, her careful lifting of each foot high, as if the grass were tall and wet. She kept an even pace, in no hurry to reach him, yet reach him she must.

His mind ratcheted back to their meeting on the *Thetis*. The ship safely docked, Commander Schley led him to his own spacious cabin afronting Portsmouth harbor, the water a brilliant blue, small boats, filled with men and women dressed for a holiday in light-colored clothing fluttering in the breeze, Schley saying, "They've all come out to welcome you. Sit where you can look out in comfort. I'll bring your wife."

He gazed on the sunny harbor scene of sloops and schooners, pennants flying, small cat boats weaving in the swells, a summer-fresh painting by Winslow Homer. He couldn't make it seem real. Too nervous to remain in the chair, he stood to circle the room. The light, shafting across the floor, soft and mild, unlike the hard, brittle Arctic light. He held his hands in this moisture-filled light, his legs trembling by the time he regained the chair. He was so afraid she would find him changed. And her? Would her hair have turned gray? He drew out his handkerchief and was blotting his palms and the back of his neck when he heard footsteps, quick and light, forcing him to rise. He hurried to place himself in the center of the room, desperate that she should see him standing. The door handle turned; he drew himself to the fullness of his six feet.

She was before him, so tall. He had forgotten how close they were in height. She was stately and lovely and she was in his arms, and Lieutenant Greely cursed himself for a fool to have anticipated anything but this easy coming together. "You are home, Dolph," she murmured and held him. He felt himself relax; he grew calm in her embrace. *He was home.*

The pen-and-ink illustrated stories that swept the country the next day showed Lieutenant Greely knocking over a chair in his hurry to press Henrietta to his bosom. "Rettie!" he cried, according to the caption, while she sobbed out, "Husband!" as she rushed into his arms. She was pictured wearing a high-necked, tight-bodiced dress whose linen skirt brushed the floor. Even Commander Schley was included, relishing a backward glance at this touching scene that had them both laughing, since there was no one anywhere about Commander Schley's room when they met. But even as he had laughed with Henrietta over this sentimentalized sensational depiction of their meeting, he felt a sudden stab of fear at the *other news* he had not told her, far more sensational, that was bound to unleash a storm that would surely ruin him.

She stood before him, now, under the apple tree.

"I could not keep this from you, my dear husband," she said as she sat down by his side.

He continued to stare out toward the sea. He could not look at her. Yet he knew she looked the same as she did at the breakfast table, helping him and their two daughters to eggs and toast and bacon, before the newspaper was delivered. Though, at this moment, he felt a heightened focus to her attention and could sense her concern. She placed the *New York Times* quietly on his lap, but he could not make himself look down. She took his hand. This gave him strength and he cast a glance at the headlines, lying face up on his knees. "HORRORS OF CAPE SABINE." He saw these words. "BRAVE MEN, CRAZED BY STARVATION AND BITTER COLD, FEEDING ON THE DEAD BODIES OF THEIR COMRADES." He raised his eyes to her face. She had not changed. Nothing had changed from the way she looked at him every morning when she brought him the paper. "Charles Miller"—Greely bit out the name of the *Times* editor—"helped you out with editorials when you and Lockwood's father were fighting to get me home."

"Yes. Brother Otto's Dartmouth classmate. Mr. Miller was very helpful. He said circulation had fallen in recent years and running these editorials about your expedition drove it up."

"Well." Greely gave the paper a vicious shake. "It seems he could not resist the opportunity to drive it up still further."

"Dolph." Henrietta's grip on his hand tightened. "Do not grow bitter."

"I cannot bear to think of James Lockwood's parents reading this." He forced himself to read aloud: "'*It has been published that after the game gave out early in February they lived principally on sealskins, lichens, and shrimps. As a matter of fact, they were kept alive on human flesh.*'"

"I knew," she said. She was perfectly calm.

"You knew?"

"I knew of the possibility. And when I saw you so troubled, so disturbed, it came to me this was what you could not talk about. But, my dear husband," Henrietta went on, "the article leaves out the good things that happened there. Those brave acts you have told me about. Sergeant Brainard's keeping everyone alive with the shrimp, tedious hours in the wind and the cold to make sure you'd have something not just for supper but for breakfast, too. The victory of Long and Eskimo Jens shooting the Good Friday Bear. Jens, who drowned while hunting seals for you. George Rice! He pushed himself too far to bring you food. Dolph, you told me he did. Corporal Elison, so terribly frostbitten, just by remaining cheerful kept up all your spirits. It's these small human actions that can make heroes of men, and then to think of him dying on the ship when all of you had kept him alive for months; it makes me weep." She put her hand over the headlines. "These would have made inspiring stories for the *Times* readers."

"Look at this!" Greely had scarcely heard what his wife has just said. "The *Times* calls Henry's death 'tragic.' Why, they've made him out to be the martyr of the expedition!" Greely read aloud. "'*Driven to despair by his frightful hunger, Henry saw an opportunity to steal a little more than his share of rations. He was found out and shot for his crime.*' A little more than his share! Gross inaccuracy! Miller will pay for this."

"Say nothing, my husband. You will only make it worse."

"But I am wronged!"

"Then you must learn to live with it. Do not add Miller's name to the list of men you resent. The ones you cannot forgive."

"Henrietta. General Hazen himself called Henry 'a desperate vagabond.' I cannot bear to think of the men's families, of Ned Israel's mother reading this. Ned's body was not cut. Pavy and Henry had not cut into it, and Brainard and I agreed to use only the bodies that had been already cut. Oh my God!" Greely's eyes grew wide. He was staring straight ahead at a scene he knew his wife could not imagine. They were in the tent below the cemetery. Brainard had crawled in. His eyes, deep in their sockets, expressed a kind of resigned anguish as he handed Shorty Frederick something wrapped in a ragged handkerchief that Shorty slid into the cookpot. Greely covered his mouth with his hands.

"I am not shocked, my husband. I have thought it out."

"We didn't shoot the man to eat him. Connell went after Henry's corpse. I am sure of it. Connell was angry when we dragged Bender's body and the doctor's down to the tidal crack. He wanted to cut them all. Brainard could stand cutting the human flesh for shrimp bait, but that other purpose . . . even so, Brainard handled everything. I never touched the knife."

✳

The next day Lieutenant Greely received clearance from his doctors and left for Newburyport. He and Henrietta moved into the upstairs bedrooms with their two daughters. The family was united in his mother's house behind the picket fence on Prospect Street. On August 14, his expedition was honored in a celebration that claimed to outdo the city of Portsmouth's.

The day after Newburyport's celebration, Henrietta came to him with the *Rochester Post-Express*. Mother Greely had taken the girls out after breakfast for a walk to the park. She wanted to show her granddaughters New England flower beds, so different from flowers that bloom in southern California, and these beds, she told them, have been planted in their father's honor.

"You will not welcome this news, Dolph," his wife said, "but since you will learn of it anyway, I want to be the one who tells you." He was sitting on the back porch. The wisteria was blooming, making a shady spot on a warm morning. Greely was tired from the events of yesterday. He doubted if he could take more disturbing news. Lieutenant Kislingbury's remains had been sent to Rochester. "What is this about, Henrietta?" he asked.

"I will tell you, Dolph. You do not have to read it." She sat down beside him on the bench.

He felt a terrible dread. "Tell me, don't read it," he whispered. "I want only your words."

"This newspaper"—he watched her fist tighten and land hard on the *Post-Express*—"made an arrangement with Lieutenant Kislingbury's brothers. In exchange for the exclusive rights to the story, the paper agreed to pay for an exhumation."

"What?" Greely exclaimed. "The families were ordered by the war department to leave the caskets closed."

"I know, Dolph, I know. I will not go on if this is too distressing."

"You must tell me, Henrietta." He could feel her anger, not at him but at what was in the newspaper.

"Two doctors were on hand, the brothers' attorney, and other public officials. The casket was opened in the chapel of the Mount Hope Cemetery. This happened yesterday."

"As I was feted here."

"Yes, my husband, while you and your men were being celebrated by your hometown."

"Read to me, Henrietta, what the paper reported."

"You do not want to hear this."

"Read it." His voice was harsher than he intended.

"The paper details how the cuts were made. I will not read that, Dolph." She stood up, her skirts rustling in that distinctive way that assured him he was home. She was so feminine. Never frail, but tall and strong and womanly. The *Rochester Post-Express* was in her grip.

"Then I will read it myself."

It would be wise of him, he knew, to let it go, but he reached for the paper. She did not try to stop him. She sat down again beside him as he took in how those gathered on either side of Kislingbury's opened casket saw how "all flesh had been cut from the limbs and shoulders as if by an expert." He let the paper drop. He covered his eyes in an attempt to erase the horrible images called up by these words. She reached for his hands, holding them in her own. The wisteria, swaying in the gentle breeze, could not shelter them from the day that was growing hot. Finally Greely said, "Bring me ink and paper, Henrietta. I mean to write a reply to go out to any paper that will print it."

"Write nothing, Dolph. You will only make it worse."

"I must clear myself."

"There is no need. The sooner you let it go, the sooner forgotten."

He could not let it go and walked inside the house, the house he was born in, to his desk. "If there was any cannibalism," he said to his wife, "the man-eating was done in secrecy and entirely without my knowledge. The body of the last man dead, Schneider, was not mutilated. For God's sake, we kept Elison alive. That ought to convince anybody we were not cannibals." But she was right. He shouldn't be writing anything. He sould be writing lies, yet he picked up the pen. He and Brainard had shaken hands on this just last night, on the back porch of his mother's house, agreeing to remain silent about what had gone on during those last weeks. But Brainard left on the early morning train. Those newspaper reporters, they weren't there, they could not know what men would do to stay alive. Besides, if he wanted a future in the army, he, Brainard, each of the survivors understood the importance of denying personal involvement with what went on during those final days at Camp Clay.

When Henrietta came in later and laid a hand on his shoulder, he felt such shame for writing anything at all that he covered his writing with his arm. She hardly glanced at what was on his desk, merely saying in her quiet way, "Come, dear, you must rest. You have done enough."

Afterword

Cosmos Club, Washington, D.C.

22 June 1930

Our stories about our own lives are a form of fiction, even as we
try to make them come out some other way.

Roger Angell, *Let Me Finish* (2006)

He was an old man now. He had continued his career and distinguished
himself in various ways. Three years after his return, in 1887, after General
Hazen's unexpected death, Greely succeeded him as the chief signal
officer. He held that post for the next nineteen years. He was innovative
and bold and found ways to use science and technology in the army. He
modernized weather reporting. He laid a telegraphic cable in Alaska. In
1906, when earthquake and fire nearly leveled San Francisco, he was
called in to lead the recovery. He was a founding member of the National Geographic Society and the first president of the Explorers Club.
He retired with the rank of general. His was a career any man could be
proud of.

He had lost his beloved Henrietta too soon. She died unexpectedly
on March 15, 1918, from pleurisy and pneumonia. They had added two
more daughters and two sons after his return from the Arctic. She had
never failed in her support of him. He was well aware that no one understood him better. "Henrietta," he said to her once, quoting Santayana's

357

well-known phrase, "those who do not know history are cursed to repeat it."

"But you knew the history," she said. "You knew about Franklin and the others."

"I know," Greely said.

"So why did you say what you just said?" she asked.

"Because we who know the history firsthand are cursed to relive it in memory ever after."

"What is it, Dolph, that you relive in your mind? You have never told me." But he could not tell her. Or perhaps he would not. "Dolph," she said, "you know I love you very much."

"I know that, Henrietta," he replied.

"Because I love you I can say that I do not think you have ever faced your mistakes."

He winced and turned away. She was right. His wife was right about most things. He was so often driven by pride. And a burning ambition. Yes, he had made mistakes. He should have taken the doctor's advice and spent the winter at Fort Conger. There was food enough. Lockwood and Brainard wanted this. But what if even one man had died? He would be held accountable. He played it safe, followed orders, and ended up losing two-thirds of his men. He had saved his career though. He was not proud of this. What he had done was shameful. But the Lady Franklin Bay Expedition, or, as the men in power called it, the Greely Expedition, had, as he had intended, made him. And he could not admit to Henrietta—the one person whose good opinion he valued most—that he had taken the coward's way out.

✳

It was June 22, the anniversary of their rescue. Greely stood at the entrance of the Cosmos Club, his residence since Henrietta's death, and greeted his old sergeant, now Brigadier General David Brainard, with the words, "Was I too strict with the men when we were at Fort Conger?" They passed through the reading room with its life-sized statue of General Lafayette astride his horse in the center. They prefered to dine in the garden, but they day being inclement, they retired to the members' dining room, where the headwaiter ushered them to their accustomed table under the arched windows.

A stranger contrast to their dining arrangements at Camp Clay could hardly be imagined: the white linen napkins, the fine china and heavy silverware, the solid comfort of the chairs. Because it was the anniversary, their conversation about those three years flowed more easily on this day, and when they were seated, Brainard said, "Your question takes me back to our first winter. The weather had closed us in. Outside work had become impossible, and you allowed us to rest in our bunks during the day. Then you changed your mind." He paused and edged his fork to make a parallel line with the smaller fork next to it. "Exerting this kind of control," he said, giving his commanding officer a straight look, "denying us comfort in a comfortless place was hard on us. You must remember the grumbling."

"I can say to you now, Brainard, nothing I had experienced in my army life prepared me for what we encountered in the Arctic. I did not know how to fit discipline to the place or to the men." He sat looking out the window at the rain. "Stefansson said that my poor eyesight should have made me ineligible for the command."

"I can't agree with that," Brainard said.

"Stefansson," Greely went on, "was not fit to lead men. When things were moving too slowly for him, he took off, dead-set on discovering new land in the High Arctic. His ship got crushed and more than half his men died. He never took responsibility for any of that." Greely stopped and looked down at his hands gripping the white linen table-cloth. "While I'm getting things off my chest"—he looked across the table at Brainard—"I'll mention that Robert Peary said that the horrors of Cape Sabine were a blot on the records of Arctic exploration. The deaths."

"He meant"—Brainard lowered his voice—"the body cutting."

"I followed orders," Greely said. "But when we got back, there were men who refused to shake my hand. Peary was one of them."

"He lost eight toes." Brainard smiled. "But our Fort Conger saved his life."

"I'll never forgive him, though Henrietta would hate to hear me say that, tearing down our building to erect three smaller ones, said we'd left pots on the stove, clothing scattered, beds unmade, benches over-turned. The man was an egoist. Obsessed with the pole as his god-given right."

"Do you think he thought he reached it?" Brainard asked.

"Whether he did or not, he went to his grave claiming it."

Brainard leaned back in his chair. "It's so easy to forget what really happened when you've been through a bad time. You want to forget. At Camp Clay, we went right up to the limits of being human. We crossed it. You can't explain what we were forced to do. It doesn't translate in civilized society." Brigadier General David Brainard straightened himself to a fully upright position. "We're old men, now, General. I should have told you what I knew about Henry."

"You told us his history on the day of his execution."

"I should have told you at the beginning of our second winter."

"Why didn't you, for god's sake!"

"By the time I found out, it was clear to me I had to keep this to myself. The men absolutely couldn't know. If they had, at Camp Clay they would have killed him. If I had told you, General, you might have had him executed sooner because of what I'd said. I thought the man a perfect fiend, but I could not be responsible for any man's death in that way."

Greely reached across the table and squeezed his friend's arm. "That was a big burden, a lot to carry."

"I took it a step further. I never wrote what I knew about Henry after we got back. It's in none of my government reports. I'll tell you now my reasons for concealment. As you know, when Private Henry passed the forged checks, he was with the Seventh Cavalry. I didn't have it in my heart to smear the Seventh further by drawing attention to Private Henry's crimes. They were still smarting from Custer's ignominious defeat at Little Big Horn."

"You did the right thing, Brainard," Greely said. "You have the ability to see the results of your actions. You're like my Henrietta that way."

"You're kind to say that, General, but frankly, I wasn't thinking very clearly."

"Well, I will tell you, Brainard, I feel a perfect fool when I look back on wanting to abort to the floes. Everything about being in those boats terrified me."

"There is no doubt you had us all alarmed by that daft idea." Brainard smiled at his commanding officer. "But I truly believe we did as well as men could do at Camp Clay. You kept us from splintering. If we'd broken into factions, we would have ended up killing each other." The Brigader General picked up his water glass and drank half of it. "Don't you find it interesting, General, that Private Frederick named his two daughters Thetis and Sabine?"

"I heard he wouldn't talk about his Arctic experiences," Greely replied. "He must have wanted to keep the memories alive if he named one daughter after the ship that saved us and the other after where we spent the most hellish months of our lives."

"And Long," Brainard said, "his returning to the Arctic. What do you make of that?"

"A private expedition," Greely mused, "a wealthy American on a quest to claim the North Pole."

"And poor Private Long was trapped in the ice for two years!" Brainard laughed.

"Some men can't stay away. Did I ever tell you," Greely continued, "that once when I was coming back through customs in New York, Biederbick was on duty? 'Anything to declare, General?' he asked me. 'Nothing at all to declare, Biederbick,' I said, and he waved me through without opening my baggage."

"Biederbick was a good man. Did you know that Connell died fondly calling you 'his dear old commander'?" Brainard said with a grin.

Greely chuckled. "He continued to give us trouble with his notion of joining Kislingbury's brothers to write a book about the expedition."

"Connell was mostly Irish blarney. And now he is gone," Brainard said.

"They're all gone. We're down to the two of us," Greely said.

"In that case," said Brainard, "I'd say it was time to order." He tossed aside the menu. "May I propose, for this anniversary dinner, that we partake of beefsteak and onions in honor of Private Henry?"

Greely smiled. "Hamburg beefsteak. My heavens!" He smote his hand on his brow. "That puts me in mind of a food dream that would visit me on those particularly bad nights when I would lie in a half-conscious state, my stomach drilled out as if by an auger. I would be in a large and well-appointed room, like this." His hand swept upward, taking in the high ceiling, the chandeliers above their heads. "Waiters rushed around, carrying sirloins of beef, balancing steaming vats of potatoes, carrots, beans simply smothered in butter, juggling towers of my favorite Parker House rolls—all for somebody else. They slid by my table without a glance."

Brainard nodded in response. "You might recall, General, that between Long and myself we had shot enough foxes so that I could set some aside. We could have one fox a week. That meant each man would receive two or three ounces of extra meat *a week*. Long and I were pretty proud of what we had been able to do for the party. We'd convinced ourselves that these two or three ounces were a great piece of good fortune. Yet there could not have been a man who believed that these fragments could save him."

The two friends sat facing each other across the linen tablecloth. "Let me read to you what Lockwood wrote." Brainard pulled a paper from his coat pocket.

"Lockwood," Greely said, "had a penchant for recording food that verged on madness."

"On the contrary, General, for him it kept madness at bay. I'll read to you what Lockwood wrote on December 2nd in the hut." And he began: "'I am to eat a cold roast turkey with Linn down at the farm on my return—turkey to be stuffed with oysters and eaten with cranberries. With Ralston, some hot hoecakes. With Ellis, spareribs. With Long, pork steaks. With Biederbick, 'buffers,' old-regiment dish. With my other neighbor, Connell, I am to eat Irish stew. Connell is to cook this himself. With Bender, a roast suckling pig. With Schneider, tenderloin. With Brainard, peaches and cream. With Frederick, a black cake to be cooked by one of my sisters, with preserves. With Salor, veal cutlets and lettuce salad. With Whisler, flapjacks with molasses. With Jewell, roast oysters, on toast. With Rice, clam chowder. With Israel, hashed-up liver. With Gardiner, Virginia Indian pone (hot). With Elison, Vienna sausage. With Dr. Pavy, pâté de foie gras. With Henry, hamburg beefsteak. With Kislingbury, hashed-up turkey, chicken, and veal. With Lieutenant Greely, Parker House rolls and coffee, cheese, omelet, chicken curry and rice, and preserved strawberries. The Parker House rolls are to be baked at his house, and I am to furnish the preserved strawberries. With Cross, I am to eat Welsh rarebit, with eggnog and black cake.'"

David Brainard set down the paper on which he had copied his friend Lockwood's words. "We were all alive then," he said. "Lockwood named all of us but the two Eskimos who would be returning to their native Greenland after the expedition, and so unavailable for these meals." He picked up the paper again. "One last thing before we order Henry's hamburg beefsteak." But he stopped, swaying in his chair, jolted by the vision of Henry's body, his chest gutted by his first shot, the head nearly blown off by his second. "Brainard! Brainard!" His commanding officer's voice, sounding as weak and faint as it had in the hut, alarmed him, and this pulled him back to himself. Sergeant Brainard had never told him that he shot Private Henry. Greely had, in all these years, never asked. For a startled moment, he wondered if he had spoken the words, but the general's look, full of concern, told him he had not. His heart slowed and he was able to think it out again. He had fired point-blank at a man with a cold mind. To do that, he had to become something that wasn't human, and he had spent his life living with it. He did it—the killing—because he believed this responsibility fell to him. He would go on keeping that secret because he did not want to cause his C.O. the distress of realizing he had placed the responsibility for shooting Henry on one individual since there was only one serviceable gun. He had kept the two bullets. They were wrapped in a cloth in a small silver vegetable dish at home along with his Camp Clay diary. He had held on to them because he didn't want to let himself forget what he had done. "Nothing to be alarmed about, General," Brainard said. "A bit of a stab to the heart, reading Lockwood's list. I miss him." He picked up the paper. "Here's what we had for supper that night of December 2nd: seal stew. Lockwood wrote it was 'very filling.'"

The general smiled at his old friend across the table. He had come as close as he needed to of speaking of his cowardice. Of his shameful reason for not remaining at Conger that had cost so many lives. He could admit this to himself now. He would take responsibility in his heart for those lost lives. Of Ned Israel and Lockwood, even the doctor, of Joe Elison, who had so sadly died on the voyage home. He was quite sure Henrietta would be proud of him. The sun had come out and the glassware sparkled. This anniversary dinner was a high point in the year for both men. "Shall we begin, General Greely?" Brainard asked, and his commanding officer smiled and nodded. Both men picked up their white linen napkins and spread them across their knees. Brainard signaled the waiter.

Laura Waterman has coauthored books on hiking, climbing, and environmental issues with her husband, Guy Waterman. *Backwoods Ethics: Environmental Issues for Hikers and Campers*, first published in 1979, received a National Outdoor Book Award Honorable Mention and was republished in 2016 as *The Green Guide to Low-Impact Hiking and Camping*. Their books also include *Wilderness Ethics: Preserving the Spirit of Wildness* (1993, 2014), *Forest and Crag: A History of Hiking, Trailblazing, and Adventure in the Northeast Mountains* (1989, 2003, 2019), and *Yankee Rock & Ice: A History of Climbing in the Northeastern United States* (1993), which was updated by Michael Wejchert in 2018. *A Fine Kind of Madness: Mountain Adventures Tall and True* (2000) was the Watermans' last book together. For nearly twenty years, the couple maintained trails in the alpine areas of New Hampshire's White Mountains, notably the Franconia Ridge. In 2000, after Guy's death, Laura and friends who cared deeply about Guy and what he stood for in the mountains started the Waterman Fund, a nonprofit that supports education, research, and stewardship in the alpine zones of Northeastern North America. The American Alpine Club awarded Laura and posthumously Guy their David Brower Conservation Award in 2012. Laura and Guy combined a life of climbing with homesteading and living self-sufficiently on the land, which they sustained up to Guy's death. Laura wrote about this twenty-eight-year experiment in her memoir, *Losing the Garden: The Story of a Marriage* (2005), which was a *Boston Globe* Editor's Pick. She has published her writing in various literary magazines, journals, and anthologies, including *Alpinist, Yankee, Appalachia, Vermont Life,* and *Climbing.* She lives in East Corinth, Vermont.

Also by Laura Waterman

Losing the Garden: The Story of a Marriage

Also by Laura and Guy Waterman

The Green Guide to Low-Impact Hiking and Camping,
previous editions published as *Backwoods Ethics*

*Forest and Crag: A History of Hiking, Trail Blazing,
and Adventure in the Northeast Mountains*

Wilderness Ethics: Preserving the Spirit of Wildness

*Yankee Rock & Ice: A History of Climbing
in the Northeastern United States*

*A Fine Kind of Madness: Mountain Adventures
Tall and True*

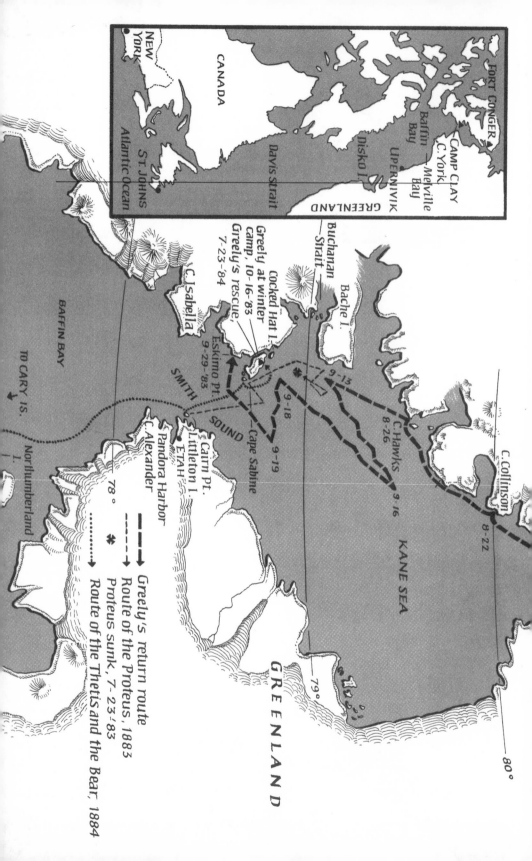